ISABEL WOLFF

RESCUING ROSE

HarperCollins*Publishers*

HarperCollins*Publishers*
77–85 Fulham Palace Road,
Hammersmith, London W6 8JB

www.harpercollins.co.uk

Special edition
A Paperback Original 2003
3

A catalogue record for this book
is available from the British Library

ISBN 0 00 711863 5

Typeset in Meridien by Palimpsest Book Production Limited,
Polmont, Stirlingshire

Printed and bound in Great Britain by
Clays Ltd, St Ives plc

For Eleana Haworth, agony aunt

and

Matthew Wolff, agony uncle

with love

Acknowledgements

I am indebted as ever to my agent Clare Conville, and to my editor Rachel Hore. I am also very grateful to the agony aunts who gave me such wonderful advice, especially Virginia Ironside whose excellent book, *Problems! Problems*, was a very helpful resource; Irma Kurtz, Kate Saunders, Jane Butterworth, Suzie Hayman and Karen Krizanovich. Thanks too to Alan Greenhalgh and Hester Lacey. For her insights into adoption, I'd like to thank Sandra Forster of NORCAP; for information about spinal cord injury, Danny Anderson of the Back-Up Trust; for an understanding of twinship I'm indebted to Chantal and Belinda Latchford, and to Jonathan and Catherine Pollard. For educating me about astronomy I'd like to thank Jerry Workman, Simon Singh, Simon Batty, Andy Carroll and Dough Daniels of the Hampstead Observatory. I'm grateful to George Butler for telling me about tabloid newspapers, Jonathan Curtis for giving me the lowdown on human resources and Sarah Anticoni for information about divorce. For background on assistance dogs I'm indebted to Stephanie Pengelly and Frodo, Allen Parton and Endal, Caroline Scott of *The Sunday Times*, as well as the staff of Canine Partners for Independence and Dogs for the Disabled. I'm grateful once again to my parents, Paul and Ursula, and to Louise Clairmonte for their very helpful feedback and advice. At HarperCollins I'd like to thank Jennifer Parr for her hawk-eyed copyediting, as well as Nick Sayers, Lynne Drew, Fiona McIntosh, Sara Wikner, Esther Taylor, Jane Harris, Martin Palmer, James Prichard, Becky Glibbery, Maxine Hitchcock and Sara Walsh. Finally, special thanks to Greg, who helped me in so many ways.

Why did not somebody teach me the constellations and make me at home in the starry heavens which are always overhead and which I don't know to this day?

Thomas Carlyle

Chapter One

Fear and bewilderment mingled in Ed's soft brown eyes as we faced each other in the garden. I stared at him, vibrant with indignation, then slowly drew back my right arm.

'Take *that*!' I shouted as a Wedgwood Kutani Crane seven-inch tea plate went whizzing past his left ear and smashed into the garden wall. 'And *that*!' I yelled as he raised his hands to fend off first the matching saucer, then the cup. 'You can have these too!' I spat as I frisbeed three dinner plates in his direction. 'And *this*!' I bawled as the accompanying soup tureen flew through the air.

'Rose!' Ed shouted, dodging bits of projectile china. 'Rose, stop this nonsense!'

'No!'

'What on earth do you hope to achieve?'

'Emotional satisfaction,' I spat. Ed successfully deflected the gravy boat and a couple of pudding bowls. I lobbed the milk jug at him and it shattered into shrapnel as it hit the path.

'For God's sake Rose – this stuff's bloody expensive!'

'Yes!' I said gaily. 'I know!' I picked up our wedding photo in its silver frame and flung that at him, hard. He ducked, and it hit the tree behind him, the glass splintering into shining shards. I stood there, breathless with exertion and raised adrenaline as he picked up the dented frame. In that picture we looked radiantly happy. It had been taken just seven months before.

'It's no-one's fault,' he said. 'These things happen.'

'Don't give me that crap!' I yelled.

'But I was so *unhappy* Rose. I was miserable. I couldn't cope with coming second to your career.'

'But my career *matters* to me,' I said as I slashed the matrimonial duvet with my biggest Sabatier. 'Anyway it's not just a career, it's a vocation. They *need* me, those people out there.'

'But I needed you too,' he whined as a cloud of goosedown swirled through the air. 'I didn't see why I had to compete with all those losers!'

'Ed!' I said, 'that's low!'

'Desperate of Dagenham!'

'Stop it!'

'Betrayed of Barnsley.'

'Don't be mean!'

'Agoraphobic of Aberystwyth.'

'That's so nasty.'

'There was never any room for *me*!'

As I gazed at Ed, the knife dropped to my side and I caught my breath, once again, at his looks. He was so utterly, ridiculously good-looking. The handsomest man I'd ever met. Sometimes he looked a little like Gregory Peck. Who was it he reminded me of now? Of course. Jimmy Stewart in *It's a Wonderful Life*, all happy and covered in snow. Except it wasn't snow on Ed's shoulders but white feathers, and life wasn't wonderful at all.

'I'm sorry, Rose,' he whispered as he spat out two tiny plumes. 'It's over. We've got to move on.'

'Don't you love me then?' I asked, tentatively, my heart banging like a Kodo drum.

'I did love you Rose,' he said regretfully. 'I really did. But . . . no, I don't think I love you any more.'

'You don't love me?' I echoed dismally. 'Oh. Oh, I see. Well you have now hurt my feelings Ed. You have really got to me. I am now *very* angry.' I rummaged in my arsenal and found a Le Creuset frying pan. 'And suppressed anger is bad for one's health, so you'll just have to take your punishment like a man.'

As I picked up the pan with both hands, horror registered on Ed's handsome face.

'Please Rose. Don't be silly.'

'I'm perfectly serious,' I said.

'You've had your little game.'

'It isn't over. At least not yet.'

'You're not really going to hit me with that, are you?' he pleaded as I advanced across the feather-strewn lawn. 'Please Rose,' he wheezed. *'Don't.'* And now, as I moved towards him, smashed china crunching underfoot, his voice began to rise from its normal light tenor, to contralto, until it was a kind of odd, soprano whine. *'Please* Rose,' he whimpered. 'Not with that. You could really hurt me, you know.'

'Good!'

'Rose, don't. Stop it!' he wailed, as he tried to protect himself with his hands. *'Rose.* ROSE!' he screamed, as I lifted the pan aloft and prepared to bring it down, hard, on his head. 'Rose!' And now, from somewhere, I could hear banging, and shouting. 'ROSE!' Ed shrieked. 'ROSE! *ROSE!'*

Suddenly I was sitting bolt upright in bed, heart pounding, eyes staring, my mouth as dry as dust. I was no longer in Ed's garden in Putney, but in my new house in Camberwell.

'ROSE!!' I heard. 'OPEN *UP!!'*

I staggered down the unfamiliar stairs, still shocked by the dream which churned in my brain like a thunder cloud.

'Rose!' exclaimed Bella as I opened the front door. 'Rose, thank . . .'

'. . . *God*!' sighed Bea.

'We've been banging for *hours*,' Bella breathed looking stricken. 'We thought you might have done something . . .'

'. . . silly,' concluded Bea. 'You wouldn't, would you?' she went on anxiously. I looked at them. *Would* I? No.

'I'd fallen asleep,' I croaked. 'Didn't hear you. It's knackering moving house.'

'We know,' they said, 'so we've come to help you.' They came in, then gave me a hug.

'Are you okay, Rose?' they enquired solicitously.

3

'I'm fine,' I said, wanting to cry.

'Wow!' gasped Bella as she surveyed the sitting room.

'Blimey!' said Bea. 'What a mess.'

The room was crammed with cardboard packing cases, bisected by shiny black masking tape. They were stacked up like miniature skyscrapers, almost totally obscuring the floor. I'd paid good money for Shift It Kwik but now I regretted my choice, for far from putting the boxes in their designated rooms, they'd just dumped them then buggered off. 'KITCH,' said a box by the window. 'BATH' announced the one by the stairs. 'BED 1,' said the two by the fireplace. 'STUDY,' declared the one by the door.

'This is going to take you ages,' said Bea, wonderingly.

'*Weeks,*' added Bella. I sighed. Bella and Bea's gift for stating the screamingly obvious can drive me nuts. When I broke my arm ice-skating when I was twelve, all they said was, 'Rose, you should have taken more care.' When I failed my 'A' Levels they said, 'Rose you should have done more work.' And when I got engaged to Ed, they said, 'Rose, we think it's too soon.' That didn't seem at all apparent to me then, but it sure as hell does now. Oh yes, Bella and Bea always state the obvious, but they have twenty-four carat hearts.

'Don't worry,' said Bella. 'We'll . . .'

'. . . help you,' concluded Bea. They're like an old married couple in many ways. They finish each other's sentences, for example, and they bicker a lot of the time. Like many an old married couple, they even look alike; but that's not surprising – they're identical twins.

'Give us the guided tour,' said Bella. 'It's quite big,' she added. This was true. I'd gone looking for a large garden flat but had ended up with a three bedroomed house. The twins admired the size of the kitchen, but thought the bathroom was a bit small.

'But for a single person it's fine,' said Bea helpfully. I winced. Single. Fuck. That was me.

'Nice garden though!' exclaimed Bella, changing the subject.

'And it's a sweet little street,' added Bea. 'It looks a bit scruffy,' she remarked as we peered out of the landing window. 'But friendly.'

'Hope Street,' I said with a bitter laugh.

'Well,' added Bella brightly, 'we think it's just . . .'

'. . . lovely!'

'It's fine,' I shrugged. 'It'll do.' I thought with a pang of Ed's elegant house in Putney with its walled garden and yellow drawing room. Moving into that had been exhausting too, but in a nice way as we'd got engaged just two weeks before. As I'd unpacked my stuff the future had seemed to stretch before us like a ribbon of clear motorway. But we'd hardly set off before we'd crashed and had to be ignominiously towed away. So now here I was, my marriage a write-off, upping sticks yet again.

Some women in my situation might have been tempted to move a little further afield – to Tasmania, say, or Mars, but though I was keen to put some distance between us I reckoned Camberwell was far enough. Plus it would be convenient for work and the area was still relatively cheap. So, a month ago, I dropped into a local estate agents and before I knew it, One Hope Street was mine.

'It's vacant for possession,' said the negotiator with unctuous enthusiasm, 'and it's semi-detached.' Just like me. 'It's been empty for a few months,' she added, 'but it's in pretty good shape – all it really needs is a clean.'

When, ten minutes later, I saw the house, I took to it at once. It had this indignant, slightly abandoned air; it exuded disappointment and regret. It was the first in a short terrace of flat fronted houses, and it had a semi-paved garden at the back.

'I'll take it,' I said casually, as though I were spending twenty quid, not four hundred grand. So I inflated my income to the building society and exchanged in ten days flat. But then I'm the impatient type. I married very quickly, for example. I separated quickly as well. And it took me precisely two and a half weeks to buy and move into this house.

'Can you afford it?' asked Bella, tucking her short blonde hair behind one ear.

'No,' I said simply. 'I can't.'

'Why did you get it then?' demanded Bea, who can be overbearing.

'It was an impulse buy.'

'We'll help you decorate,' said Bella as she scissored open a packing case.

'You can be our first client,' said Bea.

'Have you got a name yet?' I asked.

'Design at the Double!' they chorused.

'Hmm. That's catchy,' I said.

The twins have just given up their respective jobs to start an interior design company. Despite a conspicuous lack of experience they seem confident that it'll work out.

'All you need's a few contacts, then it snowballs,' Bea had said blithely when they first told me about their plans. 'A nice mention in one of the glossies and we'll soon be turning them away.'

'You make it sound unfeasibly easy,' I'd said.

'But the market for it is *huge*. All those rich people,' said Bella happily, 'with big houses and horrible taste.'

'We'll get you things at cost,' Bella offered as she unpacked some dinner plates. 'I think you should *definitely* get a new bathroom suite . . .'

'With a glass basin,' said Bea.

'And a jacuzzi,' Bella added.

'And a hand-built kitchen of course.'

'Yes, Poggenpohl,' suggested Bella enthusiastically.

'No, Smallbone of Devizes,' said Bea.

'Poggenpohl.'

'No, Smallbone.'

'You *always* contradict me.'

'No I don't!'

'Look, I won't be getting any of that fancy stuff,' I interjected wearily. 'I'm not going to have the cash.'

As the twins argued about the relative merits of expensive

kitchens I opened boxes in the sitting room. Heart pounding, I gingerly unpacked the wedding photo I'd flung at Ed in my dream. We were standing on the steps of the Chelsea town hall in a blissful, confettied blur. Don't think me conceited, but we looked bloody good together. Ed's six foot three – a bit taller than me – with fine, dark hair which curls at the nape. He's got these warm, melting brown eyes, while mine are green and my hair's Titian red.

'You're my perfect red Rose,' Ed had joked at the start – though he was soon moaning about my thorns. But it was so wonderful to begin with I reflected dismally as I put the photo, face down, in a drawer. Ours had been not so much a whirlwind romance as a tornado, but it had already blown itself out. I surveyed the trail of marital debris it had left in its wake. There were dozens of wedding presents, most – unlike our abbreviated marriage – still under guarantee. We'd decided to split them by simply keeping those from our respective friends; which meant that Ed got the Hawaiian barbecue while Rudolf came with me. Ed didn't mind: he'd never really taken to Rudy who was given to us by the twins. We named him Rudolf Valentino because he's so silent: he's never uttered a word. mynah birds are meant to be garrulous but ours has the conversational skills of a corpse.

'Speak to us, Rudy,' I heard Bella say.

'Yes, say something,' added Bea. I heard them trying to tempt him into speech with whistles and clicks but he remained defiantly purse-beaked.

'Look, Rudy, we paid good money for you,' said Bella. 'Two hundred smackers to be precise.'

'It was three hundred,' Bea corrected her.

'No it wasn't. It was two.'

'It was three, Bella: I remember distinctly.'

'Well you've remembered it wrong – it was *two*!'

I wearily opened the box labelled 'STUDY' because I'd soon have to get back to work. Lying on top was a copy of my new book – this is embarrassing – *Secrets of Marriage Success*.

As I say, I do things very fast, and I wrote it in less than three months. By unfortunate coincidence it was published on the day that Ed and I broke up. Given the distressingly public nature of our split the reviews were less than kind. 'Reading Rose Costelloe's book is like going to a bankrupt for financial advice,' was just one of the many sniggery remarks. 'Whatever next?' sneered another, 'Ann Widdecombe on *Secrets of Fashion Success*?'

I'd wanted my publishers to pull it, but by then it had gone too far. Now I put it in the drawer with my wedding photo, then took my computer and some files upstairs. In the study next to my bedroom I opened a large box marked 'Letters/Answered', and took out the one on top.

Dear Rose, I read. *I wonder if you can help me – my marriage has gone terribly wrong. But it all started well and I was bowled over by my wife who's beautiful, vivacious, and fun. She was a successful freelance journalist when we met; but, out of the blue, she got a job as an agony aunt and suddenly my life became hell. The fact is I hardly see her – answering the letters takes up all of her time; and when I do see her all she talks about is her readers' problems and, frankly, it gets me down. I've asked her to give it up – or at least tone it down – but she won't. Should I file for divorce?*

Clipped to the back was my reply.

Dear Pissed-Off of Putney, Thank you for writing to me. I'd like to help you if I possibly can. Firstly, although I feel certain that your wife loves you, it's obvious that she adores her career as well. And speaking from experience I know that writing an agony column is a hugely fulfilling thing to do. It's hard to describe the thrill you get from knowing that you've given someone in need great advice. So my suggestion, P-O – if I may call you that – is not to do anything rash. You haven't been married long, so just keep talking and I'm sure that, in time, things will improve. Then, on an impulse, which I would later greatly regret, I added: Maybe marriage guidance might help . . .

It didn't. Far from it – I should have known. Ed suggested we went to Resolve – commonly known as 'Dissolve' – but

I couldn't stand our counsellor, Mary-Claire Grey. From the second I laid eyes on her she irritated the hell out of me, with her babyish face, and dodgy highlights and ski-jump nose and tiny feet. I have been hoist with my own petard, I thought dismally, as we sat awkwardly in her consulting room. But by that stage Ed and I were arguing a lot so I believed that counselling might help. It wouldn't have been so bad if Miss Grey inspired any confidence, but the idiotic little woman simply did not. She was thirty-five(ish), divorced, and a former social worker she told us in this fey, squeaky voice.

'What I shall do,' she began, smiling winsomely, 'is simply to listen to you both. I shall then reinterpret – or, to give it its technical name, re*frame* – what you both say. Got that?' Catatonic with embarrassment, and already hating her, I nodded, like an obedient kid. 'Okay, Ed,' she said. 'You first,' and she actually clapped her podgy little hands as though this were nursery school.

'Rose,' Ed began quietly, as he looked at me. 'I feel that you don't care about me any more.'

'What Ed is saying there,' interrupted Mary-Claire, 'is that he feels you don't *care* about him any more.'

'I feel,' he went on painfully, 'that you're more concerned about the losers who write to you, than you are about *me*.'

'Ed feels you're more concerned about the *losers* who write to you Rose, than you are about *him*.'

'I feel neglected and frustrated,' Ed went on sadly.

'Ed feels *neglected* and –'

'Frustrated?' I snapped. 'Look, my marriage may be a bit rocky at the moment, but my hearing's perfectly *fine*!'

And then, I don't know, after that, things went from bad to worse. Because when it came to *my* turn, Mary-Claire seemed not to hear what I'd said.

'Ed, I'm really sorry we've got these problems,' I began, swallowing hard.

'Rose admits that there are *huge* problems,' Mary-Claire announced, with an expression of exaggerated concern.

'But I love my new career,' I went on. 'I just . . . *love* it, and I can't simply give it up to please you.'

'What Rose means by that, Ed,' said Mary-Claire sweetly, 'is that she doesn't really *want* to please you.' *Eh?*

'You see, until I became an agony aunt, I'd never really felt professionally fulfilled.'

'What Rose is saying *there*,' interjected Mary-Claire, 'is that it's only her job that makes her feel fulfilled.' *Huh?*

'And I guess I *am* a bit over-zealous on the domestic front,' I went on uncertainly, 'and I know that's been an issue too.'

'Ed,' said Mary-Claire soothingly, 'Rose is acknowledging that at home she's been a' – theatrical pause here to signify sadness and regret – '*control freak*,' she whispered. *What?*

'But I do love you Ed,' I went on, heroically ignoring her, 'and I think we can work this through.'

'What Rose is saying, there, Ed,' 'explained' Mary-Claire benignly, 'is that, basically, you're through.'

'I'm *not* saying that!' I shouted, getting to my feet. 'I'm saying we should try again!' Mary-Claire gave me a look which combined slyness with pity, and Ed and I split up within three weeks.

Looking back, I think I'd been semi-hypnotised by Mary-Claire's squeaky, sing-songy voice – like Melanie Griffiths on helium – otherwise I'd have been tempted to give her a slap. But for some reason I found it impossible to challenge her bizarre interventions. It was only later on, that I twigged . . .

Now, as I came downstairs again, I could hear Bella and Bea in the kitchen, arguing about flooring.

'– hardwood would look good.'

'– no, natural stone would be better.'

'– but a maple veneer would look fantastic!'

'– rubbish! She should go for slate!'

They should call their business '2 Much' I decided as I went into the sitting room. I unpacked a pair of crystal candlesticks which had been a wedding present from my aunt. Shift It

Kwik had wrapped them in some pages from the *Daily News*, and as I unfurled the yellowing paper I was gripped by a sense of *déjà lu*. 'AGONY AUNT IN SPLIT' announced the page 5 headline in my hand. *Rose Costelloe, the Daily Post's agony aunt, is to divorce*, it explained gleefully beneath. *Her husband, Human Resources Director, Ed Wright, has cited 'irreconcilable differences' as the cause of the split. However, sources close to Miss Costelloe claim that the real reason is Wright's close friendship with Resolve counsellor, Mary-Claire Grey (pictured left).*

'The *bitch*!' I shouted as I stared at my rival.

'She certainly is!' yelled the twins.

'Oh dear,' said Bella, as she came in and saw me clutching the article. 'Want a tissue?' I nodded. 'Here.'

I pressed the paper hanky to my eyes. 'She was supposed to be neutral,' I wailed.

'You should have had her struck off,' said Bella.

'I should have had her bumped off you mean.'

'But why the hell did you suggest marriage guidance in the first place?' asked Bea.

'Because I genuinely thought it might help! Ed had been going on and on about my job, and about how much he hated what I did, and about how he hadn't married an agony aunt, and how he was finding it all "very hard." And I'd been sent a book on marriage guidance that day so the subject was in my mind. So, in a spirit of compromise I said, "Let's get some counselling." So we did – and that was that.'

As the twins disposed of the offending newspaper article, I agitatedly pinched a stray sheet of bubble wrap.

'Miss Grey,' I spat as the plastic bubbles burst with a crack like machine-gun fire.

'Miss Conduct,' suggested Bea.

'Miss Demeanour,' said Bella.

'Miss *Take*,' I corrected them. 'I mean there she was,' I ranted. 'Smiling at Ed. Looking winsome. Batting her eyelids like a Furby. Sympathising with him at every turn, and twisting everything I said. By the time she'd finished you could have used my statements to take the corks out of

11

pinotage. She knew exactly what she wanted and she went for it, and now thanks to her I'm getting divorced!'

I thought of those embarrassingly abbreviated marriages you read about sometimes in *Hello!* Kate Winslet and Jim Threapleton three years; Marco-Pierre White and Lisa Butcher – ten weeks. And Drew Barrymore split up with her first husband so fast they didn't even have time for a honeymoon.

'You got married too . . .'

'Young?' I interjected sardonically.

'Er no. Soon, actually,' said Bea. 'But we *warned* you . . .' she added shaking her head like a nodding dachshund.

'Yes,' I said bitterly, 'you did.'

'Marry in haste,' Bea went on, 'repent at . . .'

'. . . haste. I'll be divorced in just over six months!'

But the twins are right. It *had* happened too fast. But then when you're older, you just know. I mean I'm thirty-six . . . ish. Well, thirty-eight actually. Oh all right, all *right* – thirty-nine: and I'd never believed in instant attraction, but Ed had proved me wrong. We met at a Christmas drinks party given by my next door neighbours in Meteor Street. I was making tiny talk by the Twiglets with this pleasant tree surgeon when I suddenly spotted Ed. He shone out of the crowd like a beacon, and he had clearly noticed me; because he came strolling over, introduced himself, and that was that. I was concussed with passion. I was bowled over. I was gobsmacked, *bouleversée*. I felt my jaw go slack with desire, and I probably drooled. Ed's incredibly distinguished-looking; elegant, a young forty-one, with strong cheekbones and an aquiline nose. You can fall in love with a profile, I realised then, and I fell in love with his. As for the chemistry – there was enough erotic static crackling between us to blow the lights on the Blackpool tower. He told me he was Head of Human Resources at Paramutual Insurance and that he'd just bought a house near Putney Bridge. And I was waiting for some gimlet-eyed glamour puss to zoom up and lay a ferociously proprietorial hand on his arm, when he added casually, 'I live there alone.'

If I believed in God – which, by the way, I *don't* – I would have got down on my knees there and then and thanked Him, but instead said a silent Hurrah! Ed and I talked and flirted for another hour or so, then he offered to take me home.

'But I only live next door,' I protested with a laugh.

'You told me that,' he smiled. 'But I'm not having a gorgeous woman like you wandering the streets of Clapham – I shall see you safely back.'

When you're almost six foot one, as I am, you don't get many offers like that. Men tend to assume you can take care of yourself – and of course I can. But at the same time I've always envied those dinky little girls who can always get some man to take them home. So when Ed gallantly offered to escort me to my door, I just knew that he was The One. After years of false sightings he'd arrived. Sometimes, in my single days, I'd been tempted to have him paged. *Would Mr Right kindly make his way to Reception where Miss Costelloe has been waiting for him for the past fifteen years.* Now, suddenly, there he was – *phew*! We spent Christmas in bed, he proposed on New Year's Eve, and we were married on Valentine's Day . . .

'I had reservations,' said Bella judiciously. 'But I didn't want to spoil it for you. Ed's charming, yes,' she went on. 'Handsome, yes, intelligent yes . . .' I felt sick. 'He's successful –'

'And local,' added Bea meaningfully.

'He's amusing . . .'

'Okay,' I said.

'He has, moreover, a magnetic personality,' Bella continued, 'and sex appeal in spades. But, at the same time there was something I didn't quite . . . like. Something . . . I can't quite put my finger on,' she added thoughtfully.

'I thought he was all right,' ventured Bea. 'And you can sometimes be a bit abrasive Rose.'

'That is hypocritical bollocks!' I snapped.

'But you didn't seem to have much in common with him,' Bea went on calmly. 'I mean what did you do together?'

13

'Well there wasn't a lot of free time because we were so busy . . .' I racked my brain. 'We went swimming,' I remembered, 'and we played Scrabble. We did the crossword too. He was *useless* at anagrams,' I added with a twist of spite, 'so I'd do those. But soon all we were having were cross words.'

The problems had started almost immediately – within a month of our honeymoon. Ed and I had gone to Menorca – not my first choice admittedly, but on the other hand it seemed perfect in some ways as the anagram of Menorca is 'Romance'. Between you and me, though, I'd thought he might whisk me off to Venice, say, or Sandy Lane. But his mum has a little flat on Menorca and so we went there. We had a lovely week – it was too cold to swim, but we walked and played tennis and read.

Then we went back to work – I was doing a stint at the *Post* – when this *amazing* thing happened to me. I was sitting at my desk one lunchtime, putting the finishing touches to a rather vicious profile of the P.R. king, Rex Delafoy, when suddenly there was this commotion. Doors were banging, people were running, and an air of tension and panic prevailed. It turned out that Edith Smugg, the *Post*'s ancient agony aunt, had gone face down in the soup at lunch. No-one knew quite how old she was because of all the face-lifts, but it turned out that she was eighty-three! Anyway, before Edith's stiffening body had even been stretchered out of the building, I'd been deputed to complete her page. And I remember standing, shocked, by her paper-strewn desk and wondering what the hell to do. So I stuck my hand in the postbag and pulled out three letters as if drawing the raffle at some village fete.

To my astonishment I found the contents riveting. The first was from a chap with premature ejaculation, the second was from a woman who'd sadly murdered her boyfriend five years before, and the third was from a seventy-three-year-old virgin who thought he might be gay. So I answered them as best I could and the next day I was asked to carry on. I didn't mind at all, because I'd enjoyed it; in fact by then I was hooked. I didn't care how many letters there were – I'd have done it for free if they'd asked. The feeling it gave me – I can't quite describe it – this delicious, warm glow inside. The knowledge that I might be able to *help* all these total strangers filled me with something like joy. I suddenly felt that I'd been *born* to be an agony aunt: at last I'd found my true niche. It was like a revelation to me – a Damascene flash – as though I'd heard a voice. 'Rose! Rose!' it boomed. 'This is Thy God. Thou Shalt Dispense ADVICE!'

I kept expecting to hear that they'd hired some B-List celeb to take over, or some publicly humiliated political wife. I thought they'd be handing me my cards and saying, 'Thanks for helping out, Rose – you're a *brick*.' And indeed there was talk of Trisha from daytime telly and even Carol Vorderman. But a month went by, and then another, and still no change was announced, and by now they were putting *Ask Rose* at the top of the page, and my photo byline too. The next thing I knew, I'd got a year's contract; so there I was – an agony aunt.

I'd always read the problem page; it's like the horoscope, I can never resist. But now, to my amazement, I was writing the replies myself. It's a role I adore, and the sight of my bulging postbag just makes my heart sing. All those people to be helped. All those dilemmas to be resolved. All that human muddle and . . . *mess*. There are lots of perks as well. The money's not bad and I get to broadcast and I'm asked to give seminars and talks. I also do a late-night phone-in, *Sound Advice*, at London FM twice a week. And all this simply because I happened to be in the office on the day that Edith Smugg dropped dead! I thought Ed would be pleased for me, but he wasn't – far from it. That's when things began to go wrong.

'Ed – what's the problem?' I asked, one Sunday in late June. He'd been in a funny sort of mood all day.

'The problem Rose,' he said slowly, 'or at least the *main* problem – because there are several problems – is other people's problems. That's the problem.'

'Oh,' I said uncertainly. 'I see.'

'I wish you'd never become an agony aunt,' he went on wearily.

'Well I'm sorry, Ed, but I did.'

'And I don't like you bringing your work home.'

'I have no option, it's a huge job. In any case I'd have thought you'd be understanding given that you work in Personnel.'

'It's called Human Resources these days,' he corrected me stiffly.

'So it is. But you sort out people's problems too.'

'I sort out "issues" actually,' he said. Not "problems". And it's precisely because I have to listen to people whining to me about their maternity leave or the size of their parking space, that I don't want *more* whingeing when I get home. In any case I thought agony aunts made it all up.'

'A common misconception,' I said.

'Well how many letters do you actually print?'

'I answer eight on the page, twice a week.'

'And how many do you get?'

'About a hundred and fifty.'

'So why bother with all the rest? I mean, why don't you just put a line at the bottom saying, "Rose regrets that letters cannot be answered personally".'

'Because, Ed,' I said, irritated by now, 'those people are *depending* on me. They've confided in me. They've put their faith in me. I have a sacred duty to write back. I mean, take this woman for example.' I waved a piece of Basildon Bond at him. 'Her husband has just run off with a dental hygienist thirty years his junior – don't you think she deserves a reply?'

'Well do other agony aunts write back to everyone?'

'Some do,' I said, 'and some don't. But if I didn't then it would make me feel . . . *mean*. I couldn't live with myself.'

Gradually it became apparent that Ed couldn't live with me either.

'Will you be coming to bed tonight?' he'd ask me sardonically, 'and if so, how will I recognise you?

'I shall cite the letters as correspondence in our divorce,' he'd quip with a bitter laugh.

Then he began getting on at me about all my other alleged shortcomings as well: my 'total inability' to cook for example – well I've never learnt – and my alleged 'bossiness'. He also objected to what he impertinently called my 'obsessive' tidiness – 'It's like living in an operating theatre!' he'd snap.

By July conflict had long since replaced kisses and we were sleeping in separate beds. That's when, in a spirit of compromise, I suggested marriage guidance – and that was that . . .

'Ed was supposed to get the seven *year* itch, not the seven month itch,' I said to the twins as I fumbled for a tissue again. 'I don't know what I'm going to do. It's so humiliating.'

'Well what would you advise a reader in this situation to do?' asked Bella.

'I'd advise them to try and get over it – fast.'

'Then you must do that too. There's an equation for post relationship breakdown recovery,' she added knowledgeably. 'It's supposed to take you half the time you were actually in a relationship to get over it. So in your case that would be five months.'

'No,' Bea corrected her, 'it takes twice as long, not half – so it's going to take her a year and a half.'

'I'm sure it's half the time,' said Bella.

'No, it's double,' insisted Bea. 'Look, I'll show you on a piece of paper if you like. Right, where x = the time it took him to ask you out and y = the number of times he told you he loved you and z = his income multiplied by the number of lovers you'd both had before then –'

'Oh stop arguing you two,' I said. 'Because you're both wrong – it's not going to take me five months or eighteen months – it's going to take me the rest of my *life*! Ed and I had our problems but I *loved* him,' I wept. 'I made this public commitment to him. He was The One.'

'No, he wasn't,' Bella said gently. 'If he really *was* The One, he would not have a) objected to your new career – especially

17

as he knew it made you happy – and b) carried on with Mary-Claire Grey.' At the sound of her name my tears slammed on the brakes and did a rapid U-turn up my cheeks. 'May I inject a little reality here?' Bella added gently as I felt a slick of snot slither down my top lip. 'You've been let down; your marriage has prematurely failed; you're nearly forty . . .' – OH SHIT!!!!!!! – '. . . so you've got to move on. And I think you'll only be able to do that successfully if you expunge Ed from your life.'

'You've got to expel him,' said Bea forcefully.

'You've got to eject him,' agreed her twin.

'You've got to exile him,' said Bea.

'Erase him,' Bella went on.

'Evict him.'

'Excommunicate him.'

'You've got to exorcise him,' they both said.

'Exorcise him?' I whispered. 'Yes. That's *it*. I shall simply Ed-it Ed out of my life.'

I felt better once I'd resolved to do that. Ed and I live eight miles apart, we have no mutual friends, my mail's redirected, and we don't have kids. We don't even have to communicate through lawyers as we can't start proceedings until we've been married a year. So it can all be nice and neat. Which is how I like things. Tidy. Sorted out. Nor do we have any joint financial commitments as the house belongs solely to Ed. I sold my flat when we got engaged and moved in with him. Ed wanted me to put in my equity to pool resources but Bella advised me to wait.

'Rose,' she said, 'you haven't known Ed long. Please, *don't* tie up your cash with his until you feel certain it's going to work out.'

Ed seemed disappointed that I wouldn't do it, but as things turned out, Bella was right. As for letting all our friends know about the split – that had been taken care of by the popular press.

I shall simply carry on as though I'd never met him I

decided as I opened more packing cases the next day. I shall be very civilised about it. I shall not get hysterical; I'll be as cool as vichyssoise. In any case the unpalatable image of him canoodling with our marriage guidance counsellor would keep sentiment firmly at bay.

And now I masochistically replayed the scene where I'd found them together that day. I'd been invited to speak at a seminar on Relationship Enrichment and told Ed I'd be coming home late. I hadn't thought it relevant to mention that it was being held in a conference room at the Savoy. But when I left at nine I had to walk through the bar and, to my astonishment, I spotted Ed. He was sitting at a corner table – behind a large parlour palm – holding hands with Mary-Claire Grey.

My unfailing advice to readers in such disagreeable situations is, Just Pretend You Haven't Seen Them And *Leave*! But in the nanosecond it took my brain to clock their combined presence I had walked right up to them. Mary-Claire saw me first and the look of horror on her snouty little face is something I'll never forget. She dropped Ed's hand as though it were radioactive, and emitted a high-pitched little cough. Ed swivelled in his seat, saw me, blinked twice, blushed deeply and simply said, 'Oh!'

I was relieved that he didn't try and cover it up by saying, for example, 'Gosh, Rose, fancy seeing *you* here!' or 'Darling, do you remember our marriage guidance counsellor, Mary-Claire Grey?' or even 'Can I get you a drink?'

'Oh . . . Rose,' Ed stuttered, getting to his feet. 'Well, *what* a surprise! I, er expect you're wondering what we're . . .'

'Yes,' I interjected. 'I am.' I was so frosty I gave myself goose bumps, but inside I was as hot as a flame.

'Well, I . . . we . . . we were just having a chat, actually.'

'A chat?' I echoed. 'How nice. Well, don't let me interrupt,' I added with a chilly little smile. Then I turned on my heel, and left.

Looking back, the only thing that gives me any solace is the knowledge that I retained my dignity. It's only in my dreams that I throw things at him, and swear, and rage and hit. In real life I was as cool as a frozen penguin, which might surprise people who know me well. I'm supposed to be 'difficult' you see – a bit 'complicated'. A rather 'thorny' Rose – ho ho *ho*! And of course my red hair is a guaranteed sign of a crazy streak and a wicked tongue. So the fact that I didn't erupt like Mount Etna in this moment of crisis would almost certainly confound my friends. But I felt oddly detached from what was going on. I was numb. I guess it was shock. I mean, there was my handsome husband, of barely six months, holding hands with a troll! This realisation astounded me so much that I was able to retain my sang-froid.

'Rose . . .' he ventured an hour and a half later in the kitchen where I was tidying out a drawer. 'Rose . . .' he repeated, but I was having difficulty hearing him over the deafening thump, thump of my heart. 'Rose . . .' he reiterated, 'you must think badly of me.'

'Yes,' I said quietly. 'I do.'

'I just want to say that I'm truly sorry. I know it doesn't look good.' Now that elegant little apology really annoyed me, because I was enjoying being on the moral high ground. The air's very bracing at ten thousand feet, and of course there's a *wonderful* view. 'But I'd like to . . . explain,' he suggested impotently.

'No. Spare me, Ed. Please don't.'

'I want to,' he insisted. 'There are things I'd like to say.'

Suddenly I noticed that one of the cupboards was grubby and began wiping it with a damp cloth.

'I'm not remotely interested in why you were holding hands with that pigmy,' I said stiffly as I swabbed away.

'Look, Rose. We've got to talk.'

'You sound like the B.T. ad.'

'Mary-Claire and I were just . . . chatting,' he added lamely.

'Ed,' I said serenely, 'that's a lie: a) you were not just "chatting", you were holding hands; and b) there was a pool of drool under your table big enough to support aquatic life. What's the attraction?' I added breezily as I reached for the Ajax. 'She looks like a pig in a tutu to me.'

'Well . . . she . . . she . . . Mary-Claire *listens* to me Rose,' he said with sudden emphasis. 'She hears what I say. You don't. You take everyone else's problems seriously, don't you – but not mine, and would you please put that cloth *down*?'

'There's a nasty mark here,' I said. 'It's very stubborn. I'll have to try Astonish if this doesn't work.'

'Will you *stop cleaning*, Rose, for Chrissake!' He snatched the cloth out of my hand and hurled it into the sink with a flaccid slap. 'You're always cleaning things,' he said. 'That's part of the problem – I can never relax.'

'I just like things to be shipshape,' I protested pleasantly. 'No need to snap.'

'But you're always at it. It's bizarre! If you're not at work or the radio station you're cleaning or tidying, or polishing the furniture, or you're sorting drawers. Or you're colour spectrumming my shirts: or filing stuff away, or you're hoovering the floor, or telling me to hoover.'

'But it's a very big house.'

Ed shook his head. 'You can never relax, Rose, can you? You can never just sit and *be*. Look,' he added with a painful sigh, 'you and I have got problems. What shall we do?'

At this my ears pricked up like a husky. Ed was talking my lingo now. This was just like one of my monthly 'Dilemmas' when the readers, rather than me, give advice. *Rose (name changed to protect her identity), has just found her husband Ed (ditto), canoodling with their vertically-challenged marriage guidance counsellor, Mary-Claire Grey. Rose, understandably, feels shocked and betrayed. But, despite this, she still finds her husband desperately, knee-tremblingly, heart-breakingly attractive, so is wondering what to do.* And I was just about to open my mouth when I heard Ed say, 'Maybe we should have a trial separation.' Separation. Oh. S, e, p, a, r . . . I reflected as I pulled the knife out of my heart.

'One is apart,' I said quietly.

'What?'

'One is apart.'

'Well, yes – we will be. Just for a while.'

'No, it's the anagram of separation,' I explained.

'Oh,' he sighed. 'I see. But I think we should just have a breather . . . take a month off.'

'So that you can shag that midget again?'

'I haven't shagged her – and she is a not a midget!'

'Yes you have – and she *is*!'

'I have . . . not . . . slept with Mary-Claire,' he insisted.

'I have a diploma in Advanced Body Language! I *know*.'

'Well, I . . .'

'Don't bother to deny it, Ed.'

He clenched his jaw, as he does when he's cornered, and a small blue vein jumped by his left eye. 'It's just . . .' he sighed, 'that I was feeling neglected and she –'

'Paid you attention I suppose?'

'*Yes*!' he said defiantly. 'She did. She *talked* to me, Rose. She *communicated* with me. Whereas you only communicate with strangers. That's why I wrote you that letter,' he added. 'It's the only way I could get a response! You're . . . neurotic, Rose,' he snapped, no longer contrite now, but angry. 'Sometimes I think you need help.'

At that I put my J Cloth down and gave him a contemptuous stare. 'That is ridiculous,' I said quietly. 'Help is what I provide.'

'Look Rose,' he said exasperatedly, running his left hand through his hair, 'our marriage is not going well. We rushed into it because, being older, we thought we knew what we were doing – but we were wrong. And I found you so vibrant and so attractive, Rose – I still do. But I'm finding it hard to live with you, so for the time being let's give each other some space.'

'You want more space?'

'Yes,' he said. 'Space.'

'Well you can have *all* the space in the universe,' I said calmly, 'because I'm going to file for divorce.'

'Oh,' he said. I'd shocked him. I think I'd shocked myself. But I knew exactly what 'let's give each other space' really meant, and I was going to be the one to quit first.

'We'll discuss it tomorrow,' he added wearily.

'No,' I said, 'there's no need.' I'd been chewing so hard on my lower lip that I could taste the metallic tang of blood.

'You want to call it a day already?' he asked quietly. I nodded. 'Are you really sure?' I nodded again. 'Are you quite, *quite* sure?' he persisted. 'Because there'll be serious consequences.'

'Yes,' I lied. 'I am.'

'Right,' he said faintly. He shrugged. 'Right. Okay . . . if that's what you want. Well then,' he said bleakly, 'I guess that's . . . it.' He inhaled through his nose, gave me a grim little smile then walked away. But as he reached for the door handle I said, 'Can I ask you something Ed?'

'Of course.'

'I'd just like to know why you asked me to marry you?'

'I didn't, Rose. You asked me.'

Christ – I'd forgotten. How embarrassing! I could have sworn it was the other way round. I certainly don't have any memories of getting down on bended knee. All I recall is whizzing round the London Eye, drunk as a monkey, and finding myself engaged by the time we got down. But if, as Ed ungallantly claims, *I* was the one who popped the question, then it's right that I should also be the one proposing divorce.

I was thinking about all this as I emptied the last few packing cases and cleaned the house after the twins had gone. The interior isn't bad – just a bit dusty, that's all. Off-white walls, limed wooden kitchen units, cream silk curtains (included in the price) and a perfectly respectable oatmeal Berber carpet everywhere. The house is the colour of string. It looks etiolated. Drained. Like me. I quite like it, I thought as I scrubbed and swabbed – too much colour would get me down. I decided I'd redecorate it later; I could live with this for a while.

And now, bearing in mind what the twins had said, I prepared to expunge the memories of Ed. I'd given this very careful thought. I went to the Spar round the corner and bought a packet of party balloons. When I got back I laid

23

them out flat, then wrote 'ED WRIGHT' in black biro on each one. Then I inflated them, watching his name grow and expand on the rubber skin. Ears aching from the effort I watched the balloons bobbing up and down on the sitting room floor. They looked incongruously, almost insultingly, festive as they bounced against each other in the breeze. Then I found my sewing box, took my largest needle and stabbed them, one by one. BANG! went Ed's name, as it was reduced to rubbery shreds. CRACK! exploded the next. POP! went the third as I detonated it, feeling the smile spread across my face. I derived enormous and, yes, childish satisfaction from this – it gave me a malicious thrill. Ed was full of hot air – his vows meant nothing – so this was what he deserved. I burst nine – one for each month I knew him, then took the last one, which was yellow, outside. By now the wind had picked up, and I stood in the middle of the lawn for a moment, then let the balloon go. A sudden gust snatched it and lifted it over the garden fence, before it floated up and away. I could still make out Ed's name as it rose higher and higher, bobbing and jerking in the stiff breeze. By now it was just a yellow blob against the sky, then a smudge, then a speck, and then gone.

I heaved a sigh of relief then went inside for Stage Two of my ritual. I took a piece of string and tied knots in it, one for each happy memory of my time with Ed. The first knot was for when we met, the second was for New Year's Eve; as I tied the third I thought of our engagement party; I tied the fourth for our wedding day. As I tied the fifth I remembered how happy I had felt when I moved into his house. Then I lit the end of the string and watched a neat yellow flame take hold. It climbed slowly but steadily, leaving a glowing tail of embers and a thin coil of smoke. Thirty seconds later and my memories were just a thread of ash which I washed down the sink. Finally, I riffled through a wallet of snaps and found a photo of Ed. He's usually extremely photogenic, but in this one he looked like shit. The camera must have gone off by mistake, because it was looking straight

24

up his nose. He was scowling at something, it exaggerated his slight jowl, and his face was unshaven and tired. So I pinned it to the kitchen noticeboard and made a mental note to have it enlarged. Then I went into the bathroom to perform the final part of my cathartic rites. Suddenly my mobile rang.

'It's us,' said the twins, one on each extension. 'Where are you?'

'In the bathroom.'

'You're not taking an overdose are you?' they shrieked.

'Not at the moment. No.'

'And you're not slashing your wrists or anything?'

'Are you crazy – just think of the mess!'

'Well what are you doing in the bathroom then?' asked Bea suspiciously.

'I'm doing my *exorcises*,' I said.

I rang off, took my wedding ring out of my pocket, and looked at it one last time. Ed had had it engraved inside with *Forever* – I emitted a mirthless laugh. Then, holding it between thumb and forefinger, like a dainty titbit, I dropped it into the loo. It lay there, glinting gently in the shadeless overhead light. Now I took our engagement photo, ripped it into six pieces, threw them in, then pulled the flush. I watched the cauldron of water swirl and boil then it cleared with a glug, and refilled. Everything had gone – the ring and the photograph – all except for one piece. To my annoyance it was the bit with most of Ed's face on and it was resolutely refusing to go down. It was unnerving, having him bobbing about like that, smiling cheerfully up at me as though nothing were amiss. So I flushed it again and watched the fragment spin wildly but, to my intense annoyance, it kept popping back up. After ten tries, defeated, I fished Ed's still smiling face out with the loo brush, and scraped him into the bin.

'Now Wash Your Hands,' I said wearily; then I went downstairs.

I felt a little, well, yes, flushed from my exertions so I made a cup of tea. And the kettle was just boiling when I heard the loud clatter of the letter box. On the mat was a cream-coloured envelope, marked, *To Our New Neighbour* in a large, round hand. Inside was a floral card, inscribed, *Welcome to Hope Street, from* ... Hey! I've got celebrity neighbours! ... *Beverley and Trevor McDonald.*

Chapter Two

I realise, of course, that my neighbour is very unlikely to be the *real* Trevor McDonald. Why would a famous broadcaster choose to live at the wrong end of Camberwell? No, if Trevor McDonald had chosen SE5 then he'd have one of those vast Georgian numbers on Camberwell Grove. I mean, don't get me wrong, I'm not complaining about Hope Street, even if it is at the Peckham end. I had to move fast, it met my needs, and it has a kind of unpolished charm. And the mix of cars – Beemers and Volvos nose to bumper with clapped out Datsuns – suggests that the area is 'coming up.' But I guess my neighbour simply shares the same name, which must be a bit of a bore. Constantly being asked over the phone if he's *the* Trevor McDonald, for example, or receiving *the* Trevor McDonald's mail, or being introduced as 'Trevor McDonald' at parties and hearing everyone go 'BONG!' But on the other hand it's probably useful for booking tables in restaurants, or getting tickets for Wimbledon.

This train of thought diverted me from my thermonuclear fury with Ed as I found my way to the bus stop this morning. And I was standing there feeling perfectly calm, mentally backing a steamroller over Mary-Claire Grey, when suddenly the man standing in front of me did this distressing thing. He took out a pack of Marlboro, peeled off the cellophane, screwed it up, then chucked it down. And as I watched the wrapper skittering about in the gutter I realised that I felt *exactly* like that. I feel as though *I've* been screwed up and discarded. Thrown away. You might find that weird, but after what's happened to me I see rejection in everything.

So to keep negative thoughts at bay I started doing the crossword, as usual tackling the anagrams first. The skill with these is not in rearranging the letters – that's easy – but in spotting them: you have to know the code. 'Messy' for example, usually indicates an anagram, as do 'disorder', and 'disarray'. 'Mixed up' is a good anagram clue as well; as is 'confused' and also 'upset'.

Doing anagrams makes me feel oddly happy: I often anagrammatise words in my head, just for fun. Perhaps because I was an only child I've always been able to amuse myself. I particularly enjoy it when I can make both ends of the anagram work. 'Angered' and 'Enraged' for example; 'slanderous' and 'done as slur'; 'discover' and 'divorces' is a good one, as is 'tantrums' and 'must rant'. 'Marital', rather appropriately, turns to 'martial'; 'male' very neatly becomes 'lame', and 'masculine' – I like this – becomes 'calumnies', and 'Rose', well, that's obvious. 'Sore'.

At least my journey to work was going to be easy I noted as the bus trundled up Camberwell New Road. The *Daily Post* is bang opposite Tate Britain, in a brown smoked glass block overlooking the Thames. This is the home of Amalgamated Newspapers which also publishes *Celeb!*, and the *Sunday Post*.

I got the lift to the tenth floor, swiped my security tag (for keeping out nutters), then prepared for the fray. I passed the News Desk, the Picture Desk and the back bench where the sub-editors sit. I smiled at our gossip columnist Norris Hamster and our new features editor, Linda Leigh-Trapp; I said good morning to 'Psychic Cynthia', our astrologer, and to Jason Brown, our Chief Sub. Then right at the end of the huge newsroom, by the window, I reached my 'pod' with its cupboard and files. I know quite a few agony aunts – we have lunch sometimes – and we all claim to be marginalized at work. Our (mostly male) bosses seem to view us askance; we're like the white witch who lives down the lane. But I don't feel slighted at being sidelined like this, not least because it's relatively quiet. There's always such a *noise* at the *Post*. The day starts calmly enough, but by eleven o'clock as the stories firm up, the background babble builds. There are people arguing, shouting and laughing; the incessant chatter of TV screens; computers are humming, printers spewing, and there's the polyphonic trill of mobile phones. But being seated about two miles from everyone else I don't usually notice the din.

'Hi Serena,' I said brightly to my assistant. 'How are you?'

'Well . . .' – I braced myself – '. . . can't complain. And at least,' she added, with a glance outside, 'the weather's nice for the time of year.' Serena, let me tell you, inhabits Cliché City: she could win the Palme d'Or for her platitudes. She's one of these people who are perennially perky; in fact she's so chirpy I suspect she's insane. Especially as she invariably has some dreadful domestic crisis going on. She's late thirties and mousy with three kids and a dull husband called Rob (anagram, 'Bor').

'How was your weekend?' I enquired as I sat at my desk.

'Oh it was lovely,' she replied with a smile. 'Except that Jonny got his head stuck behind the radiator.'

'Oh dear.'

'He was there for three hours.'

'Gosh.'

'He'd been looking for Frodo, his white mouse, but then, somehow, his head got jammed. We tried olive oil and butter, even that low-cholesterol Flora, but it just wouldn't budge. In the end we dialled 999 and the fire brigade got him out.'

'What about the mouse?'

'Well, sadly, after all the palaver was over, we discovered he'd been eaten by the cat.'

'Oh.' I felt unaccountably crestfallen.

'Still, it could have been worse. All's well that end's well,' she concluded breezily. Not for Frodo. 'And how was *your* weekend Rose?'

'It was fine,' I replied with a tight little smile. 'You know, settling in. New house.'

'Onwards and upwards,' she said encouragingly.

'Mmmm.'

'No use crying over spilt milk.'

'Quite.'

'I mean, life's not a . . .' Oh *God* . . .

'Bowl of cherries?' I interrupted. She looked slightly non-plussed.

'No. Dress rehearsal I was going to say.'

'Okay Serena,' I said mentally awarding her a Bafta for banality, 'let's get down to work.'

I stared, with anticipatory pleasure, at the envelopes in my over-flowing in-tray. There were brown ones and white ones, airmail and Basildon Bond. There were typed ones and hand-written ones, some strewn with flowers and hearts: I fancied I could hear the voices inside, crying out for my help.

My practised eye had already identified from the writing the likely dilemmas within. Here were the large, childish loops of repression, and the backwards slope of the chronically depressed. There the green-inked scorings of schizophrenia and the cramped hand of the introvert. While Serena logged and dated each letter for reference, I sorted out my huge index file. In this I keep all the information sheets which I send out with my replies. I've got over a hundred leaflets covering every human problem under the sun, from Abandonment to Zoophilia, via (and this is just a selection) Acne, Blushing, Body Hair, Confidence, Death, Debt, Insomnia, Jealousy, Nasty Neighbours, Nipples, Pregnancy (both wanted and unwanted), Race Relations, Snoring and Stress. Seeing the problems neatly ranged in strict alphabetical order like this gives me a satis-fied glow. Having tidied the drawer – Smoking had somehow strayed into Smacking – I opened the day's jiffy bags. Serena always has these X-rayed in the post-room because occasion-ally we get sent vile things; used condoms for example – dis-gusting – or lacy knickers, or porn. Usually, however, the bags simply contain self-help books of which I get loads. They're sent to me by publishing P.R.s all desperate for a plug. I rarely oblige but can't blame them for trying – I have three million readers after all. *How to Start a Conversation and Make Friends* announced the first one. *Helping People Cope With Crime*, *How to be a Happy Homosexual*, and *Breathe Away Your Stress*. I put them in the cupboard, arranging them neatly by height, then felt ready to face the day's post. In my column I answer letters on any issue 'Moral, Medical or Miscellaneous', but I knew more or less what I'd find. At this time of year it's failed holiday romances, dreadful second honeymoons, and disappointing exam results.

Dear Rose, I read, as I switched on my computer, *I am 19 and have just failed my GCSE's again . . . Dear Rose, last month I went to Ibiza and met this wonderful man . . . Dear Rose, I've just come back from a purgatorial cruise with my wife . . .* Then there are the hardy perennials like low self-esteem and of course, Am I Gay? And I get so many letters from cross-dressers I can never meet a man without checking his feet for high heels. Then there are the weird sexual problems – this looks like one – I'm never judgemental, of course. Oh Christ that is so disgusting!! *Dear Rose*, I read, appalled. *I'm a farmer, I've been married nearly twenty years, and to put it bluntly, I'm a bit bored in the sack. I'd like to 'experiment' a bit, shall we say, but my wife won't oblige and this is causing a rift. She says it's just 'not on' and that we should leave Grunty alone. Could you give me some guidance please?*

Dear Jeff, I typed smartly, my fingers stabbing at the keys with distaste. *All sexual activity with other species is illegal. I agree wholeheartedly with your wife. Interfering with animals is, moreover, an abuse of their rights – I suggest you stick to eating them instead!*

I have my principles you see. Agony Aunts tend to be liberal, but we all have certain bees in our bonnets. Mine are zoophilia (gross) smacking (unacceptable), and infidelity (absolutely ditto). The number of women who write to me asking how they can persuade their married boyfriend to leave his wife! Take this letter here for example. Typical. *Dear Rose, Please could you advise me what to give my lover for his birthday? I'd like to give him something personal rather than aftershave or a tie which his wife might spot.*

31

Dear Sharon, I typed energetically. *Thank you very much for your letter. I know the perfect birthday present for your married boyfriend – may I suggest that you give him the boot!*

I mean, what do these women seriously expect me to say? Sleeping with someone else's husband is the pits. Why can't they find themselves a single man – God knows there are enough out there. And now I mentally pushed Mary-Claire Grey off the top of Tower Bridge before ploughing through the rest of the mail.

I get, on average, a hundred and fifty letters a week. I type half the replies then record the rest on a dictaphone and give Serena the tape. She also leaflet-stuffs the envelopes, shreds the old letters – *so* important – and organises the helplines which appear on the page. We ring the changes with these but we usually have five or six on the go. *Fighting Phobias* is a popular one, as is *He Wants Me To Dress Up*. We also have helplines on *Prostate Problems, Impotence* and *Bad Breath*. Obviously we have to be careful not to mix up the phone numbers alongside each one. *Dear Rose,* I now read. *I am f**g pissed off because yesterday I phoned your f**g Hair Loss helpline and got Haemorrhoids instead! Those lines cost a pound a minute so I wasn't f**g impressed.*

I wrote back enclosing a conciliatory fiver and my leaflet on *Self-Control*. And now I tackled my e-mails which account for about a quarter of my mail. I find e-mails much harder to analyse than letters. There's no handwriting with all its tell-tale signs and the language is cold and concise. You can see the problem itself very clearly, but not the person who's having it. Because the main thing about the problem page is that the letters are often not quite what they seem. You have to work them out, spot the clues – like a crime novel – or deconstruct them like a piece of prac. crit. For example, someone might spend sixteen pages whining on about how they're not getting on with their partner any more and how he's always shouting at them and picking fights, blah blah *blah*. But then they'll add, in the very last line, 'but he's only like this when he drinks.' At which point I am frantically digging out my *Alcohol* leaflet and the number of their local AA. And that's the *real* skill of being an agony aunt – you have to read between the lines.

At parties people often ask me what other qualities are required. Curiosity for starters – I've got that in spades. I've always loved sitting on trains, staring dreamily out of the window into the backs of people's houses, and wondering about their lives. You have to be compassionate too – but not wet – your reply should have a strong spine. There's no point just offering sympathy, or even worse, pity, like that *dreadful* Citronella Pratt. What the reader needs is practical advice. So that means having information at the ready: information and kindness – that's what it's about. Having said which I'm not a 'cuddly', 'mumsy' agony aunt – if need be I'll take a tough tone. But the truth is that my readers invariably know what to do, I simply help them find the answer by themselves. Take this letter, here, for example. What a nightmare. Poor bloke.

Dear Rose, in 1996 my adored wife died in a car crash, leaving me distraught. Three years later I met someone else and, after a short courtship (too short I now realise), I married again. Although I don't claim to be a saint, I believe I have treated my second wife well. She is a pleasant-looking, but unfortunately rather aggressive woman in her mid forties – she broke my finger very badly last year. I can just about put up with her mood swings, what I can't put up with is her affairs. I know that she's had at least two during our marriage, and now have evidence that she's on her third. And please don't tell me to get marriage guidance counselling because she flatly refuses to go. All I know is that I'm miserable: I feel so lonely and I don't sleep well. I often fantasize about being free (we don't have children). What do you think I should do?

Dear John, I typed. Thank you for writing to me and I'm sorry you've been having such a hard time. I know from my own experience that infidelity is unacceptable – it's humiliating, it's corrosive and it hurts. Any kind of physical aggression from your partner is also beyond the pale. You've already been forgiving twice, so maybe it's time to say 'no more'. John, only you know if your marriage can go on, but it does sound as though you might be at the end of the road. Then, because I always try to add some kind words, I added: *You're obviously a very nice man, and I hope you find the happiness you deserve*. Now, I don't really know whether he's nice or not because we've never met, but because he's placed his trust in me I want to lift his morale a bit. Note that I didn't actually tell him to start proceedings; that's something I never do. In any case it's pretty obvious that he's coming round to that idea himself. What he was doing – and I often get this – was seeking permission to go ahead. Basically, he was asking me to sanction his decision to divorce and so, indirectly, I did.

Then there are all the sad letters – some so dreadful it breaks your heart. Letters with cheerful smileys all over them from children whose parents drink. Letters which start, *I'm so sorry to bother you with my problems, but I have cancer, and have three months to live* . . . Occasionally, there are the begging letters – like this one. I read it and sighed.

Dear Rose, My three-year-old daughter Daisy needs a heart and lung transplant – she's been desperately ill since the day she was born. The doctors here say she's inoperable, but we've just found a surgeon in the States. But the cost of the operation is thirty thousand pounds – money we just don't have. Please, please, Rose, would you print this letter, as we're sure you have many kind-hearted readers who'd help?

I heaved a sigh. I couldn't print it because that's not the function of my page and in any case it might not be true. But if it *were* true I couldn't forgive myself for not having taken it seriously. So I wrote back enclosing the numbers for five children's medical charities, and a cheque for seventy-five pounds. Ed used to get really cross when I did that so I stopped telling him after a while.

And now I read a letter from one of my many Lonely Young Men. *Dear Rose, My problem is that I'm 35 and have never had a girlfriend. Girls just don't seem interested in me, probably because I'm very shy with them, and I'm not at all good looking* . . . I glanced at the enclosed photo – typical! He was very attractive . . . . *so I've been feeling very depressed lately and I spend every evening at home, on my own. But I would love to get to know a special lady who would be kind to me, and perhaps even love me. Please, please Rose, can you help?*

Dear Colin, I wrote. *Thank you very much for your letter and I'm sorry that you're feeling so low. But let me assure you that you are a very handsome young man and I'm sure lots of girls would like to go out with you. But the point is you have to make a real effort to meet them – sitting at home's no good! I think you should a) do an assertiveness course to help build your confidence and b) join an evening class (not car maintenance) where I'm sure you would soon make some female friends. I enclose my Confidence leaflet and the number for your local community college, and I wish you really good luck.* I felt so sorry for him that, on the spur of the moment I added: *P.S. If you feel you'd like to, do let me know how you get on.* But as I sealed the envelope I realised that this was unlikely, and that's the weird thing about what I do. Every month over a thousand total strangers tell me about their problems and their intimate affairs. I give them the very best advice I can, but I rarely, if ever, hear back. My replies go out into the void like meteorites hurtling through space. Did what I write help them, I sometimes wonder? Are things going better for them now?

I was suddenly aware that our new editor, Ricky Soul, ex-*News of the World*, was standing by my desk. R. Soul – as he's respectfully known – has been brought in by the Amalgamated lowerarchy to try and jack up our sales.

'How's it going in the Agony and Misery Department?' he asked with a smirk.

'Oh, fine,' I replied casually. 'Fine.' As he hovered beside me I made a mental note to leave a copy of my *Personal Freshness* leaflet on his desk. Then he reached for my letters – in total breach of confidentiality! – so I quickly swept them into a drawer.

'Anything spicy you can lead with on Wednesday Rose?'

'Like what?' I enquired innocently though I knew.

'Like "Dear Rose," he said in a lisping falsetto, "I am a nineteen-year-old glamour model with a huge bust and long blonde hair and my boyfriend likes me to dress up as a nurse.

I'm tempted to tell him that I don't really enjoy it but am worried that he'll feel hurt."'

I groaned. Our old editor, Mike, who was sacked last month, used to leave me alone; but ever since Ricky arrived I've been under pressure to put in more sex.

'Got any problems like that?' he enquired with a leer.

'No, I'm afraid not,' I replied. 'However I have an accountant who likes to wear silk knickers under his pin-stripes; a farmer who wants to commit pigamy, and I've had a letter from a fifty-five-year-old nun who'd like to become a man.'

'I said spicy, Rose – not pervy,' said Ricky pulling a face. 'And not too many woofters, okay?'

'Ricky, kindly don't trivialise my readers' problems. My column isn't entertainment.'

'Of *course* it is,' he guffawed, 'that's *exactly* what it is: other people's problems give us all a lovely warm glow.' I suppressed the urge to club him to death with *Secrets of Anger Control*.

'I've also had this,' I said, handing him the letter about the sick child. He scanned the paper and his face lit up.

'Great!' he beamed. 'A Tragic Tot! We'll run with it – if she's cute.'

As he sauntered away I turned back to my final letter with a frustrated sigh. It was from a girl whose fiancé had just gone off with someone else.

Can't believe it... she wrote, *wedding four weeks off ... the shame and humiliation ... can't eat, can't sleep ... should I ring him? ... suicide ...*

'Poor kid,' I said handing it to Serena. 'I'll make this one my lead.' And, as I quickly drafted the reply, it was as though I were writing to myself.

Dear Kelly, Thank you very much for your letter: you've obviously had a terrible time. But your ex is clearly the WRONG man, otherwise he wouldn't have done what he did! So the sooner you're able to put this behind you the sooner you'll meet someone who's right. You've had a huge emotional shock, Kelly, so you need to be radical now. All those nice memories? Erase them! Remember your

ex at his worst. Remember him picking his nose, for example, or clip-
ping the hair from his ears. Remember him drunk and snoring, or
correcting you in front of your friends. Do this often enough, and
you'll find that pleasant thoughts of him will soon go. Do NOT
remember the time he mixed you a Lemsip, or the time he played
'Only You' down the phone. Next, get rid of everything that reminds
you of him – 'vanish' him from your life. All the gifts he gave you
– chuck them! And the photograph albums. Then tear up his letters
– and the Valentine's cards. Flog the engagement ring and treat your-
self to a week at a health farm with your best friend. Finally, post
up the ugliest photo you have of him and draw a red circle round
it with a line through. You ask me if you should contact him. NO,
Kelly! Do NOT!!! And in the unlikely event that he should call you,
then I suggest you tell him to get stuffed! Salvage your dignity, Kelly
– it's so important – and just be angry instead. Those homicidal
dreams you're having? Indulge them! Don't feel guilty – enjoy! Those
sadistic little fantasies in which you pull out his nails – go right
ahead. And if it helps why not simply pretend that your ex is dead?
Kelly, you've clearly had a dreadful time, but I know that you're
going to be fine. And remember that none of these things will work
nearly as well as finding another – and much better – man.

I breathed a cathartic sigh as I signed the letter. As I say,
I sometimes take a tough tone. But if a man lets you down
that badly then you have to kick him right out. And as I
made my way home that evening I decided I'd follow my
own advice. There were a few marital mementoes I hadn't
had the heart to discard but now I resolved to throw them
away. I took the wedding photo out of the drawer, together
with our engagement announcement, and my dried bouquet.
In a file I found the air tickets to Menorca and the wallets of
honeymoon snaps. There was a particularly nice one of Ed,
standing on the beach in the evening sun. I could have delivered a deranged monologue to it – I was tempted – but instead
I put it, with the other things, in an old shoebox which, to
my bitter amusement, came from 'Faith'. I tied the box tightly
with string, pressed my foot on the pedal bin and prepared
to let go.

'Goodbye Ed,' I said firmly. 'I am ex-iting from you; I am ex-pelling you; I am ex-cising you. You are ex-traneous,' I added firmly. 'You are ex-cess. I am making an ex-ample of you, because I do not want you any more. I do not want you any more,' I repeated as the bin began to blur. 'I do not . . . want. You. I . . . do . . .' – my throat began to ache and a tear splashed my hand – '. . . want you.' Oh fuck. My heart had been hijacked by nostalgia, and I couldn't let my memories go. As I reached for the kitchen roll I decided instead simply to hide the box; for if I was going to get through this I couldn't let myself be ambushed by sentiment. So I went up to the top floor, into the large spare room, and pushed the box under the bed. As I straightened up – feeling better already – I detected a wisp of smoke. I glanced out of the window into Trevor McDonald's garden. There, at the end of the short lawn, a bonfire was smouldering away. But what was being burned on it wasn't autumn leaves, but two hockey sticks – *how odd*.

Chapter Three

After a nasty break-up it's a good idea to put a few post-codes between yourself and your ex. The further the better in fact. There's nothing quite like it for distracting you from the fact that you've just been given the push. Dumped in Devon? Then why not move to Dumfries? Given the big E in Enfield? Then uproot to Edinburgh. You'll be too busy focusing on the newness of your environment to give a damn about *Him*. Not that I am thinking about *Him*. He's history. My campaign to exorcise Him is going well. It's already eight weeks since we split and I can barely even remember Ed Wright's name. I've done what I advised that girl Kelly to do – I've neatly excised him, like a tumour; I haven't even sent him my new address. So I think it's all going to be plain sailing from here. Were it not for one thing . . .

I was coming downstairs yesterday morning when I had this terrible shock. I heard Ed's voice, quite clearly. My heart zoomed into overdrive.

'You are IMPOSSIBLE!' he shouted as I clutched the ban-ister. 'This marriage is HELL!' By now I was hyperventilating while a light sweat beaded my brow. I stood, paralysed with amazement, in the kitchen doorway, staring at Rudolf's cage.

'I don't know *why* I married you,' the bird muttered shaking his head.

'Don't talk to me like that!' Rudy sobbed in my voice now. 'You're really upsetting me.'

'Oh Rose, please don't cry' 'Ed' pleaded as Rudy bounced up and down on his perch.

'Uh, uh, uh!' I heard 'myself' sob as Rudy lifted his glossy black wings.

'Please Rose,' 'Ed' added. 'We'll work it out. Please, Rose – I'm sorry. Don't.'

I gazed, horror-struck, at Rudy as the dreadful truth sunk in: he was obviously a very slow learner but he'd got us both off to a tee. I reached down the mynah bird handbook to have my diagnosis confirmed. *With a young Java Hills mynah there can be a delay of several months between it learning its vocabulary and actually speaking,* the book explained. *But don't worry – once they've started, nothing will stop them!* Oh God. *They tend to repeat words spoken with enthusiasm or excitement,* it went on. *So be very careful what you let your bird hear.* Oh. Too late for that.

'Problems problems!' Rudy yelled in Ed's voice.

'Don't be horrid,' 'I' replied. 'And take your shoes off before you come in!'

I glanced at the book again. *The thing about mynah birds is that they are truly brilliant mimics. Parrots only ever sound like parrots, but mynahs sound like human beings.*

'Anorexic of Axminster!' shrieked Rudy. 'Your cooking's awful too. You couldn't put Marmite on a cracker with a fucking *recipe*!'

'Ed, that is SO unfair!'

'It's true!'

I stared in stupefaction at Rudy, as the implications of his sudden loquacity sunk in.

'You're *selfish*!' he shouted as he stared at me, beadily.

'And you're Rude,' I replied. I pulled down the cover to shut him up.

'Nighty night!' he said.

Having my marital rows re-enacted at top volume by a bird had shaken me to my core, so I did what I always do when I'm feeling upset – I got out the ironing board. And as the iron sped back and forth, snorting a twin plume of steam, my heart rate began to subside. I find there's nothing more therapeutic than a nice pile of pressing when I've had a nasty shock. I iron everything, I really don't mind – tea-towels, knickers, socks. I even tried to iron my J cloths once, but they melted. I've never really minded ironing – something my friends find decidedly weird. But then my mum was incredibly house-proud – 'a tidy home means a tidy mind!' she'd say – so I guess I get it from her. Now, as I felt my pulse subside, I thought about how appalled she and Dad would be: my marriage only lasted seven months, while they made it to fifty years. I wondered too what they'd have thought of Ed – they never met him – but then they were already middle aged by the time they had me. When I say they 'had' me, I don't mean in the conventional sense. They acquired me; got me, rather than *be*got me – I was adopted at just under six months. But since you're asking I don't mind telling you that my childhood was idyllic in every way. We weren't well off but my parents were *great* – we lived down in Ashford, in Kent. Dad was the manager of an upmarket shoe shop and Mum worked in the town hall. She'd been told years before that she'd be unable to have kids, but then they got the chance to have me. Right from the start they told me that I was adopted, so there were *no* nasty surprises. At least not then.

When I was little my parents would tell me this story about how this pretty lady, seeing how sad they were at not having any children of their own, came up to them in the street one day and asked them if they'd like to have *me*. And they looked at me lying in her arms, and said, 'Oh what a sweet baby – yes please!' So she handed me over, and they took me home and I lived happily *ever* after with them. It was a nice story – and I believed it for a very long time. I used to imagine this well-dressed woman walking around with me in her arms, scanning the crowd for the kindest-looking couple who were keen to look after a special baby like me. Her search wasn't easy, because she was very, *very* fussy, but then, at last, she spotted Mum and Dad. She took one look at their kind faces and just knew that they were right.

Mum and Dad were great churchgoers – *really* keen – and

41

they said that God had sent me to them. And I did sometimes wonder what God was up to allowing my real mum to
give me away. I remember once or twice asking them to tell
me about her, but they suddenly looked rather uncomfort-
able and said that they didn't know. And I guessed that my
question had hurt their feelings so I never asked them again.
But I thought about her a lot and I convinced myself that
she'd had a good reason for doing what she did. I imagined
that she was very busy caring for sick children in India or
Africa. And although I was blissfully happy with Mum and
Dad, I also thought about how my 'real' mum (as I thought
of her in those days) would one day visit me. I imagined her
walking up to the house looking very pretty, wearing a
flowery dress and a pair of white gloves; and I'd run down
the path to greet her, just like Jenny Agutter in *The Railway
Children*. Except that I wouldn't be shouting, 'Daddy! My
Daddy!' I'd be shouting 'Mummy! Mummy!' instead. Then
I'd imagine her picking me up and cuddling me, and she'd
be wearing some lovely scent; then she'd take off her hat,
and her hair would be red and very curly, like mine; it would
almost spring out of her head, in long corkscrews, like mine
does, and she'd exclaim 'Rose! My darling! How you've
grown!' Then she'd hold me really close to her, and I'd feel
her cheek pressing on mine. And we'd go inside for tea, and
I'd show her all the drawings I'd done of her – dozens and
dozens of them – which I'd kept in a box under my bed.

I never told my mum and dad all this because I knew that
they'd feel hurt. So instead I let them tell me this nice story
about how I came to live with them. But later on I discovered that's all it was – a nice story.

I guess you'd like to know the truth, but I'm afraid I
simply can't tell you – because I've never told a soul. Not
Ed. Not even the twins. I never discussed it with Mum and
Dad either, although I knew that they knew. I've always
kept it to myself because it makes me feel somehow . . .
ashamed. But when I turned eighteen I found out about
my real mum, and all my nice daydreams about her stopped.

I burned all the drawings of her on a bonfire and I vowed I'd never look for her. And I never will.

People who know I'm adopted sometimes express surprise at this, especially now that my adoptive parents are dead. 'Why don't you trace your natural mother?' they ask, with staggering cheek. I'm always amazed that anyone should think I'd be interested in meeting the woman who'd given me up. It would be like tracking down the burglar who'd nicked your precious family heirlooms to shake his hand. So thanks but no thanks – I'm not interested: I've only ever had two real parents and they're dead. So I never, ever think about my 'birth mother', to use the fashionable jargon, and if I do then it's with contempt.

I guess that's probably what's put me off having children myself. I'm not really the maternal sort. When I was little I used to imagine myself with lots of babies, but later those feelings changed. Some adopted kids go the other way and have a big family, but they've probably got a nicer story than me. Anyway, enough of my 'real' mother – you must be bored with her: I mean, Jesus, I'm boring myself! All you need to know is that I had an *idyllic* childhood and that my adoptive parents were *great*.

I used to wish that they'd adopt another little girl or boy for me to play with. I was often terribly lonely and I disliked being an only child. I remember asking Mum and Dad if they couldn't adopt a sibling for me but they said I made quite enough work for them as it was! And the next day I was riding my bike and I saw a pair of ducks on the river with eight babies, all squabbling and cheeping, and I remember envying those ducklings like mad. But then, luckily, not long after that, I met Bella and Bea. They moved in next door when I was eight and they were six and a half. From the start they fascinated me, not because of their identical looks, but because they were always arguing – that's how we met. I was in the garden one day and I could hear these two little voices, disagreeing viciously.

'Barbie is HORRIBLE!'

'She is NOT horrible, she is very pretty and KIND. Sindy is UGLY!'

'No she's NOT!'

'She IS. Her head's TOO big!'

'That's because she's very CLEVER. She can speak FRENCH!'

'Well Barbie can speak AMERICAN!!!'

I remember climbing onto the garden wall and staring at them in amazement. I'd never known any identical twins before. They were dressed in the same blue shorts and pink tee shirts, with conker-brown Startrites, and red and white striped toggles bunching their short fair hair.

'Barbie's a DOCTOR! And an ASTRONAUT!'

'But Sindy's a VET!'

They looked up, saw me, and stopped arguing, then one of them said, 'What do YOU think?' I shrugged. Then I told them that I thought both dolls were silly and they seemed quite pleased with that. It was as though they wanted me to be their umpire. I've been adjudicating ever since.

I think it was the twins' sense of completeness which drew me to them – the way they belonged together, like two walnut halves. Whereas I didn't know who I truly belonged to, or who I was related to, or even who I looked like. Nor did I know whether my real mum had ever had any other children, and if they looked like me. But Bella and Bea were this perfect little unit – Yin and Yang, Bill and Ben, Tweedledum and Tweedledee. Like Tweedledum and Tweedledee they argued a lot, but the weird thing was they'd do it holding *hands*. They'd been coupled from conception, and I'd imagine them kicking and kissing in the womb. And although their mum would dress them in non-identical clothes every day, they'd always change into the same thing.

They did absolutely *everything* together. If one of them wanted to go to the loo, for example, the other would wait outside; and their mum couldn't even offer them a piece of cake without them going into a little huddle to confer. Sometimes I'd watch them doing a jigsaw puzzle, and it was if they were almost a single organism, heads touching, four hands moving in perfect synchronicity. And I found it deeply touching that they were so totally self-contained, yet wanted to make space in their lives for me. I was mesmerised by their mutuality and I deeply envied it – the power of two. They're thirty-seven now, and very attractive, but they've never had much luck with men. They were complaining bitterly about this, as usual, when they came round on Wednesday night.

'We can't find anyone,' Bella sighed as we sat in the kitchen. 'It always goes wrong.'

'Men don't see us as individuals,' said Bea.

'Hardly surprising,' I said. 'You look alike, sound alike, talk alike, walk alike, you live together and when the phone goes at home you answer "Twins!"'

'We only do that for a joke,' said Bea. 'In any case there are *huge* differences.'

'Like what?'

'Well, Bella's quieter than I am.'

'That's true,' said Bella feelingly.

'And we went to different universities, and until now we've had different careers.' Bella was a financial journalist and Bea worked for the V and A. 'Plus Bella's hair is short and mine's shoulder length; her face is a tiny bit narrower than mine, she's left-handed and I'm right-handed, and we have different views on most things.'

'Too right.'

'We're not one person in two bodies,' Bella pointed out vehemently, 'but men treat us as if we were. And the stupid questions we get! I'm sick of men asking us whether we're telepathic, or feel each other's pain or if we ever swapped places at school.'

'Or if we'd ever sleep with the same man!' Bea snorted, rolling her eyes. 'You can see what's going through their pathetic little minds when they ask us that!'

'Or they meanly flirt with both of us,' said Bella crossly, 'to try and cause a rift.'

And there's the rub.

The twins may complain about their single status but I have long since known the truth; that although they both *say* they want a serious relationship, the reality is that they don't; because they're very comfortable and compatible and companionable as they are, and they know that a man would break that up . . .

'Rudolf Valentino is speaking,' I said, changing the subject. I took the cover off.

'Don't talk to me like that Ed!' screeched Rudy. 'Boo hoo hoo. Rose, let's face it – you're a *mess*! No, I have NOT done the washing up!'

'God!' Bea shuddered. 'How ghastly. It's probably been triggered by the stress of moving house.'

'Rose you are WEIRD!' Rudy screeched. 'You need a SHRINK! No – you need an agony aunt!'

'Now you know what it was like living with Ed!' I said grimly as I gave Rudy a grape.

'Er, yes.'

'Imagine having to listen to all those vile and untrue things!'

'You've got problems Rose!' Rudy squawked. 'And will you stop stop STOP tidying up!'

'Ridiculous!' I said, as I reached for my Marigolds and began cleaning out his cage.

'Er . . . you'd better not let prospective men hear him,' said Bea carefully, as I disposed of the newspaper.

'Hmm.'

'It might, you know, put them off.'

Over supper – I'd bought a quiche and a bag of salad – the conversation turned to cash. The twins want to find a shop.

'We need premises,' said Bea. 'They don't have to be big, but that way we'll get passing trade. We're on the look-out in Kensington but it's bloody expensive and we don't have much cash.'

'Nor do I,' I said vehemently. 'I've hugely over-extended myself. I got my first mortgage statement this morning – it's going to be nine hundred quid a month.'

'Christ, that's a *lot* of money for one person,' said Bella.

'Yes.' I felt sick. 'I *know*.'

'But you must have known that when you bought it?' she added.

'I was too distressed to give it much thought.'

'Have you got the money?' asked Bea.

'Just about. It'll be fine if I never eat anything, never buy anything, never have a holiday and never, ever go out. Nine hundred pounds,' I groaned. 'I'll be totally broke. I could try and get another column,' I mused.

'No,' said Bea firmly. 'You work hard enough as it is.'

'Then I'll have to raid a bank. Or win the lottery; or get lucky with a premium bond.'

'Or get a flatmate,' suggested Bella. I looked at her. 'Get a flatmate and you'll be fine.'

'Yes, get a flatmate,' said Bea. How weird – they were agreeing! 'A flatmate would really help.'

'But I couldn't bear living with anyone else after Ed.'

'You couldn't bear living *with* Ed,' Bea pointed out. 'So how could a flatmate be worse?'

'Rose,' said Bella. 'Get a lodger – you've got that big spare room on the top floor. You could find some nice girl.'

'But I'm too old for flatsharing,' I wailed. 'Having to write "Rose Costelloe" on all my eggs, drawing up a rota for the washing up, bitching about whose turn it is to hoover . . .'

'You love hoovering!'

'. . . and arguing about the phone! I'm just not prepared to live the student life again,' I shuddered.

'But Rose,' said Bea slowly, 'you never did.' This was true. I was set to read Art History at Sussex, but flunked my 'A' levels: as I say, I had a shock at eighteen.

'We think you should get a flatmate,' the twins repeated, in unison.

'Absolutely not,' I replied.

The following morning I received this.

Dear Rose, I have a problem which is bothering me and I'm wondering if you can help. One of my most valued customers has greatly

47

exceeded her overdraft. The debt is currently £3,913.28 against agreed borrowing of £2,000. I don't want to be too heavy about it because I know that she's just moved house. But at the same time I feel that she ought to try and sort out her finances a bit. As you can imagine, I'm much too embarrassed to mention this to her myself so was wondering if you could help. Do you have any suggestions as to how this important client of mine might reduce her debt? Thank you so much for your advice in this delicate matter, Rose, and I look forward to your reply. Yours truly, Alan Drew (Branch Manager), Nat West Bank, Ashford. P.S. Please do not print.

Holy shit! Nearly four grand! That did it. The twins were right.

Dear Mr Drew, I wrote. *Thank you for your recent letter and I'm so sorry to hear that you've been having this problem with such a valued customer. How thoughtless of her to let things get out of hand like that! As it happens I do have an idea which I'll discuss with her, and I'm confident that her debt will soon be reduced.*

I sealed it, stamped it and posted it, then phoned the *Camberwell Times*.

When I opened the paper on Saturday morning and turned to the *House and Flatshare* column I found that my ad had been condensed, like a Cortina in a car-crusher, into the impenetrable hieroglyphics of the classifieds.

> **SE5. Lge O/R in lux hse nr trans/shps/pk.**
> **Suit prof sgle n/s M/F. £350 p.c.m. inc.**
> **Refs. Tel: 05949 320781**

I wasn't at all sure that the 'hse' could honestly be described as 'lux'. 'Lux' suggests marble floors and a gold-tapped jacuzzi, but the woman at the paper said I'd get a better response. And I was just reading the ad again, and wondering what kind of replies I'd get when I heard the clatter of the letter box. On the mat was a small parcel, addressed to Ms B. McDonald, so I went next door to drop it in. The McDonalds' letter box however seemed to be slightly narrower than mine and I couldn't get the thing to go through. I didn't want to push too hard in case I damaged it, so I smoothed down my hair, then pressed the bell.

Out of the corner of my eye I thought I saw the curtain twitch, then suddenly the door opened. Standing there was a large yellow Labrador with paws like tea plates and a suspicious expression on its face. I shuddered slightly as I don't really like dogs; and I was bracing myself for the thing to launch itself at me, barking and slobbering like Cerberus, when something quite different happened. It trotted up to me, took the parcel out of my hand, then went back inside, carefully shutting the door.

Feeling first and foremost surprised, but also somehow vaguely rebuffed, I turned to leave. But as I put my hand on the gate I heard rapid tapping on the window pane, then the front door opened again. There was Gnasher once more, and behind him, in a wheelchair, a very pretty dark-haired woman of about thirty-five.

'Hello, I'm Beverley,' she smiled. 'You're our new neighbour aren't you?'

'Yes, I am. Thanks for the card by the way. I'm Rose.'

'And this is Trevor,' she said, indicating the dog. 'Say hello to Rose, Trev.'

'Woof!'

'*This* is Trevor McDonald?' I said, wonderingly. 'Oh.' Trevor wagged his tail. 'I was just dropping in your packet,' I explained. 'It was delivered to me by mistake.'

'Well, why don't you come in? I promise we won't bite – or at least Trevor won't!'

And before I could manufacture an excuse because I was sure she was just being polite, Trevor had nipped behind me, ushered me inside, and then jumped up to shut the front door. I followed Beverley as she wheeled herself down the carpeted hallway into the kitchen which, like mine, is large, with pale wooden units and a dining area covered by a glass conservatory roof. Beverley filled the kettle then asked me how I was settling in, and told me that she'd been 'living in Hope,' as she put it, for three and a half years.

'Do you live here on your own?' I asked as she spun back and forth executing nifty three point turns. I noticed that she was wearing cycling gloves and wondered why.

'No, I live here with Trev. He's my partner. Aren't you darling?' He reached up and licked her ear. 'Tea or coffee?'

'Er, coffee please.'

'Get it will you Trev?' Trevor opened a lower cupboard by tugging on a cord attached to the handle, then, tail wagging, he pulled out a small jar of Nescafé, passed it to Beverley, then shut the door.

'Do you know this area?' she enquired as I stared at the dog who was staring, enraptured, at her.

'Er, no, no I don't actually,' I replied absently. 'I lived in Putney before.'

'Where exactly?'

'Blenheim Road.'

'Ooh, that's posh. Big, smart houses.'

'Yes,' I said ruefully. 'They are.'

'So what brought you to Camberwell?'

'My . . . circumstances changed.'

'You mean you've split up with someone?'

'Ye-es . . .'

'So what happened?' What happened? The cheek!

'Well, I . . .'

'Sorry,' she said, laughing, 'don't tell me. I'm a nosy parker – it's boredom you see.'

'I don't mind telling you,' I suddenly said, disarmed by her candour. 'My husband had an affair.'

'Oh dear.'

'Yes. Oh dear. Exactly. So I'm separated, pending divorce.'

'How long were you married?'

How short, rather. 'Erm . . . a bit less than a year.'

'I *see* . . . So do you know anything about Camberwell?' she asked, sensing my discomfiture.

'Not much. I just liked the house.'

'In that case I'll give you the gen. Camberwell was so called because it had lots of wells in the area, one of which was visited by the sick and crippled for a cure. Not that it's done *me* much good!' she exclaimed with a tinkling laugh. 'In the eighteenth century it was just meadows and streams and it gave the Camberwell Beauty butterfly its name and it also inspired Mendelssohn's "Spring Song". But in the nineteenth century it became more and more built up and it's been pretty much downhill since then. But it's still got lots going for it. We certainly like it, don't we Trev? Milk? The up side,' she added as Trevor passed her the carton, 'is the lovely Georgian architecture and the parks. The downside is the lack of decent shops, the wail of police sirens and the incessant screaming of car alarms.'

I found it hard to concentrate on what Beverley was telling me as I was still mesmerised by the dog. The washing machine, which had been spinning away, had now stopped. Trevor pushed on the catch with his nose, opened the door, and was now pulling out the damp clothes with his teeth.

'Thanks Trev,' said Beverley as he dropped a white bra into a red plastic basket. 'We'll hang them up in a bit. If you want the gossip on Hope Street I know it all,' she added with a laugh.

'Oh no, not really,' I lied.

'Of course you do. You're an agony aunt aren't you? I recognised you. I read your column sometimes. Right, number four opposite – that's Keith. He's in computers and calls himself "Kay" at weekends. Number six is that reporter, whatsisname, from *Newsnight* and he's getting divorced; number nine is a chartered accountant and his wife ran off with a priest. Number seventeen is a chiropodist and once did Fergie's feet. Then number twelve – Joanna and Jane – they're employment solicitors and they're both gay.'

'Right. Well, thanks,' I said vaguely as I was still transfixed by the dog. 'Trevor's . . . clever isn't he?' I added feebly as he thrust his head into the washing machine again and emerged with a pink pillow case.

'Trev's a genius,' she agreed. 'But then he's had special training. And in case you're wondering, which I'm sure you are, I did a parachute jump and it went wrong.'

'Oh, I . . . wasn't,' I lied as I took a proffered digestive.

'It's okay,' she said. 'I don't mind. It's perfectly natural so I make a point of telling everyone, then that gets it out of the way. It happened two and a half years ago.'

'I'm . . . sorry,' I said feebly. Poor kid.

'It was no-one's fault – just one of those things: I took a risk, that's all – I did a jump for charity and my chute opened late – I hit the ground with a bit of a crunch. The *hilarious* thing though,' she added with a good-natured chuckle, 'is that it was in aid of a new spinal injuries unit!'

'Really?' I said feebly. I mean – Christ! – did she expect me to laugh?

'Ironic or what!' she went on gaily. 'Mind you I raised a lot. I presented them with the cheque from my hospital bed. I had ten months in Stoke Mandeville,' she added, 'then I had to get on with the rest of my life. I'm okay now about it – I really am – I'm okay – because I know it could have been far worse. For a start I'm alive and not dead; I'm para, not tetraplegic; I'm not catheterised any more, plus I can live independently, and I've been told I'll still be able to have kids.'

'Do you have a partner?'

'No. After my accident he lasted nine months. I always knew that he'd leave,' she went on cheerfully. 'The minute I came round from theatre, I thought, that's it: Jeff'll be off – and he was. I *do* think it was mean of him to go off with my favourite nurse – but, hey – that's life!'

My God – all these confessions! They popped up like ping pong balls in a bingo hall. It was like being on Rikki Lake.

'Well, I'm . . . sorry,' I said again, impotently.

'But I decided to stay put. I loved this house, and being early Victorian it actually suits me quite well. No steps up to the front door and there's no basement. I've got a downstairs loo. And the stair-lift gets me up to my bedroom – I've got

52

another wheelchair up there. The house has been modified a bit. My kitchen worktops are slightly lower for example; but I haven't had the internal doors widened – hence the gloves – because I don't want to live in a "disabled" house. But I have a roll-in shower, and I had the patio doors changed to a slide system to make it easier to get outside.'

'You're amazing,' I said, awestruck by her courage. 'But I expect people often say that.'

'I'm just resigned that's all. I *was* bitter about it, but then six months ago I got Trevor from Helping Paw. He was a throw-out,' she added. 'He was found on a motorway at three months.'

'Oh. Poor baby,' I said. 'Poor little baby,' I repeated softly, although, as I say, I don't really like dogs.

'He used to be a Guide Dog,' Beverley explained, 'but it didn't work out.'

'In what way?'

She glanced at Trevor, then lowered her voice.

'He was *hopeless* at crossing the road. In fact, well, put it this way,' she added darkly as Trev stared at the floor, 'he'd had three previous owners before me. But being an assistance dog suits him *much* better – doesn't it Trevor?'

'Woof!'

And now I watched him gazing at Beverley, as he waited for his next command. It was as though she were a film star, and he her number one fan.

'What devotion,' I said. 'He really loves you.'

'Not half as much as I love him.' Suddenly the telephone rang. Trevor trotted into the hall, returned with the cordless handset in his mouth, and passed it to Beverley. She spoke briefly, then hung up. 'Sorry about that,' she said. 'It was the local radio station. They want to record an interview with us. I don't mind as I'm never that busy and it helps to publicise Helping Paw. It's a new charity,' she explained, 'so they need some good press. And we don't mind, do we Trev? By the way is it okay if I have your phone number?' she added, 'in case of emergency.'

'Of course.' I gave it to her, and she programmed it in, then Trevor put the handset back.

'And what do you do for work?' I asked as I got up to leave.

'Telephone sex.'

'*Really*?'

'No! Just kidding!' she laughed. 'I teach English over the phone to foreign students. It's mind-blowingly boring but it pays the bills.'

'And is that what you did before?'

She shook her head and, for the first time in an hour, her smile slipped.

'I was a PE teacher,' she said.

So that solves the mystery of the hockey sticks I thought as I unlocked my front door a few minutes later. I felt simultaneously drained and inspired by my encounter with Bev though I was horrified to see I'd picked up some of Trevor's hairs. I carefully removed every single one with a brush, and then tweezers, as I listened to my answerphone.

'Hi! I saw your ad, my name's Susan . . . Hi, I'm a pharmacist and my name's Tom . . . Hello, this is Jenny and I'm a single mum . . .' I'd only been out for an hour and I'd already had three replies. Over the weekend I had twelve more, of whom I arranged to see five.

First was a lugubrious looking engineer called Steve. He inspected the whole house, opening all my kitchen cupboards – bloody cheek! – as though he were buying it, not renting a room. Then came Phil who sounded promising but who spent half the time staring at my legs. Then there was an actor called Quentin who was jolly, but he couldn't stand birds and he smoked. After him came Annie, who was twenty-three, and who found everything 'reely nice.' The house was 'reely nice,' the room was 'reely nice,' and she worked in marketing and that was 'reely nice' too. After five minutes of this I wanted to stab her but instead smiled and said I'd 'let her know.'

'That would be reely nice.' As I waved her off I realised that the anagram of Annie is 'inane.' Then there was Scott who was Born Again and who wanted to hold prayer meetings on Monday nights, and finally there was a student at the Camberwell Art School who wanted to bring her two cats. Disappointed with the respondents I went to the local gym I've just joined for a kick-boxing class.

'KICK it! And PUNCH it! And KICK it! And BLOCK it!,' shouted our instructor, 'Stormin' Norman'. 'KICK it! And PUNCH it! And KICK it – and *KICK* it!! C'mon girls!' As I pounded the punchbag in the mirrored studio I imagined that it was Ed. And now I visualised myself breaking down his front door with a single blow of my foot, and booting Mary-Claire Grey to Battersea. Were it not for that manipulative little Madam, Ed and I would still be married and I would *not* now be contemplating having to share my house with some stranger whom I'd probably hate.

'You're real good, Rose!' said Norman appreciatively when the class came to an end. I wiped the sweat out of eyes with my wristband. 'Done it before?'

'Just a couple of times.'

'Well, take it from me, girl – you've got a kick that could break a bank door.'

Glowing from this compliment I showered and changed and was just leaving the club when I stopped in front of the noticeboard, my eye suddenly drawn to a hand-written card:

> *WANTED: Single room in house-share in SE5 for*
> *very quiet, studious male. Up to £400 p.c.m.*
> *Privacy* <u>essential</u>. *Please ring Theo on 07711 522106.*

I scribbled down the number, phoned it, and arranged that Theo would come round at seven the following night. At five to the bell rang and I opened the door. To my surprise there were *two* well-dressed young men standing there. Theo had clearly decided to bring a friend.

'Good evening Madam,' said one of the men politely,

holding out a pamphlet. 'Have you heard the Good News?' I gave them a frigid stare. I don't mind being canvassed for my political views or being asked to buy dusters from homeless men. I have no objections to kids with sponsorship forms or fund-raisers rattling their cans. I'll submit to the interrogations of market researchers, and I'm a good sport about 'Trick or Treat'. But I absolutely *hate* finding Jehovah's Witnesses on the doorstep – it can really ruin my day.

'Have you heard the Good News?' the man repeated.

'Sorry, I'm a Buddhist,' I lied.

'But we would like you to be filled with the knowledge of Jehovah's glory.'

'Thanks but no thanks. Goodbye.'

'But it will only take five minutes of your time.'

'No it won't.' I shut the door. Ten seconds later, the bell rang again.

'May we come back another time and share God's glorious Kingdom with you?'

'No,' I said. 'You may not.' I was tempted to explain that I'd had enough religion rammed down my throat to convert half the world's godless but decided to bite my tongue. 'Goodbye,' I said pointedly, then closed the door and was halfway down the hall when ... *ddrrrnnngggg!!* For crying out loud!

'Look, I said "no," so will you kindly piss *off*!' I hissed through the crack. 'Oh.' Standing there was an anxious-looking young man of about twenty-five. 'I'm sorry,' I said sliding back the chain. 'I thought you were the Jehovah's Witnesses. Can't stand them.'

'No, I'm . . . Theo.'

'Of course.' He was about five foot eleven, with blond hair cut close to the head; a strong, straight nose, and blue eyes which were half obscured by a pair of steel-rimmed glasses. He looked like the Milky Bar kid. He seemed a bit shy as he stepped inside but was at least quite tidily dressed; and as he extended his hand I noticed with satisfaction that his nails were neat and clean. As I showed him round I noticed his slight northern accent, although I couldn't quite place it. He explained that he was an accountant working for a small computer firm in Soho and that he needed somewhere straight away.

'Where are you living now?' I asked him as I showed him the sitting room.

'Just off Camberwell Grove. With a friend. He's been very kind and he's got a big flat but I feel I should find my own place. This is grand,' he said politely as we went upstairs. Grand? Hardly. 'Have you lived here long?'

'Just a month.' He liked the room, which is large, with striped lemon wallpaper, sloping eves, Dad's old cupboard and a small double bed.

'It's grand,' he said again, nodding affably. And I realised that it was simply his word for 'nice'. 'I like the aspect,' he added as he stood looking out of the window.

'Are you from Manchester?' I enquired with polite inquisitiveness.

'Nope, other side of the Pennines – Leeds.'

As we went downstairs I decided that he was pleasant and polite and terribly boring and would probably do perfectly well.

'So are you interested?' I asked him as I made him a cup of coffee.

'Well . . . yes,' he said, glancing at Rudy, who was mercifully asleep.

'In that case let's cut to the chase. I am a very, *very* busy person,' I explained, 'and I'm looking for a quiet life. If you move in I guarantee that I will leave you alone and not bother you in *any* way providing that you don't bother *me* – okay?'

He nodded nervously.

'Right,' I said whipping out my list. 'Do you have any of the following unpleasant, anti-social and potentially hazardous habits? Do you a) smoke? b) take drugs? c) leave dirty dishes in the sink? d) fail to clean the bath? e) spatter toothpaste all over the basin? f) have a problem with birds? g) play loud music? h) nick other people's milk? i) nick other people's eggs/bread/stamps ditto? j) leave the seat *up*? k) leave the iron *on*? l) leave candles burning unattended? and, finally, m) forget to lock the front door?'

'Er, no, no . . . no,' he paused for a moment. 'No. No, no . . . Sorry, what was g) again?' I told him. 'That's no too. Er . . . no, no. Nope, no . . . no and, um . . . no.'

'Good. And do you have a mobile phone because I don't want to share my land line?'

'Yes.'

'And do you watch much TV?'

He shook his head. 'Just the odd science programme, and the news. But in the evenings I write – that's why I've been looking for somewhere quiet.'

'I see. And finally, sorry to mention it, but I really don't want women staying here. I mean, girlfriends.'

He seemed taken aback. 'Girlfriends?' he repeated. 'Oh no.' He drew in his breath, and grimaced. '*That* won't be a problem. That won't be a problem at *all*.'

'Well in that case that's all absolutely fine. I'm now very pleased to tell you that – subject to satisfactory references of course – I've decided you can have the room.'

'Oh. That's a bit quick,' he said. 'Don't you want to think about it?'

'I already have.'

'I see . . .'

'I make fast decisions.'

'Uh huh. Well . . .'

'Do you want it or not?' I interjected.

'I'm not sure actually.' Bloody *cheek*!

'Why aren't you sure?' I persisted.

'Well, because I'd like time to reflect, that's all.' Time to reflect? What a wimp! 'I mean, I do like the room,' he explained earnestly. 'And your house is grand, but I didn't think that I'd have to decide straight away.'

'Well I'm afraid you do.'

'Er, why?'

'Because, as I've already explained, I'm *extremely* busy and

I want to get it sorted out tonight.'

'Oh.' He seemed nonplussed. 'I see.' Suddenly the phone rang and I stood up. I thought I heard him sigh with relief.

'That's probably someone else ringing about the room,' I said. 'I've had *so* many calls.' I went into the hall, shutting the door carefully behind me, and picked up the handset.

'Hello?' I said. There was silence. 'Hello?' I tried again. 'Hello?' I repeated a little louder. Bad connection; but now I thought I detected a breath. 'He*llo*,' I said one final time, then I put the handset down. How weird. Probably a wrong number or a fault on the line.

'I was right,' I said airily as I went back into the kitchen. 'That was someone else ringing about the room. I've had over twenty calls since the ad went in. Anyway, where were we? Oh yes. You wanted to have a think about it. You didn't seem quite sure. So shall we leave it at that then?' I added pleasantly.

'Well . . . no. I . . .'

'Look, Theo, I haven't got all day. Do you want it, or don't you? It's a simple case of "Yes" or "No".' Theo looked at me for a few seconds, and blinked. Then he suddenly smiled this odd, lop-sided little smile.

'Well, ye-es. I reckon I do.'

Chapter Four

'This is London FM,' announced Minty Malone, as I sat in the basement studio on City Road the following Tuesday. 'Welcome back to *Sound Advice*, our twice-weekly late-night phone-in with the *Post*'s agony aunt, Rose Costelloe. Do *you* have a problem? Then call 0200 222222 and Ask Rose.'

It was five past eleven and we'd already been on air for an hour. We'd heard from Melissa who was wondering whether to become Catholic, and Denise who was going bald and Neil who couldn't get a girlfriend and James who thought he was gay; then there was Josh, a jockey with mounting debts and Tom who hated his dad, and Sally who was having a nervous breakdown – the usual stuff. On the computer screen in front of me the names of the waiting callers winked and flashed.

'And on line one,' said Minty, 'we have Bob from Dulwich.'

'Hi Bob,' I said. 'How can I help?'

'Well, Rose,' he began hesitantly, as I scribbled on my pad, 'I'm quite a, well, yeah, big bloke really . . .' Hmm . . . another fatso with low self-esteem. 'And I get my leg pulled about it at work.'

'I see.'

'Anyway, there's this girl there who's a real knockout and I think she likes me as she's always nice. But my problem is that every time I get up the nerve to ask her out she makes some excuse.'

'Bob, you say you're a big bloke – how much do you weigh?'

'About . . .' – I could hear the air being sucked through his teeth – '. . . seventeen stone.'

'And how tall are you?'

'Five foot ten.'

'Then you're just going to *have* to *lose* the *lard*! Sorry to be brutal, Bob, but it's true. I know you'd like me to say that this girl will fall in love with your great personality, but I think your great *person* is going to get in the way, and frankly, I think the only reason she's being so nice is because she feels sorry for you. Bob, take it from me, no self-respecting woman – let alone a "knockout" – is going to go out with a Sumo-sized bloke. The number for Weight Watchers is . . .' I glanced at my handbook, '. . . 0845 712 3000 and I want you to ring it *first* thing. Do you promise me you'll do that?' I heard a deep sigh.

'Yeah, okay Rose. I will.'

'And Bob I want you to phone in again a month from today and tell everyone that you've lost your first stone.'

'Okay Rose, yeah. You're right.'

'Well done Bob,' said Minty, 'and now we have Martine, on line three.'

'Go ahead, Martine,' I said.

'Well,' she began in a trembly voice. 'The reason I'm ringing is because, well, I've just been told I can't have kids.' A momentary silence followed: I could almost see the tears in her eyes.

'Martine how old are you?'

'Thirty-two.'

'And have you tried *all* avenues?'

'Yes. But I had cancer when I was a teenager, you see, and because of that the doctors can't help.'

'Well *I'd* like to help you Martine, so stay on the line. Is that what you want to talk about – the fact that you've had this bad news?'

'No,' she said. 'I'm beginning to accept that. The thing is I'd like to adopt but my husband's not keen.'

'Does he say why?'

'It's because he was adopted, and he had problems so he's afraid that any kids we adopted would too.'

'But so might any children that you had naturally. They could fall ill – God forbid – or they could fail at school or drop out. Life's fraught with difficulties and you can't not go ahead with something which could make you happy out of fear that it *might* go wrong.'

'I know,' she said in a trembling voice. 'I've told my husband that.'

'And you sound like a lovely person Martine so I'm sure you'd be a really great mum.' There was a tiny sob. Oh God, I shouldn't have said that. I could hear a Niagara of tears start to fall.

'Well ... I think I would,' she wept, 'but my husband seems set against adopting, but now I know it's my only chance.' I glanced at Minty, who's three months pregnant. There was compassion all over her face.

'Martine, do you have a good relationship with your husband?' I asked.

'Yes,' she whispered. 'In most ways I do.'

'And when did this issue first come up?'

'A month ago. We hadn't really talked about it before, because we thought I might still be okay. But then I got the final results from the hospital which told me that my chances of conceiving are nil.'

'Then give your husband a little more time. He needs to think about it – and men like to come round to things in their own way. So my advice is don't panic, and don't put any pressure on him as that could easily backfire. But I do think you should both talk to someone at NORCAP, the National Organisation for Counselling Adoptees and Parents: their number is – I flicked through my handbook – 01865 875000. Will you call them, Martine?'

'Yes,' she sniffed. 'Okay.'

'The line may be busy because this is National Adoption Week, but leave your number and they'll ring you back. And Martine, I don't mind telling you that *I* was adopted and I was absolutely *fine*. I've never had *any* problems, I had a really *great* childhood, and I'm sure that your kids will too.'

'Oh thanks Rose,' she whispered. 'I do hope so.' And I was just going to go to the next caller, when I heard her say, 'but I think the reason *why* my husband feels so negative about adoption is because he's never traced his real mum.'

'Oh . . .'

'He still seems so *angry* with her for giving him up – it's like a festering wound. He rarely talks about it, but I think that's what's *really* bothering him and the issue of our adopting has brought it all up.'

'I see, well, look . . . thanks for calling in Martine and I, er . . . wish you the very best of luck. And now we go to Pam on line five. What's your problem, Pam?'

'Well, my problem is that I'm in my thirties, I'm single and as a freelance graphic designer, I work from home.'

'Ye-es.'

'But recently I've got to know my postman quite well . . .'

'Uh huh.'

'And I really fancy him.'

'I see.'

'I even get up early to make sure I catch a glimpse of him.'

'That must be tiring.'

'Oh it *is*. I've also taken to sending myself parcels so that he has to knock on the door. I'm totally smitten,' she added.

'So what's the problem?'

'He's married – at least I think he is. He wears a ring on his left hand, put it that way.'

'Yup. He's married,' I said.

'But he's absolutely gorgeous, Rose; I've never felt this way before. What should I do?'

'Well, honey, I think you should get real. I'm sure this macho mailman is very dashing but my advice is to stamp him "Return to Sender" and try and get out a bit more. And now Kathy on line three. What's the problem Kathy?'

'The problem, Rose, is that my husband has left me!'

'I'm sorry to hear that.'

'Well I don't know *why* you're sorry, as it was you who told him to!'

'What?'

'A couple of weeks ago my husband wrote to you at the *Daily Post* and you told him to get divorced.'

'I'm sorry, but I haven't a clue what you're talking about.'

'You told him to leave me. He hid the letter, but I found it. It was you. His name's John.' Oh God, now I remembered – it was the adulterous husband-basher. 'I mean, who the hell are you Rose, to tell other people how to live their lives?'

'I don't. People simply run their problems by me; I listen, and I give them advice.'

'Well you give them crap advice! I mean, what the hell are you doing telling men to leave their wives you, you . . . marriage breaker!' I looked at Minty, she was rolling her eyes and shaking her head.

'Kathy,' I said, feeling my heart rate rev, 'I did not tell your husband to leave. And from what I remember of his letter I think he'd already decided what he wanted to do.'

'But you helped him make up his mind. He's a spineless sort of bloke so if you hadn't written to him, putting it in black and white like that, then he would never have had the guts.'

'I'm not at all sure that that's true. And in any case if he's really as "spineless" as you say, then why do you want to stay married to him?'

'Because he's *my* husband – that's why! But now he's left me because of you – you, you . . . baggage!' By now my face was aflame.

'Kathy, if you speak to him like you're speaking to me I'm amazed he didn't leave you years ago!'

'You're a wicked, *wicked* woman!' she retorted.

'And now on line three we have Fran,' Minty interjected as she made slashing gestures across her throat to the producer, Wesley, on the other side of the glass. 'Hello Fran.'

'Hello Minty.'

'You are a fucking marriage breaker Rose Costelloe . . .'

Why didn't Wesley just get *rid* of her? '. . . and you're going to be SORRY for this!' Oh! Minty's face registered alarm at the threat but I just rolled my eyes and shrugged.

'Hello Fran,' I said with a large sip of hospitality Frascati. 'And what's your problem?'

'Well,' she croaked, 'I've been dumped.'

'When?'

'Six months ago.'

'That's quite a while.'

'I know. But I just . . . can't get over it.'

'And how long were you with him?'

'Almost two years. He left me for our optician,' she added plaintively. 'I never saw it coming.' Minty was struggling not to laugh. 'I feel so depressed,' she sniffed. 'Every evening I sit at home feeling bitter: I just can't . . . forget.'

'Fran,' I said, 'this is easy to say, and hard to do, but you've *got* to try and move on.'

'But I can't because it's made me feel . . . worthless. I blame myself.'

'Fran, why do you blame yourself?' There was a stunned silence.

'I don't know really – I just do.'

'Fran,' I said firmly, 'please *don't*. If you must blame anyone, then in these situations it's much more healthy to blame others. First of all blame your ex – that's a given – then blame the other woman of course. You may also wish to blame the government, Fate, bad karma or dodgy feng shui. If all else fails, blame global warming – but please *don't* blame yourself, okay?'

'Okay,' she said with a reluctant giggle.

'Can I come in here?' said Minty. 'Fran, I had a terrible break-up three years ago. I was actually jilted – on my wedding day.'

'No!' said Fran, appalled.

'Yes. But do you know, it was the *best* thing that ever happened to me, because I met someone *so* much nicer, and I just know that you will too.'

'Well, I hope so,' she sniffed. 'I've been so unhappy.'

'Fran,' I said, 'that won't last. Heartbreak is a curable condition. And remember that your ex is only your ex because he's *wrong* for you otherwise you'd still be together, right? But it's not easy getting over someone,' I went on, thinking of Ed with a vicious stab. 'So you need a strategy to help you recover. Now were there things about him you didn't like?'

'Oh *yeah*!' she exclaimed. 'Loads!'

'Good. Then make a list of them, and when you've done it, ring your friends and read it to them, then ask them if you've left anything out. Get them to add their own negative comments, and ask your family as well. Then ask your next-door neighbours – on both sides – plus the people in the corner shop, then post the list up in a prominent place. Secondly, get *off* your bum! Get down to the gym, like I did, and take up kick-boxing or Tae-Bo. Kick the shit out of your instructor, Fran – believe me it'll lift your mood. Because it's only when you're feeling happy and confident again, that the *right* man will come along.'

'Okay,' she sighed. 'Yes. You're right. Do you think I should contact some of my exes?' she added. 'One or two of them were quite keen.'

'Should you contact your exes?' I repeated slowly. 'No,' I said firmly. 'Do *not*.'

'Oh. Why?'

'Because one of the Ten Commandments of the Dumped Woman is, "Thou Shalt Not Phone Up Thy Old Boyfriends".

'Why not?'

'Well, because they might have had a sex change, or they might be in jail, or bald, or dead. Worst of all, you might find they're now happily married with two adorable kids! So no, *don't* have anything to do with your old boyfriends, Fran – put all your energy into finding someone *new*!'

'And on that positive note I'm afraid we must leave it there,' said Minty as the hand on the studio clock juddered towards the twelve. 'Thanks to everyone who's called in, and do please join Rose and me again on Tuesday night for our regular phone-in – *Sound Advice.'*

As I pushed wearily on the heavy studio door I saw Wesley waving at me.

'I've got a call for you, Rose.'

'As long as it's not that mad woman,' I whispered, making frantic circling gestures by my head. Wesley clapped his hand over the mouthpiece.

'No it's not her. It's a bloke.'

'Hello?' I said tentatively, nervously wondering if it was Ed.

'Is that Rose?'

It wasn't Ed.

'It's Henry here.' Henry? Oh, *Henry*! My ex but three! 'Heard your dulcet tones on the radio . . . brought back some *very* pleasant times . . . just come back from the Gulf . . . yes still in H.M.'s Armed Forces . . . got a desk job at the M.o.D . . . absolutely *love* to see you . . . how about dinner next week?'

Well why *not*? I thought, as I put the phone down with a grin. True, Henry had never really lit my fire. He was the human equivalent of a lava lamp – very attractive but not that bright. But on the other hand he's harmless, generous, extremely good-natured and after what I've been through I fancy a date. I mean, where's the harm in having dinner tête-à-tête with an old flame? And yes, I *know* what I said to that caller, but the point *is* that I'm sure Henry's been to some *very* interesting places in the last three years, plus I'm keen to find out what he has to say about the role of women in the armed forces, not to mention the proposed European Rapid Reaction Defence Force and its likely effect on Britain's relationship with NATO. So I fixed to see him the following Friday, November the tenth, which was also the night Theo was due to move in.

Theo had told me he'd be arriving at around half past six. And I was just trying to tame my hair at ten to when the doorbell rang. I opened my bedroom window, to check it wasn't the Jehovah's Witnesses again and as I did so a late firework suddenly exploded with a mighty BOOOOOM-MMMM!!! spangling the night with stars. 'Ooooohhh,' I heard myself breathe, like a child, then I looked below. Standing there, looking up, was Theo with so much baggage my tiny garden resembled an airport carousel.

'You're early,' I said accusingly as I opened the door.

'Yes, er, sorry,' he said.

'And you've got a lot of stuff.'

'I . . . know. But don't worry, it'll all go in my room. Most of it's books,' he explained. As I watched him trundling up and down the stairs with it all I noticed one very odd-looking, long black case. What on earth was in it I wondered – a musical instrument? God *forbid*. And now I wished I'd asked if he was going to be tooting away on a clarinet half the night or blasting me out with a trombone; and I shivered with apprehension at the thought that I was letting this total stranger into my house. But I needed the cash I reminded myself firmly, and his references had been fine. His boss at Compu-Force had assured me that far from being a convicted axe-murderer, Theo was a 'nice, reliable chap. He's had a hard time recently,' he'd added enigmatically: I'd wondered, but hadn't enquired. All I needed to know was that he wouldn't kill me, bore me, evangelise me, steal from me, hold orgies or write rubber cheques . . .

'I'm just on my way out,' I said, as I grabbed my bag and handed him his set of keys. 'I've got to be in Fulham by eight.'

'But it's only six-fifteen.'

'I . . . know,' I said, irritated by his rather forthright and frankly impertinent intervention, 'but I, um, always allow myself lots of time.'

'Well, enjoy yourself,' he said affably. Then he suddenly added, 'you look very nice.'

'Do I?' I said wonderingly. It was ages since anyone had said that to me.

'Yes. Especially your hair. It's really, erm . . .' he began rotating both index fingers next to his head by way of illustration.

'Curly?' I suggested.

'Mad.'

'Oh. Well . . . thanks very much.'

'I mean, the way it sort of jumps out of your head.'

'I see.'

'I meant it nicely,' he explained.

'Glad to hear it.' I was so frosty, I could see my own breath. 'Now,' I said, handing him five pages of typed A4, 'this is a little list of dos and don'ts about the house, just in case you've forgotten what I told you last week.'

'Thanks,' he said uncertainly. 'Do I get a gold star for good behaviour?' he added with a grin.

'No,' I said icily. 'You don't.' But I was tempted to tell him that he was well on his way to picking up his first black mark. 'Anyway, make yourself at home,' I added grudgingly as I picked up my bag.

'Thanks very much. I'll . . . try.'

'And if you're not sure about anything, just call me on my mobile . . . here,' I gave him my card. As I slung on my caramel suede jacket and stepped outside, Theo followed me out to pick up more things. KER-ACKKKK!! Another rocket exploded above us – BOOM! RACK-A-TACK!!! BOOOOOOOM!!! Each detonation illuminated the short terrace for an instant then the houses were plunged into a Stygian dark.

'The street lighting's useless,' I warned him as I fished out my car keys, 'so be careful.'

'Yes, I've noticed. It's *really* bad.'

'In fact I intend to complain to the council about it,' I said vehemently.

'Oh no!' he exclaimed. 'Please *don't*. Well, have a good evening,' he added pleasantly, then he picked up a box and went inside.

As I turned the ignition on my old Polo I stared at Theo's retreating back and pondered that bizarre exchange. *Why* didn't he want me to get the council to do something about the shoddy street lights? How *weird* . . . I wondered whether I hadn't made a dreadful error of judgement as I released the brake and set off. 'Do I get a gold star for good behaviour?' I ask you! What a *nerve*. And that rude remark of his about my hair. My hair has been described in many ways – 'pre-Raphaelite' mainly, but also 'tumbling,' 'lustrously curly,' 'corkscrewing,' even 'frizzy,' but never has it earned the epithet, 'mad'. I mean, really! How gauche can you get! And that sinister-looking black case – what the hell was in it? Maybe it wasn't a musical instrument, maybe it was a Samurai sword? And now, as I waited at a red light, I had a sudden vision of myself being found dead in bed dripping blood like a colander – I'd probably be front page news. 'AGONY AUNT DEAD IN BED!'; 'HORROR OF AGONY AUNT!'; no – 'AGONY OF AGONY AUNT!' was better or 'DEATH OF AN AGONY AUNT!'; 'AGONY AUNT SLAIN!' was good if a tad melodramatic, or maybe, 'HORROR IN SE5!' The *Daily Post*, of course, would go to town. R. Soul, grateful for such a big story, would probably do the honours with the headline himself. He was good at those. It was, after all, Ricky who had penned the legendary, 'HEADLESS BODY FOUND IN TOPLESS BAR!'

As the car moved forward again I worried in case my murder didn't make the front page: my split with Ed only made page five. I idly wondered whether it would be on national TV – it probably would. I'd get, say, two minutes on *News at Ten* and at least, ooh, a minute on Radio Four? As I drove down Kennington Road I pondered whether I'd be obituarised in the national press. They'd no doubt print my by-line photo – it's quite flattering actually – but what would the piece say? They'd probably get some other agony aunt to write it – oh God! – not Citronella Pratt! Not her – please, *please* not her – I could imagine what she'd write. 'Rose Costelloe showed some promise as an agony aunt,' damning me with faint praise. 'How very *sad* and *tragic* that we will now never know whether that promise could have been fulfilled.' I made a mental note to phone all the Obits editors first thing and tell them to ring the twins if I croaked.

Then, feeling more relaxed, I visualised my funeral which would be a very sad but dignified affair. On my coffin would be a huge spray of white lilies – no, not lilies, *roses* of course, like my name, obviously – red ones to match my hair. The twins would be chief mourners: I was confident they'd do it well. Now, as I waited at a traffic light, I imagined them in black, tears streaming down their lovely faces, clutching each other's hands. There'd be a huge photo of me leaning against the altar, and probably, what – a hundred people or so? More if some of my readers came. A *lot* more. That might bump it up to at least, ooh, three or four hundred – maybe even five. I could hear them all reminiscing about me in respectful, hushed tones as the organ played.

'– Can't believe it! So tragic!'

'– She was so beautiful and kind.'

'– That gorgeous figure of hers.'

'– She could wear *anything*.'

'– Even slim-fitting trousers.'

'– Yes – and her advice was *great*.'

I imagined Ed, arriving late, looking distraught. Mary-Claire had tried to prevent him from going, but he'd thrust her to one side.

'No!' he'd screamed. 'Nothing will stop me! And by the way, Mary-Claire – you're dumped!' And because the church was so full – I liked Trev's black ribbon in his collar, nice touch – Ed had had to stand at the back. Now, no longer able to control himself, he was incontinent with grief. And as he wept openly and loudly, heads were turning, my friends (and readers) torn between contempt for his treatment of me during my life, and pity for his distress at my death.

'It's all my fault!' he was blubbing as they sang 'Abide With Me'. 'If I hadn't betrayed her this would *never* have happened. I'll always blame myself!' Gratified by this confession, I now saw everyone at my grave, Ed still blubbing like a baby as he threw in the final clod.

'– God look at him – he's gone to pieces!'

'– He'll never get over it.'

'– He didn't deserve her.'

'– He didn't appreciate her.'

'– C'mon on Ed, it's time to go.'

Now I imagined everyone leaving, and the south London cemetery lonely and dark; and I realised that the only reason I was there was because I'd let that weirdo, Theo Sheen, into my house. I was feeling pretty appalled by now and thinking that yes, I'd taken a huge and *very* stupid risk and for what – a bit of cash? – when suddenly my mobile rang.

'Rose?' I heard as I slipped in my earpiece.

'Yes?'

'It's Theo here.' Aaarrrggh! 'I just wondered if you'll be coming back tonight?'

'Why do you want to know?'

'I wasn't sure what to do about the front door, that's all.'

'What about it?'

'Should I put the chain on?' Oh. 'I know that Camberwell can be a bit dodgy on the burglary front. So I just wanted to know whether I should put the chain on when I go to bed, that's all.'

'No,' I said, exhaling with relief. 'Don't bother. I'll be back by twelve.'

'Right then,' he said cheerfully. 'Anyway, have a nice evening. Bye.'

I heaved a sigh of relief as I rang off, but then Suspicion raised its ugly head again. And I thought maybe, reading between the lines here, he's just trying to find out whether or not I have a bloke. Yes . . . the enquiry about the security chain is just a front. A red herring. Maybe he *is* a homicidal weirdo after all . . .

PARP! PARP!! *PARP*!!!

'All *right*!' I yelled into my mirror as I moved off the green light. I pulled myself together and banished Theo from my mind as I negotiated the fume-filled roads. I skirted Brixton then drove towards Clapham, passing my old flat in Meteor Street. As I spotted a sign for Putney I felt my pulse begin to race. It was ten to seven – over an hour until I had to meet

Henry, so I still had plenty of time. To calm my nerves I turned on the radio and found myself listening to a phone-in on LBC. I recognised the voice: it was Lana McCord, the new agony aunt on *Moi!* magazine.

'We're discussing relationship breakdown,' she said. 'And now we have Betsey on line five. Betsey, you're a divorcée I understand.'

'Yes, but I'd rather be a widow!' she spat. 'Bereavement would be preferable to betrayal.' I know how she feels. 'I'm so *angry*,' she went on tearfully. She'd clearly been drinking. 'I gave him the best years of my life.'

'Betsey,' said Lana gently. 'How old are you?'

'Forty-one.'

'Then you've still got a *lot* of life left. So why spend it being bitter?' she went on. *Exactly!* 'Do you enjoy your negative thoughts?' *Quite.* 'Do they contribute to your happiness?' *Of course not.* 'Do they move you forward in any way?' *Good point!*

'I just can't deal with this blow to my self-esteem,' croaked Betsey.

'What positive steps have you taken?' asked Lana McCord.

'Well, I went out with someone, on the rebound, but that didn't work.' *Surprise surprise!* 'I've seen one or two old boyfriends.' *Hopeless! What a twit!* 'But I loved my husband and I just can't get him out of my mind. What really *gets* me is the thought of him with *her*,' she went on, in a drink-sodden drawl. 'The thought of them having – uh-uh – you know, just makes me feel ill.'

'So why torment yourself with that unpleasant thought?' *Bullseye!*

'Because I can't stop myself from doing it – that's why. I do these awful things,' she confided with a wet sniff as I drove down Putney High Street.

'What sort of things?' said Lana.

'I ring him then I hang up.' *Sad!* 'I drive past his flat as well.'

'Oh dear,' said Lana with a sigh. And now, my heart beating

74

like a tom-tom, I drove slowly down Chelverton Road.

'In fact I've driven past it so often I've worn a groove in the tarmac – but I just can't *help* it,' she wailed.

You are one *very* sad bunny, Betsey, I thought to myself as I turned left into Blenheim Road. Seventeen, twenty-five, thirty-one – mustn't let him spot me: then there it was. number thirty-seven. Ed's navy company Beemer was parked outside. Blackness filled my chest as I pulled into a space opposite and a little to the right, away from the tangerine glare of the lamp. Then I switched off my lights, turned up my collar, and sunk down into my seat. The downstairs curtains were drawn but a wedge of light shone through a chink at the top. Ed was at home. My husband. He was on the other side of that wall. And now I wondered with a crashing sensation in the pit of my stomach, if *she* was there as well. Perhaps she was standing at the Aga, cooking supper. I imagined sneaking up behind her and bashing her over the head, then chopping her into tiny pieces, mixing her with Kitty-Bics and feeding her to next door's cat. I was interrupted from this pleasant reverie by a light going on in Ed's room.

'Your behaviour is very destructive,' I heard Lana say. Yes it is, I thought. 'Not only are you not trying to recover from this, you seem determined to pour acid in the wound.' *True*. 'I mean, why do you want to torture yourself? Why?'

'Why?' I whispered as Ed's face suddenly loomed up at the window.

'Yes. Tell me. Why?'

'I don't *know*,' I wept, as he threw wide his arms and shut the curtains. 'Oh God, oh *God*, I don't know.'

Actually, I do know. You see, what *I* was doing was quite different from what that sad woman on the phone-in was doing. She was obsessing about her husband – poor thing – whereas I was actively trying to get *over* mine by laying a ghost. Because I thought that if I could just sit outside his house, and feel absolutely *nothing*, then that would help me move on. So I did. Okay, I cried at first, but then I dried my eyes and I sat there for – ooh, not that long, maybe half an hour or so – just watching as though I were a twitcher and the house some exotic bird.

'I can *do* this,' I told myself. 'Yes, Ed's there, and I'm still married to him, and yes, I *was* besotted with him, but the fact is I'm in control.' Remembering some tips from the *Breathe Away Your Stress* book I shut my eyes and inhaled through my nose. As I exhaled, counting slowly to ten, I could feel my heart rate slow, and my eyes were still closed when I heard the throaty chug of an approaching cab. And I expected to hear it go past me, but instead I heard the squeal of its brakes. I opened my eyes. It had stopped right outside Ed's house, and now the door was clicking open like the wing of a shiny black beetle, and Mary-Claire Grey stepped out. She paid the driver, then tottered up to Ed's front door, her stilettos clacking up the path like sniper fire. And I was waiting, stomach churning, for her to lift her hand to the brass bell and ring it, when instead she opened her bag, took out a bunch of keys then proceeded to unlock the door. The *bitch*! She was letting herself into Ed's house – *my* marital home – for all the world as though she *lived* there! Which she quite clearly did.

'She's moved in,' I breathed, outraged, as the door closed behind her. 'She's known him three months and she's already moved in.' Ignoring the small voice telling me that I had moved in with Ed after only *one* month, I started the car and pulled out of the space, hands trembling like winter leaves. I was so distressed I almost pranged the car in front, then with a sickening, tightening sensation around my sternum, I drove away. Dizzy now with a blend of misery, panic and nausea I sped off to meet Henry at Ghillie's on the New Kings Road.

'Rose!' he exclaimed, as I was shown to his table at the back. Still feeling sick and wobbly I allowed myself to be enveloped in one of Henry's familiar, bone-crushing hugs. 'It's *great* to see you again,' he said planting a trademark fat kiss on my cheek. 'You're a major media star these days!' I began to feel better.

'And you're a Major – full stop!'

'About bloody time!' he laughed. 'But then I always was a late developer,' he added with a good-natured smile.

Now, as I had my one glass of champagne, my stress levels plummeted from their Himalayan heights and began to stroll calmly around at Base Camp. So what if Mary-Claire was living with Ed? It didn't make any difference to me. In fact it'll make it easier for me to get over him I thought, knowing that he's moved on so fast. I'm not bothered about Ed, I said to myself. Ed's over. The credits on our marriage have rolled. As things turned out, it wasn't the major motion picture it was meant to be – it was only a short.

As Henry chatted away to me I gazed at his handsome face. His sandy hair was retreating a little, but he looked much the same as before. The lids above the forget-me-not-blue eyes were a tiny bit crinklier and there were two parallel lines etched on his brow. He'd put on a little weight since I'd last seen him, and there was an incipient jowl beneath his square jaw. But he looked so attractively manly in his sports jacket, smart cords and polished brogues.

Henry and I had met at a barbecue in Fulham five years before. We were involved for a while, but it didn't go anywhere – well, he was always away. Which, funnily enough, was exactly the same problem I'd had with my previous boyfriend, Tom. He was a pilot with British Airways flying the Australian route; we'd had a few nice stopovers here and there but otherwise things didn't really take off. Anyway, Henry was posted to Cyprus for a year, then Belize, then Gibraltar, so our affair soon fizzled out. But we'd remained in touch intermittently and I'd retained a soft spot for him the size of a swamp. It was two years since I'd last seen him and as we ate we reminisced about old times.

'Do you remember the fun we had re-enacting famous battles with your old Action Men?' I asked fondly.

'With you doing the explosions!'

'Playing Warships in bed.'

'You always beat me.'

'Making Lego tanks.'

'Oh *yes*.'

'Watching reruns of *Colditz*.'

'And *The World At War*.'

'We had fun didn't we?'

'Ra-ther.'

He told me about the NATO manoeuvres he'd been on, the Balkan skirmishes – 'Fabulous stuff!' His stint with the UN Peacekeeping force in Bosnia – 'bloody hairy!'; a recent tour of duty in the Gulf. Then I told him about my marital battles, and about Mary-Claire Grey; he squeezed my hand.

'She's moved in with him,' I said dismally, feeling the shock of it all over again. 'I've just found out. I can't *believe* it, Henry. He's only known her three months.'

'That's tough.'

'Still, I guess it'll make me a better agony aunt,' I admitted grudgingly. 'You know, been there – suffered that. And what about you?' I asked as the waiter brought my lemon sole.

'Well,' he said, picking up his knife and fork. 'I'm newly single too. I got dumped by my latest girlfriend.' My ears pricked up. That was clearly why he'd wanted to see me.

'I'm sorry,' I lied.

'Well, Venetia's a super girl – but it didn't work out.'

'Wouldn't she make the explosion noises?'

'No,' he laughed. 'It wasn't that. It was just that' – he sighed, then pushed a piece of steak round his plate.

'You don't have to tell me if you don't want to,' I said quietly.

'No, really, Rose, I do. I do want to tell you,' he repeated sadly as I sipped my water.

'So what happened?'

'Well,' he went on, awkwardly, 'it was just that there was . . .' he exhaled painfully then drew the air through his teeth, '. . . another woman.' Oh. Now that didn't sound like Henry at all – he's never been a ladies' man.

'And Venetia found out?'

'Yes. But it's slightly complicated actually,' he said, his face aflame. 'In fact Rose, do you mind, if I . . . well, if I pick your brains a bit? You see I've got this, um . . . well . . . problem, actually.' My heart sagged like a sinking soufflé. *That's* why he'd wanted to see me again – he just wanted to ask my advice.

'I don't want you to think I asked you out under false pretences,' he said with a guilty smile, 'but it's just that I know I can trust you. I know that you won't judge. And I was feeling so dreadfully low the other night, and I couldn't sleep, so I switched on the radio and, to my amazement, there *you* were. And you were giving such good advice to all those people, so I decided that I'd ask you for some too.' I looked at his open but anxious face, and my indignation melted like the dew.

'Don't worry Henry,' I murmured. 'Of course I'll help you. Just tell me what it's about.'

'Well,' he tried again, with a profound sigh, 'the other woman. You see . . . the other woman, as it were . . .' he cleared his throat. 'This other woman . . .'

'Yes?'

He glanced anxiously to left and right to check we couldn't be overheard. 'Well,' he whispered, running a nervous finger round his collar, 'the other woman . . . is . . . erm . . . *me.*'

'Sorry?'

Henry had flushed bright red, his face radiating a heat that could have melted Emmenthal. Now he discreetly pulled aside his speckled blue silk tie and undid a button on his striped shirt. Then he parted the fabric to reveal a square inch of black filigree lace. I stared at it in stupefaction. Henry? Never. Henry? No way! *Henry*? Not on your life! On the other hand, I suddenly remembered, cross-dressing is not uncommon amongst men in the forces, something which has always struck me as strange. The thought of all these big, macho, military types dolled up in frocks and high heels.

'When did this . . . start?' I enquired with professional curiosity, trying not to show I was shocked.

'About a year ago,' he replied. 'I'd always been fascinated

by women's clothes,' he admitted in a whisper. 'In fact, when I was a boy, I used to "borrow" Mum's petticoats. I suppressed it of course but then, as I got older, I got this unbearable . . . urge. I found I couldn't get dressed without putting on a pair of lacy pants first. But then Venetia caught me going through her knicker drawer and went crazy: she said I must be gay, but I'm not.'

'Of course you're not gay,' I said. 'Ninety-five per cent of cross-dressers are totally straight and in fact most are married with kids.'

'I know I'm definitely attracted to women,' Henry went on, 'always have been, but there are times when I simply want to *be* one. I can't explain why. This strange compulsion grips me and I know I've just got to go and put on a dress. But it freaked Venetia out and she walked.'

'Well some women are very understanding about it,' I said. 'It's a common . . .' – I avoided saying, 'problem' – '. . . thing. You wouldn't believe how many letters I get about it,' I added casually.

'Well I thought you'd have come across it before. You won't tell anyone,' he whispered.

'No, I won't.'

'And you see, there's no-one else I felt I could ask.' I looked at Henry's honest face, then dropped my gaze to his large, paw-like hand and tried to imagine Rouge Noir on the nails. Then I tried to visualise a string of pearls around his thick, sinewy neck. I opened my bag, took out a piece of paper and began scribbling on it.

'What you want is the Beaumont Society – it's a trans-vestites' support group. I give the phone number out so often I know it off by heart. If you ring them, someone there will send you an information pack and you don't have to give your real name. There's also Transformation, a specialist place at Euston who'll teach you how to stuff your bra, pad your bum, wear high heels – that sort of thing.'

'But it's the shopping,' he said with a groan. 'I mean, where can I get size eleven sling-backs? And what about make-up?

I haven't a *clue*. I can't ask my mum or my sister as they'd go crazy.'

'Well, if you like, *I'll* come with you. We can go to a department store and pretend the things are for me. I'm as tall as you so it wouldn't be unfeasible.'

'Would you really do that for me?'

I gave him a smile. 'Yes. Of course I would.'

Henry's swimming pool blue eyes shimmered with speechless tears. 'Thanks Rose,' he breathed. 'You're a *brick*.'

Chapter Five

The letters I get! Listen to this!

Dear Rose, I am on probation for arson, but my probation officer has changed and I'm starting to get itchy fingers again. I'd really like to set fire to something so I'm getting in lots of matches and petrol – please help!

Good God! I don't like to go behind my readers' backs – confidentiality is absolutely *sacred* – but sometimes it's something I have to do. So I've just phoned up the woman's social services and someone's going to go round to see her right now. And how about this one – in green ink of course.

Dear Rose, I have messages from Martians coming through my bedroom radiators. But that's not my main problem. The main problem is the volume which keeps me awake at night. I've asked them to keep it down, but they just won't. How can I stop them disturbing my sleep in this way?

Dear Phyllis, I wrote, Thank you for your letter. How very annoying for you having noisy Martians in your radiators. But did you know that doctors have a very clever way of dealing with this problem these days, and I do suggest that you go and see your G.P. straight away. With best wishes, Rose.

Then here was a letter, sixty pages long, written on graph paper and signed, 'King George'. The next three were from people with flatmate problems – all the usual stuff: *He slobs in front of the TV all night . . . she never does the washing up . . . he's always late with the rent . . . she has her friends round all the time . . .* As I composed my replies I thought about my own flatmate, Theo. Despite my initial – and wholly justified –

anxieties I've scarcely seen him – we're like those proverbial ships that pass in the night. Sometimes I hear him pacing
above me in the early hours because, since my split with Ed,
I haven't been sleeping well. Theo does go out sometimes in
the evenings but, strangely, only when it's dry – not when
it's wet. It's all a bit peculiar really, especially with that strange
remark of his about the lights. I mean, he seems too whole-
some to be a Jeffrey Dahmer, but then still waters and all
that . . .

I dealt with the flatmate problems, enclosing my leaflet on
Happy Cohabitation, then I opened what turned out to be one
of my very rare letters back. It was from Colin Twisk, that
Lonely Young Man.

Dear Rose, he'd written. *Thank you very much for your very,
very kind letter. I carry it about with me all the time. And whenever
I'm feeling low I get it out and read it again. Knowing that a famous
– and very attractive – person like you thinks I'm good-looking makes
me feel so much better about myself. I'm doing everything you advised
me and – guess what? – I think I may have now found my Special
Lady Friend! With deep affection, Colin Twisk.* xxxx.

Ah, I thought, isn't that nice? That's what makes my job
so worthwhile. The knowledge that I've been able to help
alleviate someone's distress and pain. I put Colin's letter in
my 'Grateful' file – that's just my little joke – then suddenly
a cry went up. Ricky, who had been away for two days, had
evidently just returned.

'Who the fuck wrote this fucking headline?' he shouted at
Jason Brown, our Chief Sub. As he jabbed his finger at the
offending page, my heart sank. Jason was about to get what's
known in the trade as a 'bollocking'. '"SOMETHING WENT
WRONG IN JET CRASH EXPERTS SAY"'? Ricky shouted. 'It's
shite! And as for this – "PROSTITUTES APPEAL TO POPE!"
Total shite! "STOLEN PAINTING FOUND BY TREE"? – that is
effing shite as well!' This was true. Now he went over to the
features editor, Linda, while Serena and I exchanged nervous
looks.

'The features are shite too,' Ricky shouted. "Why Not

Include Your Children When Baking?" Crap! "Unusual Applications for Everyday Household Objects – Try polishing your furniture with old tights and conditioning your hair with last week's whipped cream"? It's all shite,' he repeated truculently. 'It's a pile of poo! It is complete and utter ca-ca. No wonder our circulation's going down the khazi – what this paper needs is R.'

'R?' said Linda miserably. We looked at each other.

'R,' Ricky repeated slowly. 'As in the R factor.' Ah. 'As in aaaaaaaahhhhh!'

'Aaahh . . .' we all said.

'What we want,' he said, slamming his right fist into his left palm, 'is Triumph Over Tragedy, Amazing Mums, Kids of Courage. And animals!' he added animatedly. 'I want more animals. The readers like them and so do I. So get me Spanish donkeys, Linda, get me orphaned koalas, get me baby seals . . .'

'It's the wrong time of year.'

'I don't give a flying *fuck*!' he shouted. 'Get me baby seals. And while you're at it get me puppies with pacemakers and kittens with hearing aids too. And if I don't see some *fucking* heart-warming animal stories in this paper within a week, Linda, you're for the fucking chop.'

'Well, someone got out of bed on the wrong side this morning!' Serena remarked briskly as Ricky stomped back to his office. 'Still, we *all* have our problems. Oh yes, we all have our crosses to bear,' she added with a tight little smile. I looked at her as she turned on the shredder.

'Nothing serious, I hope.'

'Oh nothing we can't deal with,' she replied serenely. 'It's just that Rob crashed the car last night.'

'Oh dear. I hope he wasn't hurt.'

'Not really. Just a large bump on his head. But unfortunately the garage door's a write-off – he demolished it.'

'Oh no!'

'Still, these things are sent to try us, aren't they?' she said perkily. I smiled blankly and nodded my head. As Serena fed the old letters into the shredder – we keep them six months – I glanced at Linda, who was ashen-faced. I'd had an idea. Trevor and Beverley. That would make a good, heart-warming animal feature. Linda agreed.

'It sounds *brilliant*,' she said gratefully after I'd told her. 'We could do a big spread with lots of photos. Will you ring her for me right now?'

Beverley was in – well she usually is in, poor kid – and she sounded quite keen.

'Are you *sure* you and Trevor wouldn't mind?' I asked her. 'It would probably mean having to talk about your accident, so I wouldn't like you to say yes if you didn't feel comfortable about it.'

'No, we'd be happy to do it,' she replied. 'And it would be great publicity for Helping Paw.'

Having given Linda Bev's number I now tackled my huge pile of post. The run up to Christmas is an incredibly busy time of year for agony aunts. In fact there were so many letters to answer that I didn't leave work until eight. When I got in I felt pretty tired, but even so I decided to give the kitchen a thorough clean. I wiped down all the cupboard fronts – and the worktops, not forgetting to empty the toaster crumb tray of course; then I went into the hall and polished the telephone table. When I'd finished I noticed that the spindles on the banisters were looking *disgusting*. Being white, every speck of dust shows. As I rubbed away at them with the Astonish, I heard Theo's door open. He was on his mobile phone.

'Are you up for it?' I heard him say as he came downstairs. 'Right then. I'll be there in fifteen. Don't start without me!' he added with a laugh. 'Oh, hello Rose,' he said pleasantly as he put his phone in his pocket. 'Haven't seen you for a while.' His eyes suddenly narrowed. 'What the heck are you doing?' What the heck was I doing?

'What the heck does it look like?'

'Er, cleaning the banister spindles.'

'Correct.'

'Oh,' he said. He looked dumbfounded for some reason. 'I'm just on my way out. Well, er, have a nice evening,' he added uncertainly. 'See you.'

'See you,' I replied. As he left, carefully locking the front door behind him, I wondered about that remark. 'Are you up for it?' Hmm . . . that could only mean one thing. He'd obviously got someone. Well, that's fine, I said to myself broad-mindedly – as long as he conducts his romantic affairs elsewhere. There'll be no hanky-panky under *my* roof I decided firmly as I went into the kitchen and found a pack of instant soup. 'Country-Style Leek and Asparagus' said the box. Disgusting but it would have to do. I loathe cooking – I've never learned – and I don't bother with food that much anyway so I simply buy things that are quick. Pot Noodles for instance – yes, I know, I *know* – bought pies, that kind of thing.

'This is Radio Four!' yelled Rudy as I emptied the greenish powder into a saucepan. 'Scilly Light Automatic. Five or six. Rising. Occasionally good.' Oh no. I've been leaving Radio Four on for him during the day and he's started regurgitating selected bits. 'Viking North Utsire. Steady. German Bight. Showers. Decreasing. Good.' However, unlike the radio, I can't turn Rudy off. 'And welcome to *Gardener's Question Time*!' he announced warmly.

'You start singing the theme tune from *The Archers* and you're in big trouble,' I said as I opened the fridge in search of some grapes to keep him quiet. Normally there's not much in it. A heel of cheese maybe, two or three bottles of wine, half a loaf and Rudy's fruit. But today the fridge overflowed. In the chiller were tiny vine-ripened plum tomatoes, three fat courgettes, and a glossy aubergine; on the shelf above a roll of French butter and a wedge of unctuous Brie. There were two free-range skinless chicken breasts, a tray of tiger prawns, and some slices of rosy pink ham. Theo was clearly a *bon vivant*.

As I stirred my monosodium glutamate, I wondered who he was meeting – 'Are you up for it?' – and what she was like. Or maybe . . . yes. Maybe she wasn't a she, maybe she was a *he*. Theo had told me he wouldn't be having women over – 'that won't be a problem' he'd said: and he'd laughed, and grimaced slightly, as though the suggestion was not only ludicrous, but somehow slightly distasteful. Maybe he *was* gay. Now I wondered why this hadn't occurred to me before. After all, there was plenty of evidence that he might be. For example, he'd been living with this 'friend' of his, Mark, before, and then there'd been that gauche comment of his about my hair. He was obviously *totally* inept with women – he clearly hadn't a clue. And he was quite well dressed and toned-looking, plus he had suspiciously refined tastes in fresh produce. I mean, I really *don't* think a straight man – especially a Yorkshireman – would be seen dead buying miniature vine-ripened plum tomatoes, or, for that matter, free-range skinless chicken breasts. Yes, he probably was gay. What a waste, I thought idly. Oh well . . .

As the soup began to simmer I suddenly realised that I'd found out next to nothing about Theo. So far we'd avoided contact – treading warily around each other like animals forced to share the same cage.

Now I thought about Ed again – but then he's always on my mind – with a dreadful, knotting sensation inside. Then I suddenly remembered: the shoebox . . . Oh God. It was still under Theo's bed. Heart pounding, I rushed upstairs, pushed on his door, and got down on my hands and knees. There it still was, undisturbed. Phew. The chances of Theo finding it were slim but I wasn't taking the risk. So I fished it out, but as I straightened up I turned round and suddenly stopped. For, positioned by the window, on a shiny tripod, was an old brass telescope. Hmm. So that, presumably, is what had been in the mysterious-looking black case. I listened at the door for a moment to make sure he hadn't come back; then I went up to it, removed the lens cap and peered through the end. Although the thing was clearly antique the magnification was very strong. To my surprise I found myself looking right into the backs of the houses opposite. There was a woman lying on her bed: her legs were bare and I could even make out the pink nail polish on her toes. I swung the telescope to the left and saw a small boy watching TV. In the next house along I could see a human form moving behind frosted bathroom glass. So that's why Theo said he liked the room's aspect so much – he was a peeping Tom! His ad had said he'd wanted 'privacy' – other people's privacy it appeared!

I just *knew* that there was something odd about that boy and I was absolutely *right*! That's why he spent so much time in his room and why I heard him pacing the floor late at night. Snooping on people is the *pits* I thought crossly as I decided to take a good look round his room. It was a complete and utter shambles – I had to fight the urge to tidy it up. The floor was strewn with discarded clothes, piles of old newspapers, rolled up posters and boxes of books. On the desk was a laptop computer surrounded by a mess of paperwork. His writing was appalling but on one pad I could just make out the words, 'heavenly body,' and there was a pair of binoculars – well! So he clearly wasn't gay, he was a bit of a saddo I reflected crossly, or maybe he was a Lonely Young Man. But what a *disgusting* invasion of privacy I reflected indignantly as I inspected the rest of his room. On the mantelpiece were some strange-looking bits of rock, and, in a silver frame, a black and white photo of an attractive blonde of about thirty-five. She was laughing, her left hand clapped to her chest as though she'd just heard the most wonderful joke. Now I glanced at the bed. A maroon duvet was pulled loosely over it, but from underneath – oh God, not *another* one – protruded a square of floral silk. I lifted up the quilt. Under the pillow was a short silk nightie with a Janet Reger label. Well, well, *well*! And I was just thinking about leaving my *Am I A Transvestite?* leaflet lying casually about when I heard the telephone ring. I quickly replaced the nightie, swung the telescope back into position, then grabbed the shoebox and ran downstairs.

'Hello,' I said breathlessly. There was nothing at the other end. 'Hello?' I said again. Suddenly the silence was broken by the sound of heavy breathing. Goose bumps raised themselves up on my arms. 'Hello?' I repeated, more sharply now. 'Hello, who *is* this please?' I suddenly remembered the silent call I'd had the night Theo had first come round. Now all I could hear was deliberate, slow, heavy breathing. I shuddered – oh God, this was vile. Tempting though it was to let loose with a stream of unbridled abuse I decided just to put the phone down.

'I think I'm getting nuisance phone calls,' I said to Henry as we walked around the Windsmoor concession in Debenhams the following Saturday. 'How about this?' I held up a stretch lace, high-necked blouse. He cocked his head to one side.

'I'd prefer a scoop neckline,' he said.

'Not advisable – you've got a hairy chest.' I showed him a red crushed velvet jacket – size twenty. 'This take your fancy?' He shook his head.

'So what happens with these calls?' he asked as I riffled through a rack of large frocks. 'Do they speak to you?'

'No they don't. All I hear is heavy breathing.'

'Oh, nasty. So what do you do?'

'I do what I advise my readers to do. I don't speak to them, or try and engage them in conversation, and I don't blow a whistle down the phone. I simply wait a few seconds, say absolutely nothing, then quietly put down the phone. They want you to react Henry – that's why they do it; so it's much better to spoil their fun. Eventually the tiny-minded wankers realise that they're wasting their time and they stop.'

'How many calls have there been so far?'

'I've had four in the last two weeks. It's not that many but it's unnerving and it makes me feel jumpy about answering the phone. How about this?' I held up a blue floral skirt the size of a windbreak. He pulled a face.

'Too chintzy. Well if it carries on then complain.'

'I probably will, but to be honest I'm so busy and it all takes time. No, not that bubble-gum pink Henry, it's much too "Barbie" – try this fuchsia. But no shoulder pads, okay?'

'Okay. And do you press 1471 afterwards?'

'Of course, but it always says that the number's been withheld.'

'Hmm,' he murmured, 'that's significant.'

'I know it is. It's beginning to bother me,' I added as we passed through Separates on our way to Eveningwear to the sound of synthesised 'Jingle Bells'. 'But until they say something malicious or threatening it's rather hard to complain.'

'Perhaps it's Ed?' Henry suggested as he surreptitiously fingered a taffeta ball gown.

'I doubt it. It's not his style. In any case he doesn't even have my new number – we've been on total non-speakers since our split.'

'I still think you should check.'

'But how? I can hardly ring him up and say, "Hi Ed, this is Rose. I was just wondering if you've been making nuisance phone calls to me lately." Anyway, I *know* it's not him.'

'Have you fallen out with anyone lately?' Henry asked.

'Not that I can think of, al*though* . . . I did have a bit of a run in with a mad woman on my phone-in the other week.'

'I know,' he said. 'I heard her. I must say she sounded a bit of a brute.'

'And she's convinced I advised her husband to leave her; she said I'd be "sorry," so maybe it's her. Though God knows how she got my number.'

'That's the trouble with what you do,' Henry said as he held a pink feather boa under his stubbled chin, 'you get some *weird* people contacting you.'

'I know. Now I think you'd look lovely in this,' I went on as I pulled out a black bias cut silk satin dress. 'Ooh, and it's got thirty per cent off!'

'Really?' he said.

'Yeah, shall we give it a whirl?' He nodded enthusiastically and we headed off to the fitting room.

'That's not your size Madam,' said the sales assistant peremptorily, 'it's a twenty, I'd say you're a ten.'

'But I like things nice and loose. My husband will be coming into the cubicle with me,' I added briskly, 'as he always likes to see what I buy.'

We pulled the curtain shut and Henry quickly undressed. Then he strapped on a pair of silicone-jelly breasts he'd got from Transformation, and struggled into the dress. As I did up the zip he looked at his reflection and sighed with happiness.

'Oh yes!' he said, turning this way and that, 'it's just so . . . me.' He looked like a gorilla in a ball gown. That hairy back! 'What accessories should I wear?'

'A velvet scarf maybe, or some pearls. Or better still, a choker, to cover your Adam's apple. And you'll need some black tights, sixty denier at least unless you're prepared to shave.'

'Can't I have fishnets?'

'No, Henry. Too tarty.'

'Really?' He looked disappointed.

'Yes, really. Your mother would be horrified.'

'That's true.'

He bought a sparkly handbag and then we went down to cosmetics on the ground floor.

'Were the Beaumont Society helpful?' I enquired *sotto voce* as we perused the make-up.

'Yes,' he said, 'they were great. They told me how to avoid being "read" when I go out.'

'You're not planning to wear this stuff in public are you?' I whispered.

'Not at work, no; I might get the hem caught in my tank. But, who knows,' he breathed, 'when I'm on leave, if I'm feeling daring, I might.'

'But you're six foot one Henry!'

'So are you!'

'But I'm feminine.'

'Well you're not the only one!'

'Now, your skin-tone is fair,' I said, changing the subject. 'I think you'll need this Leichner extra-thick foundation to

92

hide the five o'clock shadow and of course translucent powder – pressed or loose? Coral lipstick, rather than red, would suit you for that English Rose look, and eye-liner should be navy not black. We'd better get you a good pair of tweezers too while we're here and something to minimise those pores.'

'Christ, you're right,' he said, as he peered, horrified, into an adjacent mirror. 'They're the size of a grapefruit's. And I need a wig and some scent.'

'I think you should go for something really feminine, like Ô de Lancôme or Femme.'

We emerged from the store two hours later with six large carrier bags, Henry beaming from ear to ear.

'You'll look ravishing in that lot,' I said as he hailed a cab. 'Really gorgeous.'

'Gosh thanks, Rose. You're a real sport.'

'My pleasure,' I said, as he gave me a hug, and it was. As I walked down Oxford Street in the milling crowds I realised that I'd loved going shopping with Henry whereas with Ed it was always a trial. Not because he didn't like doing it but because he'd always try and beat people down. If something cost eighty quid he'd knock them down to sixty; if it was fifteen he'd try and get it for ten. 'What's the best price you can give me?' he'd ask while I'd blush and look the other way. He once bargained ninety pounds off a fridge-freezer.

'Why do you bother?' I'd said.

'Because it's fun, that's why. It gives me this adrenaline rush.'

But I knew that that was a lie. The real reason was because Ed's family were incredibly hard-up and there was never any cash. His dad had been foreman at a builder's yard, but he'd died from asbestosis when Ed was eight. Ed's mother didn't get the government compensation for ten years and there was often barely enough to eat. That kind of start in life leaves an indelible mark, so I knew where Ed was coming from. But the fact that he was one of five children was one of the things that drew me to him; although, well, it's rather sad really, because he hardly ever sees them these days. Only his mother and one sister, Ruth, came to our wedding; as for the others, they've drifted apart. For example, Ed hasn't seen his youngest brother, Jon, for six years; they fell out badly, over money, I think. Nevertheless, Jon still sent us a lovely alabaster lamp for our wedding, even though Ed hadn't invited him. It made me feel terribly sad. Anyway, I liked Ed's mother, and the thought of her looking after all those children, on her own, *and* working full-time fills me with total awe. Whereas some stupid women well, it's too pathetic, they can't even cope with *one* . . .

Now, as I sat on the number thirty-six a woman came and sat in front of me with her little girl who was about two and a half, maybe three. The bus was full so the child sat on her lap, encircled by her arms like a hoop. And as I looked at them I felt the old, old pang and thought, *my* mother never held me like that . . .

I always try and distract myself at bad moments, so I got out my *Daily Post*. There was the photo of Bev and Trev on the masthead and inside a big, two page spread. It was headed 'LABRACADABRA!' and there were pictures of them at home, 'Clever Trevor' – dressed in his red Helping Paw coat – drawing the curtains and bringing in the milk. There was a shot of him getting the washing out of the machine and passing 'Tragic Bev' the pegs while she hung up the clothes. There they were in Sainsbury's, at the check-out, with Trevor handing over Bev's purse. Finally there was a shot of them both at the cashpoint, Trev getting out the money with his teeth. 'Trevor's much more than my canine carer,' Bev was quoted as saying, 'he's saved my life.'

I realised now, how modest Beverley had been in describing herself to me as a 'PE teacher'. She'd been so much more than that. Yes, she'd taught games at a girls' school, the article explained, but she'd also been an outstanding sportswoman in her own right. As an eighteen-year-old she'd been county tennis champion, and in her mid-twenties, as a middle distance runner, she'd won silver in the Commonwealth games. After retiring from the track she'd taken up women's hockey and had played for the national side. She'd been selected to play for England at the Sydney Olympics but her injury had shattered that dream. Her accident had left her 'suicidal' and 'devastated' until Trevor transformed her life. 'He's my hero,' she said. 'We adore each other. Without him I just couldn't go on.' It was touching stuff and at the bottom was the number for Helping Paw.

When I got home Theo was in the kitchen, cooking. I could hear him singing to himself. Repelled by the thought of him spying on my neighbours dressed in a floral nightie, I decided to give him a wide berth. And I was just taking off my coat when I glanced at the half-moon telephone table and saw a pile of unopened post. There were my first utilities bills, a cashmere brochure and an Oxfam Christmas catalogue. Underneath, in a white plastic cover, was some magazine or other, it looked like *Newsweek* or *Time*. I turned it over and saw that it wasn't either of those: it was *Astronomy Now* magazine. *Oh.*

'Hello Rose,' Theo called out suddenly.

'Oh. Hi!' *Astronomy Now*? But that didn't explain the Janet Reger nightie did it?

'Had a good day?' he enquired politely as I went into the kitchen.

'Er, yes. I've been shopping with a . . . friend. You've got some post, you know.'

He wiped his hands, ripped the cover off the magazine, glanced at it, then put it down. *Star Clusters in Close-Up!* announced the headline and beneath, *Magellanic Clouds and Nebulae!*

'*Astronomy Now*? I said with studied casualness. 'I've never seen that before. May I look at it?'

'Course you can. I get *Sky and Telescope* too.'

'So you're interested in . . . astronomy then?' I said feebly as I glanced at an article about the Leonid meteor showers.

'It's my passion,' he replied as he got out a knife. 'I've been mad on it since I was a boy, I –' Suddenly his mobile rang. Or rather it didn't ring; it played 'Would you like to swing on a star, carry moonbeams home in a jar?' He took the call, but it was clearly an awkward conversation for his throat become blotched and red.

'Hi. Yes. I'm okay,' he said slightly tersely. 'Yes. Fine. That'd be grand. Whatever you want. Yes. Yes. I'll drop the keys off at your office on Monday. No, I don't want to come to the house. Sorry about that,' he said with fake brightness as he put his phone back in his pocket, 'where were we?'

'Astronomy.'

'Oh yes. It's my . . . passion,' he said as he sliced a courgette with a trembling hand.

'So do you have your own telescope then?' I enquired innocently.

'Yes. It's in my room. You can have a look at it if you like.'

'Ooh, no, no, no, I wouldn't do that. I mean, I wouldn't go in your room.'

'That's okay. I don't mind if you do – I've nothing to hide. It's a three-inch refracting telescope rather than one of the more modern reflectors, but the optics are really good. It has a magnification of 150,' he added proudly as he got out a frying pan. 'It belonged to my granddad – he used to run the Leeds observatory – it's old but it's excellent.' He opened the fridge and took out a beer. 'I feel like a drink. How about you?'

I felt guilty about having mistrusted him so I nodded. 'Thanks. That'd be nice. So where do you do your . . . star-watching?' I asked as he got down two glasses.

'The best place is Norfolk – I used to go there with my grandparents. You can do it in London, but you have to choose your spot carefully because the sky-glow's so bad.'

'Sky-glow?'

'The light pollution. That awful tangerine glare. I'm involved with the Campaign for Dark Skies,' he went on as he poured out my beer. 'We ask local councils to install star-friendly street lighting which throws the light down, where it's needed, not up. It's tragic that people living in cities don't get to see the night sky – they miss so much. I mean just look up,' he said suddenly. He switched off the light, plunging us into darkness, and I peered up through the conservatory roof. Through the glass I could see five, no . . . eight stars twinkling dimly against the inky night and a sliver of silvery moon. 'City folk miss so much,' he repeated as I craned my neck. 'How often do they see the Milky Way and the Pleiades, Orion's belt, or the Plough? You don't even need a telescope to be an amateur astronomer. You can see so much just with your eyes.'

'So that's why you didn't want me to complain about the street lamps?' I suggested.

'Yes, that's right.' And that explained why Theo went out when it was dry and clear, not when it was wet. 'Actually this area's not too bad for observation,' he continued as he turned on the light and the stars vanished, 'which is why I like living here. That little park at the end of the road is quite good for example.'

'Holland Gardens?'

'Yes. I've taken my 'scope there a couple of times. There are no tall buildings around it so you get a big piece of sky, and I've a filter which cuts out the glare. And my friend Mark has a large garden so sometimes I go round there. I ring him and say "Are you up for it?"' he added. 'That's what we amateur astronomers say. It's our little in-joke. Are you up for it?' He shook his head and laughed. So he wasn't the Milky Bar kid after all – he was the Milky *Way* kid.

'What a . . . fascinating hobby,' I said with a relieved smile.

'It's more than that. I've been writing a book. I'm doing the final edits at the moment – the page proofs have just come back.'

'A book? What's it called?'

'*Heavenly Bodies –*' Ah. '*– A Popular Guide to the Stars and Planets.* It's coming out in May. But I'm under terrible pressure timewise which is why I needed to live somewhere quiet.'

'And where did you live before?' I asked as he sliced the aubergine.

'I told you, with this friend of mine, Mark.'

'But you said that that was temporary; that he was helping you out – so where did you live before that?'

'I lived in Dulwich . . .' The knife stopped in mid-air and he repeated, quietly, 'I lived in Dulwich. With my wife.'

'Oh,' I murmured, trying not to look astounded. 'You, er, didn't say you were married. You look so young.'

'I'm not. I'm twenty-nine. I was married for five years. But I didn't tell you because . . . well,' he stopped. 'Because it's too painful and to be honest it's not relevant.' Now I remembered his boss's odd remark, when I'd phoned for a reference, about Theo having had 'a hard time'.

'Why did you . . .' I began, with a sip of beer. 'No, I'm sorry. It's none of my business.'

'Why did we split up?' I nodded. 'Because I disappointed my wife.'

'Really? Er . . . how?'

'She felt I was letting her down. She's a solicitor at Prenderville White in the City,' he explained. 'She's very driven and successful, and she expected me to be the same. She wanted me to put everything into my accountancy career to match her success, but I couldn't. I did all the exams but by then I'd become far more interested in astronomy than in spreadsheets. So I left Price Waterhouse and took an undemanding book-keeping job so that I'd have more time to write. Fi said I was being self-indulgent and that I should knuckle down to my career. She kept on and on and on about it, but I couldn't bring myself to go back. So five months ago she said she wanted out.' Poor bloke. There were tears in his eyes. 'That was her actually, just now, on the phone,' he explained, his voice quivering. 'I'd forgotten to give her my keys. To be honest, I find it painful even talking to her. I mean, I can see why she felt as she did. I can understand why we broke up. But understanding is different from feeling isn't it?' I nodded. It certainly is. 'I'm still deeply attached to her. In fact,' he added, with another swig of beer, 'I do this silly thing. I –' he lowered the bottle, 'promise you won't laugh?'

'I promise.'

'I sleep with one of her old nighties.' Ah ha, I thought. So it wasn't my *Cross-Dressing* leaflet he needed but *Relationship Breakdown* instead. 'I'm sorry,' he added with that lop-sided smile of his. 'You hardly know me and here I am, showing you my emotional underpants.'

'I don't mind,' I said, and I didn't – people often tell me personal things. 'Anyway, that's my sad tale,' he concluded with a grim smile. Then he suddenly said, 'How about you?'

'How about me?'

'Yes.'

'Oh. You mean, my story?' He nodded. 'Well . . . do I have to?' I added slightly irritably. 'Yes,' he said rather bluntly. 'Fair's fair.' That was true enough, so I quickly gave him the bare bones.

'So that's why you've only been here a short time?' he said as he poured in more olive oil.

'Yes. I needed to make a clean break.'

'But why do you think your husband had the affair?' he asked as he got out a wooden spoon.

'Because he felt like it I suppose.'

'But there's usually a reason,' he said as an aroma of Mediterranean vegetables filled the air. 'I mean people don't just have an affair for nothing, do they?' he added.

'Oh I don't know,' I said.

'You're a fucking nightmare!' yelled Rudy in Ed's voice. 'This marriage was a mistake!' *Shit.*

'That silly bird,' I laughed as I pulled down the cover. 'He probably got that from the afternoon play. Anyway, I'm sorry you've had so much unhappiness,' I said.

'Well, ditto, but life has to go on. That's why I like cooking,' he added. 'It's relaxing – it helps me unwind.'

'So you like astronomy and gastronomy,' I pointed out, and for the first time that evening, he smiled. 'What are you making?' I added.

'Ratatouille – would you like some?'

'Oh, no thanks.'

'I've put some of my cook books on the shelf,' he added, 'I hope you don't mind.'

'Of course not,' I said, 'except . . .' I went over to them and began shuffling them about . . . Jane Grigson . . . Sophie Grigson . . . Ainsley Harriot . . . there. Alastair Little . . . that was better: Delia Smith . . . Rick Stein.

'What on earth are you doing?' he asked.

'I'm just tidying them up.'

'But why?'

'Because I like books to be in alphabetical order – and CDs – it's better. Don't you ever do that?'

'Er, no.'

And I was about to point out the benefits of having a properly alphabetised system when I heard the clatter of the letter box. On the mat was yet another flyer from the Tip Top Tandoori House and two from Pizza Hut. I picked them up, and went to throw them in the waste paper basket by the hall table when a sound from next door made me stop. It was muffled at first, but becoming louder now. I stood there, rooted to the spot. For it was the sound of suppressed, but anguished weeping. My heart expanded. Poor Bev.

Chapter Six

I stood there transfixed with pity, not knowing quite what to do. If I'd known Beverley better I'd have phoned her up, or made some excuse to go round. But I didn't feel I could intrude, not least because whenever we've met she's presented such a strong, cheerful face. If she knew I'd heard her crying she might well have been mortified. And then I'd felt awful in case doing the *Daily Post* feature had made her feel worse. Seeing it in black and white like that, with everyone reading about 'Tragic Bev' and her accident, and about her boyfriend leaving, and about what an outstanding sportswoman she'd been. Perhaps she'd regretted being interviewed. Perhaps *that's* why she was in tears. That thought made me very depressed, but as it turned out, I was quite wrong; because the next afternoon she phoned me to say that Ricky had liked the piece so much he'd offered her a regular slot.

'He called me this morning to tell me, Rose – on a Sunday! He wants me to write a weekly column – he thinks it'll lift the *Post's* circulation.'

'It probably will.'

'But I'm terrified, Rose, I'm not a journalist.'

'So what? You're very articulate. You'll do it well.'

'But he wants me to write it in Trevor's voice.' Ah. Now *that* could be hard to pull off. 'Will you read the trial pieces before I submit them and tell me what you think?'

'Sure.'

So the following Thursday evening we went down to the

Bunch of Grapes at the end of the street and Bev showed me her two sample columns. I'd worried that the tone might be a bit twee or sentimental, but it wasn't at all. Far from it. It was endearingly blokey. I thought they were great.

Bev's pretty ropey in the mornings, but I'm quite chirpy, I read. *I give her a lick to wake her up, maybe a bit of a cuddle, then root about under the bed to find her slippers, drag them out with a minimum of slobber, and we're away.*

'This is brilliant,' I giggled. 'Ricky will love it.'

Bev goes down for breakfast in the stair lift, then I have a tiny snooze while she has her cup of tea. But I'm on red alert. I can be snoring my brains out but the second I hear her move, I'm up.

'It's wonderful,' I said, 'you're a natural.'

'But that's just how he'd speak, isn't it Trev?'

It wasn't always like this, I read on. *Ooh, no, to begin with it was dire. It was, 'Trevor do this, and Trevor do that,' and I'm like, 'Sorry? What did your last slave die of?' Drove me nuts. But then I felt a bit guilty because maybe I could have been a bit more helpful, but bless her, Bev's a forgiving little soul and we're mad about each other now.*

'If it comes off I'm going to give the fee to Helping Paw,' Beverley added as we drank our Becks. 'I got quite a big insurance payout after the accident so I don't need the cash. And it'll be a great opportunity to publicise the charity, speaking of which, I've been meaning to ask if you'll come to our first big fund-raiser – it's just before Christmas?'

'Of course I'll come,' I said.

'It's a ball. Fancy dress,' she added. Fancy dress? Oh *shit*! 'But it's not ordinary fancy dress,' she explained as she slipped Trevor a pork scratching. 'It's in a marquee at the Courtauld, everyone comes as a work of art, and the best costume gets a prize. Fancy another pint?'

'Wouldn't say no to a half.'

'Okay, Trev, our shout.' She wheeled her chair to the bar, Trevor barked for service, then she passed him her purse. He stood up on his hind legs then placed it on the counter while the barman took the cash. Then Beverley carried each drink in turn back to our table, whilst Trevor collected her change.

'I bet he drinks Carling Black Label,' said the barman with a guffaw.

'Nah, he's teetotal,' Bev replied.

So thanks to Beverley, Ricky's happier so there've been no 'bollockings' for a while. But my workload's piling up what with pre-Christmas depression; well I'm feeling pretty gloomy myself. I spent last year's in a blissful romantic blur; I'll spend this one alone and semi-divorced.

'Christmas . . . suicidal,' said Serena perkily as she logged the letters yesterday. 'Christmas, just can't cope. Christmas, want to kill myself,' she went on briskly. 'Christmas, I wish I was dead . . .'

'Okay Serena, I get the picture.'

'Mind you, I think Christmas is going to be pre-tty grim for *us* this year,' she went on serenely as she tucked her hair behind one ear. I looked at her when she said that and realised that she's suddenly going rather grey. 'I mean, it's such an expensive time,' she said with a shudder. Well, yes, but she and her husband both work. 'And you see Rob's been a bit traumatised since his little *accident*,' she went on delicately, 'so he's been missing his targets; and what with the school fees . . .' her voice trailed away. 'Still!' she exclaimed brightly, 'mustn't complain! There's always someone worse off than yourself isn't there?' Was that a slight twitch in her right eye?

At lunchtime I phoned Henry about the ball and he said he'd come; 'as the Mona Lisa!' he added with a guffaw. The twins were equally game.

'Sounds like a lark,' said Bea, 'and we might pick up some clients. Yes, we'll definitely be up for it.' Up for it . . . ? Yes, I thought, why not? And I'd be doing Theo a big favour by inviting him – after all the poor bloke's depressed.

'A ball?' he said when I spoke to him about it the following Thursday. 'Sounds very posh, but yes. That might be . . . fun. Thanks for asking me,' he added politely.

'That's okay; and it's in a good cause.'

103

'I'll put it in my diary right now.' As he groped in his jacket pocket he pulled out various bits and pieces including his mobile phone. I looked at it lying on the kitchen table and realised that it's *exactly* like mine. It's a Motorola 250 Timeport with the same galvanised silver case.

'Courtauld . . . twentieth December,' he muttered as he scribbled away, 'that's only three weeks off. I'll come as a modern portrait so I don't have to wear anything too barmy. How about you?'

'I'm not sure. I might go as Damien Hirst's bisected cow. It's called "Mother and Child, Divided" so it would be very appropriate in my case,' I added with a bitter laugh. Theo gave me a puzzled look. 'Or maybe I'll play it safe and go as Tracey Emin's unmade bed.'

'I think you'd look good as the Botticelli Venus,' he said suddenly. I felt blood suffuse my face. 'I mean,' he stammered, 'with your long red hair – that's all I mean.' Suddenly the phone rang. I picked it up.

'Hello?' I said. There was silence, then stertorous breathing. 'Hello?' Oh not *again!* I slammed the phone down then hit 1471. Number withheld. Of course.

'Problems! Problems!' yelled Rudy.

'You're telling me,' I replied.

'Are you all right Rose?' said Theo.

'Oh I'm fine, it's just that I've got this nuisance caller.'

'What a drag. My wife had one of those once. She never said a thing, she just put the phone down. Drives them mad.'

'That's what I do.'

'Then with any luck they'll stop.'

Whoever it was went quiet on me for a few days, so I forgot about it and in any case I was very busy at work. Plus I had my phone-ins and I went on *Kilroy* to discuss 'Couples Reuniting' and I had to give a talk to the Bath W.I. So what with all that I hadn't had time to plan my outfit – and by now the ball was only ten days away. What on earth should I wear? Looking through my pre-Raphaelites book I had a stroke of inspiration. I decided to go as *Flaming June*, by Lord

Leighton, as I shall be Flaming Forty that month. Plus the girl in the painting's got hair rather like mine, though she's much more pneumatic than me. Beverley said she was also desperate about her costume so on Friday night I took my art history books next door. Trevor lay by her chair, contentedly sucking the head of his toy gorilla while Bev and I looked at the plates.

'Do you fancy Baroque or Rococo?' I asked her as I flicked through my Gombrich. 'You've got a lovely high forehead so maybe Renaissance would be more your style . . .' I gazed at the Raphael Madonna clutching the infant Jesus tightly to her and felt the familiar stab in my heart. 'Maybe you should go for Gaugin,' I went on, as she picked up another book. 'You'd make a lovely Tahitian maiden or perhaps Impressionism's more your thing. How about – yes! – a Renoir bathing beauty in frilly swimmers – no, on second thoughts you're too slim. Or a Joshua Reynolds – or a pretty Gainsborough – what do you think Bev? Bev?' I looked up. She was crying. 'Bev! What's the matter?' I grabbed her hand.

'I should go like this,' she wept, showing me a pitiless Breughel portrait of a beggar with mangled limbs. 'Or maybe I should go as that screaming Munch, or as a deformed creature from a Hieronymus Bosch.'

'Beverley – don't,' I said. 'You're lovely.'

'That's not *true*! I'm a *cripple*,' she wailed. 'I'm a fucking *cripple*, Rose: a Raspberry Ripple.'

'Bollocks! You're beautiful.'

'Not any *more*. Everyone thinks I'm so brave,' she sobbed, her face red and twisted with grief. 'Brave Bev. Battling Bev. But I'm not like that inside. I'm not like that at *all*. Don't tell anyone this,' she confided with a teary gasp, 'but I get so upset sometimes.'

'*Do* you?' I said.

'Yes,' she murmured with a sniff. 'I do. But I can't help it because I know I'll never – uh-uh – walk, or run again: I've got to sit down for the rest of my life. And I tell people that I've – uh-uh – got over it – but the truth is I *haven't* and I never *will*!' I thought again of the suppressed sobbing I'd heard through the wall and of the hockey sticks she'd burned on the fire. 'And all these paintings of these lovely – uh-uh – women with their – uh-uh – lovely, perfect, strong legs . . .'

'I'm sorry,' I said as Trevor passed her a hanky. 'It's my fault for bringing them round. Have a good cry,' I said as she buried her face in his fur. 'Why shouldn't you cry? Something awful happened to you. But Bev I know you'll be . . .' – my throat ached: I find crying catching – 'I know you'll be fine.' Her sobs subsided, and she looked up and wiped her eyes.

'Yes,' she croaked. 'Maybe I will. I'm sorry,' she said, 'I know things could be worse. The way I hit the ground I'm lucky not to be a tetraplegic, or dead. Perhaps I should go to the ball as a still life,' she added with a bleak smile. 'I mean, there is still life.'

'Oh *yes*.'

Suddenly Trevor went into the hall, then reappeared with the walkabout phone in his mouth.

'Oh,' she laughed, then hugged him again. 'It's okay, Trev, Rose is here. Whenever I'm depressed he goes and gets the phone,' she explained, 'so that I can ring up a friend.'

'How lovely,' I said as my heart turned to mush and I reached out to stroke his ear.

'Actually Rose,' she said swallowing her tears, 'the real reason why I'm crying is not so much my accident as the fact that I'm very . . .' Her voice trailed away. 'I'm very . . .' she shrugged then stared, red-eyed, into the distance; 'I'm very . . .'

'Lonely?' I murmured. She nodded slowly, then looked at me.

'*Yes*. Yes, I am. I could deal with what happened so much better if I had someone to share things with. But I haven't been out with anyone since Jeff left and it's getting me down.'

'But you know people,' I said. 'You get invited.'

'That's not the problem. The problem is Trev. Every time I meet a nice bloke it turns out that he's only really interested in me because of him. You know, the novelty of it. The Bev 'n' Trev show. Something to gas about down the pub. But if I try and meet a man *without* Trevor, they seem disappointed. They don't fall for *me*, first, on my *own*.' This conversation sounded oddly familiar – it reminded me of the twins. 'I've got a date with this chap on Friday,' she went on. 'But I'm terrified that he'll just fall in love with Trev.'

'Then don't take him with you.'

'But he gets anxious. I don't like to leave him.'

'Then he can come to me. Trevor do you want to have dinner with me on Friday night?' He thumped his tail. 'Okay, seven-thirty for eight. Let me know if you're a veggie. Right – back to the task in hand.' I picked up one of the books again, flicked through it, then suddenly stopped. I looked at the picture, then looked at Bev. Perfect.

'I've got it,' I said. I showed her the Degas ballerina, in her gossamer tutu, waiting in the wings to go on.

'That's the one, isn't it?'

Beverley gazed at it for a few seconds, then suddenly smiled.

'Yes – I think that's the one,' she said.

'So what's your problem then Sarah?' I said on my Thursday night phone-in.

'Well my problem's that I'm thirty-nine and I'm terrified of turning forty. What can I do?'

'Listen honey,' – I adopt this feisty tone on the phone-in: it's part of the entertainment – 'listen honey,' I said. 'Forty is the new thirty. Everyone knows that. This is boom time for Middle Youth. Look at Nigella. Look at Madonna . . . Hey! Got it! Problem solved! Why don't you just change your Christian name to something ending with "a"! And now on line four we have . . .' I peered at the computer screen. 'Kathy . . .' Kathy? Oh *God!!*

'I just want all your listeners to know what a *wicked*, WICKED woman you are Rose Costelloe! My husband left me because of you. You sit there in that comfy studio of yours dispensing advice like some high priestess but you ruined my life you interfering cow. And you are going to PAY for what you did to me, destroying my marriage you baggage! You are going to *pay* for that – mark my words, you'll be *really* sorry that you ever crossed me and –' Crazy Kathy was quickly faded out and I looked daggers at Wesley through the studio glass.

'And I'm afraid that brings us to the end of *Sound Advice* for tonight,' said Minty with professional calm. 'But I hope you'll join us again. And remember, if you've got a problem, don't worry about it – but *do* ask Rose.'

'Wesley,' I said crossly as I pushed on the studio door. 'Please don't put that Rottweiler through to me ever again! If I want abuse and intimidation, I can get it from my editor any day of the week.'

'I'm sorry,' he whined, his bald head gleaming in the studio lights. 'She just, you know, slipped through the net.'

'Did you get her number?'

'She withheld it.' Ah *ha*.

'Well someone – and I think it's her – has been harassing me with nuisance calls at home, and it's beginning to get me down.'

Sitting in the cab on the way back to Camberwell I thought, what if the woman's not just mad and sad but actually dangerous? Daphne, the *Daily Herald*'s agony aunt, once had a stalker, and he turned up at her office with an axe. He's currently enjoying a maxi-break at Broadmoor. What if Crazy Kathy's like that?

In the meantime the twins are being very secretive about their costumes for the ball, while Theo's still trying to decide. He ought to go as a Giacometti, I thought as I surreptitiously scrutinised his slender physique. Meanwhile Bev and I went to 'MadWorld' costume hire in Gray's Inn Road to get ourselves kitted out. In the cab there she told me about her date the night before – she wasn't impressed.

'I had to go Dutch! What a creep!'

'I've always gone Dutch,' I said. 'Does it really matter Bev? Aren't we modern women now?'

'I don't want to be modern on a first date,' she said indignantly. 'It's so unromantic.'

'I always went Dutch with Ed.'

'What? Right from the start?'

I'd never really thought about it. 'Yes,' I said. 'Right from the start. He'd just bought this big house so I felt it was only fair to go halves.'

I fetched the costumes from the rail while Trevor helped Bev get changed. He removed her shoes with his teeth, then pulled off her track suit bottoms with the command, 'Tug Trev! Tug!' I handed her the tutu through the curtain, then tied the ribbons of her ballet shoes.

'You look . . . lovely!' I said. 'So dainty.'

'And you look like the setting sun!' I was wearing a blazing orange floor-length Grecian tunic, with pleating as fine as Fortuny silk. 'The Pre-Raphaelite look really suits you,' said Bev. 'You know, this is going to be fun.'

On the night of the ball Beverley's mother came to look after Trevor as he doesn't like loud music or late nights. Then Bev, Theo and I got a cab together to the Courtauld. This was the first time that Theo and Bev had met and they seemed to have struck up an instant rapport; and although she's very independent, she allowed him to push her chair. As we walked through the arched entrance of Somerset House into the huge courtyard I caught my breath. Illuminated fountains threw up jets of water like ostrich plumes, while behind, on the open-air ice rink, skaters spun dreamily around to the strains of a Viennese waltz. And now, as we walked towards the large marquee on our left we spotted the guests arriving for the ball. The inventiveness of the costumes was amazing – everyone had gone to town. Checking in their coats with us were a Medici Pope, a Frida Kahlo self-portrait and the Holbein Henry VIII. Standing by the Christmas tree was Caravaggio's Young Bacchus, his hair festooned with vine leaves and grapes. Nearby a dignified Rembrandt chatted to a wanton-looking Salome who was gaily clutching John the Baptist's head. There were some amazing modern works too. A tall, bony woman with a long, angular face made an authentic Modigliani; a curvy girl in a cobalt-blue body-stocking was clearly a late Matisse. Chatting to the Van Gogh *Self-Portrait with Bandaged Ear* was a woman dressed as Marilyn Monroe. This was the Andy Warhol Marilyn complete with lemon-yellow hair, pink face and blue legs. She'd even put wire all around the hem of her *Seven Year Itch* plunging white dress. The surrealists were out in force too. One man had the Dali lobster telephone balanced on top of his head and, most spectacular, a man who'd come as *The Therapist* by Magritte. His top half was a birdcage, containing two white doves, half obscured by red velvet drapes, but from waist down he wore conventional pin-striped trousers and a pair of shiny black shoes.

'What amazing costumes,' I breathed. 'And it looks like a sell-out.'

'It is,' said Bev. 'I managed to sell the last two tables only yesterday, to a firm of city solicitors – they're always on for this kind of thing.'

'Which firm is that then?' asked Theo with studied casualness.

'Prenderville White.'

Prenderville White? That was where his wife worked. Shit! I glanced at Theo. He'd gone red.

'There you are Rose!' It was the twins clutching flutes of champagne. 'Flaming June!' they both cried.

'And you're – what are you? Of course. You're tubes of oil paint!'

'Correct!'

They were wearing identical white boiler suits, with 'Windsor and Newton' printed on them, front and back, with coloured belts. On their heads were flat white, hexagonal hats – or rather tops – with a matching stripe.

'I'm Burnt Sienna,' explained Bella.

'I'm Scarlet Lake,' said Bea. 'We should have got you to come as Rose Madder, Rose! It would have been rather appropriate, what!'

'This is my neighbour Beverley,' I said frostily, ignoring her.

'You look tutu gorgeous!' Bella cried – and it was true. Beverley's white silk chiffon dress was knee-length, cut fairly low and tied with a sky-blue satin sash. Her motionless legs looked thin but elegant in their pearlescent opaque tights; her feet, in be-ribboned pink satin ballet pumps, were placed carefully on the wheelchair plate. She'd pulled her hair back into a chignon and had a velvet choker around her slim throat.

'And this is Theo, my flatmate.' Theo smiled politely at the twins as they shook hands but I could see the tense, unhappy expression in his eyes.

'So how are you enjoying Rose's regime Theo?' asked Bea with a snort. 'She's fanatically tidy and she doesn't so much clean the house as give it a chemical peel!'

'Really Bea!' I'm very fond of her, but she does talk rubbish sometimes.

'Honestly Theo, she's just like Jack Lemmon in *The Odd Couple*, don't you think?'

'ROSE!!' Thank God. Here was Henry, looking like an upmarket pantomime dame. 'Isn't this fun?' he said, tossing his silver ringlets and hugging me. 'Ooh, mind my beauty spot!'

'Madame de Pompadour?' I ventured.

'No, Marie Antoinette. Let them eat canapés!' he added with a snort as a waiter offered us miniature cheese on toasts. The girls stared incredulously at Henry as I introduced him – well he did look rather strange.

'I think I'll go and find my friends, Sue and Phil,' Bev said slightly awkwardly. 'I haven't caught up with them yet.'

'Would you like me to come with you?' Theo asked.

'Well, if you're sure you don't mind.' She smiled. 'It's much easier to have someone pushing the chair in a crowd like this.'

As they set off I watched Theo anxiously scanning the throng. It would be awful if his wife were here, but she was a partner in that firm so she well might. How upsetting, I

111

reflected, when he's already feeling so raw, to bump into her at something like this; and it's not even as though he has the comfort of being with people he knows really well. But I can't torture myself about it, I decided: either she's here or she's not. Now as I circulated with Henry and the twins I looked at all the couples, having fun.

'– We've just bought a house in Clerkenwell.'

'– We're going to Val d'Isère.'

'– Of course we knew Nick Serota when he was at the Whitechapel.'

'– We've got my mum coming this year.'

'– We argue *all* the time, don't we darling?'

'– We'll be twelve on Christmas Day.'

Couples, I thought dismally; cosy couples. No wonder the anagram of couples is 'up close.' Now, as the champagne kicked in I idly wondered why my relationships have never worked out. Leaving Ed's betrayal out of it it's not as though I've made a habit of dating cads. Before Henry there was Tom, the pilot; and before Tom there was Brian. Brian was a cameraman, but he was always away on location, which was a shame, as he was really good fun. Then before Brian there was Toby, who had his own marketing consultancy, which meant he was going to and fro to the States. And before *him* – we're going way back now – there was Frank, a foreign correspondent for ITN. And before *him* – ooh, we're talking mid-eighties – was Nick, an actor, who did touring rep. But at least they've all been nice men, I reflected fair-mindedly. For some reason it just didn't work out.

A few yards away Beverley was chatting to her friends while Theo studied the seating plan.

'Are you okay?' I asked him.

'Yes,' he said with a relieved smile. 'I'm fine. For one awful moment I thought my wife might be here but I've looked at the list and she's not.'

A large gong sounded and an MC announced that dinner was served. Knowing that Theo was feeling fine I relaxed –

the evening was turning out well after all. As we slowly made our way towards our tables, a girl dressed as a Toulouse Lautrec can-can dancer asked us if we'd like to buy raffle tickets.

'We've got some great prizes,' she explained. 'The tickets are five pounds each, but if you buy four you get one free.'

'That sounds like good value for Monet,' I quipped handing her twenty quid.

'I'll have five too,' said Bev.

'I'd like ten,' said Theo. His relief at his wife's absence had made him generous. Bev gave him a grateful smile. 'We're on table sixteen,' he pointed out, 'I think it's over there, by that pillar, towards the back.'

'Would *you* like to buy a raffle ticket Sir?' I heard the girl ask someone behind us.

'No thanks,' said a familiar voice. It was as though I'd been pushed off a cliff.

'Are you sure?' The girl tried again as my heart did a drum roll.

'Quite sure, thanks,' said Ed. How bitterly, bitterly ironic. I felt blood suffuse my face. Theo's spouse *wasn't* here after all – to his huge relief – but mine *was*!

'Are you all right?' Theo asked, staring at me. 'What is it?'

'My ex-mother,' I murmured miserably.

'Your ex-mother?'

'I mean . . . my ex-*husband*. He's right behind.'

'Rose!' hissed the twins slithering up to me like a pair of sidewinders, 'Ed's here.'

'Yes, I know. Presumably *she*'s with him,' I said bleakly.

'Yes,' Bella whispered, ''fraid so. But she looks hideous,' she added. 'She's come as Vermeer's *Girl with the Pearl Earring*. It doesn't suit her at all.'

'No, that's not right,' said Bea. 'She's come as his *Portrait of a Young Woman*, actually.'

'It's *The Girl with the Pearl Earring*,' Bella insisted.

'No – it's the *Portrait of a Young Woman*. They're very similar but the headdress is slightly different.'

'I'm telling you Bea, it's *The Girl with the Pearl Earring*, I've got a book on Vermeer.'

'I don't care if she's come as the Duchamp urinal,' I hissed, 'what about him?'

'He's a Van Dyck *Laughing Cavalier*.'

'But he looks a bit sad,' said Bella.

'He looks bloody silly,' added Bea.

'I can't take it,' I muttered miserably. 'I'll have to go home.'

'No!' said the twins. 'Just ignore them and try and have fun!'

'Has anyone got any valium?' I muttered with a bitter laugh. In the absence of pharmaceutical sedation I anaesthetised myself with another gulp of champagne.

'Don't worry,' Bella whispered conspiratorially, as we found our table, 'they're sitting miles away.' Hyperventilating gently behind my palette-shaped menu I now discreetly peered through the centrepiece flowers. There Ed was, with that human Pokémon, by the window, on the far side. They were with my ex-neighbours, Pam and Doug, who were dressed as the *Arnolfini Marriage* by van Eyck.

'Bottoms up!' said Henry genially as he filled everyone's glass with Chablis. Then he began talking to the twins about their interior design business and about some empty shop he knew of near High Street Ken. I tried to chat to Bev's friends, Sue and Phil, but it was an effort to concentrate; not just because Ed was in the same room but because, by some hideous stroke of synchronicity, it was a year to the day since we'd met. This was our first anniversary, I reflected miserably. Bloody marvellous. *Great*.

I glanced at Pam and Doug and bitterly wished I'd never gone to their party that night. I'd been in two minds about it as I was busy, and I didn't know them that well. If I hadn't gone, I now reflected, I would not have met and married Ed, and he would not have been unfaithful to me with our marriage guidance counsellor and I would not now be dismal and almost divorced. I would still be living in my perfectly nice garden flat in Clapham, with a manageable mortgage, instead of in a house in Camberwell which I can barely afford.

After the duck – I couldn't touch mine – there was a speech by the charity's chairperson, that glamorous but somehow rather irritating TV vet, Ulrika Most. She'd come as a Klimt in a flowing Art Nouveau gold-speckled devoré dress. She thanked the ball's sponsors, Dogobix, in her lilting Scandiwegian, then talked about the charity's work.

'There are many thousands of people with serious disabilities,' she began. 'A Helping Paw can change their lives . . . increased independence . . . a whole new lease of life . . . but training each dog costs eight thousand pounds . . . thank you for your support tonight.' And now, after five – or was it six – glasses of wine I had begun to relax. I could cope. Oh yes, I could deal with this. Stuff Ed and his ghastly Miss Trust.

'Ed should have come as *The Rake's Progress*! I hissed across the table to the twins as the *crème brûlée* arrived. 'As for that pigmy he's shagging,' I added gaily, 'she should have come as that Turner Prize-winning pile of elephant dung!' Amused by my caustic observations I emitted a hollow laugh. But at the same time I was aware that *I* should have come as Picasso's *Weeping Woman*.

As Henry got up – 'I have to powder my nose,' he announced – the twins began to fight.

'You're flirting him with Bella, stop it!'

'I'm not – you're paranoid.'

'You are!' Bea hissed 'You always have to try and spoil things don't you?'

'Oh for God's sake – don't be ab*surd*!'

The auction followed. I tipsily submitted a closed bid for a painting – unsuccessful fortunately as I don't have the cash – then the raffle was announced: no dice. I stared miserably at my strips of pink cloakroom tickets, then the band struck up. Sue and Phil got up to dance and the twins both rushed onto the floor with Henry – still competing for his attention like mad. Theo was talking animatedly to Beverley – now

115

they were getting on like a house on fire and uu . . . uuuu . . . . uuuhhh! Someone was pushing a blunt skewer into my heart – there was Ed dancing with Miss Match; or rather Mish Mash I thought blearily as I drained my glass again. I averted my eyes, but it was like passing a car crash: I didn't want to see but somehow couldn't not look. Ed was so gorgeous, even in that ludicrous curly black wig, I thought my heart would break. I willed the glittering chandelier to fall on Miss Fortune and crush her to bits. And now, from the table behind, I heard an animated conversation taking place.

'Yes, he got this call – out of the blue.'

'What? From his mum?'

'Yes. She hadn't seen him for thirty-five years.'

'*Amazing!* thirty-five years?'

'That's right.'

'So what happened?'

'Well, apparently she was terrified that he'd tell her to get lost, but he didn't, and now they've become best of friends.'

Christ, that was all I needed – Happy Families: I poured myself some more wine. And now, after seven glasses – or was it eight? – the dancers seemed to swirl and coalesce before my eyes. Lowry stick men, thin as thermometers, danced with bosomy Rubenses; bespectacled Gilbert and George suits with frilly Fragonards; a Seurat Bather in red swimming shorts was twirling a bustled Tissot. I glanced at Theo and Bev, still chatting away animatedly as if they'd known each other for years. Hmmmm . . .

'No, I really *do* think men are from Mars and women are from Venus,' she exclaimed hotly.

'Oh that's not true,' he replied. 'For a start there's no water on Mars, and the atmosphere is mostly carbon dioxide making it impossible to support life. Ditto Venus where the average temperature is 870 degrees Fahrenheit, plus it rains sulphuric acid all day.' Bev giggled and rolled her eyes. 'Would you like to dance?' Theo added.

'Well, I'd love to,' she replied, 'but the floor's a bit too crowded. Maybe later on when there's a little more space.'

'Are you sure?' She nodded. 'How about you Rose? Rose?'

'Wha . . . ?' I lowered my glass.

'Would you like to dance?' he asked politely.

'Er . . .'

'Would you?' Would I?

'Um . . . well . . . 'kay then. Why no'?' As Bea returned to the table with Henry – Bella was dancing with a Jackson Pollock – Theo and I headed onto the floor.

'So isn't there *any* life on Mars then?' I asked him tipsily. 'I find that *ver'* disappointing.'

'No – at least not during the week. But on Saturday nights it can get pretty lively apparently . . .'

I giggled, then saw Ed and stopped.

Do you really want to hurt me? crooned the singer.

Yes, Ed, I really *do*.

Do you really want to make me cry?

I'd *love* to make you cry, I reflected bitterly as Theo spun me round. Ed and Miss Guided were less than six feet away but I heroically ignored them. And now, the tempo slowed.

I believe I can fly . . . crooned the lead singer.

I saw Mary-Claire's porky little arms go round Ed's neck. I flung my arms round Theo.

I believe I can touch the sky . . .

I saw her trotters caress his back – well two could play at that.

I think about it every night and day . . .

I saw her stand on tiptoe to grunt sweet nothings in his ear, so I whispered in Theo's.

Spread my wings and fly away . . .

'Thish lov'ly . . . s'reely nice,' I said. I hiccuped, loudly. 'Oh sorry.'

'I'm glad you're enjoying yourself,' said Theo, slightly awkwardly.

'Iss *bldy* gd fn!'

'Your costume's grand by the way.' Grand. That was *such* a nice word.

'Oh! Snks ver mush.' I hiccuped again – it was really

117

painful. Then, suddenly exhausted, I laid my forehead on Theo's shoulder – and felt my head start to spin.

I believe I can soar . . .

Now as we slowly revolved again I looked up and focused for a second on Bev.

See me running through that open door . . .

She was looking crestfallen and tense, a deep frown pleating her brow. What was up? Oh God – of *course*. She'd been chatting to Theo all night and didn't like me dancing with him. I wanted to rush over and tell her she had nothing to worry about: a) he was ten years my junior – he was a baby for God's sake! – and b) we were just having a bop. He simply felt sorry for his poor lonely old landlady so he thought he'd give her a twirl. To our left Henry and Bea were getting on *very* well, dancing cheek to cheek. Hmmmm. And now – still conspicuously ignoring them – Theo and I shimmied past Ed and Miss Lay. I was grateful, as we did so, that Theo was at least quite good-looking. Then, emboldened by booze, I looked Ed straight in the eye. Just for a nanosecond. I looked him square in the face. And drunk though I undoubtedly was by now, I registered hurt in his eyes. Well he'd brought it on himself, I reflected sourly. Suddenly I felt a sharp pain in my brow.

'Ooh.'

'What's up, Rose?' whispered Theo.

'My head really aches.'

'Would you like to sit down?'

'Yes please. Oh, no!' Because now the band was playing 'Every Little Thing She Does is Magic', one of my favourite songs; and there was Henry, bouncing around with Bea, twirling her this way and that; then I saw him dash over to Bev. He wheeled her onto the floor, then danced with her, prancing around her chair and spinning it vigorously with both hands. Then he suddenly grabbed her by the waist, lifted her clean out of it, and whirled her around. Her blue satin sash streamed behind her like a comet's tail as she turned her laughing face up; then he spun her round twice more – it made me feel giddy – before replacing her, giggling helplessly, in her chair. Now Theo cut in and danced with Beverley while Henry danced with Bea and me. Stuff Ed and Miss Alliance; this ball was really good fun. It would have been even more fun, however, if my head wasn't hurting so much. And I was just about to go and sit down when Ulrika Most stepped onto the podium again.

'Ladies and gentlemen, I'd just like to interrupt the dancing briefly for the awarding of the prizes for the best costumes.' To a trumpet fanfare and the roll of a snare drum, we all retreated to the edge of the floor.

'This has been a very difficult task,' Ulrika added as she clutched three gold envelopes. 'You *all* look wonderful. But the ball committee and I have now cast our final votes for the best dressed guests. So, in unfashionable descending order, I'd like to announce that the first prize goes to . . .' She opened the envelope. '. . . Magritte – *The Therapist*!' We all applauded like mad, as the amazing half birdcage, half businessman, came slowly forward to claim his prize. 'The second prize goes to . . . the Andy Warhol Marilyn Monroe!' We all cheered as the Marilyn screen print stepped forward, received her envelope, twirled twice, then took a deep bow. My head felt as though someone was trying to bore a hole in it with a blunt Black and Decker so I shut my eyes. But that only gave me the whirlies, so I reopened them, aware as I did so of Theo's steadying hand on my arm. 'And the third prize,' announced Ulrika, 'goes to a very authentic *Flaming June* by Lord Leighton . . . *Flaming June*?'

'That's you,' Theo hissed.

'Oh. Yeah.' I weaved through the people in front of me and crossed the floor towards the podium which suddenly seemed a very long way off. As I did so I was dimly aware of three things. That my head was about to go off like a grenade, that Ulrika's shoes really sparkled in the lights, and that the man to whom I was still married was standing there. I glanced at Ed. Correction – he wasn't standing there; he and Miss Deed were on their way out.

119

'Congratulations!' said Ulrika politely, holding out an elegant hand. But I didn't shake it, so much as grab it, for fear that I'd fall down. Ulrika's face blurred for an instant then swam back into focus. 'Well done,' she said with a smile which I now noticed didn't quite reach her eyes.

'Thank eeuuuhh,' I groaned as I took the proffered gold envelope.

'Are you okay?' she asked.

'Wha . . . ?' My head was hurting so badly I wished someone would guillotine me. 'I'm . . . fine,' I muttered, ''slutely fine.' And I was about to turn round and make my way back when I felt a jet of saliva spurt into my mouth. I leaned forward and grabbed the mike stand for a second then closed my eyes, surprised when I opened them again to see a pool of bright yellow puke on Ulrika Most's spangly shoes.

Chapter Seven

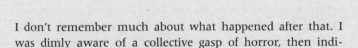

I don't remember much about what happened after that. I was dimly aware of a collective gasp of horror, then individual voices.

'– Oh God she's chundered.'

'– Maybe she's ill.'

'– Get a doctor.'

'– No – get Charles Saatchi! He'd pay a fortune for that!'

I also vaguely recall being wheeled out of the Courtauld in Bev's wheelchair with her sitting on my lap; and the twins congratulating me for throwing up on Ulrika's feet – not her dress.

'But they were such lovely shoes,' I groaned as we waited in the Strand for a cab. 'They were really sparkly. Oh God.'

'She was Most unimpressed,' Henry quipped.

'On the other hand Klimt is a bit nauseating,' said Bella.

'Yes, disgustingly decadent,' said Bea. 'And let's face it, once you've had your arm up a cow's backside, what's a bit of sick?'

'And don't worry Rose,' added Henry comfortingly, 'loads of people had left by the time you vommed.'

'Had Ed definitely left?'

'Yes,' said the twins.

'Definitely?'

'*Definitely*.'

'Thank God.'

The shame, nevertheless, was excoriating; and it was all Ed's fault. If he hadn't been there with Miss Adventure my behaviour would have been fine.

*   *   *

When I awoke the next morning, still clothed, a hangover enveloping me like a black shroud, I realised that Theo had helped me upstairs, removed my shoes, put the duvet over me, and left a bucket and a jug of water by my bed.

'Thanks,' I croaked in the kitchen as I swallowed two Neurofen, 'and . . . sorry. I must have embarrassed you, behaving like that.'

'Well, a bit,' he said bluntly. That boy doesn't mince words.

'Ha ha *ha*!' Rudy yelled.

'I'm going to make myself reread my Alcohol Abuse Leaflet,' I added blearily. 'I haven't been that drunk since I was eighteen. It was emotional stress,' I explained.

'About your ex-husband?'

'Well, soon-to-be ex-husband, yes.'

'You referred to him as your "ex-mother,"' said Theo quizzically.

'Did I?'

'What did you mean?'

'Nothing. It was a slip of the tongue. Anyway, did you enjoy yourself?' I enquired as I sipped my black tea.

'Oh yes,' he said. 'It was grand.' He smiled that lop-sided little smile of his. 'You've got some really nice friends. By the way, I retrieved this.' He handed me the gold envelope. Inside was a voucher for dinner for two at the River Café. I took it next door to Bev. I wanted to atone for getting plastered, and for cheaply flirting with Theo whom I *knew* she liked.

'But it's yours,' she said, as I held out the prize. 'You won it.'

'I want you to have it.'

'Why?'

'It's my penance,' I explained blearily as Trevor let me in. 'Please. I ruined your ball. It wouldn't have happened if Ed hadn't been there. I don't know why he *was* there,' I added miserably as we went through to the kitchen. 'It was a hell of a shock.'

'Well I think I *do* know,' said Bev carefully as she ran water into the kettle. 'I noticed that they were on the same table as one of the ball committee members, Gill Hart. I had to speak to Gill this morning and she told me that she's an old school-mate of your husband's, er, . . . *friend*,' she concluded delicately.

'His mistress you mean. And before that she was our marriage guidance counsellor.'

Bev grimaced. 'Yes, you said. You know how nosy I am,' she went on with a grin. 'Well, I asked Gill about that – I couldn't resist – and she said that Mary-Claire's about to be struck off for breaching Resolve's ethical code. Apparently they conducted an internal enquiry and after Christmas she'll get the boot.'

'Great!' I said. 'Perhaps they'll allow me to administer it personally – my Tae-Bo instructor says I've a fabulous kick. She's supposed to *save* marriages,' I said bitterly, 'not break them. She blighted my troth. It was hateful seeing them together. If I'd known I would never have gone.'

'That's understandable,' said Bev. 'If Jeff had turned up with his new woman I'd have been in much the same state. But it's hard in London; people *do* know each other. Six degrees of separation and all that.'

'Six?' I repeated sceptically. 'It's more like three, or even two. Anyway I'm sorry I spoiled the ball,' I added as she poured me some coffee. 'That's what I came to say.'

'You didn't spoil it. It was a *wonderful* evening. Gill says we raised forty grand – that's enough to train five puppies – and I thought all your friends were great.'

'And on that front,' I interrupted her anxiously, 'can I just say that the only reason I flirted with Theo is because Ed was there with Mary-Claire.'

'Oh,' she said quietly. 'I see.'

'Plus I was terribly drunk, as you know. But I have no interest in him whatsoever other than as his landlady and so . . .'

'Yes?'

'. . . the coast is clear. I'm just telling you that so that you know.'

'But whatever makes you think I'm interested?' she asked, with tell-tale touchiness and a give-away red spot on both cheeks.

'Well, because you . . . talked to him so much and also . . . Look, I'm not being funny, Bev,' I added, 'but when I was dancing with him I noticed that you didn't exactly look pleased.'

'Didn't I?' she said vaguely. She looked genuinely bemused.

'No. In fact you looked rather pissed-off. It was a slow number, and I *was* a bit over the top, what with being squiffy, so I thought . . .' I gave her a meaningful look. 'I thought . . .'

'Well you were wrong. It was –' she sighed, '– because of that song, "I believe I can fly." It always depresses me because I *don't* believe I can fly, let alone soar, and I'm certainly *not* going to be running through any open doors; plus I might have been feeling a bit down, sitting there, dressed as a bloody ballerina, thinking "I can't dance."'

'I'm sorry,' I said. 'I just thought that you might, you know, like him so I wanted to reassure you, that's all.'

'Theo is *very* nice,' Bev agreed as she stroked Trevor's head; 'he's very attractive too.'

I thought about that for a moment. 'Yes, I guess he is.'

'And he's obviously had a hard time.'

'He told you about that, did he? About his wife?'

'Yes he did, and well, I'd just like to be friends. But I have absolutely *no* romantic interest in him *whatsoever*, Rose. I hope you *believe* me.'

'Of course I do,' I lied. I realised that I'd hit a nerve so I thought I'd better change tack. 'The twins had a good time,' I went on. 'Bella got picked up by that Jackson Pollock – now he's *very* good-looking – and Henry and Bea got on really well.'

'Yes,' she said, stirring her coffee.

'And your friends seemed to enjoy themselves.'

'Oh they did; they had a great time.' An awkward silence enveloped us for a moment during which I registered the

124

slow tick of the kitchen clock. 'Rose,' said Bev, diffidently, 'there was something I wanted to ask you actually . . .'

'Anything.'

'I was wondering . . .'

'Yes?'

'Er . . . I just wanted to ask you . . .'

'What?'

'Well, it's slightly awkward actually . . .'

'Don't worry. Just ask me.'

She looked at the floor, then looked at me. 'Well . . . if . . . if you'd mind taking my costume back to the hire place for me, that's all.'

'Of course I will,' I replied. And then I wondered, what was awkward about asking me that?

It's three days now since the ball and I've put my embarrassing performance out of my mind. I've apologised to everyone and sent Ulrika a large cheque, so why go on torturing myself? I have agony aunted myself to the conclusion that although I behaved very badly I can't put the clock back so I might as well try and forget. In any case I'm very good at not thinking about unpleasant things. I shut them away in my mind. I neatly compartmentalise them and lock the door: a skill which I learned as a child. So I'm not going to dwell on my humiliation: it's over; what's done is done. In any case some good things have come out of that evening and so, despite everything, I'm still very glad that I went.

Firstly, Theo and Beverley have met. And yes, I know what she said, but I just don't believe her – why else the strenuous denials? And look, I'm not being conceited or anything, but, as you know, I'm pretty good at reading between the lines. And my guess is that Bev's simply embarrassed about the six-year age gap, so she's trying to play it all down. Plus she's naturally going to be a bit wary because Theo's been through a lot. But I can see them together quite easily actually. I sensed some Karmic bond. Now, as I swept leaves in the garden, I had a sudden, happy vision of their wedding in about, what, eighteen months' time? There was Trevor, chief usher at the register office, with a white ribbon round his neck. Then we were going on to the Planetarium for the reception, or maybe Greenwich Observatory. And now we'd had the wedding breakfast and Theo was making his speech.

'This is a wonderful day for me,' he began, his voice quivering with emotion, 'after a painful and difficult time. But meeting Bev has changed everything: she's brought the sunshine back into my life. But our happiness would never have been possible without . . .' he was looking at me, '. . . our dear friend, Rose. To Rose Costelloe!' he said, raising his glass as I blushed and smiled. And now I fast forwarded to the christening of their first child. They'd asked me to be godmother to the baby who – you'll never guess – they'd named after *me!* It was incredibly touching, and as I dug a large dandelion out of the ground I had to fight back the tears. The privilege of making other people happy. The joy of sorting out their lives. Take Henry and Bea for example: I'd brought them together as well. Now I was suddenly at *their* wedding, in Ashford, as the twins' parents still live down there. In fact – yes – of course – it was a *double* wedding – *two* have and *two* hold – because Bella was getting hitched too. She was marrying the Jackson Pollack whom she'd *also* met, indirectly, through *me!* The twins had on identical cream silk Vera Wang dresses, though strangely, Henry was wearing one too . . . And I was just trying to imagine how this would look in the wedding album when the phone rang. I picked it up.

'Hi,' said Bea. 'What are you doing?'

'Wedding. I mean, weeding.'

'In December? You must be mad. Anyway, I've got some news, about Henry.'

'Don't tell me – he's asked you out.'

'No. I've asked him out actually.'

'That's jolly brave.'

'Well I've decided I'm not going to hang about. I'm thirty-seven, I really like him, so I'm going to be upfront and direct.

Henry's *such* a good sport,' she giggled. 'I mean, what a great sense of humour – going to the ball in drag!'

'Er, yes.'

'You don't want him back yourself do you Rose?' Bea suddenly asked, sounding stricken. 'After all, you did know him first.' I visualised Henry in his black silk cocktail dress, slingbacks and pink feather boa.

'No,' I said. 'He's *great*. But I don't.'

'And you know he told us about this empty shop near High St Ken? Well yesterday Bella and I went to see it and this morning we signed the lease. It's slightly out of the way,' she went on, 'so we got it at a good price. But it's perfect.'

'That's great news. And how's Bella?'

'Smitten with her new bloke. It's Andrew this and Andrew that – it's enough to make you throw up. But I'm not really bothered because I hit it off with Henry. You can tell when a man likes you,' she went on expansively. 'We had this instant rapport. Speaking of which, I thought Theo and Bev really got on.'

'Yes,' I agreed. 'They did. Beverley's being coy about it; and of course he's got baggage what with his separation and everything but, well . . . watch this space.'

'I've been meaning to ask what you're doing at Christmas?' Bea added. 'Do you want to come home with us? We're going down tomorrow.' Christmas in Ashford? No thanks.

'That's really kind, Bea,' I said carefully. 'But I'm not sure I want to go back. You know; all those memories . . .' My voice trailed away.

'Mmm . . . thought you might say that. So what will you do?'

'I'll be here, on my own.'

'Sounds absolutely *ghastly*.'

'No, I shan't mind.'

'What about Bev and Trev?'

'They're going to her parents in Stevenage tomorrow and then to Scotland for Hogmanay.'

'And where will Theo be?'

'In Leeds with his folks. But I'll have Rudy to talk to, and I've got a huge backlog of letters. Honestly Bea, I'll be fine . . .'

'I'm dreaming of a white Christmas,' crooned Rudy on Christmas eve. 'Hello, this is *The World Tonight*!'

I heard the clatter of the letter box and went to pick up the second post. There was an invitation to the next Agony Aunts' lunch in January and a handful of Christmas cards. There was one from 'The Editor's Office' signed – or stamped, rather – by Ricky, and his deputy, Pete. There was one from Accounts signed by fifteen people none of whom I'd ever met. There was a card from Pyschic Cynthia with my astro-logical chart for the coming year. Thanks to 'generous Jupiter' I could look forward to 'stunning changes ahead.' I don't want any more stunning changes, I thought, I've had more than enough this year. I'd moved house twice and my marriage had failed. I needed only a death to complete the hat trick of traumatic life events. There were five cards from the pub-licity departments of various publishers and the rest were from assorted friends. 'Hope you're okay,' was the most fre-quent message – a tactful reference to my forthcoming divorce. 'Must catch up soon,' was another favourite – i.e. 'tell us what's been going on.' I scribbled back a few from my emergency pack – they'd arrive late but I didn't care. I wasn't even bothering to keep up appearances, I was saying Bah Humbug! to Christmas this year; my only concession to the festive season was a strand of tinsel through my weeping fig. If I'd had the money I'd have gone off to some remote Pacific island, alone. Now I opened the last card which had been forwarded to me from London FM. It was of a Christmas tree decorated with shiny red hearts and it was inscribed, *To dearest Rose, my favourite agony aunt in the whole wide world and a very Special Lady. With lots of love, Colin Twisk. xxxxx P.S.*, it said in the bottom left hand corner, *your wonderful advice has worked!* I stared, slightly queasily, at the crosses by his name, then the phone rang. I picked it up.

'Hello?' I said. There was silence; then heavy breathing, more rasping than before. I took a deep breath, put the phone down, then shouted '*Wanker!*' Suddenly I heard Theo's tread on the stairs.

'Are you talking to me?' he said with a smile.

'No. I had another nuisance call. I keep getting them, Theo. It's such a . . .'

'Nuisance?'

'Yes.' I pressed 1471. 'Number withheld.'

'You should ring BT or the police.'

'I don't feel I can – I haven't been threatened yet.'

'Well if it carries on I would. Anyway, I'm off to the, er, familial bosom,' he said rolling his eyes. 'I'll be back on the twenty-eighth. I hope you'll be all right on your own, Rose.'

'I'll be fine,' I murmured. 'Thanks.'

'Don't forget to put the chain on the door.'

'I won't.'

'And do screen your phone calls.' I nodded, touched by his forthright concern. 'Well, then, I guess I'll love you and leave you,' he said brightly as he put on his coat. I felt a sudden stabbing sensation in my sternum.

'What's up Rose? You look pained. What's the matter?' he repeated. 'Did I say something wrong?'

'Yes. You did actually.'

'What?'

'Well . . . it's just that I *loathe* that expression.'

'What expression?'

'"I'll love you and leave you".'

'Oh,' he looked nonplussed. 'Why?'

'Because Ed always used to say that – "I'll love you and leave you." And that's exactly what he did.'

Theo looked at me. 'Then in that case I'll just wish you a very Happy Christmas,' he said, then he opened the door.

'That's better. Thanks. You too.'

I felt oddly disconcerted by Theo's absence – well you get used to people don't you? – so I decided I'd have a bit of a sort out – I find it pleasantly distracting. So I sorted out my wardrobe – I like to keep my clothes neatly arranged by colour (and of course, season), then I lined up my shoes. I tidied out my handbag – restoring everything to its designated compartment – then I gave the house a bit of a clean. I washed the kitchen floor, then vacuumed the hall, then went all up the stairs. I hoovered the landing on the top floor by Theo's bedroom and, as his door just happened to be open a crack, I decided to give his carpet a quick blast. He'd had a bit of a clear-up I couldn't help noticing as I pushed the cleaner inside. The books were unpacked and ranged on the shelves, the posters blu-tacked neatly to the walls. There was one of a star-chart, like a child's join the dots puzzle, white on midnight blue. I stared at the constellations: Ursa Major, Canis Minor, Taurus and Gemini – that's my sign. Most of the others I'd never heard of: Bellatrix, Carina, Delphinus, Sculptor, Phoenix, Aquila and Lynx. There was also a large map of the moon, the craters speckling the grey surface like rising bubbles: these had lovely names too. 'Oceanus Procellarum', 'Mare Humorum' and 'Mare Serenitas'. I wished *I* could feel serene I thought as I glanced around the rest of his room.

The silk nightie still peeked from under his pillow – poor chap. And now I looked at the photo in its silver frame: this, I guessed, was his wife. She was blonde, very pretty, with an oval face and she had this fantastic smile. It struck me again that she looked a little like Theo, but then we often are drawn to our own physical type. To my surprise, she didn't look hard, as I'd imagined her, but humorous, as though she could be easily delighted or amused. Poor Theo. He'd clearly adored her – breaking up with her must have been hell. I closed his door, went downstairs where the answer machine was winking – the Hoover had masked the sound of the phone.

'Rose it's Henry!' I heard, to my huge relief. 'Just down to Wiltshire to see my folks. Thanks for taking me to the ball. It was . . .' he paused, '. . . a very special night. I expect you know that Bea's called a couple of times,' he added with a self-conscious laugh. 'She's a super girl – really good fun –

and I'll be seeing her again quite soon. Anyway, I wish you a Cool Yule Rose, despite everything, and a brilliantly Happy New Year.' Then he crooned, in his attractive baritone, 'Have Yourself a Merry Little Christmas . . .' blew me a long, noisy kiss, like bathwater being sucked down the plug, and was gone.

The one thing this Christmas wasn't going to be was merry, but what could I do? I was right not to go back to Kent. The truth is – and I don't know why I'm telling you this – I never enjoyed Christmas there. We'd spend half the day in church, and there was no television because my folks disapproved. We'd listen to the Queen on the radio and when the National Anthem played we'd all have to stand! Then my mum's two unmarried aunts would come over, but to be honest, they were dreadfully dull. And I'd hear the twins' laughter ringing through the wall, and the sound of their TV. So I'd ask my parents if I could go next door, and eventually they'd agree. 'But only as long as you're no trouble,' Mum would say. She was always saying that. 'You mustn't be any trouble,' she would tell me every time I was asked out. 'I do hope she wasn't any trouble?' she'd enquire anxiously when she came to pick me up. And the other mums would always say, very nicely, 'Oh not at all – good as gold.'

Looking back, I think that was true. I was much too quiet to be naughty. My height had made me horribly shy. I don't mind it now – in fact I quite like it – but when I was a kid I hated being so tall. And it was as though my parents felt they had to apologise for me the whole time; as though they were embarrassed by their freakish-looking 'daughter' who, anyone could see at a glance, wasn't theirs. But then they can't have known, when they adopted me, that I'd be almost six foot by the time I was twelve. But in any case I didn't get invited that much because my friends weren't often allowed back. As I say, Mum was fanatically house-proud and she didn't want too much 'noise' and 'mess'.

To be perfectly, yes, perhaps even brutally honest, I don't think my parents liked children that much. So much so that

I'd often wonder why on earth they'd wanted me. I mean, why would a forty-three-year-old couple, childless for fifteen years, suddenly decide to adopt? It was only after they'd died, and I was sorting through their things, that I found out the answer to that. Anyway, Christmas in Ashford holds few happy memories, which is why I prefer to stay here.

By contrast Christmas last year was bliss. Ed and I joked that it was 'Kissmas,' in love and alone in his house. As I switched on the radio, I thought bitterly of him and my porcine replacement all cosy in front of the fire. I had a sudden happy vision of her on one of our Wedgwood platters, trussed, stuffed and honey-glazed, with an expression of surprise on her piggy little face and a large apple in her mouth . . .

Once in Royal David's city, piped the boy treble from King's College, Cambridge, *stood a low-ly cattle shed. Where a mother, laid her baby* . . . Lucky baby I thought. *In a man-ger for its bed* . . . Carols always get to me. I felt the familiar ache in my throat. *Mary was that mother mild* . . . Wish mine had been. *Jesus Christ, her lit-tle child*. As my eyes started to brim with tears of self-pity I switched the radio off. The best remedy for pain is distraction, so I went into my study and started to work. There's nothing like immersing yourself in other people's worries to make you completely forget your own.

He's finished with me, I can't bear it, I read. *My wife's met this man over the Net* . . . *My son hasn't seen me for twelve years* . . . *My neighbour's rows keep me awake all night.*

I'd got through about twenty replies before realising that it had got dark. So I went down to the sitting room to draw the curtains when I heard the distinctive squeak of the gate. I looked through the spyhole and my heart sank. Not again. Heaven's bait.

'Good evening Madam!' said the first one pleasantly, lifting his hat.

'I'm sorry, but I've asked you not to call.'

'But we would like to share the joy of God's love with you. Have you five minutes of your precious time to spare?'

'No.'

'But Jehovah is waiting to welcome you into his glorious Kingdom.'

'Then he'll be waiting a long time.'

'But Jesus loves you Miss Costelloe!'

'That's what they all say . . .' What? 'How did you know my name?' I snapped.

'Because you're on the electoral roll.' Oh. Of *course*.

'Look,' I said wearily, 'you're wasting your time. I dislike organized religion and I *don't* believe in Jesus. Happy Christmas. Good*bye*.'

I double locked the door, put the chain on again, and settled down in front of the box. On the screen was a euphoric Jimmy Stewart, running through Bedford Falls.

'Merry Christmas everybody!' he was shouting. 'Merry Christmas!' It was *A Wonderful Life* wasn't it? *Not* . . .

The next day, while most of the country stuffed themselves senseless, watched telly and quarrelled, I worked. At seven-thirty, I bagged up my thirty-three replies, all ready to be posted, then got out a bottle of wine. And yes, I know, I *know*, you shouldn't drink alone, slippery slope and all that. But I thought, why shouldn't I? It's Christmas Day; I'm pissed-off and I've been working non-stop. Forty minutes later I'd had most of a bottle of rather good Merlot when I heard the gate squeak again. Then the doorbell rang and I stiffened, bracing myself for more grief.

Away in a manger . . . piped childish voices. Relieved, I groped for my bag. *No crib for a bed*. Where was it? Oh. Right here. *The little lord Jesus* . . . I peeped through the spyhole, then drew back the chain. *Lay down his sweet head* . . . There were five of them standing on the step aged between about seven and twelve. They were obviously local kids, on a late trawl for pocket money, but their voices were clear and sweet. *The stars in the bright sky* . . . I opened my purse. *Looked down where he lay* . . . What on earth should I give them? A fiver would be about right. I didn't have one. I only had a twenty quid note. *The little lord Jesus . . .* Oh, what the hell . . . *asleep on the hay*.

'That's to share,' I said, handing it to the biggest boy. 'And don't spend it on cigarettes.'

'Oh no. Thanks Mrs,' he said.

'Yeah. Fanks,' said a younger boy. 'You can have another carol for that if you like.'

'She can have two more,' said a small girl generously.

'It's okay,' I said. 'One was fine.'

'Happy Christmas!' they said as they left. 'God bless!'

'God bless *you*,' I replied. 'Think I'll turn in, Rudy,' I said, dizzy with drink. I covered his cage.

'Nighty night!'

It was only ten to nine but I ached for sleep: the combination of work, wine and seasonal sadness had exhausted me. My head hit the pillow like a brick. But I had strange dreams. I had the dream I sometimes have about my mother – my 'real' one I mean. We'd met at last, but it was at the Old Bailey, where she was in the dock. I was the prosecuting lawyer, in a wig, and I was cross-examining her. And my voice, which had started quiet, got louder and louder until I was really shouting at her. I was letting rip about how she'd deserted me and never, ever, ever come back.

'How could you *do* it?' I yelled. 'How could you? How *could* you?'

She looked ashamed and appalled. I have this dream every now and then and it always makes me feel happy and light. Then I had an erotic dream about Ed, which upset me, followed by a nightmare about Citronella Pratt. She was looking at me pityingly and saying, 'Oh *poor* Rose. You've got *so* many problems haven't you? Oh I *do* so *feel* for you.' And I was about to ask her what she was being so bloody smug about what with her husband famously running off with a man, not to mention the fact that she'd lost her crappy column in the *Sunday Semaphore* and was now reduced to being the agony aunt on that cheap weekly, *Get!* magazine, when something suddenly woke me up.

I sat bolt upright, eyes staring into the blackness, listening as intently as a border collie on *One Man and His Dog*. I'd heard something. Definitely. What was it? There it was again! The squeak of the gate. It kept stopping and starting as though someone were trying to inch it open without being heard. I glanced at the luminous dial on my clock and my scalp prickled – it was half past two. Heart pounding, I tried to remember if I'd left the chain on the door. I'd taken it off when the carol singers turned up, but had I remembered to put it back on? I'd been exhausted, depressed and squiffy by then so there was a chance I might not have done.

I flew to the window and, careful not to touch the curtains, peered down through the tiny gap. The gate *was* open, but I couldn't see anyone – maybe it had been a cat, or a fox. I watched the garden for a minute or so, then sighed with relief – whatever it was, it had gone. I switched on the light and was just about to go down and check the front door when there was a creak on the stairs. Oh *God* . . . And now another. Then another. There was someone in the house. Sick with fear I turned off the light; and a wave of panic engulfed me as I tried to think where I'd left my mobile phone. Then I remembered – it was in the kitchen, charging up. Oh *fuck*. I frantically searched for something I could defend myself with: a marble bookend perhaps, or an umbrella, or my alabaster bedside lamp. I wondered whether I'd be able to kick-box him, but he might well have a knife. I heard another step creak, and then another. By now I was almost crying with fear. The only reason I'd seen nothing when I'd looked out of the window was because the intruder was already inside. I *had* left the chain off. I had. I had! And I was about to pay with my life.

My pulse had doubled and my breath was coming in ragged gasps. I got down on the floor and rolled under the bed, trying to breathe silently through my nose: and the steps on the stairs were getting nearer and nearer as adrenaline sped through my veins like fire. My entrails were coiling and twisting and I could feel beads of sweat stinging my eyes. My heart was beating so wildly I thought it might burst from my chest. For now the creaking had stopped, and there was silence . . . He was standing outside my door. My ribcage hurt with the effort of holding my breath as I waited for the handle to turn. Please help me God, I prayed. I'm sorry I said I don't believe in you but I had it rammed down my throat as a kid. But please I whimpered, please, please, please, please, *please* – don't let me die. And as I mentally uttered those words the steps restarted, then faded slightly as the intruder went into my study next door. He was in my study. He was clearly looking at stuff there, and then he'd come in here and find me. He'd come in here and find me and kill me. All of a sudden I knew what to do. I'd belt downstairs – I could be out in the street in a flash.

I rolled out from under the bed, tremblingly groped for my trainers, then waited silently for a second. NOW! I burst out of my room then hurtled downstairs, two at a time, reaching the bottom in three or four strides. I flew to the front door and pulled on it, but – oh God, oh God – it was locked! I couldn't believe it – the evil fucking bastard! He'd locked me in – I was trapped! Hyperventilating, I fumbled in the hall drawer for the spare key – where was it? Oh *God* . . . I couldn't find it – *shit*! Suddenly I heard footsteps – oh sweet Jesus! – he was coming downstairs. I'd have to escape through the back door, into the garden and over the fence. As I sprinted into the kitchen, panting like an elderly Alsatian, I could hear his descending tread. And as my shaking hand sprang to the back door handle I heard, 'What are you *doing*?' *What*? I whipped round.

'What do you mean what am *I* doing what the hell are *you* doing you *maniac* creeping in at this time of night without telling me, I nearly fucking DIED!'

'I'm sorry,' Theo said. He looked stricken. 'Didn't you get my messages?'

'NO!'

'But I phoned you a few hours ago to tell you I was on my way back and that I'd be coming in late. I left two messages on your answerphone and one on your mobile asking you not to put the chain on. As it was off I assumed that you'd got them.'

'No! I didn't! I'd gone to bed.' I sank shakily onto a chair, weeping now with shock and relief. 'I'd gone to bed very early,' I sobbed, 'so I didn't hear the phone. I thought you were a burglar,' I wept, 'or even my phone pest. I was totally terrified.'

'I'm sorry,' he said quietly. He looked grey and exhausted. He ripped off a piece of kitchen roll and handed it to me. 'Don't cry.'

'And why did you go in my study?' I asked, my voice an octave higher than usual.

'Because you'd left a lamp on. I was trying to turn it off but I couldn't find the switch.'

'But what the *hell* are you *doing* here?' I asked. 'You said you'd be back on the twenty-eighth.'

'Well,' he sighed. He looked at me, then looked away. 'I . . . was worried about my book. There's still loads to do so . . . I thought I ought to get back.'

'So you left?'

'Er, yes. That's right.'

'But you'd only just *got* there.'

'I know. But I . . . realised I'd made a . . . mistake and that I should be working.' How *weird*.

'But Theo, how on earth did you get from Leeds to London on Christmas Day without a car?'

He shrugged his shoulders. 'I hitched.'

Chapter Eight

For the past week I've hardly laid eyes on Theo; he's been working hard, as have I. The house exudes the air of concentration you'd find in a college library during finals week. He's also been uncharacteristically withdrawn since his abbreviated Christmas break. If I make a cup of tea, he waits until I've gone back up to my study before going into the kitchen himself. If I'm watching TV he doesn't come into the sitting room to see what's on as he sometimes has. He's not interested in talking – that's obvious: the sign round his neck says *Do Not Disturb*. I've heard his mobile ring a few times but he always keeps the conversation short. Then this evening, I heard him emerge . . .

It was a little after ten-thirty and I was lying on the sofa reading a letter from a swinging granny who was getting divorced for the fourth time and who was worried that her pregnant daughter might be lesbian, when I heard his tread on the stairs.

'I've finished my book,' he announced quietly.

'Congratulations,' I replied.

'I went through the manuscript seven times, and each time I found more mistakes. But now I know that it's perfect. No glitches. It'll go off for printing next week.'

'And when does it come out?'

'In May.'

'That's a fast turnaround.'

'I know.' He went over to the window and parted the curtain. 'It's a nice night.'

'Really?' I murmured as I scribbled on my pad.

'Mmm. Think I'll go out.'

'New Year's Eve party?' I enquired.

'No. I've never liked the forced jollity of New Year's Eve. I'm just going to look at the sky.'

'Uh huh.'

'Would you like to come with me?' he asked suddenly.

'What?'

'Are you up for it?' he added with a smile. 'It's really clear; and the moon's not too full so I think we'll see quite a bit.'

'Well . . .'

'Go on. Why don't you?' Why didn't I . . . ? Good question. The swinging granny could wait.

'Okay, I'm up for it,' I said with a laugh.

'But you'll need your thermals,' he advised me. 'With astronomy there's a lot of standing about.'

I put on my thickest jumper, my coat and gloves; then Theo reappeared with his binoculars and the telescope in its large black case. As we walked to Holland Gardens the pavement spangled with a sugaring of ground frost and our breath came in cushiony clouds.

'I'll set it up by the playground,' Theo explained as we crunched across the ice-stiffened grass. 'You have to have the telescope on a flat surface; if there's even a tiny wobble you can't see.' As he fiddled about with the tripod I sat on a swing, looking up. 'You get a big piece of sky here,' I heard him say. 'And it's really quite dark.' This was true. Above the Lucozade tinge the sky was obsidian, and I could see scattered points of light.

'Twinkle twinkle, little star,' I sang softly. 'How I wonder what you are. Up above the sky so high . . . How many stars are there?' I asked him.

'Oh, trillions, gazillions,' he replied. 'Numbers so vast the human brain can't comprehend them. Just in our own Milky Way galaxy there are over a hundred billion stars – which makes our solar system equivalent in scale to nine grains of sand in a cathedral.' Nine grains of sand in a cathedral . . . *Wow*.

'I know so little about astronomy,' I said regretfully.

'Don't tell me – it's always gone over your head.'

'I wouldn't know an asteroid from a black hole,' I replied matter of factly.

'Well I hope you'll know a bit more after tonight.'

'Are you going to unveil the mysteries of the universe to me then?' I added with a laugh.

'I shall do my best. You know what a galaxy is?'

'Sort of.'

'It's a city of stars. There are over a hundred billion galaxies in the universe,' he went on. A hundred billion . . . Good God. 'Some are elliptical,' he explained, 'some are irregular, and some are spiral, like ours. Our galaxy has four arms like a Catherine wheel, with a bulge in the centre. Can you see the Milky Way?' Craning my neck, and shielding my eyes, I could just make out a very pale band.

'I *think* I can see it, but it's terribly faint – just a smear.'

'It's so called because the Greeks thought it looked like a river of "gala" or milk. Okay,' he said, as he took off his glasses and peered through the eyepiece. 'We're ready to go. Have a look.'

I jumped off the swing, removed my right glove, pulled back my hair and peered. I felt almost faint with awe as I found myself staring at the hugely magnified face of the moon. It was as though I were standing right next to it, so clearly could I see all the craters and shadows and seas.

'That is *amazing*!' I breathed. 'It's just so . . . *beautiful*!'

'It is. The moon has highlands and lowlands,' I heard him say as I feasted my eye. 'The highlands are covered with craters from meteorite impact billennia ago; that huge crater middle left is Copernicus – can you see it?'

'Yes – I can!'

'The lowlands are areas in which large craters have been filled by solidified lava to form lunar seas. That dark area above Copernicus is the Mare Imbrium, and the one next to it is the Mare Serenitas, or the Sea of Serenity.'

'How incredible to think that we've *been* there,' I said as I straightened up and looked at it with my naked eye. 'I remember the moon landings so vividly,' I went on warmly. 'It was July 1969, and we watched it at school. It was just so *thrilling* wasn't it?'

Then I remembered.

'I wasn't born then.' Of course. 'I'd love to have seen it live, like you did, but I was born in seventy-two. Right!' he said brightly, as I stood there feeling 120, 'let's try something else.' He swung the telescope to the right, fiddled with the eyepiece then said, 'oh yes. That's nice. *Very* nice,' he repeated tantalisingly. I wanted him to hurry up and let me see.

'This is Saturn,' he explained as I looked through the end. 'It's magnified thirty-two times, so you should be able to make out the rings.'

I bent over the telescope and a shining disc, girdled with a silvery hoop, filled my field of view. 'That is INCREDIBLE!!!' I shouted. 'That is *incredible*! My GOD!!! I can see the rings! I can see Saturn's rings!' I repeated disbelievingly. 'It's just . . . so *magical*!!' I wanted to dance. 'What are they made of?' I asked as I stared at them.

'Particles of ice most no bigger than a sugar lump. The Assyrians believed they were writhing serpents.'

'And how big is it?'

'Saturn's huge. It's a gas giant, made largely of liquid hydrogen so it's actually very light. If you could find a bath big enough to put it in, it would float. Now . . .' He removed the eyepiece and slotted in a different one. 'This is magnified ninety-six times.'

'Oh! How FAN*TASTIC*!!' I gasped as I peered through the eyepiece. 'I can even see the gap between the rings!'

'That's the Cassini division. You should be able to see the moons as well. That blob on the left is Titan, the biggest. Can you see it?'

'Yes – I CAN!!!'

'Saturn has eighteen moons,' he explained. 'One of them, Iapetus, is black on one side and white on the other: okay, let's give Jupiter a whirl.' I waited impatiently for Theo to move the telescope again, my face and fingers tingling with cold.

'Right,' he said, as I stamped my feet. 'Take a gander at that.'

'OOOOOHHH!!!' I moaned as I looked through the eyepiece. 'AAAAAAAHH!!!!!!!' I whimpered again. 'It's just so *amazing*, Theo, and it's ENORMOUS!'

'It is. It's well over a thousand times bigger than the earth. In fact it's bigger in volume than all the other planets combined.'

'Oh that is FABULOUS!! It's just so . . . HUGE!!'

'Rose, don't shout,' he whispered with a giggle, 'people will wonder what we're up to.'

'What do you mean?'

'The, er, rapturous noises.'

'Oh, sorry, but I can't help it,' I laughed. Indeed I felt as overawed as a blind man who's just been given the gift of sight. I wanted to jump up and down and shout. I'd seen photos of the planets in newspapers of course, but seeing them with my own eyes was something else.

'Jupiter's so *gorgeous*,' I said as I looked through the telescope. 'That amazing marbling effect.'

'That's just gas. Jupiter spins at an incredible speed producing ever changing bands of coloured cloud. And can you see the moons?'

'I *can*!!!'

'The one on the right is Io – which is very volcanic – the one on the left is Europa, the two close together at the bottom are Calypso and Gannymede.'

'Calypso and Gannymede,' I repeated dreamily. 'What lovely names. This is heavenly,' I breathed. 'Literally.' I shook my head. 'I feel . . . overwhelmed.'

Theo smiled. 'I'm glad. I often think that people who aren't moved by the sight of the night sky have no soul. Right, let's take a look at some stars. The Orion constellation is always a good bet at this time of year.' He repositioned the telescope, peered into it, then stood back to let me look. 'Can you see Orion's belt? Those three stars in a line?'

'Yes.'

'Go down to the right, at about five o'clock, do you see that large white one?'

'Mmm.'

'That's Rigel which is the brightest star in Orion and is sixty thousand times more luminous than our sun. Then go up a bit and to the left . . . can you see that fuzzy white patch around four stars in a trapezium?'

'Yes, I can – just.' He put in a different eyepiece, checked it, and then I looked at it again.

'That's the Orion nebula,' I heard him say. 'Basically, it's a stellar nursery, in which new stars are being born.'

'Baby stars!' I said. 'How adorable! Or are they called starlets? And how are the little poppets made?'

'Well it's not quite like human reproduction,' he said seriously. 'You don't need a mummy star and a daddy star.'

'You don't?'

'No. What happens is that a new star condenses out of a great swirling cloud of gas and dust. Gravity squeezes these clumps together and the pressure at the centre makes them heat up. Once they get to about ten million degrees centigrade, nuclear reactions begin; this releases huge amounts of energy, which causes the star to burn. They usually burn for a few billion years,' he went on. 'For example our sun has been burning for about five billion years and has got about another five billion or so to go.'

'So it's middle-aged.'

'Yes.'

'Like me,' I added with a sardonic laugh.

'No,' he said softly. 'Not like you. Now, up beyond Orion's left shoulder we pass a very bright star called Betelgeuse – the Americans call it Beetlejuice – see it? – then we go into Gemini.'

'That's my sign.'

'Do you see those two bright stars, up there?'

'Which ones? There are rather a lot.'

'Here,' he said, 'follow my hand.' He stood behind me, and placed his left hand on my shoulder – the sudden contact made my heart jump. Then he extended his right arm in front of me, the sleeve of his ski jacket brushing my cheek. Despite the stinging cold I felt a warmth rise up from my chest to my face. 'Can you see now?' he asked softly, and as he spoke I was aware of his breath, warm on my ear. Feeling strangely disconcerted, I squinted at the sky and could now see two bright stars of equal size.

'Those are Castor and Pollux, the heavenly twins,' I heard him say. 'They were the sons of Leda and were transformed by Zeus into the constellation Gemini so that they would never be separated.' I thought of Bella and Bea.

'And Orion was the hunter wasn't he?'

'Yes. He boasted that he could kill any creature on Earth. But he forgot the Scorpion, which crawled out of a hole, and killed him. When the Gods brought Orion back to life and placed him in the heavens, the Scorpion was put there too, but as far away from him as possible so that the two can never meet again. Here,' he removed a silver hip-flask from his pocket. 'It's brandy. Would you like a swig?'

'Have you put all this classical stuff in your book?' I asked him as I had a sip.

'Oh yes. People like all the stories and myths. Do you see that winking star – over there? That's Algol, which marks the head of the Gorgon, the snake-headed monster which Perseus slew. Algol's actually a binary star,' he went on. 'Binaries look like one star from a distance, but in reality they're two, one often brighter than the other. They orbit each other, pulled together by gravity into a kind of eternal embrace.'

'And where does gravity itself come from?' I asked as we sat side by side on the swings.

'No-one knows. All we know is that gravity is the mutual attraction between every bit of matter in the universe. And the closer the matter is,' he added softly, 'the stronger the attraction.'

'Oh,' I murmured. 'I see.' A strange silence enveloped us for a minute or two as we sat staring up at the sky. And as we swung gently back and forth Theo told me about galaxies that kiss and collide; about supernovae, stars in their death throes, which explode with the brilliance of billions of suns. He told me about nebulae, towering clouds of luminous gas which float through space like vast jellyfish.

'It's . . . amazing,' I said impotently, as I gazed upwards. 'The mind-blowing immensity.'

'It is. For example, our nearest star, Alpha Centauri, is just over four light years away, which doesn't sound much but is in fact twenty-five *trillion* miles. And our galaxy alone is so vast that it takes the sun 225 million years to go round the centre once. Which is even slower than the Circle Line.'

'That's incredible,' I breathed.

'It puts our daily struggles into perspective doesn't it?' he added with a laugh. 'Tax returns, parking fines, dental appointments – even divorce.'

'It certainly does.' My fury with Ed suddenly seemed ludicrous and absurd. We were both less than a billionth of a sub-atomic particle in the cosmic scale of things.

'It's just . . . grand,' I said. 'That's the only word for it.'

'Yes,' he said, 'it's grand. And what's really interesting is that when we look at the stars we're actually looking into the past.'

'How?'

'Because of the time it takes for their light to reach our eyes. For example, when we look at Sirius, the brightest star in the sky – that one there – we're actually seeing it not as it is now, but as it was eight years ago, because it's eight light years away. And some of the galaxies that Hubble has photographed are *billions* of light years away. Their light has been travelling across space for so long that by now they may well no longer exist. That's what astronomy is really about,' he added quietly. 'It's about looking *back*. It's about the search for our origins.'

'The search for our origins . . .' I repeated softly. 'Moonstarer,' I said suddenly.

'What?'

'It's the anagram of astronomer – it's just come to me.'

'Moon-starer,' he repeated. 'That's nice. You're good at anagrams aren't you?' he added.

'It's just a knack. Finding parallel meanings by rearranging the letters; sorting them out.'

'You like sorting things out, don't you Rose?'

I shrugged. 'Yes I do. I always have. I often anagrammatise people's names for example.'

'And the anagram of Rose is –'

'Sore.'

'Eros, actually, I was going to say.'

I looked at him. 'Yes, that too.'

He glanced up again. Suddenly a phosphorescent streak flared overhead. 'Oooh – a meteor!' I exclaimed. 'Oh no it's not,' I laughed. 'It's just a firework.' I glanced at my watch: it was twenty to twelve.

'Would you like some more brandy?' he asked. In the distance we could hear party revellers. 'Perhaps we should be drinking champagne. I'll be right glad to see the back of this year though.'

I heaved a sigh. 'So will I. I've moved house twice, got married, and separated, all within twelve months. In terms of major life events that's really going it.'

'It certainly is. I wonder what this year will bring?' he added quietly.

'If you were an astrologer, rather than an astronomer, you'd know.'

'I'll be turning thirty,' he went on seriously.

'When?'

'On August the first.'

'August the first?' I repeated.

'Yes, why? What's special about it?'

'Oh . . . nothing.' I couldn't explain why I always feel very depressed on that date.

'Is that your birthday too then?'

I laughed darkly. 'No. Mine's in June. So . . . what else will happen to you this year?' I asked, changing the subject.

'I've got my book coming out in May, and I'll be getting divorced.'

'No going back then?'

'Oh no. Fiona's quite clear about that. In fact I think she might have met someone else.'

'Really?'

He nodded. 'She wouldn't like to rub my nose in it, but I get that feeling.'

'Well, maybe you'll have a new relationship,' I said, thinking of Beverley.

'Yes, maybe. I don't know. All I know is that the universe is expanding – it's never static – and I want my life to expand too. I miss my wife,' he added, 'it's been . . . awful; but it's clear that her feelings have changed.'

'Can I ask you something Theo?' I said, feeling suddenly brave.

He looked at me. 'If you like.'

'Did you really come back early from Leeds just to work?'

'Ye-es,' he replied as he got off the swing and looked through the telescope.

'You were in such a hurry you left on Christmas *Day*?'

'That's right.'

'You couldn't even wait until the next morning? Or until the trains were running?'

'You're dead right,' he said quietly. 'I couldn't wait.'

'How long did it take you to hitch?'

He considered the question. 'Five and a half hours, give or take. There wasn't much traffic, obviously, so I had to wait for a lift.'

'And you left at night?'

'Yes.'

'But why?'

'Because I . . . was in a sudden panic about the book.'

'Then why didn't you simply take your manuscript home with you so that you could work on it up there?'

'I was . . . worried that I might lose it, or, you know, leave it on the train.' I stared at him incredulously. 'You don't

148

believe me, do you?' he added.

'No,' I replied quietly. 'I don't.'

He sat on the bottom of the slide and rested his chin in his hands. 'All right then, I'll tell you the truth. The real reason I left early was because Christmas was so *awful*, I couldn't stand it. I had to get out.'

'You had a row with your parents?'

'No. I had a row with my father's wife.'

'With your stepmother, you mean?'

'No I don't mean that. I won't attach the word "mother" to her in any way; she's just the woman he married, that's all.'

'And what about your mother? Where's she?'

'My mother's dead. She died when I was nine.' How strange, I thought. After six weeks I know so many things about Theo. I know what brand of toothpaste he uses, and what aftershave; I know his tastes in music and food. I know that his childhood holidays were spent in Norfolk, and I even know how he votes. I know the reason why his marriage broke up; and yet I didn't know that his mother had died.

'I never talk about it,' he went on quietly. 'She died of a brain haemorrhage. She was only thirty-six. My father was on his own for a very long time. But three years ago he married Jane – who I hate.'

'Why do you hate her?'

'Because she's just . . . vile. She has no fellow feeling for other people, no imaginative sympathy. She can't empathise.'

'But what's she actually done?'

'She's eradicated all the memories of my mother. There weren't many – my dad's not insensitive – but Jane won't allow even a photo of my mum in the house.'

'Even though she died, what – twenty years ago?'

'Yes. It's hard to understand, I know,' he added quietly. 'But she's the jealous type; she knows my father really loved my mother, plus my mum was very attractive, and Jane's not.'

'But what actually happened to make you leave?'

His shoulders slumped forward suddenly, then he heaved

a weary sigh. 'It was awful,' he began quietly. 'We'd had Christmas lunch, and that had gone just about all right. And we were sitting in the living room watching telly when I looked at the wall and saw that the small portrait of my mother had gone. So I mentioned it to Dad and he looked embarrassed, so then I asked Jane, outright, but she claimed not to know. So I pressed her about it and I wouldn't let up, and she finally admitted that she'd thrown it away. She threw my mother away,' he said, his voice fracturing with feeling. 'She threw my mother away.'

'But why does your father tolerate her behaviour?'

'Because he's sixty-three and she's thirty-seven.' For the second time that night I felt *ancient* – Theo had a stepmother who was younger than me! 'Dad's terrified that she'll leave him and that he'll be alone in his old age. But when I knew what she'd done, I just put on my coat and walked to the motorway.'

'How far?'

'Six miles.'

'God.'

'My mother was . . . lovely,' he said simply. 'She was always joking and laughing and she had this fantastic smile. Then, one perfectly ordinary Friday morning, she collapsed and I never saw her again.' And now I suddenly realised that the woman in the photo in Theo's room wasn't his wife – it was her.

'I'm very sorry,' I murmured. 'How terrible. I thought you'd seemed down since you returned.'

'I was. In fact I was completely miserable, so I buried myself in the book.'

'Shall we go back now?' I suggested after a moment, 'it's freezing.'

'Yes, but can I ask *you* something now?' That sounded ominous. I gave him a sideways look. 'Who's your "ex-mother"?' Oh *shit*.

'My ex-mother?' I repeated. 'I'm not sure what you mean.' I glanced at my watch; it was ten minutes to midnight. I stood up to leave. 'My mother died three years ago,' I explained, 'so she's ex in that sense I guess.'

'That's not what I mean,' Theo said. 'At the ball you referred to your "ex-mother". You said it was a slip, but I wasn't convinced. The expression "ex-mother" has a very bitter edge. Who is she?'

I flinched. 'Why do you want to know?'

'Because, well, I'm . . . curious, that's why. I mean, I know all sorts of things about you now, Rose. I know what brand of shampoo you use, and what toothpaste, and what perfume and what soap. I know what you eat – or rather don't really eat – and I know a bit about your marriage, and your friends. But I don't know anything about your family and I'd been wondering who your 'ex-mother' could be.'

'Well . . .' I began. Then stopped. 'Well . . .' I sighed. Oh fuck.

'Are you adopted?'

I looked at him. 'That's a very blunt question.'

'I'm sorry. I am a bit blunt. So are you?'

My heart did a swallow dive. 'Yes.'

'I thought so. I was looking at that photo of your parents in the sitting room, and I could see you weren't related to them. And there are a few other things you've said that I've picked up on, so I reckoned your "ex-mother" might be your real mother.'

'She's my birth mother, that's correct.'

'And you've never traced her?' he asked softly.

'No.'

'Why not?' He really was *very* forthright.

'Well, because it's very . . . personal,' I said. 'Not everyone does.'

'But surely life's too short to neglect something so huge.'

'Life's also too short to *waste*. And in order to earn the epithet "mother" you surely have to do a bit of mother*ing* first! I *used* to want to find her,' I confided quietly as I looked at the sky. 'When I was a child I'd scan the crowds for any woman who I thought could possibly be her. I once followed a woman round Safeways for two hours because I thought she looked like me. I was convinced my real mum would come for me one day, but I knew that if she didn't, I'd look. I'd home in on her like a heat-seeking missile, and I'd find her, wherever she was. But then when I was eighteen I discovered something . . . bad about her, and I changed my mind. I vowed then that I'd never search for her; I never have, and I never will.' Now, from one of the houses to the left of the park I could hear the New Year countdown begin.

'TEN . . . NINE . . . EIGHT . . .'

'What was it you discovered?' Theo asked quietly.

'It's none of your business!' I saw his face flinch.

'Sorry,' he murmured. 'You're obviously very sensitive about it.'

'I'm not "sensitive" about it,' I snapped. 'But the point is you're extremely direct. And I've answered your questions, even though I didn't want to, and I'm not answering any more.'

'SIX . . . FIVE . . .'

'My apologies,' he said as he stood up and began to dismantle the telescope. 'You're quite right. But because I lost my mum so young I'm envious of anyone who still has theirs. And the thought that your mother might be out there – somewhere – maybe even living close by . . .' I felt sick. 'I mean, she'd only be, how old – fifty-five, fifty-six? Maybe even less.'

'THREE . . . TWO . . .'

'I'm not looking for her,' I said, as he folded the tripod. 'And that's all there is to it, okay?'

'ONE . . .'

'But don't you wonder about her?' he persisted as I walked away.

'ZERO!!!!!'

'NO!' I shot over my shoulder. 'I *don't*!'

In the distance I could hear the peal of church bells, and now we heard the revellers sing.

Should auld acquaintance be forgot . . .

'You don't think about her?'

And never brought to mind . . .

'Never!'

We'll tak' a cup of kindness yet . . .

'And I'm not thinking about her now.'

For auld lang syne.

'How old are you Rose?' he asked as he drew level with me, 'thirty-six? Thirty-seven?'

'I'm thirty-nine.'

'So you've still got half your life left.'

'Maybe.'

For auld lang syne, my dear . . .

'If it were me,' he said as we crossed the park, 'I'd be crossing continents; I'd leave no stone unturned.'

For auld lang s-y-y-y-n-e . . .

'You only say that because your mother was a good person, but mine wasn't.'

'How do you know?'

'I just do. I have enough . . . information about what she did to know that I'm not going to go knocking on her door. In any case,' I added as we headed for the park gate, 'it's much too late.'

We'll tak' a cup of kindness yet . . .

'No it's not.'

'It *is*!'

For auld lang syne . . .

'It's never too late, Rose.'

I turned and faced him. 'Yes it *is*! She blew it Theo! Don't you understand? My mother blew it almost forty years ago. And if she'd ever wanted to come and find me and get down on her knees and beg for forgiveness, then she could have done – but she didn't!'

It was as though we'd stepped on a landmine – our earlier rapport had been blown apart. And as we walked through the park gates in clumsy silence I wished I hadn't gone out with him. Yes, it was very nice seeing the universe and all that, but his interrogations had got me down. It's not even as though I know him well, so he had *no* right to quiz me like that. And I think Theo must have realised he'd over-stepped the mark because when we got back he went straight upstairs.

'I'm off to bed,' he said from the first step. 'Thanks for coming out.'

'That's okay,' I said stiffly.

'It was really clear,' he went on, 'and I saw some very . . . interesting things. Well, good night Rose,' he added breezily.

'Good night.'

'And, oh yes – Happy New Year!'

Chapter Nine

'Happy New Year,' I said to Serena when I went into work two days later.

'I hope it is happy,' she replied. 'The signs are not exactly –' she began briskly, then stopped herself.

'Are you okay Serena?' I said, narrowing my eyes.

'Oh yes,' she said chirpily. 'I'm *fine*. Except that we had a flood on Boxing Day. The washing machine blew up. I'd put it on the delicates cycle and then we'd gone over to Rob's mother for lunch. When we got back the house looked like the Serpentine; the carpets were *ruined*. Still, nil desperandum,' she added twitchily.

'But surely you're insured?'

'Well, we *were* . . . but unfortunately we hadn't got round to renewing our accidental damage cover what with things being a little bit tight. But never mind,' she added with platitudinous perkiness, 'mustn't complain. I mean, worse things happen at sea don't they?' She really was the Doyenne of Denial. 'The show must go on and all that,' she added with a heroic, but tense little smile. 'No, really, Rose, I'm fine. I'm ab-so-*lute*-ly fine. Unlike our poor readers,' she said patting the vast pile of mail.

'So what have we got today?' I sighed.

'Christmas quarrels, money worries, acne, bedwetting, internet infidelity and – this . . .' Grimacing slightly, she handed me a tiny plastic bag in which, by peering closely, I could just distinguish two or three black . . . things.

Although they appeared to be organic I hadn't a clue what they were.

'What the hell are these?' I asked, pulling a face. 'Spiders?' She shook her head. 'Ants?'

'No?'

'Woodlice?'

'Uh uh.'

'Fleas?'

'Nope.'

'Ticks?'

'Getting warm.'

'Well what does the letter say?'

Serena blushed, then cleared her throat. 'Dear Rose, I found these in my pubic hair this morning and I wondered . . .' 'WHAT????' I wanted to hurl. 'GOD!!!! How revolting!' I exclaimed. 'Is it a hoax?'

'No. It's perfectly serious. They've given an address.'

'Then please write back pointing out that I run a problem page not a diagnostic service for STDs. That's the most repulsive letter I've ever had,' I added crossly – 'How utterly vile.' Although at the same time I was also aware that it would be an absolute cracker of a story at the agony aunts' lunch next week. Those dos can get very competitive. Oh yes, that one would be a winner all right. I vaguely wondered about taking the evidence with me to confound any sceptics but decided it was simply too gross. As Serena disposed of it, I glanced at the pile of new books. *Understanding Obesity* – very appealing. *You Want Me To Do What?* Oh, nice. And, oh . . . this one looked quite interesting – *Older Women: Younger Men, New Options For Love and Romance*. Hmm . . . I thought as I switched on the computer. Might give that one a plug.

My Outlook Express icon revolved several times like a tiny comet, then delivered my e-mails with a quiet 'pop'. I quickly whizzed through them one by one.

When we're in bed my husband accidentally calls me 'Gary' for some reason . . . I've fallen in love with my boss . . . I have a very low sperm count (12 million) . . . My mother-in-law's run off with my dad.

There was an e-mail from the fat young man who'd called my radio show telling me that he'd lost his first stone; another from the parents of the little girl who'd had the heart and lung transplant, telling me she was doing well. Then I opened the last message which, to my dismay, was headed, *Watch Out!!!* It was from 'you'llbesorry@hotmail.com' – clearly a fictitious address.

Dear Ms Costelloe, I read, *As I am now unable to get through to you on your poxy phone-in I decided to contact you this way to tell you that I hope you had a really horrible Christmas and to wish you a miserable New Year. K. Jenkins (Mrs).*

'Have you made any New Year resolutions Rose?' I heard Serena ask.

'Yes,' I replied. 'I have. Not to let vile people intimidate me.' I showed her the message, then told her about all the silent phone calls to my house.

'Some people!' Serena exclaimed with stock indignation. 'I mean, really – what a nerve! And how often do they call?'

'It seems to be random. I can get silent calls three days running, then nothing for a week and a half. I didn't have any over Christmas for example, but then I had another one late last night.'

'And do you really think it's this Kathy woman?'

'Yes. I think it probably is. She's obviously desperately childish, and extremely unpleasant.'

'Al*though*,' said Serena, as I pressed the 'Delete' button, 'if she's always been so aggressive on your radio show, why would she keep quiet when calling your house?' I looked at Serena. She was a genius. Of *course* – it didn't add up. And now, as I went down to the canteen for a *cappuccino*, I remembered something else. That the first silent phone call had been the night Theo came round – several days *before* Kathy first rang my radio phone-in. As I sat staring out of the plate glass window across the Thames I tried to work it out. It wasn't Kathy. No. It wasn't. It was someone else – but *who*? Were they male or female? I didn't even know that much as they never spoke. And was their attitude towards

me nakedly hostile, or were they an obsessive creep . . . ?
Ah.

I suddenly thought of Colin Twisk, the lonely young man.
He'd sent me several more very peculiar missives lately
including that kiss-covered Christmas card. I hadn't responded
to any of them, so maybe he felt rebuffed. But on the other
hand, I thought, it could be absolutely *anyone*. Three million
people read the problem page, and another half million listen
to *Sound Advice*. If even 0.0001 per cent of that lot were loonies
– a generous estimate – then that's already several individuals. But what really got to me was the thought that they'd
somehow found out my number at home. And now I wondered if they intended simply to intimidate me at a distance,
or whether they were planning to raise the stakes? What if
they found out where I lived and actually came to the house?
That thought fuelled my paranoia so I decided to keep on
with the kick-boxing class – God forbid that it should ever
come in handy, but one of these days, it might.

'KICK it and BLOCK it and KICK it and *PUNCH* it!' shouted
Stormin' Norman the following night. 'KICK it and BLOCK
it and power! *Power*!! POWER!!'

Sweat pouring off my face I slammed my leather-gloved
fists into the punch-bag again and again.

'KICK it and BLOCK it and KICK it and *PUNCH* it! Use
your fists – now your feet! Power! *Power*!! POWER!!!'

I collapsed, wheezing like an asthmatic shih tzu as the shat-
tering techno-beat finally stopped.

'Wow Rose, you are one *angry* lady tonight!' Norman
observed almost admiringly. 'It's awesome.'

'Thanks,' I panted as I reached for my towel.

'I wouldn't pick a fight with you, girl – you'd kick my ass
to Timbuktu.' I wiped the sweat off my forehead and smiled.
'So who's the punch-bag?' he added with a laugh as I poured
a bottle of Evian down my throat.

'What?'

'Who's the punch-bag?' I wiped my mouth.

'What do you mean?'

'Well, I've been teaching this for five years and I ain't never seen a woman kick as hard as you. You lash out like it's really *personal*, Rose.'

'Do I?' I said quietly.

'Yes, babe, you sure as hell do. It's as though you really *mean* it.'

'Oh.'

'So who is it you're hitting girl?'

I stared at him blankly. 'To be honest, I'm not quite sure.'

'I'm not quite . . . sure,' I said to Ricky carefully a few days later. I was trying hard not to lose my rag.

'Well, think about it,' he said as he put his feet up on his vast desk. 'I keep saying we need more sex in the paper, and a photo-story would do the job.' A photo-story? One of those vulgar strips with semi-naked girls and moronic young men with speech bubbles coming out of their mouths! I could see it now.

Get us another beer will you Tracy?

No Kev, from now on you can get your own beer . . .

The wife's working late, Sharon. Fancy a drink?

Hmmm. Wouldn't say no . . .

A photo-story? How awful. I recoiled from the idea like a salted slug.

'The readers would love it,' Ricky went on expansively. You mean *you'd* love it you sleaze-bag, I thought.

'With respect, Ricky,' I ventured as he placed his hands behind his head, revealing two dark patches the size of France, 'I feel that a photo-story would only cheapen the page, reflecting badly on the paper as a whole. After all, the *Daily Post* is a quality tabloid,' I reminded him sweetly, aware of the acrid smell of his sweat.

'Quality tabloid?' he reiterated mockingly. 'Bollocks! It's a populist rag.'

'But a photo-story would also mean I'd have less space to answer the readers' letters,' I pointed out, 'and I feel my first duty is to them.'

'Crapola!' he proclaimed loudly. 'Your first duty is to me. I'm your editor, so you do what I say. Your contract's up for review quite soon, isn't it?' he added with casual menace. My God he was low.

'Tell you what Ricky,' I said reasonably. 'I'm willing to compromise. Let's put the photo-story idea on hold for a while, but I'm prepared to spice up the helplines a bit. And of course that would also bring in more cash for the paper as they're charged at a pound a minute.' Ricky leaned back in his reclining chair again and contemplated the ceiling. Then he suddenly brightened as he seemed to glimpse the possibilities of the situation.

'Yeah – that might be good. We could have, Hot Sex, Fantastic Sex, Three in a Bed Sex, Swinging Sex.'

'Sex after having a baby,' I added helpfully.

'Sex when you're pregnant,' he leered.

'Sexual Fantasies,' I added with a smile. 'Sexual Fetishes.'

'Yeah,' he repeated happily. 'I like the sound of that. But we'll review the photo-story idea in six months.'

'Great. Well, that's settled then,' I said breezily. 'Ooh must dash. I've got a lunch.'

That man is sex-obsessed I thought crossly as I shot downstairs in the lift. Whatever next for the *Post* I thought rolling my eyes – a page three girl? But I'd bought myself six months I reflected as I left the building, and with any luck, if the circulation didn't rise, Ricky might have been kicked out by then. Spicing up the helplines was one thing, but I wasn't having a photo-strip on my page. The agony column is not a forum for cheap entertainment – it's a public service, like the number twelve bus. After all, I'm not just an advice columnist, I reflected as I hailed a cab. I'm a Samaritan, a social worker, a grief therapist, a marriage guidance counsellor, a Citizens' Advice Bureau and sometimes almost a priest.

The agony aunts' lunch was being held at Joe Allen's in Covent Garden. I was slightly dreading it – some of those women are *so* egotistical! – but on the other hand it's fun to swap notes. There'd be at least ten of us, maybe more. What was the collective noun for agony aunts I wondered as we drove over Lambeth Bridge. A 'misery' maybe, or a 'worry'; a 'dismay' was pretty good too. A 'distress' of agony aunts, possibly or, no – even better – an 'angst'. As we drove up the Strand I idly wondered who'd be there. Lana McCord at *Moi!* magazine probably and that nice Katie Bridge at the *Globe*. I've got a lot of time for Mary Kreizler at the *Sunday Star*, and of course Dr Kay Stoddart at *Chick* magazine. I prayed that Citronella Pratt wouldn't be there, but she was at the last one, so she probably would. She'd made it clear on that occasion that she loathed me, but then she'd badly wanted my job. She'd lost her awful social affairs column at the *Semaphore* and was desperate for a new string. Serena told me that Edith Smugg had only been dead two hours before Citronella had phoned up, sliming away. She'd even come in for an interview, but Linda had been distinctly unimpressed. But Citronella's hide is made of Teflon and the constant rebuttals just don't stick. She has a kind of notoriety which is due in part to her poisonous opinions, and also to the fact that three years ago her husband famously ran off with a man. So on the back of that she got picked up by *Get!* magazine; but her 'advice' is dire. In fact it's not really advice, so much as naked pity – in short, malicious crap. Because having total strangers confide their unhappiness gives Citronella a psychological lift. She's obviously a miserable woman, so she gets off on others' pain. Whereas I'm an agony aunt for the simple reason that I just love helping people in need. My motives are wholly altruistic; I want to comfort and advise, that's all.

The cab pulled up in Exeter Street and oh God – there she was! Coming down the street, with that stompy walk of hers, bottom out, dumpy inelegance incarnate in one of her sack-like frocks; her thin sandy hair lifting in the wind. I discreetly turned my back to her as I paid the cab driver so that I wouldn't have to smile. I followed her into the restaurant at a safe distance, and found that our table downstairs was already full. There were twelve agony aunts all enthusiastically air-kissing despite the fact that at least half of them don't get on. The ones on the magazines would much rather be on newspapers, and the ones on the newspapers are very hard pressed.

To my irritation I found I'd been placed opposite Citronella. I managed to arrange my features into a pleasant smile although my polite salutation was not returned. So instead I briefly chatted to June Snort from the *Daily News*: our papers might be deadly rivals but I always try to be civil to her. As we all perused the menu, the atmosphere was polite, respectful and restrained.

'– Does anyone happen to know if the incest crisis-line is still running?'

'– Have you read that marvellous new book on stress?'

'– Did you hear that the National Council for Confidence Building has been closed down?'

'– Has anyone got the number for the Dipsomaniacs' Trust?'

Then, once we'd had a drink, the atmosphere became more relaxed. Mavis Sackville began her usual pious spiel about the importance of us being properly qualified.

'Agony aunts should be professionally trained counsellors and therapists,' she insisted as our starters arrived. 'Ours is not a job for dilettantes – agony arrivistes – who risk giving bad, if not *dangerous*, advice.' But we all knew why she was saying that – she'd just been dumped by *Female* magazine for a celebrity agony aunt, that fat actress, Valerie Tooth.

'With respect, Mavis, I believe that professional training is less important than experience, compassion, and emotional insight,' said Mary Kreizler firmly.

'And empathy,' I pointed out. 'The reader needs to know that we can truly imagine how they feel even if we haven't been through exactly the same thing ourselves.'

'I think our job is to direct our readers to the right source of information,' said Katie Bridge matter-of-factly. 'We're simply the person standing there at the crossroads, map at the ready, advising them which way to go.'

Then we discussed the future of agony aunting, which we all agreed is looking bright.

'There are so many sources of information available these days,' said Lana McCord, 'in the media and on the net. And yet the need to confide in an anonymous stranger remains stronger than ever.' We all nodded seriously at that. Then, as our main course arrived, the conversation became slightly more animated as we discussed brushes with unstable readers – a hazard of the job.

'I had a stalker,' said Karen Braithwaite from the *Daily Moon*, 'he was apprehended in reception with a knife.'

'I had two stalkers,' said Sally Truman from the *Echo*, 'and they both had baseball bats.'

'I had three stalkers,' said June Snort, not to be outdone, 'and they all had Ruger forty-four semi-automatics.'

'Really?' we all said.

'No!' she shrieked. 'Just kidding you!' How we laughed. 'But two of my readers have ended up in Rampton High Security,' she added with an odd kind of pride.

'Wow,' we all said.

'While we're on the subject, has anyone heard of Colin Twisk?' I asked looking round the table. 'He's nerdy but quite good-looking, thirty-five, he works in computers, can't get a girlfriend, a classic Lonely Young Man.'

'Oh yes, I've had him,' said Katie Bridge. 'I made the mistake of writing back to him and then had him on my back for six months.'

'Oh,' I said feebly. 'I see. Do you think he could be . . . dangerous?' I added casually.

'Well, maybe. Put it this way, I wasn't prepared to risk it, so I took out a restraining order. Top me up will you Rose?' I felt sick. And now, as we had pudding, we began talking about the most disgusting letters we'd ever received.

'I had a letter from a man who said that his penis was too big,' said Lana McCord. 'Complete with a photo to prove it!'

'What did you do?' I asked.

'I sent him my home address of course!!'

'Well I was sent a dead mouse,' said June Snort with a superior smirk.

'I was sent a dead *rat*,' said Katie Bridge.

'– I once got a letter in which every other word was the "c" word.'

'– I had a pair of old Y fronts.'

'– I had a pair of old Y fronts – with skid marks.'

'Well,' I said, as they all gagged, 'last week I was sent some pubic lice!'

'*No!*' Their faces were a mask of shock. I felt triumphant.

'There were three of them,' I explained. 'In a small plastic bag – it was totally gross.' Beat *that*!

'Well, *I've* had famous people writing to me,' said June Snort casually.

'Who?' we all asked.

'I can't say, obviously.'

'No, no, of course you can't,' we agreed.

'But let's just say that she's a very famous Australian pop singer.'

We all looked at each other. 'No way!'

'Look, just because people are loaded and gorgeous doesn't mean they're happy – even the stars need advice.'

'Well I had Madonna once,' said Lana McCord with a guffaw, 'she was very concerned about Guy!'

'Yeah – and I had the Pope – he's worried about his love life!' said Karen Braithwaite with a tipsy laugh.

By now the atmosphere was one of inebriated abandon. Even Citronella was getting pissed.

'But, oh God, what a job, eh, being an agony aunt,' said Lana McCord dismally.

'Oh I don't know,' I said.

'The way we take on other people's suffering. I mean, why the *hell* do we do it?' Why?

'Because we can make a difference,' I said. 'We can save relationships – and even lives. We can rescue people from their troubles,' I added. '*That's* why we do it.'

'I don't agree,' said Mary Kreizler. 'I think we do it because we like peeping into the chaos of other people's lives. We find it reassuring.'

'No – it's because it's a vocation,' I persisted, 'and, crucially, because we know that our readers *need* us.'

'No,' interjected Katie. '*We* need *them*. Let's be honest girls, we do it because we're suffering as well – that's why. And as we help others we help heal some damaged part of ourselves. I mean, I had a *terrible* upbringing,' she drawled on as she sipped her Cointreau. She shook her head and sighed. 'My parents divorced when I was eight.'

'Well that's nothing,' said June Snort indignantly, 'my parents divorced when I was two.'

'I've been in therapy since I was ten,' countered Katie, biting on a petit four.

'So?' said Sally Truman. 'I've been in therapy since I was five!'

'And I've taken just about every drug you care to mention,' said Lana McCord. 'Cannabis, cocaine, the works.'

'– I was neglected as a child.'

'– My mother was an anorexic. We were always hungry.'

'– My father was a drunk!'

'– *My* mother wouldn't let me have a pet – not so much as a *kitten*!'

'– I had a kitten – but it died.'

'– Well my puppy died – on my fifth birthday!'

'And I was bullied at school!' announced Citronella tipsily. We all stopped talking and looked. Her round, slightly goitrous face was sagging with self-pity, her semi-circular eyebrows in a theatrical droop. 'The other children victimised me,' she confided in her deceptively soft voice. I felt incredulous. It was far more likely that she had victimised *them*. 'They were so beastly,' she said, 'and what made it so much worse was that it was a very *expensive* school.' Boast, boast. 'But they were jealous of me,' she added with an inebriated sigh, 'because I was so much more intelligent than them.'

'Than *they*,' I corrected her.

'What?'

'So much more intelligent than *they*,' I explained sweetly. 'The subject of the subordinate clause is *they*.'

Citronella shot me an evil look. 'It was . . . *awful*,' she said with a lachrymose expression.

'Poor you,' I said. I couldn't resist. She looked at me with loathing then lifted her head, like a cobra about to strike. She drew back her thin lips and I found myself momentarily distracted by her teeth. They were large, square, yellow and strangely grooved, with a wart in the centre of the top gum.

'Mind you Rose,' she whispered with a smile, 'you've had *your* problems, haven't you? I mean, with your husband leaving you like that after, what – only seven months? And for a marriage guidance counsellor,' she added spitefully. '*So* unfortunate. Especially in *your* position.' Right.

'But *your* husband left you for a hairdresser, Citronella.'

'He was an *international* hairdresser!' she shot back.

'Well my husband left me for his secretary,' said Mavis Sackville tearfully. 'After thirty years. He broke it to me at the airport. What do you think of that?'

'My mother used to smack me for no reason,' said Mary Kreizler.

'My father beat my mother,' said June Snort.

'That's nothing, my father *ate* my mother,' said Lana McCord. And as the competitive misery restarted I suddenly realised what the collective noun for agony aunts should be – a 'torture'. I blotted their voices out with more booze.

'– My parents never said they loved me. Not once.'

'– My parents loved my sister more than me.'

'– Well my parents loved my hamster more than me!'

'– My mother said she wished I was *dead*.'

Right. Enough of their self-pity. They didn't know they were born. That was *it*. I stood up.

'Well then just wait till I tell you what MY mother did to ME!' I shouted.

The table fell silent, and everyone looked at me, agog. My legs felt shaky, and my head was spinning. I suddenly knew I'd had too much to drink.

'What *did* your mother do to you?' asked Stephanie Wyman wonderingly.

'Yes, what did she do?' said Katie Bridge.

'Yes, tell us,' they all demanded. 'Go, on, Rose. Tell us.'

All right then. I would.

'She . . .' I sighed. 'She . . .' Oh God. I was pissed and I was miserable. There was a pit of blackness in my heart. 'She . . .' I could have told them there and then. I could have just said it out loud and finally got it off my chest. But I didn't. 'It doesn't matter,' I croaked. 'Doesn't matter. Gotta go. 'S getting late.' Feeling slightly sheepish we paid the bill and staggered out into the street, waving a little too energetically at passing cabs in the way that inebriated people do.

'Vauxhill Bridge please,' I said. 'The Agalmagated Newspapers building.'

'The Amalgamated Newspapers building?'

'That's what I said.'

I slumped back in the seat, watching the Aldwych spin by in a blur. Suddenly my mobile rang.

'Rose! It's Bella.'

'Hi!'

'How are you?'

'I'm okay. Just 'd lunch. How was Christmas?'

'It was fine. Look, Rose, I can't talk for long as we're busy doing up the shop, but will you have dinner with me next week? I want you to meet Andrew,' she added. Who the hell was Andrew? Oh yes, Andrew; of course, her new man.

'The Jackson Pollock?'

'That's right. He's *terribly* nice.'

'So iss all going well then is't?'

'Oh *yes* – which is why I haven't called. So will you meet us for dinner next week? On Wednesday?'

'Yeah. 'Course,' I said.

167

'Rose, have you been drinking?' she asked tentatively.

'Have I been dr'nking? *Yup*!'

'Well, if I can give you some advice.'

'No! S'*my* job!'

'Well, just . . . go easy a bit.'

As I put my mobile away with a tipsy sigh I realised that Bella was right. I do drink too much these days. Any excuse, and it's down the hatch. I'd say I've been like that since my parents died – I'm not really sure why. But I'll have to take myself in hand, I told myself as we crossed the Thames. That was one hell of a lunch though, I reflected as the taxi drove down Lambeth Palace Road. Although I thought Katie Bridge was talking bollocks about how we're all agony aunts because we're suffering inside. Speak for yourself why doncha Katie! I'm an agony aunt because my readers *need* me I reminded myself as the cab stopped outside Amalgamated House.

'How much issat?' I said as I groped in my handbag. It wasn't quite as tidy as usual: my standards are slipping; I couldn't find my purse. 'How much?' I tried again as I rummaged amongst the receipts and sweet wrappers.

'Nothing,' the driver replied.

'Wha'?'

'Nothing,' he repeated. 'I know who you are. You're Rose Costelloe.'

'Yeah.'

'I listen to your show when I'm doing nights. And I phoned in six months ago and the advice you gave me was great. In fact, I don't mind telling you that it saved my marriage.'

'Really? Oh. I'm *ver'* glad.'

'That advice was free Rose, and so is this cab ride.'

'Well . . . thass *really* kind.' There! What did I tell you? I *am* needed. I *can* make a difference. I'd rescued a marriage. My heart sang.

'So, thanks then, Rose.' He smiled at me, and I felt my eyes fill with grateful tears.

'No. Thank *you*,' I replied.

Chapter Ten

'This is Radio Four,' announced Rudy warmly on Thursday. 'Now – *Desert Island Discs*!' He's been saying that all evening, silly bird. 'And your first record?' Hmmm. I stared at my list. Should my choice be posh or populist? A healthy mixture would go down best. On the highbrow front I definitely wanted the slow movement of the Scriabin Piano Concerto, and the 'Fair Winds' Quartet from *Cosi*. A Schubert lied would be lovely, and one of those gorgeous 'Songs from the Auvergne'. Something Latin would go down well with the punters, maybe the 'Buena Vista Social Club'. That's how many records so far? Five – so I've another three to go. Pop-wise I like 'Stars' by Simply Red and I love 'Here Comes the Sun'. I'd also be expected to choose some piece which really *means* something to me. I glanced into the garden, then laughed a bitter little laugh. 'Bye Bye Baby'. Of course. Or maybe, if I was really going for it on the heavy irony front, 'Mamma Mia'! Oh yes. Not that I'd want to go into too much detail with Sue Lawley – I mean, it's not *In the Psychiatrist's Chair*. And what piece of music would tie in well with my career? Hhhmm . . . 'Bridge Over Troubled Water'! *Perfect*. That would have them in floods. I reappraised my choices with a deep sense of satisfaction, it was a nicely eclectic mix.

Obviously I wasn't going to be invited onto the programme *quite* yet but it's good to be prepared. Mind you, Edith Smugg was nearly eighty before she got on, so I hoped I wouldn't have to wait as long as that. Maybe I should get Serena to put out a few subtle feelers? And then there was *This is Your*

Life! Suddenly I heard the click of the key in the lock, and Theo came in. I'd been a little frosty with him since his impertinent interventions on New Year's Eve but, buoyed up by my pleasant encounter with that taxi driver, I was feeling indulgent and warm.

'Hi. Nice day?' he enquired pleasantly.

'Yes thanks. Not at all bad.'

'Still working?' he asked with a nod at my list.

'Er, that's right.'

'It's crazy Rose – you never stop. I've never met anyone – apart from my wife – who works quite as hard as you. What is it about the women in my life,' he muttered. 'They're all such workaholics.' Women in my life? I smiled.

'Well,' I said, with another sip of white wine, 'I can't let the letters pile up. When someone's taken their courage in their hands and written to me, then they should at least get a prompt reply.' Theo put the newspaper on the table then got out a saucepan. 'Oh, I didn't know you read the *Daily Post*.'

'I don't,' he replied as he opened the fridge. 'It was left on the bus. I read your column by the way.'

'Oh yes. *And* . . . ?'

'Well I thought it was grand. But I don't think Carol from Coventry should give her boyfriend another chance.'

'Oh?'

'He's been unfaithful to her.'

'I know. But they've got three kids and he had been under terrible stress.'

'That's true . . .'

'And she had that fling five years ago, remember?'

'Mmm,' he murmured. 'I guess.'

'I'm normally very hard on infidelity,' I said, 'but sometimes couples have to look at the wider picture and see if they can't get over it.'

'Maybe. But I also don't believe that joining a twelve-step programme is necessarily going to crack Lisa from Luton's co-dependency problem.'

'Oh *really*?' I said. 'Do let me know if you need any help

with your black holes or quasars or anything won't you?' Theo raised both hands in playful surrender, then smiled. 'Do you want a Becks?' I added.

'Thanks. It must be strange trying to sort out other people's lives all day though,' he said as I poured him the beer. 'Doesn't it get boring after a while?'

'Boring?'

'Dealing with the same old issues again and again.' He opened the newspaper at *Ask Rose*. 'I'd have thought there's a limit to the amount any one person can write about eating disorders, infidelity, alcohol and thinning hair.'

'Actually, Theo, that's not true. When you're a connoisseur of human frailty, as I am,' I said with mock grandiosity, 'believe me, it is *never* dull.'

'But don't you get tired of it?' he asked as he got out a saucepan.

'No,' I said, shifting in my chair. 'That's like me asking you if you don't ever get tired of staring at the same old planets, or the same old meteor showers?'

'I find astronomy infinitely interesting,' he said serenely.

'So is being an agony aunt. It's so human,' I pointed out. 'It's the stuff of people's lives. Whereas, with respect, what you do, however fascinating, has no personal dimension at all. You are actively looking away from your fellow beings onto the cold and lifeless stars.'

'They're not cold, they're incredibly hot actually,' he said as he shook out some rice. 'And as for lifeless – who knows . . . ?'

'I know that what I do can make a difference,' I went on, ignoring him. 'I'm at the coalface of human distress.'

'But you don't get to meet your readers, do you?' he said as he stirred the pan. 'Being an agony aunt is not as human as being, say, a doctor or an aid worker, or a nurse. It's all too easy to dish out advice to someone if you're never going to meet.'

'But I worry about them,' I pointed out. 'I lie awake at night wondering if their lives are going better now, and whether what I said to them helped.'

'But you never actually come into real contact with your readers do you? There are no "close encounters", as it were.'

'Hmmm. That's true. But it's precisely *because* we don't know each other that they feel able to confide in me in the way that they do.'

'You know, the wonderful thing about astronomy is that it's based on precise mathematical laws,' he explained, 'which means that there's always a solution.' There's always a solution? How nice . . . 'I'm making risotto,' he added suddenly, 'would you like some?'

'Oh, I –'

'Go on Rose, you hardly eat. I hope you're not dieting,' he added with an appalled expression.

'No. I'm just not that interested in food. But I take vitamins to make up for it,' I said indicating the shelf upon which, neatly lined up in their plastic bottles, was an alphabet of supplements from A to Zinc.

'Taking vitamins is not the same as eating properly. I've never even seen you cook.'

'Can't cook, won't cook,' I said loftily. 'I haven't cooked since eighty-eight.'

'So how did you manage when you were married then?'

'Oh, ready-prepared stuff from M and S. Ed used to complain about the cost – well it *is* expensive – but it was quick, and I didn't have time. There's this big Aga in his kitchen but I only ever used the microwave. It used to drive him mad.'

'You're just like my wife,' he said over his shoulder. 'She didn't cook either, because of the long hours she worked, so it fell to me. I had to learn and I found I enjoyed it. I'll teach you if you like.'

'Well . . . okay. Thanks.' He turned and smiled. And in that instant I felt suddenly, overwhelmingly happy. This was the kind of domesticity I liked. Sharing my space with a young man who was neither my husband nor my lover and whom I didn't have to impress. There was no sexual or romantic tension between us to spoil things. Suddenly his mobile rang.

'Hello pet!' he exclaimed. Oh. Who the *hell* was that? 'Yeah, I'm just having a bite to eat. I'll be with you in half an hour.'

'Got a date?' I enquired nonchalantly as he put his phone back in his pocket.

'Not exactly. I'm going next door. Bev needs a few light-bulbs changing.'

'Can't Trevor do it?'

'He won't go up ladders.'

I laughed. 'That's very neighbourly of you,' I said casually.

'I'm happy to help. Beverley's a grand girl,' he said warmly. 'She's special.' I felt a sudden stab of fear and pain: and now, as he spooned the creamy risotto onto the warmed plates I entertained this despicable thought. I hoped that Theo wouldn't hit it off with Beverley too quickly – because then, well, he might leave me. Isn't that low of me, even to think it? But, as I say, you get used to people, don't you, and I guess I'd miss him if he wasn't around.

'It's my wife's birthday,' he announced as he sprinkled on parmesan shavings.

'Her thirtieth?'

'Ooh no.' My heart sank. She was obviously even younger than he was. Twenty-five quite possibly. Or even twenty-three. I braced myself.

'She's thirty-eight.' My fork stopped in mid-air.

'Your wife's eight years older than you?'

'Your maths is brilliant. Yes, that's right. So what? That hardly makes me a granny-snatcher does it? Anyway, it's the person that matters to me. Most of my girlfriends have been my age or thereabouts, but with Fiona there was a bit of a gap. Haven't you ever gone out with anyone younger Rose?'

'No I haven't.'

'But you could easily attract a man of my age.'

'Could I?'

'Yes, 'course you could.' Oh.

'Can I ask you a really personal question, Theo?'

'Why not? I've been blunt enough with you.'

'Didn't your wife want kids?'

173

'Nope,' he replied as he passed me the salad. 'But that's not what broke us up. I'd have lived with her decision although, if I'm being honest, I would like a family. And what about you?' Hmm . . . what *about* me?

'Well, it's never really been on the cards. I was always so busy and Ed wasn't bothered – he said that being one of five had put him off. The constant struggles with his siblings; the noise; the chronic lack of space. Plus he said he was worried about the expense.'

'Oh.'

'Well I guess children *do* cost a lot. I used to want them,' I went on. 'When I was a kid. But then everything changed.'

'Why was that?'

'Well . . . because it just did, that's why.'

'Because of what you found out about your mother?' he asked softly.

'Anyway, I'm thirty-nine so time's running out.'

An awkward silence descended upon us as we finished the meal, then Theo stood up.

'Well I'd better love you and – sorry,' he corrected himself. 'I'd better get going, I mean.'

'I'll wash up,' I said. 'Thanks for supper. Send Bev and Trev my love.'

Theo picked up the newspaper, which was still open at my page, and I thought he was going to take it upstairs. Instead of which he folded it twice, went over to the pedal bin, and flipped up the lid.

'Don't!' I said.

He looked up at me. 'Don't what?'

'Don't throw it away.'

'Why not?

'Because I don't want you to, that's why.'

'Sorry,' he said, 'I thought you liked things tidy.'

'That's not what I mean.'

'Oh, do you recycle them? I didn't realise.'

'No,' I said, flushing. 'No. It's just that . . .'

'What? What is it? Rose?'

My eyes had suddenly filled with speechless tears, and now my voice was thin and high. 'My *column's* in there!' I wailed.

'I'm sorry – I wasn't thinking. I assumed you'd have your own copy.'

'I do have my own copy.'

'Oh.' He looked completely nonplussed. 'Then why can't I throw this one away?'

'Because . . . well . . . I just don't want you to, that's all.'

'But why not? I mean, you've got one.'

'Yes, but that's not the point.'

'What is the point then?'

Oh God. How on earth could I tell him?

'Rose what *is* it?'

'I can't say.'

'Why not?'

'Because you'll think it's silly, that's why.'

'No I won't.'

'You will!'

'Try me.'

'Erm . . .'

'Go on,' he added softly.

'Well . . .' My throat was aching and I could barely speak, '. . . it's just a sort of *thing* I have . . .'

'What thing?'

'That because my photo and my words are in that paper,' I croaked, 'I feel that *I'm* being chucked away too.'

'Oh. That *is* silly,' he said. 'In fact, it's a bit weird.'

'I know, but I can't *help* it,' I wailed.

'Um, don't you think you're over-reacting here?' Bloody cheek!

'No, actually. I'm *not*! I am not over-reacting at *all* Theo!'

'All right, all right – you're not.'

'I mean, did *you* over-react when your stepmother threw away the picture of your mum?'

'But Rose, that was the *only* one. Whereas there are *millions* of copies of this newspaper which means that you're being thrown away all the time.'

'Yes. But I'm being thrown away by people I don't *know*, so it doesn't matter; but I *do* know you – so it does. It's like you were putting *me* in the bin as well!'

Rudy, responding to the mounting agitation in my voice, began to shake his wings.

'You need a shrink!' he shouted in Ed's voice as he bounced along his perch. 'And that's all from *You and Yours*. Goodbye!'

'I'm sorry,' said Theo. 'I didn't mean anything. Here . . .' he handed me the newspaper then put on his jacket. 'Anyway, I'd better get next door.'

'Yes you had! You'd better get next door *right* now and change Bev's bloody lightbulbs – but I've got lightbulbs too you know.'

'Rose,' he said, as he paused in the doorway. 'Don't take this the wrong way, but I think that Rudy might be right.'

'Well thanks very much!' I yelled as he left the house. And I was standing there, speechless with rage, when the phone rang. If it's my nuisance caller he's going to get a right blasting this time I told myself as I picked it up.

'*Hello!!*' I barked.

'Er . . . Rose?'

'Oh, hi Henry, it's you.'

'I . . . just wanted . . . to ask you something, um, actually . . . er . . . ?'

'Yes? What is it?'

'Rose . . . are you okay?'

'No!' I said. 'I'm not! In fact I'm extremely pissed off! Rudy suggested that I needed a shrink and Theo agreed with him! Imagine the impertinence!'

'Well . . . whatever made him say that?' I told him about the incident with the newspaper. 'Ah,' he said, slowly. 'I *see*.'

'I mean, *you* never threw away my articles did you, Henry?'

'Ooh no no no,' he said. 'In fact,' he went on, 'I think I've still got them all. In a special pile somewhere. Yes, I'm sure I have.'

'Really Henry? Oh that's so sweet of you. But Theo just didn't get it at all. Said I was "over-reacting". Insensitive moron. He's really tactless you know.'

'Er, I hope he can't hear you Rose.'

'No,' I said, 'he's gone to see Bev.'

'Bev?'

'Beverley, you remember, at the ball?'

'Oh yes, of course. The girl in the Degas costume.'

'She lives next door. She and Theo get on like a house on fire,' I said miserably.

'Do they?'

'Oh yes,' I said feelingly, 'they *do*. He's always popping in. Any excuse. That's where he is right now. Changing her light-bulbs if you please! *Very* Freudian. Screwing them in if you ask me! He'll probably be moving in with her soon I shouldn't wonder, and then I'll be left all on my *own*. Henry are you still there?'

'Oh, yes, I just dropped my handbag that's all.'

'Anyway what was it you wanted to ask me?'

'Well . . . er . . . what was it? Oh yes. I'm seeing Bea on Saturday,' he explained. 'I'm meeting her at the Imperial War Museum.' That sounded like a barrel of laughs. 'And I thought we'd have dinner somewhere afterwards and I was just wondering what sort of food she likes? That's why I'm ringing you. To ask you that question.'

'Oh. Well, I don't really know.'

'I mean, does she like Italian?' he went on, 'or do you think she prefers French? Does she go for Indian, or Thai? Maybe she's into Chinese, or Turkish, or possibly even Polish?' What *was* he talking about?

'Henry,' I said, 'why don't you ask *her*?'

'Yes, that's a very good idea. What an excellent strategy. I will. I'll ask her myself. Maybe we could have dinner at the Army and Navy club,' he mused. 'They do jolly good prof-iteroles there.'

'Well while you're playing footsie with Bea I'll be playing gooseberry with Bella. She wants me to meet her new man.'

'Oh yes,' said Henry. 'Bea's mentioned him – not in entirely complimentary terms . . .'

*   *   *

177

'He's a total wanker and piss-artist!' is what Bea had actually said. But then Bea was hardly going to go a bundle over him I thought as I went to meet Bella and Andrew on Saturday night. She and Bea have such an odd relationship. They're like a pair of Theo's binary stars, reluctantly locked into each other's orbit – competitive yet cosy – co-dependency personified. And was their new business likely to succeed, I wondered? I had my doubts. Okay, Bella knows about money – she was a financial journalist – and Bea has artistic flair; but interior design is very recession-sensitive; at the first whiff of a slump they'll be doomed. I mean, who's going to want to have the walls crackle-glazed if the house is being repossessed?

And now, as I rattled along on the Circle Line – I'd decided not to drive – I thought about Henry and Bea. As we left Victoria I tried to work out whether or not I minded that they were seeing each other: it's the kind of thing I get letters about. But by the time we'd trundled through South Kensington I'd decided I couldn't care less. If Bea and Henry want to ride off into the sunset, good luck to them – life was short. In fact life was getting distinctly shorter I realised – I had the big four oh coming up and I was increasingly aware that time no longer stretched before me like a vast prairie. But what would Bea make of Henry's penchant for pretty frocks? To be honest, she's very conservative and I don't see her reacting well. Still, it's up to him to tell her, isn't it? Nothing to do with me. Now, as the tube train pulled into Paddington, I began to wonder what Andrew would be like. The fact that Bea wasn't crazy about him was something I took with a *big* pinch of salt. She'd find fault even if he had the brain of Einstein, the looks of Brad Pitt and the business flair of Bill Gates. I was sure he'd be perfectly *fine*. And he must at least be quite interesting I decided as I alighted at Notting Hill. I mean, his choice of costume for a start – a squiggly Jackson Pollock suit – at least suggested imagination and style. We'd arranged to meet at the fashionable Pharmacy restaurant; I'd never been there before. But as I walked down the Gate I could immediately identify it by the burly bouncer standing outside.

'I have a reservation,' I said as I went through the purple rope. The automatic door slid back with a wheezy sigh then I walked into the thronged bar.

'Rose!' Bella squealed, waving like a game-show contestant. 'Rose! Hi! We're over here!' Oh God, she was clearly over-excited – she was talking in exclamation marks. 'Rose! This is Andrew! Andrew! Rose!' Adrenaline leaked from every pore like honey out of a comb. But then, poor kid, she hasn't had a proper boyfriend for over four years.

I held out my hand and smiled. 'It's good to meet you Andrew.'

'Dee-lighted to meet *you* Rose. Heard *a lot* about you,' he added meaningfully.

'Oh. Yes. Well, same here.' I had only the vaguest recollection of Andrew at the ball. Tonight he was wearing a sixties style suit I could have cut myself on and a pair of Jarvis Cocker type specs. His slicked-back dark hair glistened with gel, and on his feet were a pair of pointy suede shoes. Meeting him now I decided that he was somehow both smooth and sharp.

'We're drinking cranberry vodkas Rose,' he said. 'How about you?'

'I'd like the same.'

'Same again for you Bunny?' he said to Bella.

'Ooh yes please!' she said.

'Bunny?' I repeated wonderingly while Bella sat there simpering.

'That's my name for her,' he grinned.

'Er, why?'

'Because she's so fluffy and lovely and she reminds me of my old pet wabbit, don't you Bunny?' Oh for God's sake! What a twat! '*Love* your column by the way, Rose,' he added seriously, 'I always read it.'

'Really?' I decided to suspend judgement for a while. 'What an . . . unusual place,' I added looking round.

'I know!' said Bella. 'It's a scream!' It was like a super-annuated chemist's shop with huge bottles of pills every-where. Lining the walls were shelf units stacked up with fake packs of prescription drugs. As Andrew made his way to the bar I peered at the names: Tagomet, Ventalin, Betnovate, Warfarin and oh, charming – Anusol. I idly wondered whether there was any Valium, for Bella, who was smiling at me with the manic enthusiasm of the chimp in the PG Tips ad.

'We love it here,' she said – using the 'we' word already! – but to be honest, I wasn't mad keen. It was packed to the rafters with noisy twenty-somethings, which made me feel terribly old. As for the interior – I found its dispensary theme completely absurd. Whatever next I wondered? A restaurant called 'Morgue' complete with mortuary slabs in place of tables, and scalpels instead of knives?

'It's great,' I lied. 'What a fun place.'

'We come here a lot. Andrew's got a fabulous flat round the corner.' I smiled. 'Don't you think he's *gorgeous*,' she whis-pered.

I looked at him. 'Hhmm. Not bad. How old is he – thirty-seven?'

'No, *forty*-seven.' Good God!

'Well he's obviously been drinking the right brand of coffee.'

'I know,' she giggled. 'He does look young; and luckily,' she went on, *sotto voce*, 'he's never been married!' Uh *oh*.

'Oh that *is* lucky,' I lied. 'And what does he do again?'

'He's in advertising.' Of course. What else? 'He's really well-connected,' she added admiringly. This certainly seemed to be true. For as he stood at the bar, Andrew was greeting the other punters as energetically as a politician on polling day. 'He knows *so* many people,' Bella said happily as Andrew genially slapped backs and pressed flesh. 'Ooh, he's coming back!'

'Sorry about that girls!' he said, rolling his eyes with mock-exasperation. 'I've got a lot of friends here tonight. Well – cheers! Nice to meet you Rose! Down the hatch!'

As we sipped our drinks I realised that Andrew's 'friends,' unless they were just as preternaturally youthful-looking, seemed to be a good twenty years younger than he. I felt like a pensioner at a school disco, but Andrew was clearly at home.

'I love this place Rose,' he said. 'It's so buzzy, and it's very handy.' Not for Camberwell, I thought.

'Bella says you live nearby.'

'Yes, Rose. Just off the Portobello Road. *Great* area, Notting Hill Gate. What I like about it, Rose, is that it's full of *real* people – they're really *real* – you know what I mean?'

'Hhm. And you work in advertising?' I went on pleasantly.

'Yeah, Rose. That's absolutely right.'

'On the creative side?'

'What I do's very creative.'

'And which agency are you with?'

'I'm not with an agency, Rose, I'm in TV.'

'He works for Channel 37,' said Bella helpfully.

'It's very demanding, Rose, but I've got a great team.' Team?

'Funnily enough,' I said, 'my assistant's husband, Rob Banks, works for Channel 37. But he's on the tele-sales side so I don't suppose you'd know him.'

'Rob Banks? He works for me. He's a cretin,' said Andrew, with casual cruelty. 'He's no good; he's on the way out.'

'So you're in advertising *sales*,' I said, ignoring his outrageous indiscretion. 'You sell air-time.'

'Yeah. I'm in advertising. Like I said.' Now I knew why he kept using my Christian name. 'Oh hi Kim!' he said leaping to his feet and air-kissing a slender blonde. 'You're looking *great*, darling,' he said appreciatively. 'Yeah, we'll do lunch some time. Sorry about that,' he said to us, rolling his eyes. 'It's all go in here tonight. That was Kim Medcalf by the way – you probably recognised her – she's in *EastEnders*. Right, shall we go up and eat?'

Dinner, needless to say, was purgatorial. Between mouthfuls of polenta Andrew dropped enough names to fill a telephone directory. We heard about his 'fun' drinks at Bafta with 'Kate' (Winslet) and 'Joan' (Collins) and about his recent lunch with 'Martine'. He expatiated upon the romantic prospects of 'Jerry' (Hall) – 'a really *lovely* lady, Rose' – and revealed his familiarity with 'Tara' (P-T). He told us that he had 'a lot of time' for Guy (Ritchie) – *'a lot* of time, actually, Rose' – and that he was on '*very*' friendly terms with Sting. And as he burbled away I was struck again by his suspiciously youthful-looking countenance, especially round the brow. This man was pushing fifty, but his forehead was as smooth as a billiard ball: and where on earth were his crow's feet? Something wasn't quite right. Andrew had that slightly glassy look I've seen before on women who . . . oh yes, of course. Men have it as well, don't they? Botox. Or maybe he'd been under the knife . . . And now, as he held forth about some party at the Groucho where he'd been 'gassing' with Graham Norton ('a *really* witty guy actually, Rose') I realised two things: a) that he had evinced no interest whatsoever in Bella or in me all evening and b) that in describing Andrew as a 'total wanker and piss-artist' Bea had seriously under-sold this guy. He was, in fact, a tiny-minded, self-pleasuring, nar-cissistic, star-fucking, fifth-rate, pretentious little prat. And I looked at Bella, as she threw back her head and laughed at his leaden bons mots, and mentally yelled. 'I know you're desperate, "Bunny," but what the HELL are you DOING with this JERK???' Instead of which I just smiled at them both benignly. And now as the rather pretty waitress cleared our plates, I noticed something else – that Andrew's eyes swept up from her feet to her head, then lingered appreciatively over her breasts.

'Any desserts?' she asked. I shook my head.

'And Bunny's watching her weight. Aren't you Bun?' he added giving Bella a playful prod. She blushed and giggled while I tried very, very hard not to stab Andrew with my pudding fork.

'Bella has a lovely figure actually,' I said censoriously. 'She doesn't need to slim.'

' 'Course you do, don't you Bunny?' he said, as he coochi-cooed her cheeks. And now, at long last the evening was nearly over; I'd done my duty and could go. I realised with a sinking heart that I had a long haul back to Camberwell. And it's not as though I'm flush enough to splash out on a cab, I'd have to go by tube: and as Andrew paid the bill – 'I can get this on expenses, Rose, as you're media,' he explained gallantly – I thought, why the hell did we have to come *here*? I'd suggested we met up in W1 but Andrew had insisted on Pharmacy. At first I'd assumed it was out of laziness, but that wasn't it at all. It was because if we'd met on neutral ground, he'd have been unable to show off his social 'success'. He'd wanted me to see him Meeting and Greeting in a fashionable watering hole in W11. For as we got up and walked through the restaurant he was at it again: nodding at diners and saying 'Hi!' then rotating his right index finger in a little pantomime of dialling and answering – it was like a fake social semaphore.

'Yeah, yeah, I'll give you a bell,' he mouthed. 'Give us a buzz – we'll do lunch.'

'Thanks for coming Rose,' said Bella. I looked at her pityingly.

'It was lovely to see you,' I said. 'And very interesting meeting you Andrew. Thanks for supper.'

'My pleasure, Rose – we'll do it again.'

No we bloody well *won't*, I said to myself crossly as I trailed home on the tube. All the way round on the Circle Line to Embankment then down the Northern Line, and then a long, cold wait at the Oval for the number thirty-six, and then a ten minute schlep to the house. I glanced at my watch. It was five to twelve. Beverley's lights were still on downstairs, but my house was silent and dark. As I opened the door I couldn't see Theo's jacket on its hook – he was obviously still next door. Hmm . . . So I left the chain off so that he didn't ring the bell and wake me, then I covered Rudy's cage and went to bed.

Because of the vodka I slept fitfully, waking in the small hours with a raging thirst. I was dimly aware of a faint noise downstairs, but didn't panic as I had at Christmas because I knew that it was only Theo coming in. And I wondered how his evening with Beverley had gone, then I drifted off again, working out, just before I lost consciousness, that the anagram of Andrew is Warned . . .

I felt a bit bleary when I awoke at seven and went downstairs to make some tea. Theo seemed to have made a bit of a mess coming in, things had been disturbed. The hall table drawer was open – he'd obviously been rummaging for a pen – and one of my pictures was askew on the wall. And – oh shit! – the front door! Not only had he *not* put the chain on, the naughty boy, he'd actually left it ajar! How *bloody* irresponsible! I shall have to have words with him about this I said crossly as I went to close it. And I was just trying to work out how I might put it – because I don't want to fall out with him – when something in the sitting room caught my eye. I looked in. It was a shambles. I knew Theo was untidy but what on earth had he been *doing*? A small table was overturned, and my CDs were strewn on the floor; my bureau had been opened and the contents pulled out, and what the hell . . . ? Oh. *Fuck*. For now I saw that there was a conspicuous gap where the TV used to be.

'SHIT!' I shouted. 'I've been BURGLED!'

'Rose! Are you all right?' I heard Theo thunder down the stairs then he rushed into the sitting room with only a white towel wrapped round his waist.

'Sorry,' he said sheepishly, 'I was in the bathroom – what's up?'

'I've been bloody well burgled! – that's what!'

'Oh no!' He looked stricken.

'Oh yes! And the reason they broke in was because you left the chain off the bloody door!'

'But I only did that because you weren't back yet.' *What?*

'But I thought *you* weren't back. I came in at twelve, and the house was all dark so I assumed you were still at Bev's; plus your jacket wasn't hanging up.'

'Oh, I took it upstairs. I went to bed very early last night.'

184

'What time was that?'

He screwed up his face. 'I got back at about ten, watched a bit of telly, then went to bed at half past. I was so exhausted I fell asleep straight away. I knew that you were still out, so I left the door unchained.'

I put my head in my hands. Oh God.

'I thought *you* were still out. I'm so sorry Theo. It's my fault, not yours. I left the chain off – and someone broke in.'

'But didn't you lock the door?'

'Of course. But these people are professionals – they have bunches of duplicate keys. I even heard sounds, but I didn't investigate because I assumed that it was you, coming in.'

Then I had this awful thought. The burglars came in while we were asleep – we could have been murdered in our beds. You hear about people being broken into at night, and the thieves actually come right into the bedroom looking for cash and jewellery and – oh God! Oh *God*! I shot upstairs, heart pounding, and yanked open my underwear drawer. I pulled out the carefully arranged knickers and bras, reached to the back and took out my leather jewel case. In it were all my old bits and pieces and my one precious, precious thing. If you saw it you'd laugh, it's no more than a bauble – but to me worth all the gold in Fort Knox. With trembling fingers, I opened the tiny blue plastic box, lifted the cotton wool, then relaxed. I put the case back, then went downstairs, still shaking like a cold Chihuahua, to find Theo ringing the police.

'They'll be round in ten minutes,' he explained as he put the phone down.

'They didn't take anything of yours did they?'

'No. My 'scope and computer are still there. I think it's just the TV and the video that have gone.'

'And a hundred quid which I had in my desk. Thank God I didn't leave my handbag downstairs otherwise they'd have taken my credit cards too. It could have been worse,' I added, calmer now, much calmer. 'And I can get another TV second hand.'

'Don't you have contents insurance?'

I shook my head. 'I was trying to economise. So all things considered' – I thought of my jewel box again – 'it could have been *far* worse. At least they didn't take anything of sentimental value.'

'Rose, I hate to say this, but I think they did. That photo of your parents – it's gone.' I looked on the sideboard. Theo was right. It wasn't there.

'Oh well,' I said with a shrug.

'That must be very upsetting. I'm sorry.'

'It's okay – the frame's only silver plate. Anyway, I'll make some tea – I believe it's traditional at times like this? What's the matter Theo?' He was looking at me strangely.

'Oh . . . nothing. Er, I'd better get dressed.' Now that the shock had subsided I found myself noticing how slim his waist was, and how broad his shoulders; and how surprisingly muscled and smooth his chest, and it suddenly crossed my mind that he should have gone to the ball as Michelangelo's *David* – obviously with at least a fig leaf in front. As he turned, I noticed that his upper back was dotted with clusters of faint freckles, like distant galaxies, and that his calves were muscled and strong. I went into the kitchen, feeling vaguely disturbed, then opened the fridge to give Rudy some fruit.

'Do you want some grapes this morning Rudy?' I asked him over my shoulder, 'or would you prefer a bit of peach? I've got half a banana here if you'd rather have that. Or there's a really nice pear. What do you think Rudy?' He was rather quiet this morning. That was funny. Not like him at all. And now I slowly turned round and saw, to my horror, that Rudolph Valentino had gone.

Chapter Eleven

'I'm really sorry,' I said to Bea when I told her about Rudy the following evening. We stared mournfully at the empty space where his cage had been. 'I feel dreadful.'

'It's not your fault. I'm just amazed you didn't hear him shouting, 'I'm being kidnapped! Help!''

'He was probably too shocked to speak. The burglars must have lifted his cover, seen he was valuable, and decided to take him as well. P.C. Plod said they're circulating his details to eighty-three pet shops in the south east.'

'Did you tell them what he says?' she asked as I poured two glasses of wine.

'I did. I said the frequent references to the Radio Four schedule would help to identify him.'

'And the reruns of your quarrels with Ed. I hope someone finds him,' she added as she bit a Twiglet. 'Bella will be very upset. Don't blame yourself, Rose; these things happen, but you'll have to get a burglar alarm. I say, it's bit of a mess in here isn't it?' she added as she looked round the kitchen. 'Is young Theo a pig?'

'No, it's not him,' I said guiltily. 'I'm afraid it's me.' I surveyed the stacks of dirty plates and unwashed mugs. 'I haven't quite felt like tidying up.'

'*Really*?' she said, giving me a peculiar look. 'Don't worry – it must be the shock. You've got post-traumatic stress disorder,' she announced confidently as I took our pizza out of its carton.

'Yes,' I said vaguely. 'That's probably what it is. Anyway,'

I changed the subject, 'how was your date with Henry?'

'Oh it was *fine*,' she replied. 'At first I thought he seemed a little distracted, but no, we enjoyed ourselves. He talked about the ball a lot – he loved it.'

'Yes, he said he did. And was the Imperial War Museum fun?'

'It was great,' she replied as I discarded the Pizza Hut box. 'And where did you eat?'

'We had a curry at Veeraswamy's and then a nightcap at the In and Out club. Henry's so nice,' she breathed as I put two large slices on our plates. 'What I particularly liked – and this *really* surprised me – was that he was in touch with his feminine side. He knows quite a lot about fashion actually,' she added as she picked up her knife and fork.

'*Does* he?'

'But at the same time he's a real *man*. *D*o you know what I mean Rose? Well of course you do,' she added hastily. 'I don't know why you didn't snap him up.'

'I never had time to,' I said as I got out the napkins. 'He was always away. Gadding about with the regiment in Cyprus, or Oman or Belize or wherever.'

'That's precisely why you went out with him, isn't it Rose?'

I looked at her. 'What do you mean?'

'I just mean that you've always chosen men with whom you could only have a long-distance relationship.'

'Oh don't be absurd.' I passed her the pepper mill. 'Ed never went anywhere did he?'

'Exactly. So instead you drove him away.'

'I did not "drive" Ed "away" Bea. As you well know he was unfaithful to me with our marriage guidance counsellor within a mere seven months.'

'It's not the seven months that's significant,' said Bea dismissively. 'It's the fact that you needed a marriage guidance counsellor at *all*. You're just no good at being in a couple,' she went on. Bloody cheek! She's no good at being *out* of a couple – the distinctly weird one she's in with her twin. 'That's your problem, Rose,' she added airily. 'It's classic avoidance.'

188

'Look, would you stop psychoanalysing me Bea. I've just been burgled. Give me a break.'

'Okay. Anyway, Henry mentioned that he might have to go to the Middle East next month. It's totally depressing.'

'Hazard of the job I'm afraid. Oh, hang on, there's the phone.' I ran into the hall. It was Beverley commiserating about the break-in.

'I wish I'd *done* something,' she said. 'I was up very late – I couldn't sleep – and I thought I heard a noise at about half past two. But the problem was Trev was snoring so loudly it was hard to tell.'

'Do you want to come round?' I suggested. 'We're just having a take-away pizza. There's loads.'

'Really?' she said, 'that might be nice.'

'Theo's out star-gazing,' I explained, 'but Bea's here.'

'Oh. Well . . . um, actually, Rose, I don't think I will.'

'You wouldn't be intruding a bit Bev, honestly. She's just telling me about her date with Henry. Why don't you come round? Go on.'

'That's kind, but actually I've got loads to do, I really ought to work.'

'Oh well,' I sighed. 'Up to you. Just come if you decide to change your mind. Shall I tell Theo you rang?'

'Er, yes,' she said carefully. 'Please do.'

'Beverley was all set to come round,' I told Bea, 'but when I mentioned that Theo was out she didn't want to bother after all. She's nuts about him. She hotly denies it, but reading between the lines, I'm sure. And I know he likes her, because he calls her "poppet", and goes to the pub with her, and he's always helping her with things and going round.'

'So it's a case of watch this space, is it?' Bea asked.

'Yes, it is,' I said with a slight pang. 'Anyway I'm glad that you and Henry got on so well.'

'Oh we did,' Bea replied. 'In fact we've got another date next week. He's taking me to a lecture on New Directions for European Security and Defence Policy at the International Institute for Strategic Studies. Isn't that lovely?'

I nodded enthusiastically. 'Sounds great.'

'I think he wants me to know as much about military issues as he does,' she said happily. 'So that we can talk about it. I've just read the biography of Field Marshal Barker-Ffortescue,' she went on. 'Did you know that, apparently, he sometimes wore frocks?'

'Gosh!' I said.

'Isn't that *hideous*!'

'Mmm. It certainly is.' Obviously I wasn't going to let on about Henry's taste for feminine attire. It was up to *him* to tell Bea if things got serious.

'Anyway, what did you think of the dreaded Andrew?' she asked me.

'He was a monumental bore. They should use him instead of general anaesthetic in hospitals – thirty seconds and you'd be out. And the way he name-dropped!' I added scornfully. 'It was pathetic! I couldn't believe he'd *really* met all those people.'

'No, I think he has. Channel 37's a small company so he gets included in their corporate events. He goes to the award ceremonies, the parties, the private screenings – that kind of thing – so that makes him feel in the loop.'

'I've always thought Bella had good taste – why's she bothering?'

'Because she's absolutely desperate, that's why. And he's quite attractive, and he takes her to glamorous events and fancy restaurants – plus she's flattered by his attention.'

'Well, I bet she's not the only one who's getting it,' I pointed out as we chomped on our Margaritas. 'He's clearly got a roving eye.'

'I know,' Bea agreed, spearing a stray slice of salami. 'I saw it myself. You must have put on a good show by the way, because Bella thinks you really approve.'

'Does she? Oh God. Well we mustn't hurt her feelings,' I added. 'He may be a nightmare but it's her life. And who knows – it might actually work out.' At this a look of naked panic swept across Bea's face.

'Work out?' she repeated. She blinked several times, rapidly. 'Oh no, I can't see that happening at *all*. So you really think it might work out do you?'

I shrugged. 'Maybe.'

She shook her head. 'No way. In fact, I haven't the heart to tell her this,' she went on, 'but I think Bella's barking up the wrong tree.'

I didn't mention to Bea the horribly indiscreet remark that Andrew had made about Serena's husband, but it preyed on my mind. Poor Serena I thought, as she arrived for work on Monday; Rob's going to lose his job. I felt awful being privy to such information, and she's got enough problems as it is. As she hung up her coat I noticed how threadbare it was, and saw that her jumper had a visible mend. And I'm sure she used to have her hair highlighted, but now it's decidedly grey. I resolved to speak to Ricky about getting her a raise . . .

'So how's everything going?' I asked her genially.

'Oh, *comme ci comme ça.*'

'So, things are okay then,' I reiterated.

'Oh yes. Not bad. And of course Rome wasn't built in a day, was it?' she said perkily.

'Serena, whatever happened to your hand?' I gasped. 'That bandage!'

'Well,' she emitted a nervous titter, 'it's just a little . . . burn. Johnny thought it would be fun to put the stainless steel teapot in the microwave. When I went into the kitchen it was arcing and making this loud buzzing – I thought the machine was going to blow up. So I opened the door and stupidly grabbed it: it was, to put it mildly, *hot*. Still, the chap in Accident and Emergency said it was only second degree.'

'My God.'

'It's really not too bad at all. And of course, boys will be boys,' she added stoically.

'I'm sorry Serena. It must really hurt.'

'Well, that's family life for you, and you have to take the rough with the smooth. But at least Rob's job's going well.'

'Really?' I tried not to sound too amazed.

'Yes,' she confided, 'it is. His boss, Andrew, told him he was doing brilliantly.'

'That's . . . incredible! I mean, that's *great*.'

'So one must be thankful for small mercies,' she concluded with a twitchy smile.

'Yes,' I agreed. 'One must.'

To save Serena's hand I opened the batch of jiffy bags containing the day's books. *God's Diet – The Divinely Simply Way to Lose Weight*. I sighed – these celebrity slimming books are such a bore. *500 Terrific Ideas for Organizing Everything*! – I couldn't be bothered with that. *A Do-It-Yourself Guide to Personal and Planetary Transformation* by David Icke. Or rather Sicke. And finally, *Baby Care: 101 Essential Tips*. I idly flicked through it. *Tip 5: Do NOT leave your baby on the bus*, it advised brilliantly. Or, indeed, anywhere else. And now I turned to the day's letters with a strangely sinking heart. *Dear Rose, I've got terrible money worries . . . Dear Rose, I think I'm gay . . . Dear Rose, I haven't been out of my house for five years . . . Dear Rose, my husband drinks . . .*

Doesn't it ever get boring? I could hear Theo's voice whispering in my ear, like Satan. *Dealing with the same old issues all the time...* Of course it's not boring I told myself sharply, I was just a bit low today, that was all. It was because of the burglary – and Rudy – I was terribly worried: I had a lot on my plate. As I picked up the next pile of letters I forced myself to buck up. They were all from people who were getting divorced, their cries of lamentation and resentment blending into one huge matri*moan*ial whine.

I've got access problems . . . and he won't meet his obligations . . . plus my mother's taken his side, and now the children won't speak to me, but what's even worse . . . my wife ran off with our au pair . . . Boo hoo hoo, I thought wearily; it was as though my shoulders were wet with their tears. But I knew why I was feeling so uncharacteristically negative – because I was about

192

to start proceedings too. It's hard giving advice to people on something very painful when you're actually going through it yourself. I've got my solicitor, Frances, lined up; Ed will get the petition next week.

Frances pointed out that because I shared costs in Putney for nine months I'm entitled to seek recompense. But I feel it's undignified to ask for a settlement, and it would only drag things out. I may be hard up, but I don't want to prolong the agony with any argy bargy about cash – I just want a quick, clean break. This time last year, I reflected bitterly, I was putting the finishing touches to my wedding plans; a mere twelve months on and I'm about to request my decree nisi. I suddenly remembered that the first anniversary is the 'paper' one – or rather 'papers' one in our case. Now I realised how reckless it had been to get married on Valentine's Day: we had given a hostage to fortune and recrimination had replaced romance.

I turned wearily to the next letter. *Dear Rose*, I read, in writing that was becoming all too familiar, *I just want you to know that even though you haven't replied to any of my eleven recent letters, you're still my Number One agony aunt and a very Special Lady. Your advice is so brilliant, and I love listening to your phone-ins! Do you know you've really changed my life! With love from your totally devoted fan, Colin Twisk*. There were six crosses and then, at the bottom of the page: *P.S. Why don't we meet up some time . . . ?*

I looked at that sentence with a combination of alarm and distaste, then I lifted my head and looked out of the window at the sheet of rainwashed February sky. It's him, I thought. It is. It's Colin Twisk. He's my silent caller. He's become obsessed. He's hung up on me, I thought wryly. And now I remembered, with a sinking sensation, what Katie Bridge had said. She'd said that Colin might well be 'dangerous' and that she wasn't 'taking the risk'. So I asked Serena to find all his previous letters, then I put them in a special file: because if he doesn't stop harassing me, or if he gets nasty, I might need them as evidence – God forbid. But he's clearly become fixated: 'I especially love listening to your phone-ins'. Well he certainly seems to like the sound of my voice. Sometimes I come home and find that he's even dialled my answerphone and left some heavy breathing on that. But how did he get my number in the first place – and what if he finds out my home address? The Jehovah's Witnesses got my details from the electoral roll; if they could do that, then so could he.

To cheer myself up, I read Trevor's latest column – *A Dog's Life* – which comes out every Monday in the *Post*'s Features section. It's been going really well, but Linda's asked Bev to make the tone a little more personal – confessional even – and so she has.

'An eventful week this one,' Trev had written:

On Tuesday we heard that yours truly has got through to round two of the Dogs of Distinction Award, so sighs of relief all round. Despite this Bev's been a bit down in the chops, but I know the reason why. The poor girl's fallen in love. She won't tell me who the object of her affection is – but she's got all the classic signs. She's listless, she's not eating, she doesn't sleep well, and she snaps at the slightest thing. For instance, on Thursday, right, I was buying some pop sox for her in M and S and she completely lost it. 'No Trev!' she yelled. 'I distinctly said I wanted navy, not black!' She even pointed to the shopping list to prove it; the whole shop was watching – I nearly died! It really bummed out my karma I can tell you: well, I felt my professionalism had been impugned. So I trotted back to Hosiery and got the right ones, but I was not a happy pup. And I wanted to say, hang on a mo, Bev, just chill out will you, and tell me what's going on. You share, and I'll care – but the silly girl won't 'fess up. I keep putting my head on her lap and looking at her with as much fetching beseechingness as a dog can muster – always monitoring the slobber thing of course – but she just won't spill the choccy drops. Maybe she thinks I'm going to blab about it to all my mates down the park – as if! I'd never bark about Bev's private affairs – but she's resolutely keeping schtum. We met one or two nice blokes at New Year, so it could be one of them. But I don't think it's on. I mean, I told her about that nice little chocolate lab I had the hots for didn't I? But I can't force her to tell. All I know is we went shopping yesterday, and she bought someone a Valentine card. She thought I didn't see – I made like I was engrossed in the soft toys, right – but my eyes swivelled to the back of my head. And I saw her pick out a large card with LOVE *ME*! in huge red glittery letters and I thought mmmmm . . . wonder who that's for then? . . .

'Trevor's column is brilliant,' I said to Linda. 'I love the cliff-hanger ending.'

'Yes, he writes really well. We get tons of positive feedback from the readers and the ratings have really risen – that was a *great* contact, Rose. By the way, don't forget to record your updated Helplines, will you: we've got to get them up and running by the end of the week.' I winced – well it's *so* embarrassing – but anything to keep Ricky off my back. So I went into the interviewing room I use for this purpose with my five new three-minute scripts.

'Hello,' I said warmly into the premium numbers recording line, 'I'm Rose Costelloe of the *Daily Post*. Thank you for calling my helpline on How to Spice Up Your Sex Life. Now, has the sparkle gone out of your love making? . . . perhaps the most exciting thing that happens in your bed is losing the TV remote . . . first admit that it's a problem . . . don't blame your partner . . . make an effort . . . relax . . . massage . . . intimacy . . . soft music . . . feathers and silk . . . Please write to me in strict confidence if you've any other problems, goodbye. Hello, I'm Rose Costelloe of the *Daily Post*. Thank you for calling my helpline on Sexual Fetishes. Now, this is *nothing* to worry about . . .'

I emerged an hour later, with a deep sense of distaste. I mean, I really *don't* think it's my job to tell people what to do with rubber masks, whips and high heels; and my unease was compounded by the fact that I could imagine Colin listening to them, breathing heavily . . . The thought of it made me feel sick.

'POST!!!' The adolescent-looking mail-boy passed me in the corridor with the second delivery.

'Ooh, anything for me by any chance?' I said ironically as I looked at his trolley. I knew there'd be ten letters at least.

'Yes, Miss Costelloe, just this.' He handed me a solitary cream vellum envelope marked 'Private and Confidential. To be opened by addressee ONLY. Suddenly I detected the distinctive aroma of Ricky's b.o. and he loomed into view. He smiled warmly at me – he was clearly in a good mood about the circulation rise – so I decided to strike while the iron was hot.

'Ricky, could I have a quick word with you please?'

'Yeah, 'course you can Rose. So what can I do for you?' he asked benignly as we went into his vast office. On the walls were industry awards he'd won, and framed front pages with a selection of his greatest headlines. There was the Moonie mass marriage ceremony headlined 'CLUB WED!' and a legendary one about the notorious rock star, Ozzy Gallagher, who'd been snapped punching an autograph hunter. 'SHIT HITS FAN!' it announced. There were also photos of the many neglected animals Ricky had rescued through his readers' campaigns. There was an abused Spanish donkey, now in a sanctuary in Devon, and two seal pups he'd airlifted off the Canadian ice. There was a baby chimp, which he'd saved from a Bosnian zoo, and three kangaroos he'd redeemed from a cull.

'What lovely photos,' I said.

'Oh yes, Rose. They are.' Suddenly he stood up, went up to the wall and took down a photo of a Vietnamese pot-bellied pig. Its vast tummy scraped the ground and its eyes were obscured by thick rolls of fat. 'This is Audrey,' he explained quietly. 'She's my particular favourite.'

'Was she named after Audrey Hepburn?' I asked politely.

He shook his head. 'No. She's just Audrey. That's her name. She was bought when she was a tiny piglet, but became a problem when she grew too big. Her owners tried to sell her, but no-one wanted her because she ate so much. So they decided that there was only one thing for it and that they'd have to . . .' his voice cracked. This was evidently difficult for him. 'Can you imagine, Rose?' he went on, his chin visibly puckering. 'This poor little thing was destined for the frying pan? Can you *imagine*, Rose?' he added, his voice faltering now, 'the horror of eating your own pet pig?' I suddenly realised that I was absolutely starving. I'd missed lunch. 'Can you imagine, Rose?' Ricky repeated, his eyes glistening.

'Yes. I mean, *no*. How *cruel*.'

'It was totally inhuman,' he agreed, swallowing hard. 'Luckily a kind-hearted reader brought Audrey to our attention. So we raised the cash to buy her, then took her to a kids' farm in Surrey where she can . . .' his voice quivered again, '. . . run free. Where she's happy, Rose, and where . . .' he bit his lower lip, '. . . she's *loved*.' And as he put the photo back on the wall I thought, what a *strange* man. A man who could happily describe Paula Yates as a 'celebrity stiff'; who could refer to the death of Princess Diana as a 'fabulous news event'; and yet who could go into paroxysms of sentiment over the fate of a pot bellied pig. Hard outside, soft centre, evidently: but then they say that Hitler adored his dog.

'That's a wonderful story,' I said. 'What a happy ending.'

'It certainly is'.

'You saved her bacon,' I said genially.

He allowed himself to smile. He sat down again, sniffing slightly, then composed himself. 'Anyway, what can I do for you Rose?'

'Well it isn't for me,' I began, as he leaned back in his leather recliner. 'It's for Serena actually.' I thought of her threadbare coat. 'I'll come straight to the point. Can you give her a pay rise please?'

Ricky raised an eyebrow. 'Why?'

'Well, because she works very hard and I feel she deserves it.'

'Don't we all?' he said with a laugh.

'But she's been loyal to this paper for fifteen years and I'd like to feel she had a bit more at the end of the month. Her family circumstances are such that . . .' – I wasn't going to go into details about Rob's work situation – '. . . she's under a lot of stress. She's got three kids, the school fees – it's not easy for her.' I was careful not to add that she was clearly more than half way to a nervous breakdown – I don't think Ricky's compassion extends to human beings.

'She gets her annual increment,' he pointed out indignantly.

'Yes, but it's only three per cent. I feel she's a deserving case for something else – maybe a long service bonus of some kind. Something which would make her feel wanted and appreciated. I know she'd never go to the union so I thought I'd take it up directly with you and –'

Suddenly one of the phones on Ricky's desk began ringing and he picked it up. 'Yeah . . . yeah . . . yeah,' he said irritably. 'No we've got the Posh and Becks too. What are they doing on Rod Stewart's new bird? Well, find out – and what about that bloke who bonked the apple pie . . . ? Right . . . right . . . yeah. Gay arch-bishop? Bor-ing. Martine McCutcheon? Done her to death. Geri Halliwell? She gets on my tits. Nah, I'm not bothered about Vanessa-Mae . . .'

I knew instantly who Ricky was talking to – one of his 'moles' at our main rival, the *Daily News*. All the tabloids have plants in each other's offices so that they can gazump each other's stories – it's well known. You never know who they are of course, but Ricky was obviously on the phone to one of his. His voice was becoming increasingly agitated and I could see the conversation would go on for a while. I suddenly remembered the letter I was holding in my hand. I decided I might as well read it while Ricky was gassing, so I slid my thumb under the flap, then removed the sheets of expensive vellum, all six sides of which were covered in an

198

elegant, forward-sloping hand. I skimmed it quickly, and decided it was a marital crisis of the kind I see every day.

My feelings towards my husband had started to change . . . begun growing apart . . . the unique stresses we're under . . . the constant pressure of being in the public eye. Oh. *Many temptations in my industry . . . very attractive . . . magnetic pull . . . just couldn't resist.*

'Nah, don't give me that crap,' I heard Ricky say. 'What we want is something big. Something that will put on at least 300 grand. We want a lap-dancing woman priest; we want Fergie running off with the Dalai Lama; we want Liz Hurley marrying Steve Bing. In short we want an A1-Five-Star-Copper-Bottomed-Prime-Time-Sure-Fire-Weapons-Grade SCOOP . . . !'

I read on, avidly, my eyes devouring the words. I had a lurching sensation in my stomach and a prickling feeling on my scalp. *Got myself in such a mess . . . it's so lonely at the top . . . friends have betrayed me before . . . didn't know which way to turn . . . you give such great advice, Rose . . . thought that maybe you could help.*

'Look,' said Ricky, 'I want something *mega*. No, I don't fucking well want Charlotte Church. Why? Because they'll *all* have that. Get me an *exclusive* you little git! I *will* talk to you like that – I pay you enough don't I? – so just get your scrawny arse into gear!'

I looked at the signature, just to check that I was right, then I turned back to read the rest. As I read the final page, I thought my eyes would drop out of my head. *I've never been involved with a woman before . . .* she'd written.

'EXCLOOOSIVE!!!' I heard Ricky shout.

But she's just so good for me – for the first time in years I feel truly alive. Writing to you is a huge risk, Rose, but I somehow know, instinctively, that I can trust you – that's why I'm placing myself in your hands.

'EXCLOOOOOSIVE!!! GOT THAT???!!!!' shouted Ricky again. Then he slammed down the phone.

I stared disbelievingly, again, at the signature on the letter, then looked at the address. That's definitely where she lives.

That's her Jacobean country mansion, I've read articles about it in *Hello!* It's near Moreton-in-the-Marsh – it cost her five million. Fucking hell!

'What's the matter, Rose?' said Ricky. 'You look a bit peaky. Anything up?'

'Ooh, no, no, no,' I said, quickly folding the letter with trembling hands and putting it back in the envelope. 'Anyway, where were we?' I added as I slipped it into my handbag. 'Oh yes, Serena's rise.'

'Serena's rise?' he echoed. 'Look, I'm not in the mood right now. I've got other things on my plate. I'll e-mail you later with my decision, okay?'

'Okay.' I was too shocked by what I'd just read to pin him down on the matter: I simply wanted to get out of there – fast. As I walked, heart racing, back to my office I knew, of course, what I *ought* to do. As an employee of Amalgamated Newspapers, there was no question that I should tell Ricky about this fabulous scoop. But my primary loyalty is to my readers – whomsoever they be – so that was something I would never do.

How unbelievable, I thought again as I walked through the newsroom. *Electra!* She could buy her own agony aunt. *Electra*, with all her money and glamour, had written to me – to *me*! – because she believed that *I* could help. I was filled with a renewed sense of purpose and I felt my heart expand. How incredible, I said to myself for the fiftieth time. Hang on . . . Maybe it is. Maybe it *is* incredible. Literally. Maybe the whole thing's a hoax . . .

I did some deep breathing and some hard thinking. It was all too easy to imagine a disgruntled employee stealing a pad of her headed paper and concocting something like this. But on the other hand I get enough fake letters to be able to sniff them out. It's easy to do this because a hoax is always so over the top. I get a letter from someone purporting to be, say, 'Ricky Soul'; and it will say that they've got terrible BO and acne and bad breath and piles and everyone hates them and they haven't had a girlfriend for fifteen years . . . And the idea is that I write back to the *real* Ricky, saying, *Dear Mr Soul, I'm so sorry to hear about your terrible BO and your acne and your bad breath and piles, and the fact that everyone hates you and that you haven't had a girlfriend for fifteen years . . .* and they're incredibly embarrassed. This didn't feel like a hoax to me: but the handwriting would give it away. I'd seen examples of Electra's handwriting in a newspaper article – all I'd have to do is compare. I sat down at my pod, still feeling sick and trembly, and locked the letter away in my desk. This was one that wasn't going to be date-stamped and filed in the normal way. It was going to be read, answered and then immediately shredded – by me – when everyone else had gone home.

'Serena,' I said. She looked up from her copy of the *Financial Times* – she was anxiously checking share prices – 'I'm giving a talk about graphology . . .'

'Are you?' she said. 'Oh you didn't tell me that. Who for?'

'For . . . the . . . Hackney W.I.'

'What date?' she enquired, as she got out the desk diary.

'Um, February the thirtieth,' I replied. 'I, er, need to read that article on celebrity handwriting the *Post* did a few months ago. Would you mind going down to the library and digging it out for me? Thanks.'

Serena returned with the cutting twenty minutes later, and I went into the interviewing room so that I could be alone. Electra had begged for my 'total discretion' and she was going to get it two hundred per cent. I looked at the article under a strong light, then studied the letter. I couldn't compare the pressure on the paper of course, but I could see that the handwriting was exactly the same. The shape of each letter was identical, so was every up-stroke and down-stroke and loop. The size of the letters was uniform, and so were the crosses and dots. There was no doubt about it – it was the genuine article. Now what the hell did I do?

I wanted to write to her from home; but what if I was mugged with the letter in my bag? – I'd just been burgled after all. So I left it locked away, and decided I'd stay late and deal with it then.

At five I came back to my desk from the ladies' loo to find a new e-mail on the screen, from Ricky, headed *Serena's Pay Rise*. *Sorry*, he'd written, *no can do*. I resolved to ask him again, in a few days' time, when I'd have less pressing things on my mind. It wasn't purely altruism that prompted me, it was self-interest – Serena needed to feel happy to do her job well. In any case I wasn't taking no for an answer because I knew it was something that Ricky could afford to do. The *Daily Post* makes a huge profit, and Serena is loyal and hard working – she deserves it. At six-thirty she put on her coat.

'I'm off, Rose. I'm going home. Are you working late?' she added solicitously.

'Yes I am. You know how it is.'

'Well, I'll be on my way then. See you tomorrow,' she added, then she left the office, along with most of the Features team. Now that everyone had gone I relaxed. I left the letter locked in my desk – only I have keys – then went down to the canteen to get something to eat. By the time I came back up half an hour later, I'd worked out what to say.

To my surprise, I found it very easy to be firm. I refused to be fazed by the fact that Electra's a mega-star: she was simply a reader who needed my help. So I told her – well, obviously confidentiality prevents me from telling you *what* I told her; but suffice to say that I indicated that her infatuation with her female backing singer was extremely unlikely to last. I also asked her to consider the effect on her kids – poor lambs. I could imagine little Cinnamon's tear-stained face, not to mention baby Alfie's cries. I typed it up, sealed it, then fed her letter into the shredder. As the strips were extruded I caught them, and cut them widthways, several times. Then I went into the ladies and flushed the confetti-sized fragments down the loo. I did not, of course, leave my reply in the office out-tray – too risky: I stamped it and posted it on my way home.

As I walked to the bus stop I reflected on how much that letter had been worth. A fortune. It was like having a five-carat diamond in my hand. And you might think that I should have given it to Ricky, but to me being an agony aunt is like being a priest. *Write to me in strictest confidence* it says on my page; and my readers know that they can. The secrets they tell me will go to my grave. Edith Smugg would have been proud of me.

Chapter Twelve

The knowledge that someone as famous as Electra had placed her trust in me buoyed me up in the run-up to Valentine's Day. I was dreading starting my divorce proceedings because it would mean contact – indirectly – with Ed. But I had only to think of his heartless indifference to my readers' suffering to strengthen me in my resolve. How would he have characterised Electra I wondered wryly: 'Glum of Gloucestershire'? 'Crestfallen of the Cotswolds'?; 'Miserable of Moreton-in-the-Marsh'? I imagined that titchy bitch, Mary-Claire Grey, smothering him with Valentine's kitsch – a chocolate heart with his name on quite possibly, or a 'cute' teddy with outstretched paws, or one of those cheap red satin cushions emblazoned with *I Luv U!* Well the only billet-doux he was going to get from me was a divorce petition, on tasteful cream vellum, citing his adultery. I'd already signed it, ready for Frances to send: it was like a cruise missile, primed for launch.

I wondered what I could expect in the way of Valentine's endearments – not much. I'd been averting my eyes from the sickly displays: why torture myself? As for all those emetic messages in the newspapers – give me a break. It's just mush-brained, unabashed baby-talk – it's totally infantile: I mean, who *cares* if Luscious-Lips loves Chicken Pie I said crossly as I opened *The Times* at the bus stop on Tuesday morning. Who gives a toss that Wombat has the hots for Twinkle Toes? I'm not remotely interested in the fact that Tiger-bum adores Jumbo Prawn or that Fat-Face sends big snogs to La-La. And no, I couldn't care *less* that *Bunny Wabbit Finks Andwoo is Weely Wundaful!* it's just sick-making sentimental *tosh*. Bunny Wabbit? I stared at the paper, eyes popping like ping-pong balls. Where the other messages were all tiny classifieds, this one was huge, and boxed. It shouted its absurd blandishments in thick capitals half an inch high. I rummaged in my bag – it's such a mess – for my mobile, then hit the speed-dial button for Bea.

'You've got to take Bella to the head doctor,' I said. 'I've just seen it.'

'I know, it cost her three grand!'

'*What*!' In the background I could hear hammering and sawing.

'That would pay half our fitting-up costs. We've just had the mother of all rows and she stomped out of the shop. She says it's her own private cash, not the company money, and she can do what she likes – I went mad! Worse, she claims it was "worth every penny" because Andrew's the "love of her life." '

'What are you going to do Bea?'

'I don't know. It's going to be hard enough to get the business up and running as it is without Bella going bonkers, plus we're arguing all the time. She says she's not happy to be the one who minds the shop and does the accounts – she wants to go out on site as well. But the fact is that when it comes to design Bella couldn't find her own backside with both hands. I mean, the other day she had to ask me what the difference was between Swedish Provincial and Rustic Guatemalan!'

'Hmmm. That doesn't augur well.'

'It's all because of that idiot, Andrew,' she added angrily. 'The excitement of having a boyfriend – however sub-standard – has sent Bella round the twist. Ooh, change the subject quick Rose, she's just coming back.'

'Okay. Er, did you send Henry something for Valentine's Day?'

'Yes. A really nice card.'

'And have you had one from him?'

'Er, no I haven't,' she said casually; 'at least, not *yet*.'

'Well I'm sure you'll get something,' I said reassuringly. 'He's terribly thoughtful like that.'

'Oh yes,' she said airily, 'I'm not worried about it. I'm not worried about it at all. Er, did he send you a Valentine's card when you were going out with him?'

'No,' I replied truthfully. 'He didn't.' He actually sent me two dozen red roses and a huge box of Bendicks. I heard Bea exhale with relief.

'And did you get anything today?' she enquired anxiously.

'Absolutely zilch. There was nothing in the post at home, and I'm just on my way to work. I know I won't get one but I really don't care – I mean, who needs it, Bea?'

Yeah, who *needs* it? I repeated as I stamped up the steps of Amalgamated House. February the fourteenth is just a silly love-fest I told myself as I crossed the foyer and got the lift up to the tenth floor. It's not even romantic – it's big business, it's ruthlessly mercantile. They should call it Interflora Day, or Hallmark Day or Veuve Cliquot Day instead. I shall simply give it the cold shoulder, like I did Christmas, I decided as I arrived at my desk. As for being taken out to dinner tête-à-tête – no thanks! Nothing could be worse than sitting in a restaurant with a load of gruesome twosomes who are simply responding to the imperatives of the calendar. And what about the notorious Valentine's Day Massacre, I reminded myself grimly as I pondered my huge pile of mail. No, I really couldn't give a *damn* about it I repeated as I quickly riffled through the pile of post. Letter, letter, letter, flyer, letter, letter, letter, post-card, letter, letter, letter, invitation, letter, letter, letter, airmail, letter, letter, letter, letter, *Valentine's card!!!* YEAAAAAHHHHHHHH!!!!!!

'GOT ONE!' I shouted, to a surprised-looking Serena.

'Got what?'

I held up a large, red envelope and smiled. 'A Valentine. Phew. Thank *God*!' I now noticed that the card felt slightly thick, squidgy almost. Hmm. 'Did you get one from Rob?' I enquired.

'Er, no. He's got a lot on his plate, with work. You know how it is.'

Thanks to Andrew, I did.

'I'm sure he'll get you something,' I said soothingly as I ripped open the envelope. Serena seemed even more tense than usual and it was only half past nine. 'Are you okay?' I asked her. She was tidying out her drawer.

'Yes, except for that awful rain last night. We had a very bad leak.'

'Oh dear.'

'I was up all night emptying buckets, so I'm rather tired. Still,' she said philosophically, 'it's my own fault for not getting it fixed. A stitch in time saves nine and all that, and they say there'll be more storms tonight.'

The card resisted slightly as I tried to pull it out of the envelope, so I gave it a good, sharp tug. As I did so a shower of something – I didn't know what – suddenly shot through the air.

'What the – ?' Tiny bits of tissue paper flew up, then floated down in a light cloud, like confetti, covering my hair and clothes. I felt like a figure in a shaken snowstorm as they gently descended, strewing my desk.

'What on earth are those?' said Serena as they fluttered and pirouetted through the air like a blizzard of bonsai ticker-tape. She picked one off her jumper and examined it. 'They've got writing on them. Look!' Printed on both sides, in neat red letters, was *CSThnknAU*.

'CSThnknAU,' I read out, wonderingly. It was like a Scrabble hand. 'What on earth does that mean? Is it Czech?' I added.

'No.'

'Polish?'

'It's a text message,' Serena explained. 'I've got a little book of them, hang on.' She opened her top drawer and took out a tiny dictionary. 'CantW82XU,' she said, 'no, that's Can't Wait To Kiss You; CUIMD – that's See You In My Dreams; ah ha! CSThnknAU – Can't Stop Thinking About You. That's what it is.'

'Oh. I see.'

There were hundreds of them – maybe a thousand – they seemed to get everywhere. As I blew them off my keyboard and brushed them off my chair I wondered who could have sent them to me. I looked at the card, which bore the same strange message, encircled by a heart: inside there was no signature, just two crosses and a large question mark. On the back was printed the name of the company, Confettimail, whose slogan was 'Spread The Word.' Well, they certainly did that all right: their words got everywhere. I called the given number, gave them my name, and asked to know who my card was from.

'I'm afraid we can't tell you that,' said the woman at the other end.

'But can't you give me a clue?'

'I'm sorry, but it's confidential.'

I had a brainwave. 'But I'd like to send him something too. I think I know who it is actually,' I lied, 'but I just need to make absolutely sure.'

'Oh, then in that case,' she said judiciously, 'I can give you a *tiny* hint. The man who ordered it sounded rather nervous, and said you'd be "annoyed" if you knew.'

My heart sank to the soles of my shoes: just what I'd dreaded – it was Colin Twisk. I'd hoped it wouldn't prove to be – but who else would come up with something like this? Something guaranteed simultaneously to capture my attention and irritate the hell out of me. He'd said I'd be annoyed and I was! I was also dreadfully disappointed I realised miserably as I pulled them out of my hair. If it were from anyone else I'd have been pleased; but with Creepy Colin it was symbolic of the way I couldn't get rid of the guy. Like these tiny bits of paper, he was ubiquitous and invasive, reaching into the nooks and crannies of my life.

All day long, I kept finding them. I'd go to the loo and at least six would flutter out of my knickers; there were even a couple lodged in my bra. They'd got into my shirt, and my shoes, and my ears – they were everywhere. Each time I thought I'd got them all, I'd be sure to find a few more.

What a bore I thought bitterly as I delicately extracted one from my left nostril; and it was depressing too, because a year ago my friends had thrown real confetti over me, on the steps of the Chelsea Town Hall. All I'd wanted today was just one simple Valentine card to remind me that I wasn't completely unloved. Trevor, by contrast, had received eighteen from his new army of devoted fans. I found myself in the novel, and morally challenging, position of being jealous of a dog.

'There are another five for Trev,' Linda announced as the second post arrived after lunch. She put them in a large jiffy bag. 'I'll send them to him first class.'

'No, don't post them,' I said, 'I can take them round. Then he'll get them today.'

'Okay, thanks. Reception called to say they've had a bouquet for him too, so don't forget to pick that up.'

'I won't.'

'And there's a large box of Bonios.'

'Right.'

'And a presentation box of Good Boy! chocolate drops.'

'Got it.'

'And a gift-wrapped squeaky toy.'

'*Okay . . .*'

At five, I wondered again about my divorce petition, and phoned Frances, who told me that it hadn't gone out.

'But I thought he'd get it today.' I felt crestfallen – I'd hoped to make a dramatic impact – then suddenly strangely relieved.

'You have to have been married for a year and a day,' Frances explained, 'which means he won't actually get it until the sixteenth.'

As I put the phone down I realised I hadn't spoken to Ed for almost five months. I'd resolved to cut him right out of my life, and I'd done it. I felt proud of my self-control, but all day I'd wondered whether he'd been thinking of me and of our wedding exactly one year ago. As I made my way home I reflected on why we'd married: well, because we were mutually attracted, that's why, and at a stage in our lives

210

when we were willing to marry. We were also available. I could hardly believe my luck that someone as conspicuously attractive and engaging as Ed was still single. But for some reason, which we'd never discussed – well, what's the point? – his previous relationships hadn't worked out. There had been women, of course – as I say, he's sex on legs – but they'd never lasted more than a few months. Perhaps he'd been unfaithful to them as well, but he would never have admitted that.

I thought of the house in Putney again with a bitter sigh. He'd only just bought it when we met – it had cost him an arm and a leg. And I remember the first time I saw it being amazed at its size. I found it odd that a single man with no kids – and no intention of having any – should choose to live in such a huge place. But Ed explained that it was the house he'd dreamed of owning one day, when he was a small boy and terribly poor. After his father died, the family had to move into this two-bedroomed cottage on the outskirts of Derby. He showed me a photo of it once – it looked *tiny* – I don't know how they all fitted in. Ed shared one bedroom with his two younger brothers – in bunks – while his mother slept with the girls. And he said that it was so unbearably cramped and claustrophobic that he'd had this obsession ever since with having *space*. So much so that, for example, he can instantly calculate the square footage of any property he enters. He should have been an estate agent I'd sometimes thought.

'All my life I've wanted a really spacious house with large rooms,' he'd explained. 'The biggest I could possibly afford.' So for the past fifteen years he'd traded up and up, buying shrewdly, moving constantly until, finally, he'd bought Blenheim Road. I used to tease him about it. I called it his 'Putney Palace'. Don't get me wrong – it's lovely – but it's just rather big for one person on their own. It's a white-fronted, stuccoed, Victorian semi-detached villa, done up in a classic English way. Yellow speckled wallpaper in the drawing room, pale green soft furnishings; a smart oxblood on the dining room walls, a soft coral below the dado on the stairs. And in his bedroom, periwinkle blue and cream, with a co-ordinating window seat. It was all so quietly elegant, so understated, so beautifully *comme il faut*. It had four further bedrooms, two en suite, and the kitchen was a dream. Lovely glazed terracotta tiles on the floor and an Aga in a distinguished dark blue. I sighed. Hope Street, though charmingly raffish, was a far cry from Blenheim Road. I put up my hand to ring Beverley's bell, but Trevor had got there first.

'Happy Valentine's Day Trev,' I said as he let me in. I handed him the jiffy bag. 'You're a very popular guy.' Tail wagging, he ushered me into the sitting room, where he and Bev were watching TV.

'He's got twenty-three cards,' I announced as he settled himself back on his beanbag. I handed her the bouquet and the gifts.

'Nice going Trev,' Bev said with a laugh. 'Some of us had to make do with one! Not that I'm complaining,' she added with a smile. I looked at her Valentine positioned in the centre of her mantelpiece. It simply said 'You're A Star!' The word 'star' gave it away; it was clearly from Theo – who else? He'd said Bev was 'special' and 'wonderful' and he called her 'pet'.

'How lovely,' I said suppressing a pang.

'I don't know who sent it,' she fibbed.

'I bet you do really.'

'I *don't!*'

'Well Trevor revealed in his column that you'd sent someone a card,' I said nonchalantly.

'*Did* he?' she replied with an enigmatic smile. But I knew who Bev had bought it for – she'd bought it for Theo of course. 'LOVE *ME*!' it had commanded in red glittery letters; he must have had it by now. As I helped Bev put up Trevor's cards – several containing photos of hopeful-looking girl dogs – I looked at all her trophies and medals and shields. We usually sit in her kitchen when I go round, so I'd never seen them before. There were twelve, all engraved with her name.

'You *are* a star Bev,' I said quietly as I looked at them.

'You're amazing. You excelled not just in one sport, but in three.' She shrugged. 'But why did you change from athletics to hockey?'

'Because I was getting too old for the track; plus I'm not really an individualist, Rose; I wanted to play in a team – I still do. I hate working on my own here all day, for example, even though I'm with Trev. I'd love to go *out* to work,' she said with sudden ferocity: 'I get so desperately lonely here; it drives me crazy . . .' Her voice trailed away. Suddenly Trevor got up, went into the hall, returned with the phone, then tried to put it in her lap.

'It's okay Trev,' she said gently. 'I don't need to call a friend, Rose is here. Put it back. If he thinks I'm sad he brings me the phone,' Bev explained again. 'He hit on that idea without me even asking him – he thought it up all by himself.'

'I hope you're not sad,' I said.

'Not really,' she sighed, 'it's just that I feel very isolated at times, and I do get a bit down working from home, and . . . anyway,' she forced her features into a grim smile, 'enough of all that. Any news of Rudy?' she asked, clearly wishing to change the subject.

I shook my head. 'The police are looking, but I don't think I'll see him again. It's terribly sad.'

Back home I looked at the empty space where Rudy's cage had been: without him the kitchen was horribly quiet. His non-stop chatter had been so irritating, but now he'd gone I missed it like mad. I just hoped that whoever had him was looking after him properly and peeling his grapes, like I do; I hoped that they were keeping him warm, and watered, and cleaning him out every day. I hoped they talked to him when they were there, and put the radio on when they went out. As I took off my coat I saw that the sleeves were covered with Trevor's golden hairs. And I was just reluctantly reaching for the clothes brush – I could hardly be bothered – when I heard a huge BOOM! and glanced outside. The semi-twilight had turned to pitch as the towering cumulo-nimbus churned and boiled; and now the rain began to strafe the windows like machine gun fire – except that it wasn't rain, but hail. White stones, like ball bearings, were driving down with such force I thought they'd shatter the panes. I dashed outside where I'd left my garden tools – I'm *so* careless these days – and as I ran back inside I glanced up. Theo's dormer window was wide open. There was no security risk because it's up in the roof but I knew that the hail would come in. So I decided to close it to protect his computer and telescope – I didn't think he'd mind. I ran upstairs and as I went to the window I saw that his table was already quite wet: the pages of his desk diary, which he'd left open, were becoming rippled and mottled with damp. As I shut the window I averted my eyes from them – but then something caught my eye. My name.

Rose is very . . . – his writing was so unreadable it might as well have been in Esperanto – *Rose is very*, I tried again, *diff* . . . *t*. Diffident obviously. Something . . . *mother* . . . *problems* . . . *feel sorry* . . . *very* something . . . *ctive*. That looked like 'active'. Well, I am very active. I've got a lot of energy. Something . . . *but* . . . *a b* . . . *pole*. Hhmmm. A beanpole? Well it's true. And on the facing page I was just able to make out, '. . . *and Henry's clearly keen on Bea.*'

As I say, I only read those few words because the journal was open, but of course I didn't read any more; because although I was quite naturally consumed with curiosity, reading someone else's diary is the pits. And I was just leaving his room when I suddenly heard, *Would You Like to Swing on A Star, Carry Moonbeams Home in a Jar?* His mobile phone – identical to my own – was lying on his bed. He'd forgotten to take it with him. I peered at it and there, on the screen, were the letters, *BEV/H* – he'd clearly programmed in her number – and there was the dancing telephone icon, and at the bottom of the screen it said 'Answer?' *Would You Like to Swing on a Star* . . . Now it had stopped, and then a few seconds later I heard the trill of his voicemail alert and the ringing envelope appeared on the screen. I stared at it, and then, involuntarily, my hand reached out and I did this awful thing. I picked up the phone, pressed the voicemail button, and held it to my ear. 'You have one new message. Message sent today at six-fifteen.'

'Hi sweetie!' I heard Bev say. 'It's only me. Just ringing for a chat. Hope you've had a lovely Valentine's Day! I've had a *very* nice one,' she giggled. ' Talk to you later darling! Byeee!!!'

'End call?' it enquired, so I pressed OK. My hand shook slightly as I put the phone down. Theo was Beverley's 'sweetie' and her 'darling'. *Well* . . . I don't know why she's bothering to deny that she's interested – I mean, what's the point of being coy? And obviously that Valentine she'd bought *was* for him, and now I wondered where it was. It wasn't on his mantelpiece, or on his desk. I ran downstairs and looked, but there was no trace of it. Perhaps he was too shy to display it: perhaps he'd tucked it away in a drawer, or, quite possibly, Beverley had sent it to his office, to add to the fun and mystery. I was distracted from further speculation by the sound of my own phone ringing. I picked up the receiver and heard snuffling and heavy breathing at the other end. My stomach clenched – it was my nuisance caller – then I realised it was Bea, in tears.

'What's the problem?' I said.

'Henry didn't get me *anything!*' she wailed. 'That's what. Not a card – not even one half-dead poxy red rose.'

'Oh dear. Are you quite sure?'

'Yes.'

'Does it really matter?'

'Well, it's not a good sign,' she sobbed. 'Whereas Andrew – uh-uh – sent Bella a huge bunch of flowers.'

'When are you seeing Henry again?'

'Next week. We're – uh-uh – going to a military tattoo.'

'But he wouldn't keep asking you out if he wasn't interested, would he Bea?'

There was a momentary silence, then a wet sniff. 'I asked him,' she croaked.

'Oh. Well he wouldn't *go* if he wasn't bothered about you. He'd make some excuse.' I heard her blow her nose.

'That's true.'

'I'm sure he likes you, otherwise he'd avoid you.'

'Really?'

'Yes, I think he would.'

'Oh Rose,' she said, audibly brightening, 'you're such a *brilliant* agony aunt. I feel so much better now. I was so mis because Andrew and Bella have gone off for a smoochy dinner somewhere and I haven't even got a date. But you've really cheered me up. I'm not going to mope,' she went on bravely. 'I'm going to spend the evening reading *Jane's Defence Weekly*, there's this brilliant article on tube-launched tactical Tomahawk cruise missiles. Then when I see Henry next time we'll have *heaps* to talk about, won't we?'

'Of course you will,' I agreed. I glanced at the clock. 'Ooh, can't chat; I've got my phone-in – the cab will be here in a sec.' As I stood up, I realised I ought to tidy the cushions and sort out the old newspapers but I simply couldn't be fagged; plus there was a layer of dust on the mantelpiece and the windows were filthy . . . I groaned. I heard the taxi pull up, so I ran out and climbed into the back; as I did so my handbag rang.

'Rose!' It was Henry.

'That's funny,' I said as I shut the door. 'I've just been talking to Bea.'

'Really?' he said suspiciously. 'About what?'

'About the . . . shop. It was really nice of you to help them find premises. Are you going to the opening party?'

'I don't know. Actually Rose, there was something I wanted to ask you . . . that's why I'm calling. I've been meaning to talk to you for some time.' I leaned forward and shut the glass partition which separated me from the driver.

'Okay, I'm all ears.'

'It's about Bea,' he began slightly wearily as we chugged up Kennington Road. 'I mean, she's a super girl . . .'

'Yes she is,' I said as I glanced out of the window onto the rain-swept streets.

'But . . . I don't, you know, feel it's quite . . . right.' My heart sank: Bea would be broken-hearted. I felt a stab of vicarious pain. 'I do *like* her and everything,' he went on, 'but, well, the fact is . . .' his voice trailed away.

'Don't you find her attractive?' I asked as we sped past the Oval.

'Yes, but that's not what it's about. It's just that I can't see it going anywhere because well, you see, the point is . . .'

'Look, you don't have to explain,' I interrupted. 'I know why it's tricky with Bea.'

'You do?'

'Of course.'

'I simply can't help the way I feel,' he said as we drove round the Elephant and Castle.

'And I don't think Bea will react well,' I pointed out.

'You're dead right,' he sighed. 'She won't.'

'I mean, cross-dressing is just not her thing.'

'What?'

'Your cross-dressing,' I repeated as we drove through Southwark. 'She won't like it. She's much too strait-laced.'

'Oh. Hmm,' he said quietly. 'That's right.'

'So maybe it's best to be honest. I mean, it's entirely up to you whether you tell her about . . . Henrietta,' I said delicately, 'but if you're not interested in her, you really shouldn't drag things out. Ooh, sorry!' I giggled. 'But you know what I mean.' There was a moment's silence during which I was aware only of the swish of the tyres on the road.

'You're right Rose,' Henry sighed as we crossed Blackfriars Bridge. 'The last thing I want to do is mess her about. Especially with this big party they're having. She keeps telling me how much she's looking forward to all her friends meeting me, but I don't feel comfortable with that. And she sent me this Valentine card.'

'*Did* she?' I asked disingenuously.

'Yes.'

'How do you know?'

'Because I recognised her handwriting on the envelope. But I didn't send her one.'

'Oh dear.'

'You're right, Rose,' he said. 'I'll have to grasp the nettle. I'll do it before I go back to the Gulf in March. How's your flatmate?' he asked suddenly, as we turned into City Road.

'Theo? Oh he's fine. He and Beverley are terribly secretive but it's Valentine's cards and sweet nothings all round. Ooh I've arrived. Sorry, I can't chat any more, I'm on air in ten minutes. But do be honest with Bea, Henry, and that way you'll hurt her less.'

'Yes. Yes . . .' he said distractedly. 'You're right.'

As I climbed out of the cab I suddenly remembered Bea's confident prediction that Bella was ' heading for a fall'. Rather ironic in the circumstances, and Theo had got things wrong too. In his diary he'd written that Henry was 'very keen on Bea'. No stars for observation there. But then they clearly haven't quite got that knack I have of being able to read between the lines.

For some reason – the knock-on effect of the burglary, per-haps, or, more likely, too much hospitality plonk – I found I wasn't really in the mood for my phone-in. I was in a funny, flippant frame of mind.

'Welcome to London FM if you've just tuned in,' said a very pregnant Minty, 'and a Happy Valentine's Day to you all. You're listening to our regular phone-in, *Sound Advice*, with Rose Costelloe of the *Daily Post*. And now it's Tanya from Tooting on line one.'

'Hello Rose!'

'Hi Tanya, how can I help?'

'Well I've got a tricky problem in that I'd like to dump my boyfriend but the problem is he hasn't called me recently.'

'Oh, I see. Well, this *is* a tricky one, Tanya,' I replied, with another sip of Frascati. 'I find it's always best to have a man's undivided attention when attempting to give him the boot.'

'Should I phone him and tell him it's over then?'

'No. That's much too crude. What I'd do is get him to come round to your place on some pretext – to help get your car started, say, or to clear the drains. Then, when he's done that, thank him effusively and tell him what a *wonderful* guy he is.

Then "break it to him" as gently as you can that you're afraid you won't be seeing him any more. This will simultaneously confuse and annoy the hell out of him, leaving you feeling *great*. And now I see we have Janice from Hampstead on line two.'

'My problem is my best friend's husband,' she said. 'He's such a bore.'

'In what way?'

'He insists on sprinkling his conversation with foreign words to show how clever he is. He talks about how he's an "aficionado" of Mexican cinema for example – I mean an "afi*thi*onado"' she corrected herself. 'He goes on about how "langlauf" is his favourite sport; and how he prefers his salad "*au naturel*"; he lets drop that Oxford was his "alma mater" and that he's into "gestalt" psychology. It's pathetic,' she concluded vehemently.

'It is: it's also "bourgeois" and "arriviste". Next time he does it, politely point out to him that English is *the* international language, "*par excellence*" – on the other hand, Janice, "*chacun à son goût*".'

'And now,' said Minty, 'we have Alan from Acton, whose problem is that his wife is a heavy smoker.'

'Really? How much does she weigh?'

'She's on forty a day,' he explained. 'It's absolutely disgusting, but she won't give it up. I keep telling her about the health risks but she just ignores me, what can I do?'

'Well, don't bawl her out about carcinogens – that's clearly never going to work – I suggest that you lie instead. Simply tell her that new research shows that smoking gives women fat ankles: I guarantee she'll stop like a shot.'

It was ten to twelve and I was terribly tired by now: I had another swig of white wine.

'And now,' said Minty, 'we have Martine on line four. What would you like to ask Rose?'

'Oh I don't want to ask her anything,' she said. 'I just want to thank her, for giving me some great advice.'

'Remind us of the story will you?' said Minty. But I'd already remembered. I don't forget these ones.

'Well, I was distraught because I can't have kids,' Martine began, 'so I wanted to adopt. But my husband wouldn't agree to it because he was adopted, but now, thanks to Rose, he has.'

'Well, that's just wonderful,' said Minty warmly.

'You see,' Martine went on, 'his problem was that he'd never really faced up to the pain he'd felt all his life at knowing that he'd been given up.' I fiddled with the stem of my wine glass. 'Psychologists call it the "Primal Wound" don't they, when a baby is taken away from its mother. But, on Rose's advice, my husband had counselling from someone at NORCAP about it, and it just seemed to – set him *free*. It was as though he'd been liberated,' she went on, her voice quivering, 'and this enabled him to search for his mum.' I raised the glass and had another large sip of wine: this was more than I wanted to know. 'And the amazing thing is that he actually found her – just ten days ago.' Oh *God*. 'He found his mother,' she repeated, 'and he phoned her; it was as though a wall in his mind had come down.' My face was suddenly uncomfortably warm and I felt the familiar ache in my throat. 'They met last week for the first time in thirty-seven years,' I heard her say. 'And now he understands why she did what she did.' I stared at my pad, and saw, with a kind of detached interest, that my scribbled notes had begun to blur. 'He'd carried this hatred around in his heart for so long, but now, at last, it's gone . . .' A tear dropped onto the page with a tiny splash and the black felt tip began to bleed. '. . . so I just wanted to say a huge thank you to Rose because now I'm hoping to be a mum.'

There was a moment's silence, then I heard Minty say, 'That's a lovely story. Isn't it Rose?' She pushed a tissue across the padded table.

'Yes,' I croaked. 'It's great.'

'Well, thanks to everyone who's called in tonight,' she added warmly. 'Do join Rose and me again on Thursday but, until then, goodbye. Are you okay Rose?' she added solici-tously as the signature tune played us out.

'Sorry?'

'Are you all right?'

'Oh. I'm fine.'

'It was a very moving story,' she said quietly as we left the studio. 'I was close to tears myself. It must be great though, knowing how much you can help other people with their problems.'

'Mmm,' I agreed with a sniff. 'It is. It's . . . wonderful,' I murmured, my throat aching. I just wished that someone could help me with mine.

I went slowly down the stairs, Martine's words still ringing in my ears as I waited for my cab. *Never really faced up to it. . . . Primal wound . . . carried this hatred around.* The rain was falling like stair rods as I pushed on the door and stepped outside. *Saw his mum for the first time in thirty-seven years . . . as though a wall in his mind had come down.* As we sped through the City, the buildings spun past the window in a blur of raindrops and strobing lights. I distractedly wiped away the film of condensation with the back of my hand. *At last he understands why she did what she did. It's as though he's been set free.* I stared straight ahead, aware only of the metronomic sweep of the windscreen wipers, and the surprising heat of my tears.

Chapter Thirteen

If just one more person thanks me for 'helping' them with their lives, I am going to puke! It happened again this morning. There I was, on the number thirty-six, enjoying the crossword, temporarily stuck on thirteen down: 'Big trouble, sis! Tread with care' – an anagram of 'sis' and 'tread', clearly – when Bella phoned oozing gratitude.

'It's thanks to you that I met Andrew,' she gushed as we trundled along. 'Because without you I wouldn't have gone to that ball.'

'In that case you should thank Beverley,' I pointed out as we drew up at a bus stop. 'After all, it was her gig, not mine.'

'Yes, but you invited me Rose: and little did I realise as I got ready that night, that I was about to meet my Fate! I'm so glad I met him,' she went on ecstatically as I showed the conductor my travelcard. 'Did I tell you we're going skiing the day after tomorrow. Klosters. You know, where Prince Charles goes.'

'You're going *skiing*? But what about the shop?'

'Oh we're only going for a week,' she said airily.

'But how will Bea manage on her own?'

'She'll be *fine*. She does most of the organising as it is, Rose, she likes it that way – you know her. And to be honest I've realised that my personal happiness is far more important than my business success.' As Bella droned on about Andrew and about how 'gorgeous' he was I glanced down at the crossword clue again. 'Sis! Tread', anagrammatised. What was it? S, i, s, t, r . . .

'There was just one other thing I wanted tell you, Rose,' I heard Bella add.

'Oh, what's that?'

'Well, you know your assistant Serena's husband works for Andrew.'

'Yes, Rob,' I said as I glanced out of the window at the clumps of daffodil buds in the park.

'The thing is, well it's rather unfortunate, but I'm afraid he's had to be sacked.' Had to be sacked?

'But they've got three young kids,' I pointed out hotly.

'I know,' she sighed, 'it's very sad. But apparently he was useless at his job. Now the reason I'm telling you is in case Serena mentions it, because if she does, she'll probably portray Andrew in a negative light, and obviously I wouldn't like that at all.'

'Don't worry Bella,' I said calmly. 'Whatever Serena said to me about Andrew couldn't possibly affect my opinion of him in *any* way.'

'Oh that's such a relief,' she breathed. And I was tempted to tell her just what my opinion of Andrew *really* was when she added, 'well must dash. Got to get my skates on – or skis rather! – see you at the party, Rose. Byeeee!'

I looked at thirteen down again. Sis, tread, anagrammatised. Got it! 'Disaster'. How apt.

When I got to work I saw that Serena was on the phone. She was still wearing her coat, which was odd, and she was whispering and looked very distressed. She glanced up, then saw me and slammed the receiver down as though it were red hot.

'Hi Serena!' I said with a cheerfulness so bright I risked damaging her retinas. 'How are you today?'

'Oh I'm *fine*,' she replied nervously. 'I'm fine. Yes, yes, yes . . . yes. I'm fine. I'm fine, I'm fine,' she gibbered, unable this morning to summon a single cheery cliché with which to console herself. 'Of course I am. I'm fine. Why do you ask?'

'Er, because I always do, that's why.'

'Well I'm absolutely *fine*,' she repeated, 'I'm fine.

Absolutely. I'm . . . Right,' she said, grabbing the pile of mail, 'let's get down to work.'

She started ripping open the letters, her hands visibly trembling, her eyeballs practically swivelling in her head. Poor Serena: this latest blow about Rob's job could send her right over the edge. But she clearly didn't want to confide in me about his dismissal, so I pretended I had no idea. As she date-stamped the letters I sent Ricky another urgent e-mail about her pay rise and got a nasty one straight back. *Rose, if you don't stop banging on about this I will not renew your contract when it comes up in March. For your information the Daily Post is a national newspaper, not a charity for life's losers. R.*

Serena and I turned to the day's mail – acne, bedwetting, blushing, male menopause, snoring and thinning hair. There was also another letter from Colin Twisk. I recognised his rather feminine, loopy handwriting and took a deep breath. What would it contain today? Another shower of Confettimail? An invitation to dinner? More absurdly lavish praise?

Dear Miss Costelloe, I read. *I am writing to tell you how disappointed I am in you.* Oh . . . *I cannot believe that a woman for whom I have always had the highest regard can behave in such a depraved way.* What??? *When I saw the new Helplines on your page I was shocked to my core – and revolted. 'How to Spice Up Your Sex Life? Sexual Fetishes? I could not at first believe that you could be responsible for such unadulterated filth. But I have since discovered not only that you had recorded these frankly pornographic pieces, but that you had actually composed them yourself! Notwithstanding the excellent advice you once gave me – which, may I say, has led to my happy association with my new friend, Penelope Boink – I have to inform you that, as from today, I will no longer be reading your page. I am henceforth switching to one of your rivals, June Snort, at the Daily News. I am also discontinuing forthwith what had heretofore and hitherto been a very pleasant epistolary association with you. Yours in disgust. C. Twisk.*

I read it again in amazement, then looked up at Serena and grinned.

'Hurrah and hallelujah!' I declared. 'I've just had some very good news.'

'Lucky you,' she replied bitterly.

'Creepy Colin's gone off. He's disgusted with me because of the helplines – that's made my day. I'll make them *really* disgusting now,' I added, vehemently, 'just to make sure he never bothers me again. What could I do Serena? Three-in-a-Bed-Sex, no, Six-in-a-Bed Sex; no Six*teen*-in-a-Bed-Sex; Sex Toys; Sex Games; Same Sex Sex; Orgiastic Sex; Sexual Perversion; Spanking; How to Swing. What do you think, Serena?'

'Well the new ones are certainly popular,' she pointed out, slightly calmer now. 'Accounts say we've had thousands of calls.'

In which case Ricky can definitely up her pay a bit I reflected crossly. I'd go and see him again tomorrow and I would *not* take no for an answer – in fact I'd bawl him out. I calmed myself again with the happy thought of Colin taking himself off. No more creepy, kiss-covered letters, I reflected ecstatically. No more silent calls. No more worrying that he'd turn up at the house. No more Confettimail. I reread his letter. *Forthwith . . . heretofore . . . hitherto . . .* What a pompous little git. Right! I fired off a short sharp letter of my own, telling him how delighted I was at the prospect of never hearing from him again either by letter – or by telephone at home, I added meaningfully; then I flung it in the post tray as joy-fully as I would skim a large, flat stone. Cheered, uplifted and invigorated I phoned my solicitor, Frances, to find out about the status of my divorce.

'We haven't had the Acknowledgement of Service back yet,' she explained.

'Well how long does it take?'

'It has to be returned within eight working days. Apparently there was a two day post strike in Putney last week which means he won't have got it until the eighteenth. So, taking account of the fact that today's Wednesday, we should have it by the twenty-seventh.'

'Well if he doesn't send it, presumably you'll chase up his solicitor.'

'He doesn't have one – he's doing it himself.'

'Why?'

'Well because it's all pretty straightforward and presumably he wants to save himself a few grand.'

At lunchtime I didn't go down to the canteen as I often do, but had a sandwich at my desk. Serena went out, which is unusual for her, but I imagined that with all her current stress she needed some air. And I was just chomping on my bacon and avocado ciabatta when Bea rang me on my mobile, in floods.

'What's the matter? Is it Henry?' I whispered.

'Oh no. It's this bloody skiing holiday. I'm absolutely frantic: is Bella being selfish or what!'

'She doesn't mean to be,' I said – I never take sides with the twins – 'it's just that she's not thinking straight. Her judgement's temporarily shot to pieces.'

'You're telling me. How the hell am I going to manage on my own?' Bea wailed. 'It's the launch party next week. I interviewed a temp this morning but she was an absolute moron. I need someone *intelligent*.'

'I'd help you myself Bea if I wasn't so busy here, but I could give you a hand tonight.'

'Thanks, but it's during the day that I need it. I don't know which way to turn,' she went on desperately. 'I didn't even have time to see Henry – he phoned up and suggested lunch. I was thrilled of course, but I'm just too busy, so we've postponed it for a few days. The painters are still here and I've got to make several trips to the cash and carry to get the booze for the party, plus I've got client meetings to attend. I need someone bright and responsible who'll supervise the workmen for the next couple of days while I'm out and answer the phone. But who could I ask? I don't know anyone.'

'Nor do I,' I said. Hang on! *I'd love to go out to work. I get so lonely.* 'Oh yes I do – Bev!'

'What?'

'Beverley would do it. She's at home all day and she was saying only last week that it drives her round the bend. And she hasn't got much teaching work at the moment. Why don't you ask her to help?'

'Do you think she would?'

'Let me try her – I'll ring you straight back.' I got through to Bev in a flash – we have each other's numbers on speed-dial – and explained. To my surprise she didn't agree immediately, but seemed to hesitate: I could hear the air being drawn through her teeth.

'I'd like to help Rose, not least as a favour to you, but to be honest, I'm not quite sure.'

'But I thought you'd like to get out of the house.'

'Yes, yes I would. But it's not that, it's just . . .' I suddenly realised what it was. How slow of me. Beverley didn't *like* Bea.

'I know Bea can be a bit over-bearing,' I anticipated, 'but she's really very kind and nice.'

'Hhhm.'

'She'll pay you of course.'

'Oh that's not the point, Rose.'

'And she's desperate for help.'

'I know . . .'

'And just between you and me, Bev, she's got boyfriend problems at the moment.'

Now, this was very indiscreet of me I know: but I didn't go into details, my aim being simply to elicit sympathy for Bea so that Bev would agree to help out.

'She's got boyfriend problems?' Beverley echoed. 'Oh, poor girl.'

'Plus Bella's just bogged off to Klosters,' I added, 'so it's all been getting too much. She only needs you for a couple of days to mind things. Would you do it?'

'Well, okay then. But where do I go?'

'The shop's in St Alban's Grove just behind Kensington High Street. Bea will send a taxi to pick you up.'

'Fixed!' I said to Bea two minutes later. 'Send a cab to

three Hope Street at a quarter to nine tomorrow morning.'

'Oh thanks Rose,' she sighed, 'you're a brick.'

I went home that night feeling vaguely triumphant, and with a renewed sense of calm. I'd inadvertently banished Creepy Colin and I'd helped Bea out of a difficult spot. Beverley would enjoy getting out of the house, and I was on top of my mail-bag too. Added to which my divorce proceedings had finally started which meant that I could move forward to the next phase of my life. At last I felt I was getting over Ed. I'd taken my own advice, and I'd stuck to it. I was moving on. I felt *strong*. The only cloud on the horizon was Serena. She'd looked so sad as she said goodbye to me at six, the poor woman was clearly under terrible stress. As I got home I resolved to tackle Ricky again about some special long-service payment which might tide her over for a few weeks.

As I opened the front door I was hit by the sweet, yeasty aroma of freshly baked bread. On the kitchen table were three brown loaves, still warm to the touch, and a scrawly note from Theo: *Bea and I . . . no – Bev and I – are in the Bunch of Grapes. Join us!* But I was tired, plus I didn't want to get in their way. Theo and Bev are obviously really hitting it off. Why else would they spend so much time together? So I went to bed with the new P.D. James and didn't see Theo until the next morning.

'You look smart,' I said as I ran water into the kettle. In fact he looked quite gorgeous.

'Thanks. I've got a meeting this morning with my publishers and this is my only suit. Aren't you going to eat anything?' he asked suddenly as I sat down with my cup of black tea.

'No, I can never be bothered. I'll have a bagel when I get to work.'

'Well you *should* bother, Rose,' he said with typical forthrightness. 'Here –' he commanded. 'Have this.' He popped up the piece of brown bread he'd been toasting, buttered it thickly, slapped on some marmalade then handed it to me.

'Thanks. Ooh, how delicious,' I breathed as I chewed on the nutty, deliciously squidgy brown bread.

'Why didn't you come to the pub?' he asked suddenly, almost accusingly.

'Oh, well, I'd been working late . . .'

'Surprise surprise.'

'And . . . I didn't want to play gooseberry with you and Bev.' He smiled his lop-sided little smile.

'Oh it's not like *that*, Rose,' he said blushing. 'We're just friends Bev and me.' Oh *yeah*.

'Is she happy about going to the shop?' I asked. He nodded. 'Good, because she wasn't quite sure at first. But I know the reason why,' I confided.

'*Do* you?' He looked surprised. 'I didn't think she'd told you. She's only recently told me.'

'No she hasn't, not in so many words. But, reading between the lines, I agree that Bea's not everyone's cup of tea.'

'Oh. Hmm.'

'But I'm sure they'll get on fine.'

Theo looked at me through slightly narrowed eyes, and nodded slowly, then we heard the diesel chug of a cab.

'That'll be her taxi,' he said putting down his mug. 'I'll go and give her a hand.'

As I left the house five minutes later, I saw Theo helping Beverley into the cab, then he handed her Trevor's lead. Beverley looked very smart, though a little apprehensive, but I was sure she'd be fine. And in any case she wouldn't see that much of Bea as she's out on site half the day.

'I'll ring you at lunchtime!' I called as I waved at her. 'Have fun!' She pulled a wry face. And I'd just shut the gate and was on my way down the street when I heard Theo call out.

'Rose! Your phone's ringing. I can hear it.' Blast.

'They can call me at work!' I yelled. I didn't want to turn back: I wanted to go forward. I was in a positive frame of mind. The recent storms had swept away leaving the sky a pure, squeaky-clean blue. The gardens blazed with golden forsythia and the sticky buds were showing slivers of green. For the first time since I'd moved to Camberwell I felt positive and upbeat. Thanks to Theo's rent I'd been able to keep within my overdraft limit, and my job was going well. I'd made some good friends in the area and I'd coped with the stress of my break-up with Ed. There were, however, still one or two flies in my ointment. My fortieth birthday for starters – the very thought made my heart thud. Plus I was still upset about Rudy; and then there was that other issue of mine . . . I caught my reflection in the Spar window, with my 'beanpole' figure and my 'mad' hair. Yes, there's still that other issue of mine.

'But things could be *a lot* worse,' I muttered to myself as I stopped at the newsagents. And I was just bending down to pick up a *Times* to do the crossword when suddenly a tabloid headline hit me in the eye.

'ELECTRA SHOCK!' it screamed on the front of the *Daily News*. 'STAR BETRAYED BY AGONY AUNT OVER LESBIAN AFFAIR! *Exclusive*! *See pages 2, 3, 4, 5, 6, 7, 12, 19, 28 and 43* it announced beneath.

As my hand reached for a copy I felt simultaneously red hot and ice cold.

Electra . . . marriage in crisis . . . attractive backing singer, Kiki Cockayne . . . husband Jez seen leaving Cotswold mansion . . . tearful star blames the Daily Post's agony aunt . . . 'I trusted Rose Costelloe . . . felt vulnerable . . . but she cynically betrayed me.' And there, taking up the top half of page 2, was a facsimile of Electra's letter to me. But *how*? Suddenly my mobile phone started to buzz – it was lucky I noticed; I must have pressed the 'vibrate' button by mistake. I fumbled in my bag, noticing as I answered it that I'd had six missed calls overnight.

'ROSE!!!'

'Yes?' Oh shit. It was Ricky.

'I've been trying to get hold of you since two o'clock this morning!'

'Oh, I didn't know. I'm sorry.'

'You *will* be sorry. *Very* sorry. I want you in my office. NOW!'

*   *   *

'HOW?' he demanded half an hour later.

'I don't know,' I replied. I glanced at the framed headline on the wall, 'SHIT HITS FAN'. Too right. 'I simply can't explain how it happened,' I said impotently. 'It's a dreadful breach of trust.'

'You're telling me,' said Ricky. 'It's a dreadful breach of trust between you and the *Daily Post*!' His face was puce and droplets of sweat pearled his gleaming brow. 'How come the opposition have got this fucking great scoop and not *us*!' he demanded as he jabbed his finger at the *Daily News*. 'You get a letter from Electra about how she's got the hots for a woman and you don't bring it to me?'

'No,' I replied firmly.

'Why not?'

'It was a matter of conscience.'

'A matter of *conscience*?' He looked at me as though I were sick. His mouth opened and closed twice with cod-like non-comprehension. 'Who do you think you are – a *priest*?' He'd been shouting at me so much that the room was filled with the sour stench of his sweat.

'I just don't know how it happened,' I said again miserably.

'Well I think we've got a little mole, haven't we Rose? Or maybe it's you!'

'What?'

'Maybe *you* sold the letter to the *Daily News*.'

'Why the hell would I do *that*?'

'Because it must have been worth at least eighty grand to whoever did do it, because that's precisely what *I* would have paid. Got money problems have you Rose?'

'Nothing that would ever make me stoop to something so low. In any case why would I want to jeopardise my career? I love my job, and I'm good at it, Ricky – that suggestion is completely absurd.'

'No, I'll tell you what's absurd,' he said. 'The idea that you're going to stay in your job after this. I've spoken to Personnel: your contract's up in ten days and you can kiss any chance of a new one goodbye.'

I was in a state close to catatonia as I returned to my desk. My face was all over a national tabloid and I was going to lose my job. My legs were weak and my cheeks felt hot and my breath came in ragged gasps. How the *hell* did it happen I wondered for the thousandth time. I'd guarded that letter like Cerberus guarding Hades: I'd taken *such* care. But someone had got hold of it, and copied it, and sold it. *I think we've got a little mole . . .* But *who*?

As I walked through the newsroom, aware of eyeballs swivelling discreetly in my direction, I mentally re-enacted what I'd done that day. The letter had been in my sole possession, and had been shredded personally by me. No-one else had seen it: it had been with me *all* the time. Ex*cept* . . . I remembered I'd gone down to the canteen for half an hour, but I'd locked the letter away in my drawer. No-one else has the keys to my desk, and my own ones were in my bag. But in any case, how could anyone have guessed at the importance of that one letter when I get so many every week? Whoever it was must have had some reason for suspecting that there was something of special interest inside . . .

Linda smiled at me sympathetically as I passed by her desk – maybe it was her. Psychic Cynthia sent me a compassionate look – maybe she'd intuited what Electra had written. Or maybe that whey-faced post-boy who'd handed it to me had x-ray eyes.

Now I thought about Electra, who'd been publicly humiliated and betrayed. The whole world would now know about her silly infatuation, poor woman: I heaved a painful sigh. As I sat down at my pod I looked at the *Daily News* again. *Rose Costelloe . . . gross incompetence . . . agony aunts in a position of trust . . .* Then there was a pious quote from June Snort, saying that she would *never* do that. *My readers know that they can write to me in total confidence*, she wrote priggishly – ha! At the agony aunts' lunch she'd been trying to convince us that she'd had a letter from Kylie Minogue!

The *Daily News*, delighted to have such a large stick with which to beat the *Daily Post*, claimed, vaguely, that Electra's letter had 'fallen into their hands'. There was no suggestion that I'd leaked it to them, but my reputation was in shreds. 'How could Ms Costelloe have let this highly sensitive letter, with its heart-rending sentiments, out of her grasp?' it enquired pompously. The accusation of professional misconduct was seared on my brain like a flaming brand. There was a photo of me, of course, and a potted biography in which the journalist questioned how a woman whose marriage had lasted 'a mere seven months' could possibly advise others on their matrimonial affairs. The rest of the coverage was devoted to the story itself. There was a grainy shot of the backing singer at her window, and several photos of Electra on her last tour. There was a photo of her actor husband, Jez, looking grim as he left their huge house with an overnight bag. There was a piece by the paper's showbiz editor, Bazza Bomberger, evaluating Electra's career. And there was the expected expatiation upon other lesbian celebrities – notably Sophie Ward and Anne Heche.

I glanced at the clock, it was ten to ten. My mail was sitting in a huge pile in my in-tray: for a fraction of a second I was tempted to walk out of the office, there and then. If I was being sacked in ten days then what the hell – why not go now? The high drama of it momentarily appealed to me but then reason prevailed. It would be totally unfair on Serena, who already had quite enough on her plate. It would also be quite wrong of me to flounce out when I still had work to do. Just because I had problems didn't mean I could neglect those of everyone else. When you're an agony aunt you have a *huge* responsibility to your readers, and I wasn't about to shirk mine. I ripped open the first envelope which was an internal one. Inside it was a letter, marked *Personal*, addressed to me in a hand I recognised.

Dear Rose, I read. *I'm writing this to you because I owe it to you and because I'm sorry. I know you don't deserve this, but things have been so hard for me lately: and when I saw Ricky's e-mail to you yesterday morning, I'm afraid it was just the last straw. I'd already had a tip-off about Electra's letter, and when I saw that e-mail I*

decided to act. But I sincerely hope that you suffer no bad conse-
quences yourself and that you'll be able to forgive me one day.

Well, I thought. Well, well, *well*. I looked out of the window – I felt a fool. It hadn't even crossed my mind that it could be cheery, chirpy, stoical Serena. Her bite was clearly worse than her bark. And now I idly wondered what comforting clichés she would have uttered as she prepared to go to the *Daily News*. 'Make hay while the sun shines,' possibly, or 'A bird in the hand is worth two in the bush.' 'Strike while the iron is hot' perhaps, or 'He who hesitates is lost.'

Attached was her formal letter of resignation, which I put in the internal mail to HR. I stared out of the window at the river for a few minutes: I was in shock, so I felt curiously calm. How naive of her to hope that I wouldn't suffer any 'consequences'. She'd effectively destroyed my career. She'd been Mount Vesuvius to my Pompeii and now my professional credibility lay in ruins. I was about to lose my column, and I'd lose my phone-in, and who would employ me as an agony aunt ever again? I thought of the huge drop in my earnings which would surely follow and my heart sank – I'd have to sell Hope Street and buy a flat. It struck me in that instant that I wouldn't be living with Theo any more; and at this I felt a terrible pang. But then, as I say, you get used to people, don't you, and I guess I've got used to him. I thought of the aroma of baking bread when I'd opened the front door last night; and now I looked up at the sky. For some reason, a ghostly half moon was visible in the expanse of bright blue. Theo would be able to tell me why.

Now I looked at Serena's desk – it was unusually tidy – she'd plainly been poised for flight. I opened her drawers, which were virtually empty, and now remembered seeing her clearing them out. I also recalled seeing her nervously phoning someone yesterday morning, and leaving the building at lunch. That must have been after she'd seen Ricky's second e-mail and had finally decided to go to the *News*. And I remembered how sad she'd looked when she'd wished me goodbye the evening before: she knew we wouldn't be meeting again.

'Take care of yourself Rose,' she'd said, and she'd smiled this odd, slightly guilty smile. Now I understood why. I pulled out her pen-tray and saw that in it were two sets of keys. A set for her desk obviously; then I tried the other one in my lock – it worked. So, unbeknown to me she'd had a spare key to my drawer. They must have been Edith Smugg's. Serena must have opened it when I'd gone down to the canteen. I'd thought she'd gone home but she'd clearly hung around, waiting for me to leave my desk.

I reread the *Daily News*. There was no denial from the Electra camp, and Kiki Cockayne, the backing singer, had said simply, 'no comment', fuelling speculation that it was all true. Which it was. Electra had come to me, genuinely seeking my advice, and she'd been completely stitched up. I'd have to write and apologise.

'Rose – the *Semaphore* are after you for a quote!' shouted Linda as I walked back towards Ricky's office. 'And the *Daily Planet* and the *Sunday Star*. And Radio Five want an interview with you as well.'

'I'm not talking to any of them,' I replied. 'They'll make me look even worse.' I knocked sharply on Ricky's door.

'Serena leaked it,' I said as he looked up. 'I've had a letter from her.'

'The bitch! I'll fire her!'

'She's already resigned. You should have given her the pay rise,' I added. 'That's why she did it: her husband had just lost his job. She'd worked here for fifteen years and she needed to feel appreciated, and she didn't. In fact when she saw your e-mail describing her as a "loser" she knew she wasn't valued at all. You made her feel completely worthless, Ricky, and so these are the consequences.'

'Give me that letter,' he commanded, holding out a fat hand. 'Give it to me!' he snapped.

'Why?'

'Because I'll sue her arse off, that's why. We'll get her under the confidentiality clause in her contract – we'll make her give back that eighty grand. We'll pursue her in a civil case, and we'll win, *and* we'll make her pay all the costs. Rose, what are you doing? Give me that letter – it's evidence!'

But I'd already turned on the shredder in the corner of his office, and now I ran Serena's letter through.

'Why the fuck did you do that?' Ricky's mouth was agape as the slivers of paper were extruded.

'Because that letter was written to me. It's my personal property, Ricky, I can do what I like with it.'

'But don't you want to see her finished?'

'No. After all, what happened is my fault. I let the letter fall into her hands and I also failed to delete your e-mails fast enough – she'd clearly spotted them on my screen. So I'm the one who should carry the can, not her. My contract is up on March the tenth, I believe, which gives you about two weeks to find someone else.'

As I returned to my desk I thought, bitterly, of Andrew. If he hadn't sacked Rob, then Serena would almost certainly not have done what she did. She did it because she was desperate – she'd simply seen pound signs – and now she was eighty grand better off. No more leaking roofs. No more threadbare coats. And no more helping me. *Shit*. The next two weeks were going to be dreadful on my own.

'Would you like a temp?' Linda asked.

'No, I couldn't be sure that they'd be discreet. That might sound a bit rich coming from me,' I added bitterly, 'but they'd take too long to train and vet. It'll be easier just to get on with it myself.'

'Okay,' she sighed. 'Well, let me know.'

By lunchtime I knew exactly how difficult it is flogging through thirty problems a day without assistance. Beverley phoned me at two to offer her support but I didn't want to talk. 'But there's something I want to tell you,' she added.

'I'm sorry, Bev, but I really can't chat. I've got a huge backlog in my in-tray, the phone's going the whole time, plus I'm devastated about losing my job.'

As I replaced the receiver I thought of all the people who knew me, and who would read the lies about me in the *Daily*

News. Ed would, and so would Mary-Claire Grey and that baggage Citronella Pratt. She'd be really cock-a-hoop about it; she'd always wanted this job. At five Bev phoned again – she said she'd had a great day – but that there was something she wanted to discuss.

'Can't it wait?' I said as I dug my *Adolescence, Mental Health* and *Jealousy* leaflets out of my filing drawer. 'I'm still frantic. How urgent is it?'

'Well, it's not that urgent. Yet. But it will get urgent, so tell me when we can talk.'

'Okay, I will – but not now.'

As I put the phone down I saw my colleagues leaving for the day, and now the shock began to sink in. I realised how much I was going to miss them, and doing the job I'd loved. I'd miss the noise and chatter of the newsroom, and even the daily argy-bargy with the subs. I looked out of the window at the gathering dusk and thought about Serena's letter again. Suddenly something suddenly struck me as strange: I'd been too traumatised to think of it before. Serena had told me that she'd had a 'tip-off' about Electra's letter. A tip-off? But from who? And *why*?

Chapter Fourteen

Dear Ms Costelloe, I was utterly flabbergasted by your recent letter, with its outrageous suggestion that I had telephoned you 'at home'. May I state categorically that I have never done so and in any case do not possess your home number. No wonder you are experiencing such grave problems in your professional life if you are capable of such a blatant misconception as this. May I suggest personal counselling? Yours truly, Colin Twisk. P.S. Kindly do not leak this letter to the Daily News.

'Wanker!' I snapped as I threw it in the bin. And he was a liar to boot. I knew it was him. Who else could it be? He'd been obsessed with me for six months. I closed my eyes, breathed deeply, then let it go – at least I'd got him off my back.

I stared dismally at my over-flowing in-tray: without Serena it now takes an age. There are the new letters to be logged and the ones I've dealt with to be filed, and I have to keep the stash of leaflets stocked up. The phones are constantly ringing, and the fax is whirring plus there's a huge pile of shredding to be done. All that without addressing a single problem. If it weren't for my friends I'd go mad.

'I just want to check that you're coping,' Bea said solicitously first thing this morning.

'I'm okay,' I lied. 'How's the shop?' I asked changing the subject.

'Well, I think we're on track. Beverley's coming in again this morning, thank God. I told her I had an important lunch – it's with Henry actually – so she agreed to an extra day. Have you seen the papers by the way?'

239

'Of course I've seen them,' I groaned.

'You'd think they'd have more pressing things to write about wouldn't you?' she said with a contemptuous snort. For the Electra story had rumbled on. The broadsheets, who regard agony aunts as unqualified busybodies doing more harm than good, said Electra had only herself to blame for her monumental lack of judgement in confiding in someone like me, while the tabloids continued to pick over the bones of the star's crisis-hit marriage. There were several photos of Electra's kids, and of the rather raunchy-looking backing singer, Kiki Cockayne. There was also a photo of Kiki Cockayne's boyfriend looking distinctly grim. On and on went the coverage, *ad nauseam* and *ad infinitum* – I wanted to throw. And if I'd had to work long hours before all this, now, without help, it was dire. I'd get home at ten, and flop in front of my tiny old portable TV – a poor stand-in for the stolen one – semi-catatonic with fatigue.

'What are you watching?' Theo asked last night as he sat down beside me on the sofa.

'I'm not watching anything,' I said. 'I'm too exhausted. I'm just letting the images flicker across my retina.'

Theo took off his shoes, and put his bare feet on the footstool, alongside mine. I looked at them, they were elegant, strong and sinewy, with nice, non-knobbly, straight toes.

'Nice ankles,' he said suddenly.

'Thanks.' I gave him a sideways look. 'I hope they make up for the fact that my hair's "mad".'

'I didn't offend you did I?'

'Yes, you did actually.' He blushed. 'But I'm used to your Northern forthrightness now.'

'Sorry. I think I was a bit scared of you.'

'Oh, I see. And are you still?'

He looked at me. 'No,' he said. 'I'm not.' I flicked the channel over to *Newsnight*. 'I like watching telly in black and white,' Theo added after a moment. 'It reminds me of being a student.'

'I'll have to get used to it again,' I said dismally. 'I won't be able to afford a new TV after what's happened this week.' I suddenly imagined myself becoming like Serena, with holes in my roof and a threadbare coat and an expression of neurotic stoicism on my face.

'Don't fret,' Theo said, soothingly, 'I'm sure you'll find something else.' He laid his hand on mine for a moment, then withdrew it.

'Yes,' I sighed, 'I probably will. But it won't be as interesting or nearly as well paid. I'm overstretched as it is so I'll probably have to sell this place and get a flat.'

'Really?' A look of regret crossed his face.

'Yes. I won't be able to afford it.'

'Well, we'll cross that bridge when we come to it,' he said. I smiled at his friendly, brotherly, use of the first person plural.

'Yes,' I smiled. 'We will.'

Now, as I stared at the screen, exhausted, my brain began to buzz and my eyes started to close and I could feel my chin begin to drop towards my chest.

'Hey.' I felt a gentle jab in the ribs. 'Hey. You.'

'What?'

'The phone's ringing.'

'Oh.' I padded into the hall and wearily reached for the receiver. 'Hello,' I said. 'Hello?' I was suddenly jerked back into consciousness. For once again I could hear loud, deliberate, heavy breathing – it was stertorous, male, and slow. I'd been working for twelve hours. I was all in. I'd had it. Stuff what the people at the phone company say.

'Fuck OFF!' I shouted, then I slammed down the handset. I pressed 1471 – number withheld.

'Who were you swearing at?' asked Theo casually as I stomped back into the living room, radioactive with indignation.

'My nuisance caller. Colin Twisk.'

'Colin Twisk?'

'Yes. Colin Twisk,' I repeated as Jeremy Paxman curled his lip at some cabinet minister. 'I wrote to him recently letting him know that I knew he'd been ringing me at home and

241

he wrote back denying it. He claimed not even to have my number, but he clearly does because he's at it again.'

'But I know Colin Twisk,' said Theo. My gaze swept from Paxman's equine profile to Theo's boyish one.

'You *what*?'

'I know Colin Twisk.' I felt my eyes widen and my mouth go slack. 'He works at Compu-Force. He's a systems analyst – he's a bit of an oddball, but I'd say he's quite harmless. You think *he's* been making these calls?'

'I do.'

'But *why*?'

'Because I once wrote him an encouraging letter about his lack of a girlfriend and it seemed to, I don't know, set him off! He kept on writing back to me, telling me how marvellous and special I was and sending me this weird Confettimail stuff on Valentine's Day.'

'Really?'

'Yes, these tiny bits of paper with a text message printed on them – "Can't Stop Thinking About You". There were hundreds of them; they got everywhere. It was extremely annoying.'

'How strange.'

'And then he started suggesting that we meet up and – oh!' Of course! 'That's how he got this number!' I exclaimed. 'Because of *you*. He knows you live with me because you've obviously talked about me to your colleagues, and you've given my number to your personnel people, in case of emergency, and Colin's read it on an internal list.'

Theo shook his head. 'Sorry, Rose. Wrong on both counts. For starters I've never mentioned you to *anyone* at work.'

'Haven't you?'

'No.'

'What, never?' I felt oddly disappointed.

'I don't talk about my private life. I sit quietly at my desk, pretending to do my spreadsheets whilst actually thinking about the Big Bang. Nor have I *ever* given out your home number, I only use my mobile.'

'Oh. I see.'

'I really don't think it *is* him,' said Theo judiciously. 'In fact, now I come to think of it, he's got this new girlfriend, Penelope Boink. She came in last week, and he was proudly introducing her to us all: apparently they met on some assertiveness course. It seems she's had lifelong confidence problems on account of her silly name. No, I very much doubt it's Colin,' he said confidently. 'He's much too happy.'

'Oh. Well, then who *is* it?'

'I haven't a clue. But why don't you just bar the calls and be done with it?'

'Because in order to do that you have to know what the number is first – don't you?'

'I'm not sure – you should ring up the phone people and check. Doesn't this person ever speak to you?'

'Never. It's just this heavy breathing. It's sick.'

'Then change your number.'

'No I won't, because then they'd have won. I've had to change it three times in the last year as it is, what with all my marital upheavals, so I'm *not* going to do it again.' As the *Newsnight* credits rolled I pushed myself up off the sofa and stifled a yawn. 'Anyway, I'm shattered.'

'Me too. Let's turn in.' Theo switched out the lights, checked the back door, and put the chain on the front one, and now we found ourselves going upstairs, together, to bed. It was funny hearing our combined tread on the creaking steps. But I was too exhausted to feel self-conscious at this sudden intimacy – in fact it felt rather friendly and nice. I had a sudden image of us actually lying *in* bed, together – in a platonic way of course – happily reading our books. A Stephen Hawking for him and a Ruth Rendell for me. I like crime fiction. The more red herrings the better. I can usually work out what's really going on, because, as I say, I can read between the lines.

'Night then, Rose,' said Theo politely as I paused by my bedroom door.

He smiled at me. I smiled back.

'Good night. Oh, by the way, how did Bev get on today?'

I asked him, 'I was too frantic to return her call.'

'Well, I spoke to her this morning and she seemed a bit low. She said she'd much rather be helping you.'

'Really?' I said, as I turned my door handle.

'Yes.'

'I wish she *had* been helping me,' I said wearily. 'I could have done with someone like her. In fact I . . . oh! What a *brilliant* idea!' Then, in an access of sudden happiness and relief, I did this peculiar thing. I stepped forward and kissed him on the cheek. I couldn't help it. 'You're a genius Theo! Good night.'

'I'd love to help,' said Bev the next morning, 'but what would the bosses say?'

'I've just cleared it with Linda and I couldn't give a damn what Ricky thinks. I'm so snowed under, but I feel that as long as people are writing to me, personally, then I have a duty to write back. And I'm getting a lot more letters because of the Electra business, so I have to answer all those ones as well.'

'Right then,' I heard Beverley say. 'I'm on my way. I'm the Hope Street temp,' she added with a laugh.

'And how was Bea yesterday?' I asked.

'Oh . . . fine,' Bev said noncommittally though I detected a slight edge to her voice. Bea must have been insensitive to her, in some way, without realising it. I didn't probe.

'How did she seem when she came back from her lunch with Henry?'

'Well . . . pretty happy, I'd say.'

'Really? And how did Henry look when he came to pick her up?'

'He looked . . . pretty happy too. He was smiling a lot, put it that way.'

'Oh, that's interesting. Maybe things are working out after all.'

By lunchtime, I knew that they weren't.

'I just bottled out,' said Henry when he phoned me from his mobile in the Army and Navy lingerie department where he was buying a corset. 'I was going to tell her, but she was yakking away the whole time about the party and about how cross she is with her sister for going skiing and about what an idiot the new boyfriend is, and about what a brilliant help Beverley's been . . .'

'So you couldn't find the right moment.'

'No. And I'm definitely expected at the opening, so it's going to be very hard not to go. No, it's not for my wife, it's for my mother,' I heard him say to an assistant. 'Yes, that's right – my *mother*. No, she likes marabou trim.'

'Well you'll have to think of some subtle way of telling Bea,' I said. 'If you don't she'll continue to hope, and hope's a killer.'

'I know. Yes, yes, *very* young at heart. Sixty-eight next May. You're right, Rose, I'll do it soon. Well if Joan Collins can, why can't she . . . ?'

'Henry and I had a super lunch,' said Bea happily ten minutes later. 'It went really well. He seemed a bit strained at first, but we were soon chatting away. He's definitely coming to the party, so that's a good sign isn't it?'

'Er, yes,' I said. 'It is.'

'You *do* think he likes me, don't you?' she said anxiously. 'Maybe he's said something . . . ?'

'Ooh no, we haven't discussed you at all. But I'm sure he . . . does. Er, actually Bea, I can't talk because Bev's arriving in a minute. Now that you don't need her she's helping me for a few days.'

'You too! She's awfully good. I really liked her,' Bea added warmly, 'and Trevor's divine. Henry seemed very taken with him: I do like a man who's fond of animals don't you?'

I thought of Ricky. 'Hmmm. It all depends.'

'Anyway, I'd better crack on, Rose. See you at the party.'

Ten minutes later Beverley was installed at Serena's desk, with Trevor, as I showed her the ropes.

'Here's the log-book for the letters, and the keys to the filing cabinet, and here, in this file down here, are the various leaflets I send out. This is the Health Address Book – that's our Bible – which lists the different support groups. The job's not hard,' I added, 'it's just rather involved, and I hope you can bear all the noise.'

'Bear it?' she repeated wonderingly. 'I *like* it!' She looked around at the frenetic activity in the newsroom. 'In fact I *love* it!' She shook her head in happy disbelief. 'I'm in an office, Rose. There are all these *people* – it's . . . great!' And I thought regretfully, yes, it is. It *is* great, and I'm really going to miss it. A wave of panic and sadness swept over me as I got back to work.

Within an hour Beverley was getting the hang of everything and my workload had suddenly halved. I didn't even have to answer the phone – I heard her fielding enquiries with discreet aplomb. Trevor, wearing his red Helping Paw coat, lay quietly by the side of her wheelchair contentedly sucking the head of his toy gorilla. It's his stress-busting executive toy.

'I like the little pocket in his coat,' I said to Bev. 'I hadn't noticed that before.'

'Yes, it's useful for putting things in. I think he's going to get some good material for his column this week,' she added as yet another person stopped by to stroke his ears. 'Anyway, back to work.' Beverley logged all the new letters, an expression of intense and sympathetic interest on her face. 'It's fascinating,' she breathed.

'What have we got today?'

'Alzheimer's, bedwetting, contraception, depression, missing persons, kleptomania and stress.'

'Okay then, I'd better make a start.'

'And here's a woman with SCI.'

'What's that?'

'Oh sorry, Spinal Cord Injury – she was paralysed from the waist down in a hit and run. She's twenty-nine, distraught, her boyfriend's left her and she's suicidal. God,' she sighed, shaking her head. 'I know *exactly* how she feels.'

'Then you answer that one.'

'What?'

'You write back to her.'

'Really?'

'Yes. I'll have to sign it of course, because she's written to me, but why don't you do the draft?'

'Well, because I'm not an agony aunt, Rose.'

'No, but you'd do a better reply than I ever could.'

Beverley smiled. 'Well . . . okay. If you're sure then. I'll give it a shot.' She picked up her pad and began making notes; and we worked in companionable silence for a while, when I suddenly remembered. I'd been too overwhelmed with work and worry to think of it before.

'Beverley, the other day you said there was something you wanted to tell me.'

'Oh. Ye-es,' she shifted slightly in her wheelchair and her neck reddened. 'Yes, that's right. Well, it might not be relevant after all, so then I wasn't sure whether or not to say anything about it to you . . .'

'About what?'

'About the fact that . . . Well . . . you see. It's quite an *awkward* situation, potentially, although, as I say, it might be all right, because, erm . . .' What on earth was she talking about?

'Is it about you?' I asked. She shook her head.

'Is it about me?'

'Sort of. Well, yes. It is about you actually. Or, to be more precise, it's about Ed . . .'

'What the *hell*'s Bella *thinking* of?' I asked Bea five minutes later. 'She's completely lost it this time.' I lowered my voice – I didn't want the whole office to hear. 'I mean it's one thing to go off on a skiing holiday ten days before you open, it's quite another to invite my soon-to-be-ex-husband to the bloody launch.'

'Oh God,' Bea gasped. 'She hasn't has she?'

'Yes, she has. Bev's just told me. She was going through the RSVPs and she went down Bella's list ticking them off and suddenly saw 'Ed Wright'. She agonised about whether or not to tell me, because she knew I'd be furious, but she felt that I ought to know.'

'And has he replied yet?'

'Apparently not – which is why Bev hesitated about telling me.'

'Well it's highly unlikely that he'll come . . .'

'I hope you're right, because if he does, then I can't.'

'But that's not on – you're our closest friend! I'm sure he won't accept,' she reiterated.

'No, he won't, because you've got to uninvite him, okay?'

'Rose, I can't do that – it's so rude.'

'I know it is. But you've got no choice because it's either him, or me. Here's his number; you've got three days. I don't *want* him there Bea, not least because he might bring *her*.'

'Rose, I'm really sorry about it,' said Bea. 'But Bella's back tomorrow, and *she* invited him, so it's up to her to stand him down.'

My fury with Bella lasted all day.

'How could she *do* that?' I said to Beverley for the twentieth time as we chugged back to Camberwell in a cab. 'It's incomprehensible.'

'I know why,' she said quietly.

'You do?'

'It's because she's so madly, deliriously happy that she wants everyone else to be happy too. It's the selfish insensitivity of the ecstatic,' she concluded sagely. 'Bliss blunts their minds to others' pain.' I looked at Beverley as she said that and suddenly saw that she was right. And I realised in that instant how wise she is, and what enormous insight she has.

'Anyway, that's why I wasn't sure whether or not to tell you,' she went on. 'I didn't want to cause a rift between you and Bella, and I didn't know whether or not he'd accept. If he'd simply sent his regrets I wouldn't have mentioned it to you, but there'd been no reply. And if he *did* come, and no-one had warned you, then . . .' her voice trailed away. 'I mean, you didn't react well at the Helping Paw ball,' she added delicately.

I cringed. 'No, I got steaming drunk. Well, I'm glad you told me,' I said as we turned into Hope Street. 'It could have been an awful shock. Are you coming in?' I added.

'No thanks,' she said as the cab driver dropped the ramp. 'I've got to get ready – I'm going out.'

'With Theo?' I asked casually, though my heart sank slightly.

'No. With Hamish. He's a lovely guy. I knew him five years ago, and we met again at New Year. He's down from Edinburgh for a week, rehearsing – he's a conductor – so we're going out for a bite.'

So perhaps Trevor was right and it wasn't Theo, but this Hamish, who was the object of Beverley's affection. Maybe she'd sent *him* the Valentine's card. My heart lifted, because, as I say, I've got used to Theo.

As I opened the front door I could hear the clattering of saucepans. Theo was busy.

'You're back early,' he observed as he rummaged in the cupboard under the sink.

'That's because Beverley was such a huge help. She even drafted some of the replies; it saved me loads of time, and her advice was great.'

'Yes,' he agreed emphatically. 'She's *very* astute. She's given me some good advice, actually,' he added over his shoulder.

'Really?' I didn't like to ask him what it was about. His separation presumably.

'And what did Trevor contribute?' he asked as he pulled out several pans. 'Envelope-licking?'

'No need, they're self seal.'

'Got it!' he said triumphantly. He held up a wok. 'I knew I'd seen one. Blimey!' he exclaimed, looking at it more closely, 'it's absolutely pristine. I don't think this wok has *ever* been used, has it?'

'No. At least not by me.'

'Well, this is its Big Night.'

'Are you expecting someone then?' The kitchen table was set, for two, with table mats, candles and linen napkins.

'Yes,' he said. 'I am.'

'Who is it?' I asked casually. 'Not that it's any of my business.'

'It *is* your business. It's you. We're having Thai green chicken curry in case you're wondering. And you're making it by the way.'

'I am? But I only do passive cooking Theo, you know that.'

He threw me an apron. 'Come on.'

Five minutes later I was happily grating gnarled bulbs of root ginger and fat sticks of woody lemon grass. The aromatic tang made me ravenous.

'That's grand,' said Theo, as he inspected my work, 'now crush the garlic cloves.'

'This is like *Ready Steady Cook*,' I said as I had a quick slurp of white wine.

'Now finely chop the coriander,' he instructed, then he poured oil into the pan. As he did so he sang, 'Are the stars out tonight, I don't know if it's cloudy or bright, for I only have fries, for you, dear . . .' I smiled. He had rather a nice voice. Then he sang, 'Don't fry for me Argentina . . .' and as he diced the chicken breasts he crooned, 'Love meat tender, love meat true . . .' He was clearly in a happy sort of mood. By now the rice was bubbling, and the oil was gently spattering; then Theo handed me the wooden spoon.

'Right, stir-fry the garlic for about forty seconds, then add the lemon grass and ginger. Now slop in some curry paste. Quick!'

'Okay, okay, don't be so bossy – but how much?'

'A couple of tablespoons should do it. That's it – don't over-do it; and keep stirring. Don't let it stick, silly. Right, here comes the meat.' He scraped in the cubes of translucent pink flesh which turned white as they sizzled in the pan. 'Keep it moving,' Theo added. 'Now pour in the coconut milk.' The creamy fluid went in in a steady stream, as smooth and viscous as oil.

I looked at him, his glasses had steamed up. He removed them, wiped them, then gave me a myopic smile and I noticed

250

how nice his eyes were, and how blue. 'There,' he said as he put them back on, and peered into the pan. 'That's it.'

'Really? That didn't take long. I thought curries were long, fiddly, drawn-out affairs.'

'Not Thai ones,' he replied. 'Indian ones rely on lots of spices, but for a Thai curry all you need are a few fresh herbs. Now we just leave it to simmer away nicely for eight minutes, then we add the roughly chopped mushrooms at the end.' Theo took the rice off the heat, and showed me how to wash out the starch, then he put it back on the flame. 'By the time the rice is done, the curry will be cooked.'

'It smells wonderful,' I said. 'I'm *starving*.'

Theo turned off the spotlights and lit the candles. 'Glad to hear it.' Five minutes later he was ladling the creamy mixture onto a pile of fragrant, non-sticky rice. I sunk in my fork, and closed my eyes.

'This is the most delicious thing I've ever tasted in my entire life,' I breathed.

'Better than packet soup and take-aways, eh?'

'Hmm. It's . . . divine. What lovely flavours.'

'I used to make it for my wife.'

'She must miss it,' I added.

'Maybe. She phoned today to say she wants to start the divorce.' I looked at him. 'She *has* met someone else. She thinks it's serious.'

'I'm sorry Theo. That's hard. But you seem quite cheerful.'

'It's gallows humour.' He drew in his breath. 'It's depressing, but it's probably for the best. Fiona and I have been in limbo city for seven months, so I guess it's better to move on.'

'I'm sorry,' I repeated, impotently.

''S'all right. I feel a lot better than I thought I would. And it means I'll be able to get my share of the house as Fiona's going to buy me out. After five years there should be quite a bit of my money in it, certainly enough for a decent flat.'

'Oh,' I said. I felt a sudden stabbing sensation. 'Oh, well, that's . . . good. Especially as I'm probably going to have to

251

sell this place – I'll probably be asking you if *I* can be *your* flatmate!'

'Well, that'd be nice. But you'd have to obey *my* rules.'

I laughed. 'And what would they be?'

'You would not be allowed to be too tidy.'

'Uh huh.'

'And you'd have to eat proper food. And, well, that's about it.'

'Sounds like you'd be an easy landlord.'

'I probably would.'

'Anyway, I'm glad you're not too miserable about Fiona,' I said.

'It's funny, but now it's happened, I'm not. For months I was that upset I could hardly function, but now I feel I can cope. I've discovered that there's life beyond every relationship, Rose,' he added softly. I felt a strange fluttering in my stomach.

'Yes,' I said. 'There is.' I looked at my plate. It was empty.

'Shall we have second helpings?' I heard him say. 'Second helpings?'

'What? Oh. Yes please.'

As I held out my plate, I told him about Bella inviting Ed to the twins' launch party. Theo looked appalled.

'It's awful,' I said, glancing at the gold-edged invitation, marked *Rose & Theo*, pinned to my notice board. 'She's got to uninvite him. I went mad.'

'Well we don't want *him* turning up,' he said bluntly.

'Er, no,' I agreed. 'We don't.' He caught my surprised expression.

'Well it would upset you.' he said.

'You're right. It would.'

'And how's it going at the *Post*?' he asked as he sat down again.

'Well, with Bev's help, it's bearable – but I finish next week.' My heart turned over. A professional chasm yawned before me. 'My contract expires on the tenth. My editor's already trying to recruit someone else,' I went on. 'The whole thing makes me feel sick. I put so much into that job, Theo. It was my whole *life*. My *raison d'être*.'

'Hmm,' he said thoughtfully. 'I know.'

'And the way Serena betrayed me was awful, especially as I was trying to get her a rise. But you know it's *funny* . . .' I told him about her claim that she'd been tipped off about the letter.

'Well who do you think that was?'

I shook my head. 'I really don't know. All I do know is, it's a bit whiffy. I guess it's someone who wanted to see Electra ripped apart in the press.'

'Well it certainly hasn't made her look good. Going-over-the-hill-rock-chick has lesbian fling. Maybe it was the backing singer's bloke,' Theo suggested. 'It could be a simple case of lover's revenge. Or maybe – and I don't like to say this – it's someone who's got it in for you.' I looked at him, my heart sinking at the thought, but I knew that he might be right. 'I mean you've suffered as much as that Electra in all this.'

'Yes,' I said bitterly. 'I have.' But *who* might want to hurt me, and why? And what could possibly connect them to Electra? I had another sip of white wine. I was too tired to try and work it out. My plate was empty again. I held it up.

'What, more?' said Theo with a laugh.

'Yes please. Is there any?'

He peered into the saucepan. 'Just a smidgeon. We'll have to make double the quantity next time.' *We. We'll* have to make. As Theo spooned it onto my plate I smiled at him, and he smiled back and held my gaze for a moment in his. And in that instant I wasn't sure whether I cared if Ed went to the twins' party or not.

Chapter Fifteen

By the next morning, however, my indignation had returned, on its high horse, all guns blazing.

'How *could* you?' I said to Bella when I phoned her at ten.

'I'm sorry Rose,' she whimpered. 'But I've been feeling so happy with life and I just got carried away. I wanted *everyone* to come to the party – the whole, wide world. And I saw Ed's name in my address book a couple of weeks ago and so on an impulse I invited him too. But I didn't put *her* name on it,' she added earnestly.

'Oh that's really thoughtful of you Bella – *thanks*.'

'I don't know how I can make it up to you, Rose.'

'By phoning him and standing him down.'

'Ooh, that'll be embarrassing,' she breathed.

'I don't give a damn. You've got to do it, otherwise I can't go.'

'Okay,' she sighed. 'Oh God, everyone's *so* cross with me at the moment. Except Andrew,' she added blissfully. 'Anyway, I will do it, Rose, don't worry. I'm sorry. See you on Wednesday night.'

On Wednesday evening I finished work at five-thirty, having had a huge row with a sub who had cut my column down *really* badly to make way for some crappy ad.

'That is one thing I won't miss,' I said to Beverley as we went into the ladies' loo to change for the party. 'The endless argy-bargy with the subs. I'm sick of having letters butchered. Do you need any help?' I called into the next cubicle.

'No I'm fine.' She emerged looking wonderful in a velvet trimmed cardigan and a calf-length black silk skirt. She applied some make-up, then reappraised her appearance several times. She slipped in a pair of dangly pearl earrings and twisted her hair into a knot like she'd done for the ball.

'I'm really glad I persuaded you to come,' I said as we went down to the waiting cab. 'It'll be fun.'

'Maybe,' she said with a shrug.

'Has the Ed situation been defused?' she asked as we sped westwards.

'Yes, Bella's done it by phone.' As we drove through Pimlico Beverley checked her appearance again.

'Does this lipstick suit me?' she asked anxiously.

I nodded.

'And am I wearing too much mascara?'

'No.'

'Are you sure? I don't want to look tarty.'

'Yes. I'm quite sure. You look gorgeous Bev. And so does Trev.'

She put her make-up away. 'It's funny,' she said, as she got a tiny dog brush out of Trevor's coat pocket and began tidying his fur, 'but when you first met Trevor, you were quite nervous of him. It was as though you didn't really like dogs.'

'I didn't grow up with one that's why. My mum was very house-proud and she said she couldn't stand the hairs and the mess so we didn't have any pets.' I glanced out of the window.

'Were you close to your parents, Rose?'

I pretended I hadn't heard her. 'But I do like Trev.'

We heard the chimes of Big Ben as we drove past Victoria station and I speculated about how many people would be there.

'Three hundred were invited,' Beverley explained as she checked her appearance again, 'including a few celebs and some hacks. The twins are assuming that about half that number will show. I hope it's no more than that because the shop isn't very big. I'm glad we're going early,' she added, as she dabbed on a little more powder, 'so that we can stake out our place.'

Now we were passing the Albert Hall, then turning left into Hyde Park Gate, then we wiggled through some back streets and came to St Alban's Grove. It was a narrow street of picture-postcard prettiness.

'What adorable shops,' I said as we drove down it. 'It's like Toy Town. What number is it?'

'Number two.' Of course. The twins had seen that as an omen of success. They should have called the business 'Two Gether,' or rather, 'Too Gether,' I thought. We trundled past a bespoke ladies' shoe-maker with colourful brogues in the window and the Raj Tent Club selling Indian tents, and there on the corner, festooned with silver balloons and flying streamers, was Design at the Double! The fascia was decked with fairy lights – the whole place seemed to sparkle and shine in the dusk. We glanced in the windows which were filled with beautiful *objets* – velvet cushions and pink leather boxes and spangly picture frames. As we pushed on the door a brass bell tinkled above us, then we were hit by the smell of fresh paint mingled with the biscuity scent of champagne. There were about a dozen earlycomers, like us, chatting in small knots. Beverley and I took a proffered glass of fizz then greeted Bea, who looked nervous and flushed.

'Congratulations!' we said. And there was Bella coming towards us looking very tanned, with visible goggle marks, the ghastly Andrew at her side. I thought of Serena and all the problems I'd suffered because he'd sacked Rob. And I thought of him persuading Bella to go skiing at a time when Bea most needed her help.

'Hi Rose,' he said extending his hand. 'Glad you could make it.' Glad I could make it! What a cheek! 'Sorry about your, er, little work problem,' he added tactlessly. 'We read about it while we were away. I know Electra's husband, Jez, quite well actually.' Of *course*. 'He wouldn't have liked her going after a bird.'

I gave him an icy little smile, then introduced him to Bev. 'Beverley was Bea's right hand woman recently,' I said pointedly. 'When she was incredibly busy and needed help.'

'Really? he said uninterestedly. Bella gave me a guilty hug.

'You did sort that out, didn't you?' I asked her *sotto voce*.

'Yes, I did. I phoned Ed's home answerphone and his work answerphone, just to be quite sure. His secretary said he was around, so there's no way he won't have got it.' I sighed with relief.

Andrew and Bella walked away to talk to some other people, and Bea was chatting to Bev so I had a quick look round the shop. On the ground floor were the pretty artefacts the twins were going to sell – tartan tea-cups, hand-blown glass vases, mother of pearl dishes – it was a feast for the eye. Downstairs were the books of upholstery fabric, the wallpaper samples and the cards of paint effects. It was all so effortlessly elegant and tasteful. Bea had done a great job. As I went back upstairs the babble was building and the bell over the door was tinkling merrily as more people arrived.

'– Isn't this divine?'

'– Ooh look at that lovely button-back chair.'

'– They've got a fabulous range of Jane Churchill too.'

'– Sort of classic with a twist.'

'– Klosters? Oh that *is* smart.'

'– We've just got back from Val d'Isère.'

I could see why Beverley had hesitated about coming; the twins' clients were a slightly grandiose lot. Still . . . I had another sip of champagne. Who gives a monkey's who they are so long as they've got the dosh? I saw Bea glance nervously at the door a few times as she chatted to her guests but of course I knew why. Suddenly it opened again, with a merry peal, and there was Theo. I saw Bev's face light up.

'Hi!' she said. 'At last.'

'Why? Am I late?' He looked at his watch. 'No, I'm in perfect time.'

Henry however had still not put in an appearance and I could see the stress building on Bea's face. As she greeted everyone, and discussed the merits of egg-glazes over sponged paint effects, her mind was clearly elsewhere.

In the by now substantial crowd there were one or two people who were vaguely familiar from TV. Andrew was talking to them with immense animation, whereas he'd hardly said two words to Bev. He didn't speak to her because to him she was just a woman in a wheelchair. He wasn't interested. What a shit . . . As Beverley and Theo chatted animatedly in the way that they do, I scrutinised Andrew more closely. Every time a pretty girl came within view she would get the discreet sweep from top to toe and then back. He'd clearly perfected the art, betraying his interest only by the merest flicker of an eyelid. As I watched him I realised that the anagram of Andrew is 'Wander' as well as 'Warned' . . .

'Isn't that woman on breakfast telly?' I asked Bev as Andrew air-kissed an attractive brunette.

'Yes,' she said, 'that's Emily Maynard, she's a new presenter on GMGB.' Even in the swelling throng I could make out snatches of Andrew's brash conversation: *'You're looking great . . . yeah just got back . . . Klosters . . . yeah, I did see Prince Charles . . . oh Wills is a really great guy actually . . . yeah, I have met him. And Harry.'* I wanted to puke.

'There are quite a few journalists from the glossies here too,' Beverley added.

'Really?'

'That tall woman over there, the one who looks like Naomi Campbell.'

'Yes.'

'That's Lily Jago – she edits *Moi!* magazine.'

'Uh huh.'

'And the woman she's talking to is Faith Smith, who does the weather on AM-UK!'

'So it is. You're very good at spotting people,' I remarked.

'It's being in a wheelchair,' she replied ruefully. 'You get to watch a lot of TV.'

As Bea circulated I saw her glancing at the door again and then, suddenly, her face lit up. It was as though she were

Mary Magdalene and Henry the risen Christ. I could practically hear the Hallelujah chorus as she stepped forward, beaming from ear to ear. As he walked through the door, I recognised the expression on Henry's face: it was one of suppressed anxiety, as though he was trying hard to appear relaxed. Bea strode up to him, kissed him, then threaded her arm through his and led him away. I saw his face flush, but I was surprised, once again, at his lack of interest. Why didn't he like her? She was, after all, very attractive, and though undeniably bossy, she had such a good heart . . . On the other hand she'd freak out once he started trying to borrow her ball gowns. No, I thought, it would never work. Henry would just *have* to tell her the truth, however painful. Perhaps he should simply have come in a frock.

'Hi Rose!' Henry waved at me apologetically, then discreetly rolled his eyes. He seemed unable to escape Bea's vice-like grip as she introduced him to all her friends. She attached herself to him in the way that Cherie Blair used to hold down Tony, as if the poor bloke were about to run off.

'Oh Henry,' I whispered. But he'd brought it on himself. 'You twit.'

'Hmmm,' I heard Bev say to Theo. I looked at them and suddenly realised that I'd been standing with them for ages and that I ought to circulate. So I got chatting to a couple of journalists from the *Sunday Semaphore* who commiserated at my recent mauling in the press. And then I spoke to a woman from *Country Living* who was going to do a feature on the twins. Then I talked to a blonde journalist called Claudia who wrote for *Heat* magazine, and whose speciality was pop.

'I'm the twins' first customer,' she explained. 'I bought a lamp here yesterday, before the shop had officially opened, so Bea kindly invited me along. Your face looks very familiar,' she added. 'Oh . . . I've got it. You're the agony aunt, aren't you? You got all that flak about Electra last week.'

'Well, yes, I did get a lot of flak,' I said bitterly. 'But I guess she came out of it badly too.'

'Oh I don't know about that,' Claudia said with a smirk.

'Ooh no,' she said, with a sip of champagne, 'I don't know about that at all.'

'What do you mean? The press trashed her.'

'Well . . .' Suddenly someone clapped their hands and the babble of voices hushed.

'Ladies and gentlemen, welcome to Design at the Double,' announced Andrew – whose party *was* this? I wondered indignantly – 'pray silence for Bella and Bea.'

The twins' faces flushed with pleasure as they looked round at the assembled throng. I glanced at Claudia's profile. What on earth did she mean? But I couldn't ask because Bea was about to speak. She clasped her hands in front of her, like a communicant at the altar, then cleared her throat and smiled.

'Bella and I just want to say a huge thank you to everyone for coming,' she began, 'it means a lot to us that you're all here. For years we've dreamed of having our own business and, finally, that day has arrived. Design at the Double is our baby, in a way, and so we wanted you to help us christen it tonight. But before we do, we have a number of people to thank: notably our bank manager, Keith, who has extended to us a generous business overdraft facility which we hope we'll never have to use. We're also very grateful to our friend Rose Costelloe, our very own agony aunt, who's supported us so much.' I blushed. 'We'd also like to thank Beverley and Trevor McDonald, who helped out so brilliantly last week.' I glanced at Beverley. She was smiling. 'But most of all,' Bea added, 'I'd like to thank my boyfriend Henry . . .' AAAAR-RRGGGGGGHHHH!!!!!! '. . . who first told us about this shop. We'd been looking for premises for ages,' she went on blithely, 'but none of them had felt quite right. But when we saw this it was, well,' she smiled coyly at him, 'love at first sight. So will you raise your glasses to Design at the Double, everyone, and do please tell *all* your friends.'

I glanced at Henry as we toasted the shop. He'd gone the colour of a Sicilian tomato and there was a polite smile superglued to his face. How could Bea be so reckless? How could she not have read between the lines? She had set herself up for a heartbreak with her flat refusal to face facts. For the facts were that Henry had never really pursued her. She had pursued him. So much for her strategy to be, what was it? – 'direct and upfront'. Men – especially macho ones like Henry – simply don't like being chased. That, I suspected, was the *real* reason he wasn't interested in her. He broke away from Bea, and came up to me, his brow glistening, his mouth still set in a rictus grin.

'Christ!' he whispered, as he ran a hanky round the back of his neck. 'What a way to be billed.'

'Well, I *did* tell you,' I whispered back.

'Hmm, you did. But it gives completely the wrong impression,' he added glancing at the assembled crowd.

'Oh well,' I said with a shrug. I helped myself to a passing tray of canapés. 'It doesn't matter, does it, Henry? No-one really knows you here. It's far worse for her.'

'Yes it *does* matter actually,' he hissed, looking anxiously round again. 'It absolutely *does*.'

'Hen-reee!' Bea was calling him over. He arranged his features into a pleasant expression again, and sped off. If only Bea realised that he was wearing lacy black knickers under his corduroys she might not be so keen. I turned back to Claudia, the pop journalist I'd been chatting with.

'I'm sorry,' I said, as she broke off from her conversation, 'we were talking about Electra. Er, what did you mean?'

'Nothing, except that you said she'd been trashed all over the papers.'

'Well, she has.'

'But she's got plenty to compensate her I'd say.'

What on earth was she talking about?

'I'm sorry, I don't understand. Her husband's left her, and she's been made to look ridiculous.'

'Aah,' she said, 'the poor love. But her new single's still going to go into the charts at number one on Sunday, so that'll make up for it.'

'Is it? How do you know?'

'Because the Midweek Chart comes out on Wednesday

afternoons – I saw it three hours ago. It's based on sales from certain shops; and according to this week's chart, "Shame On You" is heading straight for the top.'

'Oh. I know nothing about pop music,' I said. 'But, well, good luck to her.'

Claudia looked at me, through narrowed eyes. 'But don't you think that's interesting?'

'What?'

'That she's going to be at number one with this song, when her last single more or less bombed.'

'Interesting?' I looked at her blankly. 'I don't know what you mean.'

'I'll tell you what I mean. Two weeks before her new song's released, Electra gets saturation coverage, not just in the tabloids, where she'd expect it, but in the broadsheets as well.'

'Yes . . . ?'

'It's all a bit fishy don't you think? I mean, why the hell would Electra write to you about her problems?'

'Well,' I said, bristling, 'because she said I give my readers *excellent* advice, that's why.'

'But didn't you find it *surprising*, that she'd confided in you?'

'Well . . . ye-es, I suppose I did. But on the other hand, she seemed genuinely desperate.'

'Oh she was,' said Claudia. 'But not for advice about her personal life. That woman has an army of therapists so why on earth would she need you?' I felt the penny loosen, then slowly begin to drop.

'A friend of mine's writing an unauthorised biography of Electra,' Claudia explained with another sip of champagne, 'so I know quite a lot. I think someone's been spinning,' she concluded. 'Yeah . . . that's what I think.'

Ah. Now I told her what Serena had said about having had a tip-off. Claudia's elegantly plucked eyebrows went up in a knowing way.

'But who would the tip-off have come from?' I said, staring at her, as I struggled to work it all out. 'Kiki Cockayne's boyfriend is very pissed off at being dumped. Maybe it came from him.'

'I doubt it,' Claudia said. She took a packet of Marlboro Lights out of her bag. 'I think it came from her.'

I stared at her. 'But if Electra just wants publicity,' I said wonderingly, 'then why on earth involve me? All she has to do is tip off the press herself about her relationship with Kiki, then bingo! The long lenses arrive.'

'I think it's more sophisticated than that,' said Claudia, thoughtfully. A twin plume of smoke streamed from her elegant nostrils as she tossed back her head. 'You see by involving you in it, the story becomes much bigger, because you're well known too. And then the press keep going with it all week about the rights and wrongs of spilling your guts to an agony aunt, and whether or not an agony aunt's loyalty is to her readers or to her editor, and whether or not agony aunts should be professionally qualified and whether or not they give good advice. It gives it a variety of interesting angles, all of which lead back to Electra, which guarantees that she stays in the public eye.'

'But how could they have known that I wouldn't just give her letter straight to my own editor, which is what some agony aunts *would* have done?'

'Well, it wouldn't have mattered to them if you had, because then they get the exclusive in the *Daily Post*. But this way it's so much better because it involves an attack by the *Daily News* on a columnist from its deadly rival, which adds hugely to the scoop's appeal. You've become a big part of this story, Rose.'

'Yes,' I said bitterly, 'I know.'

'I guess they just knew that you wouldn't let on to your editor about Electra's letter.'

'Well it's true. The only time I'd ever breach a confidence is if I thought someone was putting themselves, or others, at risk. And I've publicly said that, many times, in the media interviews I've done.'

'So they decided to target your assistant instead. She didn't

264

have as much to lose as you. She didn't have the fancy job and the nice salary; so she was tempted – and she cracked.' I felt my lips purse up like my mother's used to, like a draw-string bag.

'She certainly did.'

'I love conspiracy theories,' Claudia went on knowingly, 'and I think I know who's behind this. I can't prove it, of course, but you might want to try as you've lost your job.' I heard the door bell ring again; it was late, people were beginning to leave.

'Who *is* it then?' I said.

'Well, in my opinion I think it's . . .'

Suddenly I felt a subtle pressure on my elbow and turned to my left. I felt as though I'd fallen down a mineshaft. I was looking at Ed. In a nanosecond my pulse had accelerated from a steady, perfectly legal seventy, to a one hundred and thirty Ferrari burn.

'Rose,' he said softly. I turned to Claudia, who was looking at Ed, slightly awe-struck, in the way that all women do.

'Claudia,' I said, my heart beating so loudly I was convinced she'd hear it, 'could I call you some time?'

'Sure. I've got to go now anyway, but here . . .' she opened her bag and handed me her business card. 'Give me a ring.'

'Rose,' said Ed again. 'I . . .' he shrugged with embarrassment, then smiled. 'You look very . . . well. In fact you look lovely,' he added.

I stared at him, my legs trembling violently. Oh shit. Ed was just so, so attractive; he eclipsed every other man in the room.

'Ed,' I said with lethal civility. 'What a surprise.' Blocks of protective ice shot up around me like the bricks of an igloo and I saw him flinch at the tone of my voice. 'I thought you weren't coming,' I added pointedly with another sip of champagne.

'Well,' he smiled guiltily, 'I've gate-crashed. I know I'm not meant to be here.' I glanced around for Mary-Claire, and couldn't see her; but my eye lighted on Bella, who was looking aghast. 'I'm here on my own,' he added, reading my mind.

265

'Oh. I see. And why's that?'

'Well,' he shrugged again. 'I just am.' How strange. Why wasn't that midget here? Maybe they were remaking *The Wizard of Oz* and she was busy playing one of the Munchkins. Or maybe there'd been an outbreak of swine fever in Putney and she wasn't feeling well.

'So why *have* you come?' I asked.

'Because, I, well, I simply wanted to, well . . .' he cleared his throat, '. . . see you actually.'

'Oh,' I said dismissively. 'How nice.' I was so cold with him I was giving myself frostbite: I was also, to be honest, intrigued. 'But, *why* do you want to see me Ed?' I asked pleasantly.

'Because you've had a very . . . hard time. It's really hurt me seeing you being attacked in the press. I, of all people, know how dedicated to your job you are,' he said with a grim little laugh. 'So I just wanted to, well, offer you my support, that's all.'

'Oh.' The warmth of his words was melting my igloo and large puddles were forming at my feet. 'Well . . . thanks. But then why didn't you just ring me up?'

'Because I don't have your number.'

'But you know where I work.'

'That's true. But I thought you might not want to speak to me. When I first got the invitation for tonight, I was amazed; and I thought you must have asked the twins to invite me. And that made me feel so happy, Rose, because, well . . .' he sighed. 'Well . . . ,' he tried again.

'Yes?'

'I've . . . missed you.'

'Ah.'

'In fact,' he murmured urgently, as though he were in some distress, 'I can't stop thinking about you.' By now my igloo had become a small lake, and I was trying desperately to stay afloat. 'Then I got Bella's messages asking me not to turn up,' Ed went on, 'and I realised I'd made a mistake. I know I shouldn't have come, and I'm sorry, but the fact is, I just wanted to *see* you again. Face to face.'

I was going to need sunglasses at this rate. But I decided I wasn't going to make it too easy for him. And I was just about to launch into some chilly little speech about how grateful I was for his generous sentiments, when he suddenly added, 'well, that's all I came to say really. Goodbye.' And with that he kissed me on the cheek, then went up to the twins, congratulated them, gave me a sad little smile, and left. I stood, staring after him, as he walked down the street, still aware of the light pressure of his lips on my face. I glanced around at the crowd. Henry was making a fuss of Trevor; Theo was talking to Bev, then the twins extricated themselves from their respective conversations and came up to me.

'Rose,' Bea breathed, her eyes like saucers. 'Are you okay?'

'Ye-es,' I lied. 'I'm fine. I . . . well, it was rather strange,' I added faintly. In fact it was an emotional hit and run.

'At least he didn't stay long,' Bella observed. 'That was decent of him.'

'What did he want?' asked Bea. What *did* he want? I looked at her.

'I don't really know. He said he just wanted to tell me that he'd been thinking of me with all this crap I've had in the press.'

'And where was *she*?'

'Good question.'

'Maybe he's dumped her,' said Bella. My heart lifted suddenly.

'Yes, maybe he has,' said Bea. 'Not that you'd want him back Rose. That would be disastrous.'

'Er, yes,' I said. 'It would. Anyway, er, it's been great, but I think I'll go home now.'

Henry was on his way out, making some excuse to Bea. He gave me a friendly wave goodbye. Theo and Beverley said that they were happy to go, too; and as we trundled back to Camberwell in the cab I was aware that Theo was staring at me.

'Are you all right Rose?' he asked as we chugged through the streets of south London. I glanced out of the window.

'I'm fine. It was just a bit weird speaking to my husband for the first time in six months.' Beverley reached out and squeezed my hand. 'Why is it,' I asked, in a voice so faint, I hardly recognised it as my own, 'that it's always at the very, very moment when you finally think you've got over someone, that they come back into your life?'

'What did he say?' Beverley asked.

'He said . . .' I began. 'He said that he can't stop thinking about me.'

'Oh.' As the cab stopped, and Theo pulled down the ramp, Ed's words spun through my head again like the 'zipper' line at the bottom of the screen on CNN. *I've missed you Rose . . . I'm sorry . . . wanted to see you again . . . face to face.* I paid the driver as Theo helped Beverley inside then lifted up the catch on my gate.

'You're such a nightmare to live with!' No, Ed hadn't said that. 'You're a mess!' No, he hadn't said that either, I reflected. He'd only said nice, kind things.

'You're always working Rose. No, I won't clear that up!' What the –? I looked at the doorstep. There was something standing on it. It was large and square and covered with a black bin liner which had two large slashes in the side.

'Betrayed of Barnsley!' I heard. 'Depressed of Dagenham!' I gingerly lifted the bin liner, and there, staring beadily up at me, was Rudy.

'Rudy!' I breathed. 'Thank God.' And now as I opened the front door and took him inside, I could see a note attached to the cage.

Dear Rose, it said in thick hb pencil, *(we assume that's your name). Sorry, but we just couldn't stick it with this bird. All the awful rows gave us the hump. We've got a lot of simpathy for Ed actually. He sounds like a pretty desent sort of bloke. Yours truly, the burglars.*

My indignation at their impertinence was swept away by my relief. 'Oh it's so nice to see you again, Rudy,' I said ecstatically. 'You can talk as much as you like. Rudy's back!' I shouted to Theo as he came into the kitchen. 'He's been returned!'

I looked in his cage – it was beautifully clean and freshly newspapered, and there was water in his bowl. A half apple lay on the floor, and a couple of large black grapes. As Theo helped me put the cage back in its place, my head reeled. What a night. I'd been told that the Electra affair was a publicity stunt, and my stolen mynah had been returned. Strangest of all, my soon-to-be-ex-husband had unexpectedly turned up and been affectionate and charming to me. *I can't stop thinking about you*. That's what he'd said I remembered as I went up to bed. *I can't stop thinking about you*. Oh. Can't Stop Thinking About You. CSThnkAU.

Chapter Sixteen

'I can't believe it,' Bea wailed the following morning. 'I just can't – uh uh . . .' She was weeping so uncontrollably that I could barely distinguish the words. 'Feel such a fool . . . thought he was so nice . . . up the garden path . . . what will my friends think? . . . he just phoned me this morning . . . *total* shock . . .'

'How did he, um, put it?' I asked. At this there was another explosive sob. It was so loud that Trevor heard it, and came over to my desk to investigate; but then he's very sensitive to weeping, that dog.

'He said,' Bea began, 'he – uh-uh – said, that there was – uh-uh-uh – another *woman*!'

'Another woman?' I reiterated wonderingly. I glanced at Beverley as she ripped open the letters. She was trying not to look as though she'd heard but she knew it was Bea as she'd taken the call. Another woman . . . ? Ah. Of *course*. That's how Henry had delicately put it to me when he'd first told me about his penchant for feminine attire. He'd said that the reason he'd broken up with Venetia was because there'd been 'another woman,' i.e. him.

'And is that all he said?' I added gently.

'Yes,' she sniffed. 'That's all.'

'Well I'm very sorry, Bea, I know you liked him . . .'

'Liked him? I *adored* him!' she shrieked. 'And all the time I spent reading up on military history has completely gone to waste. Who am I going to discuss El Alamein with now? Hm?'

'Oh, well, it might come in handy one day, you never know.'

'It's just so *awful*,' she blubbed. 'I never saw it coming. How could I be so blind?' Indeed. 'I don't know who this other woman *is*,' she added menacingly. I wasn't going to tell her the truth.

'Bea, I really wouldn't worry too much about that. There are lots of other nice men out there and in any case Henry's going to the Gulf for six weeks. Honestly,' I added airily, 'you wouldn't be happy with him as he's always away. And would you really want to be an army wife?'

Her sobs subsided. 'Probably not – uh-uh. But that's not the point!' she added crossly.

'Then what is the point?'

'The point *is* that now Bella's got someone and I *haven't*!'

Ah, I thought as I put down the phone. Poor Bea, that was a hard fall. But she's like a bull in a china shop – her lack of circumspection is dire. I mean, some people have absolutely no insight into their own behaviour do they! And I'm afraid Bea just didn't read between the lines. I breathed a sigh of relief for Henry, though; at least he'd done the deed. Now, as Beverley handed me the day's problems I revisited the strange events of the previous night. I had spoken to Ed for the first time in six months and had worked out that the Confettimail was from him: which, presumably, could mean only one thing – that he'd split up with Mary-Claire Grey.

'Beverley,' I said as I switched on my computer, 'you know your friend, the one on the ball committee, the one who knows my husband's girlfriend . . .'

'Yes,' she said, 'Gill Hart.'

'Could you do a bit of discreet snooping and find out what's happened?'

'Sure. I'll give her a ring.'

I tried hard to concentrate on the day's problems, but it was difficult given what had happened the night before. A confusing combination of surprise and yes, pleasure, at seeing Ed again, competed in my mind for space. He'd taken this

huge risk, and gone to the twins' party knowing that I'd probably be cold and remote. And I'd tried very hard to be cold
and remote but his warm words had deflected my wrath.
Which meant I no longer had the luxury of indignation – a
channel between us had opened up. It was clear that Ed had
real regrets about our split and wanted to make amends. But
did I . . . ? I determined to drive him from my thoughts for
the time being, and now, as I handed over some letters to
Beverley to draft, I thought again about what Claudia had
said. I rummaged in my bag – it's such a mess these days –
for her business card, then rang her at *Heat* magazine.

'I'm sorry we didn't conclude our conversation last night,'
I said.

'Well I don't blame you – that stunning bloke turned up!
Who *is* he?'

I explained.

'Lucky you!' she breathed. 'Anyway back to the subject in
hand.'

'So you think Electra's record company are behind this?'

'Ooh no, it's more than that. If you ask me it's got Rex
Delafoy plastered all over it.' Rex Delafoy? The P.R. king and
tabloid sleazemonger?

'I thought disgraced politicians were more his thing. Why
would he get involved with this?'

'Because he wanted to promote Electra and, at the same
time, I would say, get at you.'

'Why would he want to do that?'

'I don't know. But have you ever crossed him? He's notoriously vengeful.'

'No. Although . . . I did write a profile of him last year, for
the *Post*, just before I became their agony aunt. It wasn't that
nice, but then it didn't say anything about him that hasn't
been said before. In fact it was a bit of a cuttings job as I only
had a day.'

'Was it a signed profile?' she asked.

'No, it was anonymous, they always are.'

'But he could have found out that it was by you.'

'Yes, probably. It wouldn't be hard –' *Ah.* I suddenly remembered: Serena's sister works for Rex Delafoy. Knowing what I now know about Serena, she probably told her that it was me.

'Well,' Claudia added, 'I'd take another look at that profile if I were you.'

I went down to the library, leafed through the thick file of Delafoy clippings and found my piece near the top. *Delafoy's legendary ruthlessness . . . consummate media manipulator . . . purveyor of sleaze . . . makes reputations . . . breaks reputations . . . Fleet Street eats out of his hand . . . ruthless, rude and backstabbing . . .* And then I'd added, in a flourish of my own, *The hair is improbably luxuriant while his curiously smooth and bagless eyes suggest that he's been under the knife.*

I phoned Claudia back and read it to her.

'Oh God he'd *hate* that!' she exclaimed.

'What, ruthless, rude and backstabbing?'

'No, the last bit – he's notoriously vain. He's had hair weaving and he *has* had his eyes done – but he'd never forgive you for saying so in a million years. I'd talk to your editor about this if I were you. Good luck!'

'The Electra story appears to be a scam,' I said calmly to Ricky five minutes later. 'I believe I've been stitched up – or rather "turned over" to use tabloid-speak.' Ricky leaned forward on his desk, his balding head gleaming in the spotlights as I explained Claudia's theory to him.

'But her letter was genuine wasn't it?'

'Only in as much as she wrote it, but in every other respect it's probably fake.'

'You mean she's not a dyke?' His face expressed a strange mixture of stupefaction and disappointment.

'No, I don't think she is. I think Rex Delafoy dreamt up the whole thing with the aim of giving Electra a massive media blast to hype her new single, while at the same time getting at me. Delafoy's lot then tipped off Serena about it.'

Ricky looked at me then rubbed both temples with his

index and middle fingers as if it helped the cogs in his brain to turn. 'But how could they possibly *know* that Serena would definitely leak the letter?'

'Because her sister works for Rex Delafoy. That's why Delafoy's lot targeted Serena because they knew that she was broke. Then all she had to do was get hold of the letter, copy it, take it to the *Daily News* and Pass Go.'

Ricky steepled his fingers and stared into the distance, an expression of childlike bewilderment on his face. 'But *how* did she get hold of it? You said you were so careful.'

'I was. But what I didn't know was that Serena had a set of keys to my desk, probably a spare set of Edith Smugg's. I went down to the canteen for about half an hour and she must have opened my drawer then. She'd made a great show of saying that she was going home, but she clearly didn't – she hung around.'

Ricky's brow was pleated with concentration while his lips were pursed into a thin line. 'But in that case why didn't Delafoy's lot just *give* Serena a *copy* of the letter?'

'Because they needed her to believe it was real. She wouldn't have taken it to the *News* if she thought it wasn't genuine.'

'Hhmm. Shirley!' he shouted to his secretary, 'get me all the latest cuts on Electra!' He reached for the phone. 'I'll get my investigative boys onto this.' A wave of relief swept over me. Maybe I wouldn't lose my job. I'd felt so indignant at what had happened, but maybe things were going to turn out all right after all.

As I returned to my desk, Beverley was on the phone and I heard her say, 'Thanks Gill – talk to you soon. Rose, I've found out a bit about Mary-Claire Grey,' she said as I sat down. 'All Gill knows is that Ed didn't leave her.'

'Didn't he?'

'No. She dumped *him*.'

'*Oh*?'

'It happened a month ago apparently, but Gill doesn't know why. She said she hasn't spoken to Mary-Claire for a while – apparently she's moved up to Newcastle – but when she's got her new number, she'll tell me more.'

So . . . Mary-Claire had given Ed the push. How interesting. But why?

'Maybe he snores,' suggested Bella a couple of nights later as we were sitting in my kitchen. 'God this curry's fantastic Rose, I can't believe you made it.'

I still couldn't quite believe it myself. Theo was out giving a lecture on 'Sunspots, Aurorae and Other Cosmic Commotion' so I'd done it unaided. To my amazement it hadn't been hard.

'Ed doesn't snore,' I said.

'Does he smell nasty?'

'No. He smells of Penhaligon's Lime.'

'And he's not boring is he?'

'No,' I agreed as I passed them the nan bread. 'He's amusing.'

'Horrid political opinions?'

'Not as far as I know.'

Bella furrowed her brow. 'Then what could it be?'

'He's not a secret cross-dresser or anything is he?' asked Bea with another large slurp of white wine. She'd been drowning her sorrows all evening. 'That would be a *total* turn-off in my book.'

'Er, no,' I replied. 'He's not.' As the twins continued to speculate, I glanced at the glossy publishing catalogue lying on the table. It listed *Heavenly Bodies*, which was due out in May. There was a photo of Theo, leaning casually against my front door, his blond hair haloed by the lemony sun.

'Maybe Ed was unfaithful to Mary-Claire as well, Rose,' I heard Bella say.

'Hmm. I doubt it somehow, but yes, maybe. Pak choi for anyone?'

'Well, it's all a mystery,' said Bella as I passed her the dish of lightly steamed leaves. 'But don't you feel happy, Rose, now that she's gone?'

'Well, yes, I suppose I do. But although I've spent the past six months loathing her, the whole thing makes me feel *weird*.

I was getting over Ed – I wasn't even reading his horoscope any more – but now the blighter's popped up again.'

'That's my fault,' said Bella guiltily. 'Although from what you say about the Valentine confetti, he might have got in touch anyway.'

'Maybe.'

'Perhaps he simply misses you,' said Bea with a shrug. 'I mean, you did love each other to start with.'

I looked at her. 'Yes,' I said quietly. 'We did. In fact I was besotted with him.'

'Well you had a funny way of showing it Rose, because let's face it, you totally neglected him.' Alcohol – and her unhappiness – had made her tactless: I flinched. 'That's why he had the affair,' she went on heavy-handedly. 'Because you spent too much time working. Bella and I thought so at the time. Frankly, the burglars have a good point.'

'Well I think they're very *nice* burglars for returning Rudy,' said Bella diplomatically as she fed him a grape. 'It's so nice to see you again Rudy,' she trilled. 'We were *so* worried about you. How's he been since he got back?' she added. 'Has his trauma affected him in any way?'

'No, he seems perfectly fine. In fact I think he's got Stockholm Syndrome as he seems to have positively enjoyed himself; but he keeps shouting "Vowel please, Carol," and "You are the weakest link!" so I guess they watched a lot of daytime TV.'

'They would do because they'd be busy burgling in the evenings,' Bella pointed out.

'Where's Beverley?' Bea asked tipsily. 'I'd like to have seen her. She's nice.'

'She's got another date.'

'Lucky her,' said Bea bitterly. 'Who's the guy?'

'I think it's this Scottish bloke, Hamish, who she met again at New Year. She saw him last week too. He's a conductor.'

'Of buses?'

'No, orchestras. Apparently he goes all over the world.'

'But I thought she was mad keen on Theo,' said Bea.

'Well, she is, in the sense that they see a lot of each other – but I don't know what's going on. When it comes to her love life Beverley doesn't really confide in me and so I don't like to probe.'

Suddenly Rudy started bobbing his head, and shaking his wings. 'We've got to ditch the bloody mynah, Dave!' he shouted as he hopped along his perch. 'That effing bird's driving me mad!!'

'Dave? Oh, that's interesting,' said Bella animatedly. 'The burglar's name is Dave.'

'I've tried, John!' Rudy yelled. 'I've tried! But no-one wants him mate!'

'And John,' said Bea lifting her head from the table. 'Got that?' I wrote down Dave and John, and resolved to phone the police the next morning, idly wondering whether Rudy could be a witness for the prosecution in any trial.

'I hope Andrew's enjoying himself this evening,' Bella added, as Bea groaned and rolled her eyes. 'He's at an awards ceremony, but partners weren't invited. Still,' she said happily, 'I'll be seeing him tomorrow.'

'And the next day,' said Bea viciously as she cleared our plates. 'And the day after that, and the one after that, and you'll be seeing him next week, and next month and next year and next decade and next fucking *century* for all I know!'

'Bea, don't be like that,' pleaded Bella. 'Please try and be happy for me.'

'I *can't* – I've just been *dumped*! While you're going to go off and marry Andrew, aren't you?'

'Well,' Bella blushed, 'I don't know, I –'

'Yes you *are*!' Bea shouted as she slammed the dishes into the sink. 'You're going to go off and marry Andrew and live with him and leave me all on MY *OWN*!' She furiously squished Fairy liquid over the plates while Bella and I exchanged nervous looks.

'Don't worry Bea,' said Bella gently. 'I know you'll meet someone else soon. Henry simply wasn't right for you, otherwise he wouldn't be seeing this "other woman" would he? He'd be seeing you. Andrew knows so many people,' she added reassuringly, 'I'll ask him to find someone nice.'

Bea groaned then lifted her right hand to her brow. 'Oh God,' she said, 'I'm miserable and I'm absolutely *pissed* – we'd better go.'

Later, as I got ready for bed I wondered what would happen if Bella did get married: it's definitely on the cards, and when it happens Bea will be completely unable to cope. I imagined her at the wedding blubbing loudly in the front pew, or leaping to her feet when the vicar asked if there was any 'impediment' to them being joined together in Holy Matrimony and shouting out, 'Yes! Me!' But then she's lived with Bella for most of their lives – they're as intertwined as a figure of eight. Now there was a real danger of the link being broken and it was making Bea feel chronically insecure. As I brushed my teeth I imagined her sitting alone and desolate in their flat in Brook Green with Bella's stuff all gone.

I spat neatly into the basin, then opened the mirrored bathroom cabinet. On the bottom shelf are my few things: my moisturiser, toothpaste, and scent – Égoïste – and on the top shelf is Theo's stuff. Like me, he doesn't have much: just his razor, shaving cream and deodorant and his small bottle of Eau de Cologne. As I closed the door I looked anxiously into the mirror, as I often do these days. I studied my eyes, where the lids were beginning to crease slightly, and the shallow tramlines etched on my brow. A slight sag was just becoming evident on my jaw line, but my neck was still reasonably smooth. I patted cream onto my face then turned on the tiny tranny which I always have tuned to London FM. Minty was on, presenting *Capitalise*, the station's feature magazine.

'And now we talk to Pat Richardson, who runs Reunite, an adoption search agency . . .' I heard her say. 'Pat has dedicated her life to reuniting adopted children with their natural parents,' Minty continued. I turned it up. 'But each time it brings back the memory of the day when, as an unmarried mother of sixteen, her nine-week-old daughter was wrenched from her arms and taken away. Pat, welcome to the show.'

As I slowly massaged in the moisturiser I listened to the woman explain how she'd searched for her daughter for thirty years, finally finding her in May 1994. But, to her surprise, there had been no joyful reunion: the girl had been cold and remote. There had been just three telephone conversations, then no further contact. Her daughter didn't want to know.

'The day I knew I'd found her I was elated,' said Pat quietly. 'It was like walking on air. It never occurred to me that she might not want to know me . . .'

'More fool you, then,' I said.

'What sort of thing triggers an adoption search?' Minty asked.

'Well, very often it's when the adoptee has their first baby, or a landmark birthday can set it off. The issue has been niggling away for years, and then they suddenly hit thirty, or forty and decide that they're going to do it at last.'

'Well, also with us in the studio,' said Minty, 'is Lucy, now thirty-two who, eighteen months ago, found her mother through Reunite. And for Lucy the trigger was indeed a big birthday – her thirtieth. But your story is a much happier one, isn't it?'

'Yes, it is,' Lucy replied. 'Thanks to Pat's agency I did find my mother, and luckily we've become friends. I'd wanted to look for her since I was about twelve.'

'Not all adopted children do want to find their birth parents,' said Minty softly. 'Why did you want to find yours?'

'Well, it was two things. Firstly, I'd always felt that there were some huge pieces missing from my life – it was as though I didn't quite feel *real*. And secondly, although my adoptive parents are lovely, I'd often felt like a square peg in a round hole. I was constantly aware that I looked nothing like them or like my non-adopted siblings. That knowledge ate away at me, and I got to the stage where, for good or ill, I just *had* to know.'

'What was it you wanted to know most of all?' Minty asked

gently. 'Why your mother had given you up?'

There was a pause, and then the girl said, 'No. I thought that would be the main thing, but it wasn't. I just wanted to know . . .' There was silence. 'I just wanted to know . . .' she tried again. 'I just wanted to know . . .' I heard her swallow her tears, '. . . why I am like I *am*.'

And now, as she composed herself again and carried on speaking, I looked at my long nose, with its tilted end, and at my slightly determined chin, and I looked at the curve of my eyebrow, and at the distinct groove between nose and lip; and I thought, as I so often have thought, that's what *I* want to know. I want to know why my hair is red, and so curly – or 'mad' rather – and why my eyes are pale green. I want to know why I'm over six foot and why my collar bone is slightly pronounced. I want to know why my top lip lifts a little in the centre, and why my hands are the shape that they are. Where do these physical traits come from? Do they come from *her*, or from her parents; or do I resemble *him*? Is my character *her* character or his character, or is it simply my own? Do I have any mannerisms of theirs, and do they like the things that I do? Do I laugh – or cry – in the same way, and is my voice similar to either of theirs? I'll be forty years old in less than three months and I don't know the answer to any of this.

'Thank you for joining us on the programme today,' said Minty, 'and the number for Reunite is 0870 333111. That's 0870 333111.' Involuntarily, I reached for my lip liner and had even started to jot down the number on the mirror when I suddenly stopped.

'No,' I muttered. 'What's the *point*?'

'Do join us again tomorrow at the same time,' Minty concluded warmly as the ads began to roll.

Mother's Day will soon be here so why not spoil YOUR mum with some chocolate truffles from Chocomania?!! Go on, surprise your mum – you know she deserves it!

I smiled grimly, then turned it off. 'Mother's Day.' 'Mothering Sunday.' I ask you. What a joke.

*　　*　　*

'This week did not begin well,' Trevor wrote in his column on Monday:

I had to have a bath (horrific), plus Bev's got it into her head that dried dog food is better for me – I'd rather eat Brillo pads! Not to mention that vicious little Persian number from across the road giving me the evil eye. Then we went to Tate Modern on Sunday and this woman comes up to me and starts patting me; but then she says to Bev, 'It must be so *awful* being blind, my dear, but at least you've got a *lovely* Guide Dog.' Quick as a flash Bev says, 'YOU must be blind if you think he's a Guide Dog, his jacket says Helping Paw quite clearly!' Oooh! I wanted to die. The poor girl's been as touchy as a Thai masseuse lately what with the uncertain situation on the bloke front. But all these petty aggravations fade into insignificance compared with the things Bev and I have seen this week. We've been lending a paw in the Post's Agony department and, believe you me, there's nothing like reading about other people's problems to make you forget your own. The letters I've read! Depression, drug addiction, insomnia, serious illness – it kind of gets things in perspective, you know. Mind you, I've been a bit of an agony aunt to Bev these past few days. As I say, that girl's mood has been up and down like a Jack Russell on speed – which makes a dog's life pret-ty tough. The object of her affection – I've sussed who it is now, that Scottish bloke – is leaving London again next week, so I'm soon going to be mopping up tears. I'll just have to be ready with the box of Kleenex and hope Bev doesn't go too crazy on me. Still, at least I've got through to the next round of the Dogs of Distinction award but, hey, the competition's going to be stiff. Guide dogs, life-saving dogs, sniffer dogs (total respec', boys), gun dogs (there's one Setter who can handle a Smith and Wesson like a real pro); anyway, these guys are all up for it too so there's no way I'm going to win. No. Way. 'But it's not the winning is it, Trev?' as Bev says every time I get a bit uptight about it all. 'It's the taking part.' 'Sure,' I reply, as I secretly stick my paw down my throat. 'Course I wanna win! Anyway, office life has been providing

282

a welcome distraction from all the stress, and I like it; except for the editor slobbering over me. Bless him, he likes animals, but I do draw the line at being snogged by a man. I mean, it's really not good for the old image is it? And I thought I had a problem with saliva control . . .

'Trevor's been a bit rude about Ricky,' I said to Beverley.

'I know,' she said, with a grin. 'You really ought to be more careful,' she said, wagging an admonitory finger at him, 'we don't want you getting us sacked.' Suddenly my nostrils detected Eau de Ricky. Sure enough – he was coming our way.

'You're for it now Trev,' I said as he nervously put down his toy gorilla. 'You should never offend the boss.'

'Trevor baby!' Ricky exclaimed, throwing wide his arms. 'Our circulation's up again, and it's *all* down to *you*. Here,' he got down on his hands and knees and put his arms round the startled dog. 'Let me give you a *big* kiss.'

'That'll teach you for being so cheeky Trevor,' said Beverley primly.

'This dog writes like a dream,' Ricky said as Trev politely licked his ear. 'I'm thinking of entering him for Columnist of the Year actually – he's doing the *Daily Post* proud. And how's it going in Misery and Agony, Bev? Thanks for helping out.'

'Oh it's fine,' she replied. 'I've spent most of the morning opening letters of support for Rose, actually,' she explained pointedly, 'she gets at least ten every day. Here,' she said, handing him one, 'why don't you take a look?' She passed him a letter, and he quickly scanned it, nodding, then handed it back. 'Rose has such *huge* support from the readers,' Bev added sweetly.

'Well, yes, I, er, can see. In fact I've been getting quite a lot of letters like this myself. Erm, when's your last day Rose?' he added anxiously.

'Thursday.'

'Right, well, erm, don't do anything rash. My investigative team are making steady progress – I'll let you know.'

That afternoon Theo phoned to alert me to a small piece in the *Evening Standard*'s media diary wittily headed, *Watt's Going On With Electra?* I glanced through it, *Foul play suspected in tabloid trashing of agony aunt . . . hand of Rex Delafoy . . . lesbian love triangle scandal a stunt . . . Electra spotted canoodling in Groucho's with her husband, Jez . . . Sapphic rumours may well be untrue . . . So where does this leave the Post's disgraced problem lady? Watch this space.*

I was rereading it later that night at home, as I sat in front of the telly with Theo, when there was a knock at the door.

'Who on earth's that?' said Theo. 'It's gone eleven.' I shrugged. He glanced out of the window. 'It's a motorbike courier. Are you expecting something?'

'No.'

Theo opened the door, then came back into the sitting room with a large jiffy bag addressed to me. Inside it was a copy of the early edition of the *Daily Post*. 'SHAME ON *YOU!!!*' it announced above a huge photo of Electra. *Star Faked Lesbian Affair to Boost Single! King of Spin Behind Scam!* There was a photo of Electra walking arm in arm with her husband, a triumphant little smile on her lips; below was a smaller shot of me above the headline, *Respected Agony Aunt Wins Reprieve.* I read through the piece as Theo looked at it over my shoulder, aware of the warm pressure of his arm on mine. *Electra's husband sanctioned Rex Delafoy's publicity scam from which all parties – except the Post's Rose Costelloe – stood to gain. Electra's single shot to number one . . . backing singer benefited from ensuing exposure and is pursuing a solo career of her own . . . her boyfriend party to sting . . . Rex Delafoy, said to have been angered by hostile profile penned by Costelloe, pleased to see her attacked in the press . . . Her assistant, Serena Banks, following a tip-off, leaked the letter to the Daily News. Rose Costelloe took every possible precaution to protect the star's confidentiality but was duped in a cynical hoax . . .*

'Her behaviour has been entirely vindicated,' Theo read out loud from the leader column on the comment page. 'She retains the *Daily Post*'s absolute trust.' He rubbed my forearm affectionately. 'There you go!' The article went on gleefully to point out that the biggest loser had been the *Daily News* who a) looked foolish for being taken in and b) paid eighty thousand pounds for a 'scoop' that had been exposed as a sham. There was then a table comparing the circulation of both papers, with the *Daily Post* claiming to have put on four hundred thousand new readers in the last three months.

'The *Daily News* has merely succeeded in hugely boosting the profile of our brilliant agony aunt, Rose Costelloe,' Theo read out with a smile. 'She will continue to solve your problems with her usual combination of kindness and solid good sense.'

I read it all with a kind of detached interest: it was as though it had all happened to someone else. Paper-clipped to the front was a note, from Ricky. *I'm sorry about all this, Rose. I now accept you were right not to give me the letter. We'll sort out your new contract first thing.*

'My God, he's apologised to me,' I said wonderingly, feeling my face crease into a huge smile.

'Well make sure you get more money out of him after all this,' Theo advised me. 'At least an extra twenty per cent.'

'Five,' said Ricky the next morning.

'Twenty,' I repeated sweetly.

'That's a bit steep.'

'I don't care. My feelings have been hurt, my reputation savaged, and my word widely disbelieved.'

'Ten, then.' Screw you, I thought. I turned and began to walk out of his office. 'Fourteen.' My hand sprang to the door. 'Fifteen?' I opened it and stepped outside. 'Oh all right then! Sixteen.' I was going for broke. 'Seventeen and a half?' he shouted querulously. 'Okay, okay, twenty per cent it is.'

I turned round. 'Thanks Ricky. And the same for Beverley?'

'Why?'

'In recognition of the fact that she doesn't just do the admin, she also drafts some of the replies.'

He sighed. 'Yeah, okay, then. As it's her.'

'And she gets a transport allowance to cover her taxis?'

He nodded. 'Here,' he said, pushing the contract at me. 'Sign on the dotted line. Another year with a month's notice on either side, not that we'd want you to leave. You're just about the best known agony aunt in the country now. Our sales have shot right up.'

As I walked back to my desk I was surprised to realise that I didn't feel elated by my new contract, just relieved that I wouldn't have to sell my house.

'How did it go?' Beverley asked. I told her. She was thrilled.

'HR are drawing up your contract right now.' Suddenly my phone rang. '*Daily Post* Problem Page,' I said cheerfully.

'Rose?' My heart did a flick-flack. 'It's Ed.'

'Oh; Ed, hi,' I managed to say casually, as my stomach churned and lurched like a tumble dryer. 'How are you?'

'I'm fine. But I've just seen the papers and I simply wanted to say, well, that I'm glad at the way things have turned out. I mean, you're still my wife . . .'

'For the time being,' I said defensively.

'For the time being – yes – and I've hated seeing you got at like that. I know how much your job means to you and well, I'm glad you've got it back.'

I distractedly pulled out my pen tray, and two bits of stray Confettimail fluttered out. 'Thank you Ed,' I said as they spiralled gracefully to the floor, like sycamore seeds. 'That's very kind of you.' I picked one of them up and studied it. *CSThinkAU* . . . And now there was an awkward silence in which it wasn't clear who was going to hang up first. 'Anyway, I'd better get back to work,' I said. 'I'm pretty busy.'

'Oh, of course. I mean, you've probably got a letter from Posh Spice to deal with,' he said with a slightly forced laugh.

'Mick Jagger actually.'

'Ha ha ha ha ha!'

'And Gwyneth Paltrow.'

'Of course.'

'So . . . goodbye then Ed.'

'Goodbye, Rose.'

'Goodbye . . .'

'Goodbye.'

'Have we done saying goodbye yet Ed?'

'Er, yes we have.'

'Because you're still there.'

'Oh. Well, um, that's because – there's something I've just remembered.'

'Yes?' I fiddled with the biros in my pen pot. 'And what's that?'

'Well,' he said nervously. 'I've been doing some clearing out lately and I discovered some stuff of yours and I wondered if you'd, er . . . If you'd er . . .'

'Yes?'

'. . . like me to bring it round?'

Chapter Seventeen

On Wednesday evening, at seven, I discreetly watched for Ed out of my bedroom window, my stomach in knots, my chest heaving like an accordion, and at five past his company BMW pulled up. He got out, beeped open the boot and took out a large cardboard box. As I heard the squeak of the gate I looked in the mirror, slowed my pulse with some deep breaths, then went downstairs and opened the door. There he was, looking devastating, in cream chinos and a navy blazer and an open necked chequered shirt. But there were dark shadows beneath his expressive brown eyes, as though he hadn't been sleeping well.

'This is very kind of you,' I said civilly. 'You shouldn't have. I peered into the box. 'You really *shouldn't* have!' I repeated with a laugh. 'You should have taken it to Oxfam instead!' There was a hideous painting I'd bought in Rome, an ugly ceramic pot I'd made at an evening class, my old *Doctor Who* videos, some school files, and a dozen or so vinyl LPs'

'Well, I thought some of it might have special sentimental value,' he said gently.

'Well thanks. Actually, it does. Where did you find it all?'

'In the attic.'

'Oh yes. I'd forgotten I'd put it up there.' He handed me the box, and we stood smiling at each other awkwardly, like teenagers at a school disco. The tension was making my jaw ache.

'Er. Do you want to come in?'

'Well,' he said diffidently. 'If you're sure it's convenient.'

'Yes. I'm not working.'

'You're *not*?'

'No.'

'I thought you worked all the time.'

'Not any more. I've got this fabulous new assistant, Beverley, who helps me draft the replies so that cuts my work load in half.'

'Gosh, well, that's great,' Ed beamed. I put the box down in the hall, and Ed came inside. I looked at his aquiline nose, his fine, sculpted lips, and the two deep curving lines, etched, like brackets, into either side of his mouth.

'How's Rudy?' he asked politely as he followed me into the kitchen.

'Oh, he's fine. He was stolen, but returned a month later as they couldn't stand the noise. You see he speaks now.'

'Really? What does he say?'

'All sorts of things, none of it wildly original.' I peered into his cage. 'He's asleep, he did a lot of talking today so he's tired, but he'll wake up by and by. Would you like a drink?' I added. 'You're driving so you can either have one glass of wine or' – I rummaged in the fridge – 'one of these.' I held up a bottle of beer.

'I didn't know you were a beer drinker, Rose,' he said as he sat down at the table.

'I'm not really, they're Theo's, but we share stuff – he won't mind.'

'And, er, who is Theo exactly?'

'My flatmate. He's an astronomer; his book's coming out in May. It's called *Heavenly Bodies – a Popular Guide to the Stars and Planets*,' I explained, surprised to feel my heart swell with a kind of pride. 'He knows all about asteroids and spiral galaxies and lunar occultations,' I added. 'Theo's great.'

'And, um, how old is he?'

'Twenty-nine.'

'Oh.' A look of relief seemed to flicker across Ed's face. I flipped the lid off his beer. 'And where is he now?'

'At the Royal Astronomical Society, giving a lecture on

meteor showers. He's an absolutely mesmerising speaker. I've been to hear him a couple of times.'

'I see. Nice house,' Ed said affably, glancing round. 'It's got style.'

'It's not nearly as big and smart as yours of course, but then you can't have everything.'

'How many bedrooms have you got?'

'Three.'

'So it's about, what . . . 1500 square feet?'

'Haven't a clue.'

'And there's a garden?'

'Just a small one: semi-paved.' I saw Ed's eyes range along the cluttered work-top. 'Sorry, the kitchen's a bit of a mess. I haven't got round to tidying up much lately, what with being pilloried in the national press. In any case Theo and I seem to live in cheerful chaos a lot of the time,' I added airily. Ed looked at me as though I were ill.

'You've changed Rose,' he said quietly. He shook his head as if in disbelief. 'You seem so . . . *different* somehow.'

'Really?' I said vaguely. 'Yes . . . maybe I have. It's probably the Camberwell effect. It's all very relaxed and Bohemian around here. Are you hungry by the way? I was about to cook something.'

'What?' Ed nearly spat out his beer.

'Would you like something to eat?' I reiterated. 'I could make a quick risotto.'

'Oh, well, that would be great. But Rose,' he said wonderingly, 'you never cooked anything before.'

'No. I didn't know how. But Theo's taught me to make a few things. He's a brilliant cook,' I added warmly as I got down the packet of arborio rice. 'He's an astronomer and a gastronomer,' I explained with a smile. 'So our marriage guidance counsellor has moved on I hear?' I said as I fished out a saucepan.

'Who told you that?'

'I just heard. What happened?' I asked with friendly curiosity as I got out the chopping board.

291

'Oh,' he sighed, as I began to cut up a small onion, 'it wouldn't be gallant of me to say.'

'Go on Ed, tell me.'

'No. Well, all right then. She just . . . got on my nerves.'

'I must say she got on mine too, but I thought you were rather keen. She did move in with you, after all.'

'She was only there for a couple of months.'

'I see. So why did she annoy you? Don't tell me,' I said as I got out the butter, 'she was short with you!'

He pulled a face. 'Honestly Rose, she wasn't that small. Everyone's short to you because you're so tall.'

'I know,' I said, 'it's mean of me. Especially as she must be feeling rather *low*,' I snorted.

'C'mon, Rose.'

'And let's face it she doesn't need me cutting her down to size!' I guffawed. 'No really Ed, tell me, seriously, what was the problem with her?'

'She . . . well, she just complained all the time.'

'About what?'

'Oh, all sorts of things. It ground me down and I wasn't happy, so in the end I asked her to leave.'

I turned and looked at him. 'You dumped her?'

He reddened. 'Yes. Yes. I did.' Oh well, I thought as I lightly sweated the onion. It was a minor deception. Male pride and all that. 'Anyway, I don't really want to talk about it,' he added ruefully. 'It's over.'

'All right. I won't ask any more. So how's your mum then?' I enquired changing the subject.

'She's fine.'

'And the others?'

'They're . . . fine too.' He seemed to hesitate for a second, 'not that I see them that much.'

'I always thought that was a shame,' I said as I tipped in the rice. 'I was partly attracted to you because of your huge family, not having any siblings myself. And what about Jon?' I added. 'The one who sent us that lovely alabaster lamp when we got married.'

Ed shifted uncomfortably. 'I think he's . . . okay. I haven't seen him for years, Rose. You know that. We had our . . . differences.'

'Oh yes. You did tell me.' As I say, they'd fallen out about money and hadn't spoken for over six years. I'd seen a photo of Jon once at Ed's mother's – he taught History at a school in Hull.

'Thanks for returning the divorce papers,' I went on as I sloshed half a glass of white wine into the pan. 'And thanks for the Valentine too.' I smiled at him over my shoulder, as I steadily stirred the rice. 'I kept finding bits of confetti for days. You *are* a dark horse, Ed. I had no idea it was from you. I thought it was from my stalker.'

'Your stalker?' He looked horrified.

'Well, not really, he was just a bit of a pest. I was furious when I thought it was from him, but then I realised it was from you. I must say I was very intrigued.'

'How did you guess?' he asked, a tiny smile at his lips.

'It was something you said at the twins' launch. You said you couldn't stop thinking about me, and I suddenly twigged.' I turned my back to him again as I continued to stir the steaming risotto. A rich aroma filled the air.

'Well, it's true, Rose,' I heard him say, quietly. 'I can't stop thinking about you. And I miss you. You're still my wife after all.'

'For the time being,' I said coolly as I poured in some stock.

'Yes, I know. For the time being. And when I saw you at the ball I was longing to talk to you, but somehow I'd got myself caught up with Mary-Claire. She'd have gone ballistic if I'd spoken to you, so I just had to watch you from afar. And I thought, that's my wife, that amazing-looking woman over there; she's *my* wife, and she's dancing with someone else. Who, er, was he by the way?' he added carefully as I washed the salad.

'That was Theo.'

'Theo? Oh. I see. So, are you . . . ?'

'Are we what? Oh . . . *no*,' I said. 'Not that it's any of your business, Ed – I told you, he's my flatmate, that's all. We're simply happy cohabitees.'

'You're obviously on very friendly terms.'

'We are. I've learned a lot from Theo actually.'

'Like what?'

'Well, for example, that our galaxy alone is so big, that it takes the sun 225 million years just to go round its centre once. Isn't that incredible?'

'Mmm,' he said furrowing his brow.

'Just think, the last time it completed a full circuit the first dinosaurs were roaming the earth. I wonder what the planet will be like 225 million years from now?' I mused.

'I wonder,' he said in a bored kind of way.

'I've learned that there are galaxies which actually steal stars from neighbouring galaxies.'

'Really? They should be reported.'

'And I've learned that the Andromeda galaxy is on a direct collision course with our own one. It's going to crash into the Milky Way in a billion years.'

'Oh. Well, there goes the neighbourhood.'

I smiled. 'I've also learned that the Hubble telescope is so powerful that it could focus on a single lit match in London from as far away as Tokyo.' I shook my head. 'It's just *amazing*. It makes you view things in a different way.'

'Hhhm,' he said. 'But I don't want to talk about astronomy Rose, I want to talk about us.' And now, as I warmed the plates, and laid the table, I heard Ed's voice as if in a dream.

'Just wish we could put the clock back . . . got ourselves in a mess . . . I behaved like a complete jerk, Rose . . . but I felt so neglected by you . . . And I tried to tell you but you wouldn't listen . . . you were completely obsessed. I wanted you to take notice of me,' he concluded. 'But you wouldn't, so I decided I'd make you, and Mary-Claire was very pushy and so . . .'

'It's true, I did neglect you,' I admitted as I took the risotto off the heat. 'I wasn't very wifely, was I?'

'Well, to be honest, no. And you were so difficult to live with.'

'Yes, I probably was.'

'It was as though you didn't really *like* living with me. You were so unrelaxed.'

Suddenly Rudy woke up and began to shake his wings.

'Ed, I've told you to take your shoes off when you come in!' he shouted in my voice.

'I was difficult,' I said with a laugh.

'You're a fucking nightmare!' Rudy shouted in Ed's voice now. Ed's face was a mask of horror.

'Did I really talk to you like that?'

'You did, but then you were rather provoked. I'm sorry I wasn't a good spouse,' I said as I sprinkled parmesan shavings onto the rice. 'You deserved better, but I just got so engrossed in the new job.' I tossed the salad then we sat down to eat, saying nothing for a minute or two. Just sitting opposite each other, having dinner together in a way we'd rarely done before.

'Rose,' he said quietly. 'I know I don't have the right to ask you this, but have you met anyone else yet?' I stared at him. Why should I tell him? '*Have* you met anyone else?' he pressed me.

'Well, hhhm. No. Not yet. Why do you ask?'

'Because, well . . . I'd like to put the divorce on hold, that's why. That's really what I came round to say.'

'Why didn't you say it over the phone?'

He rested his left hand on the table, then drew in his breath.

'Because I knew it was something I could only do face to face. Getting the divorce papers was just terrible,' he went on dismally. 'It took me ages to sign them because I simply didn't want to.' So *that* was why he'd delayed. 'And then seeing you attacked in the press like that made me feel so awful; and it made me realise how much you still mean to me. I wanted to protect you, but I couldn't. Please, Rose, can't we try again? Please, Rose,' he repeated softly. 'I still love you, and I feel we never really gave ourselves a proper chance. We married far too quickly and then it all imploded, and you left, and I haven't been happy since. Have *you* been happy,

Rose?' I looked into his warm, brown eyes, and felt something inside me shift. 'Have you?' he repeated quietly.

'Not really, Ed. I've just coped. I've done what I advise my heartbroken readers to do. I've put on my clothes in the morning and I've gone to work and I've tried to block you right out.' Now I remembered the little exorcism ceremony I'd done six months before. I'd tried to flush Ed away but he kept popping back – and now here he was. 'I flushed my wedding ring down the loo,' I told him. He winced as though he'd been given a slap. 'I wanted to cut you right out of my heart.'

'Haven't you missed me?' he asked.

'Yes. Of course I have. It was just so terrible to start with – it was torture – but my anger kept my feelings at bay.'

'And are you still angry with me?' He put down his fork. Was I still angry with him?

'No. Not now.' He smiled and then exhaled with relief.

'Then do you think we could start seeing each other again, just taking it day by day, and see if we can't give ourselves another chance?'

Another chance? I stared at his empty plate.

'So you want second helpings?'

He gave me with a quizzical smile. 'Second helpings? Yes,' he whispered. 'I do.'

Sometimes people write to me complaining that although they don't have any specific problems, at the same time they don't feel happy, and they feel that they ought to feel happy. So they actually ask me how they can become happy. I usually write back saying that in my view happiness lies in being able to want the things that you've got, not the things you haven't got – that's always been my advice. Now I'm not so sure. For example, I'd wanted Ed back – I'd obsessed about him for months – and now, to my amazement, here he was, fairly pleading with me to give him another chance. But strangely, having the thing I'd so wanted didn't leave me feeling happy – it left me feeling hollow and strange. If Ed had come after me last October, I'd have been putty in his hands. I'd have forgiven and forgotten and gone back to him – I mean, who wants to get divorced? But it was six months since we'd split up and my life had changed, and now I was completely confused.

'He only wants second helpings because he hasn't enjoyed his just desserts,' said Bella contemptuously when I dropped in at the shop on the following Saturday. 'I hope you're not going to see him again?'

'That's a bit rich coming from you,' I said. 'You invited him to the party after all.'

'I know,' she cringed. 'I wasn't thinking straight. Anyway, *are* you going to see him?'

I sighed. 'I don't know. I told him I wanted to think about it and he gallantly left the ball in my court. He's not being pushy about it or anything – he's just planted the idea in my mind. His demeanour was gratifyingly contrite and he was very sympathetic and actually I'm wondering whether he isn't right. I mean, his affair is over, and I've realised my mistakes, so maybe we *could* try again. Getting divorced makes one feel such a *failure*.'

'Well I'd be very careful,' said Bella, shaking her head. 'He's been unfaithful to you once, remember.'

'But there were mitigating circumstances, Bella, viz, I was an absolutely useless wife.'

'I don't know,' she said, 'it's your life, but I've always said there was something about Ed I didn't like.'

And I was tempted to say, 'but look at the fifth rate philandering pile of shite *you're* dating.' Instead I bit my lip.

'So how's it all going?' I asked pleasantly.

'Oh it's fine. Bea's out with clients at the moment – they want Latvian minimalist apparently so it's quite a tricky commission – and I'm stuck here. But to be honest,' she said, 'it's probably the best thing as we're not getting on very well. Bea's being rather . . . *difficile*,' she enunciated delicately.

'What do you mean?'

'She's making my life sheer bloody *hell*.'

'In what way?'

'Well . . .' she lowered her voice as a customer came in and began looking at the tartan tea-cups. '. . . Andrew and I went to the cinema last night. And Bea came along too.'

'So?' I murmured.

'Well, it was a bit awkward.'

'But she's very lonely.'

'I know. The soft furnishings are downstairs Madam if you'd like to take a look.'

'And she's still smarting about Henry,' I pointed out, 'so she wants a bit of distraction.'

'Yes, and that's fair enough. But then on Monday Andrew and I went out to dinner at Quaglino's and Bea turned up there too.'

'Really?'

'Yes. Then we went to a premiere on Tuesday and she insisted on coming as well. Andrew really doesn't like it.'

'I see.'

'I think she's going slightly mad actually,' Bella concluded airily. You're one to talk I thought. 'Anyway Rose, what do you think I should do?' Oh *why* do I have to solve other people's problems all the time I thought wearily. I feel like a walking C.A.B.

'Well,' I said, feeling my lips purse, 'you'll have to take a tough line. Or perhaps just don't tell her where you're off to every time you go out.'

'But she always asks; or she rings me on my mobile and forces me to tell her. I don't know what to do.'

'It's a tricky one. Hopefully she'll become so engrossed in the business as it becomes more successful that she'll feel less insecure. I mean, you're each other's anchors. Bea's terrified that you'll leave her.'

Bella winced. 'I know. This was always going to be our biggest problem,' she said regretfully. Yes, I thought, that's right. The longer the twins have lived together the more difficult men find it, and the harder it is to break up. 'I mean, if Andrew does want to live with me,' Bella went on, 'then I can imagine Bea trying to come too. And although I'd be perfectly happy about it in some ways, I know Andrew would never agree. I mean, he doesn't actually *like* Bea that much,' she confided. 'Partly because he feels that she doesn't like him.'

'Doesn't she?' I said disingenuously. I was amazed that he had the sensitivity to detect Bea's distaste.

'No. She doesn't like him at all. So she says that the reason she wants to come out with us all the time is so that she can "keep an eye" on him.'

'Hmmm . . .'

'She said this awful thing about him actually.'

'Really. What did she say?'

'She implied that he might, well, let me down.'

'By being unfaithful?'

She nodded. 'But I know that he *never* would. Can I help you?' she said politely to the customer as she came upstairs clutching a velvet cushion patterned with snapdragons and foxgloves.

'Yes, I'd like this. It's lovely,' she breathed.

'I know,' said Bella, as she began to wrap it in tissue, 'they're gorgeous. Is it for you?' she added pleasantly as she tore off some sticky tape.

The woman smiled. 'No, it's for my mum. I always try and get her something really *special* on Mother's Day.'

When I got home two hours later there was a message on the answerphone from Henry.

'Rose, I'm off to the Gulf tomorrow for six weeks. Sorry I haven't seen you recently, I've been rather, well, involved. I hope Bea doesn't hate me too much, and I'll call you in May when I'm back.'

I hung up my coat, and looked at the house. It was a mess. There was dust all along the shelves and on the tops of the pictures, and the carpet needed a clean. The cushions were unplumped in the sitting room, and there were old coffee cups standing about. Several unread newspapers were waiting to be chucked and there was a pile of dishes in the sink.

Theo and I have become slobs, I realised. I don't know why, but I'm far less tidy than I used to be. I knew I should hoover, for example, but I simply couldn't be fagged. Instead I began to go through the box of old stuff that Ed had brought round. I put the records in the sitting room, then packed up the painting and the pot for Age Concern. Age Concern, I reflected ruefully. Yes, I'm very concerned about my age. Still, I thought to myself, as I flicked through my old school files, there's nothing I can do. There were three red ring binders, containing my 'A' level work on yellowing A4, my writing tiny and terribly neat. I'd done English, French and Art History and I'd spectacularly failed them all. It was June 1980 and I remember sitting in the school hall staring at the questions as non-comprehendingly as if they'd been written in Sanskrit or Japanese.

Comment on the use of symbolism in Madame Bovary . . . Can't. *What were the greatest achievements of the Renaissance?* Don't know. *Why is* Measure for Measure *considered a 'dark comedy'?* What does the question mean? My mind was as blank as a television screen after closedown: it was featureless, humming and grey. And I just sat there and doodled, occasionally looking at the clock, unable to write anything other than my name. I didn't need to read the official letter in August to know that I'd got three 'U's.

The twins thought I'd failed to revise the right questions but that wasn't it at all. I'd worked very hard, and I was well prepared, but I'd made this awful mistake. I'd applied to see the registration of my birth and I'd been shown it the day before. If, as I was, you were adopted before 1975, then you have to speak to a social worker first. And they give you what's called Section Fifty-One Counselling where they prepare you for what you might find. So I went to the Ashford social services place and met this woman, and she was very nice and very professional and she explained that what I was about to see might open up a can of worms for me, and was I one hundred per cent sure that I really *wanted* to see it given that I was still very young? And I said yes, I was one hundred per cent sure. I'd waited for this moment all my life. Then she asked me if my adoptive parents knew what I was doing, and I said that they did. I'd told them that I wanted to see the registration because I was applying for a passport, but it wasn't true. The real reason was that I just wanted, at long, long last, to read the names of my biological mother and father. But when the counsellor handed that piece of paper to me, and I saw what was on it, it was the most shocking experience of my life. And the following day I somehow got myself to school and sat my first 'A' level and my dreams of university went up in smoke . . .

I heard the click of Theo's key in the lock; he'd been next door helping Beverley with her VAT return.

'Look at these old LPs,' he exclaimed. 'Are they yours? The Partridge Family. Who the hell are they?' I suddenly felt very old. 'And the Jackson Five. My God – Michael Jackson looks black. What have we got here? Mud. The Bay City Rollers . . . and what's this one? Marie Osmond! This stuff must be worth a fortune, Rose!'

'Stop it. You're making me feel like an antique.'

'I'm sorry.' He smiled. 'I used to tease my wife like that, it drove her mad.'

'She's almost as ancient as I am, isn't she?'

'That's right.'

'How was Beverley?' I asked changing the subject.

'Not too bad, a bit depressed.'

'I suppose her bloke's gone off?' Theo looked at me. 'That Scottish guy? The conductor.'

'Oh yes. Hamish. That's right. He's gone abroad, so she's rather, you know, down in the mouth, plus Trevor's got a bit of a cold.'

'Does she want to come round and eat with us? I could cook.'

'I already asked her and she said no.'

I've noticed that Beverley always prefers to be left alone when she has these occasional dark moods. So Theo and I spent the evening playing Scrabble as we quite often do – and I was just thinking about my nuisance phone calls and how they seem to have stopped, when, by one of those strokes of telepathy or simple coincidence, I had another one. The phone rang at eleven, and I picked it up and it was the heavy breather again.

'Who was that?' Theo asked.

'The Poison Panter.'

He pulled a face. 'Oh dear. Again.'

'Well they say it's good to stalk.'

'You don't seem that worried about it, Rose.'

'I'm not. It's beginning to wash over me.'

'And what was it like this time?'

'It was quite heavy, and asthmatic: I almost felt sorry for him. You know,' I said as I sat down again and stared at my rack of letters, 'there's something slightly odd about it all. With other silent calls they often ring several times in a row, to annoy you, but my caller always stops after one.'

'Well he's obviously a considerate nuisance.'

'Or she is. I still don't know.'

'I thought you were going to bar the calls.'

'I've tried, but the phone company's always engaged. I hung on for twenty minutes yesterday listening to synthesised "Greensleeves"; in the end I had to give up. Anyway whose go is it? Mine. No, don't look at the letters when you're picking Theo, that's cheating.'

'But I need some more vowels. Right, what have you got?' I stared at my letters: I had two 'e's, then 'p,' 'r,' 'a,' 'o,' 'h' – that would make 'Oprah,' or 'Harpo,' but proper nouns aren't allowed.

'Okay, I've got . . . this.' I put down ORPHA on top of Theo's TENT.

'Orphan. That gives you . . . twenty-four with the double word score.'

'I'm an orphan,' I said with a rueful smile.

'Oh yeah. You should go into a children's home. Anyway, you're probably not an orphan,' he said with another swig of beer. He picked up his letters and put 'ARENTS' across the P of ORPHAN. 'Your natural mother's probably still alive. And who knows, maybe your father is too.' I looked at him. 'They might not even be sixty yet. They've probably got another twenty years left.' If anyone else had mentioned my natural parents to me I'd have given them the liquid nitrogen treatment but, coming from Theo, I didn't mind. He picked up the *Times* magazine. *How to do Mother's Day in Style!* it shouted in pink letters. *The Strongest Link!*

'I always think of my mother at this time of year,' Theo said as he flicked through it.

'I always think of mine too.'

'Your adoptive mother?' I shook my head. 'Do you mind if I ask you about your adoptive parents?' he said with uncharacteristic diplomacy as I took some more letters out of the bag.

'No, I don't mind. Fire away.'

'You don't seem to have been very close to them.'

'I wasn't.'

'I knew that from the casual way you reacted when their photo was stolen.' I shrugged. 'Rose, what were they like?'

'What were they like? Well,' I explained, as I put my letters on the wooden rack, 'they were about a foot shorter than I am. And . . . they were very strait laced, and extremely devout. We spent an awful lot of time in the Bethesda Baptist Chapel at weekends,' I added. 'Which is why I don't go to church now. I'd say that they meant well and that they were decent people, but . . .'

'But what?'

I sighed. 'Well,' I began chewing on my lower lip, as I always do when I'm stressed, 'there were a number of things. For a start, and I've never told anyone else this Theo – not even the twins – I suppose I simply never felt that I *belonged* with them. My father ran a shoe shop, semi-bespoke, and I'd watch him fitting someone with a pair of shoes, measuring their feet properly, widthways and lengthways, examining their arch and their instep – getting it just right. And I'd think that I didn't fit with them.'

'Because you didn't look like them?'

'Oh no, it wasn't that. If there'd been a stronger bond that wouldn't have mattered at all. It was because they weren't very, well, parental, I suppose. I didn't want for anything, and they weren't unkind, but nor were they ever really . . . affectionate. I felt like their guest, not their daughter. I'd watch the twins' mother hugging them when she came to fetch them from school and I'd feel the most terrible pang. And my parents didn't really know how to play with me, so I had to amuse myself. They weren't that tolerant of kids really, I was always being told not to make a mess.'

'That's probably why you're so tidy,' he said. 'Although . . .' he looked around, 'standards have been slipping a bit lately.'

'Mm. I don't know why.'

'Because you're relaxing Rose.' I realised that he was right. 'Tell me more about your parents,' he added softly.

'Well I often used to wonder why they'd adopted me,' I went on, 'and I found out the answer after they died.'

'What did you find out?'

I kept my eyes fixed on the Scrabble board while I wondered whether or not to reply. 'I found out that they'd adopted me for all the wrong reasons.'

'Which were?'

'Pity.'

He looked at me. 'How do you know?'

'Because after they'd died I was going through their things and in my dad's desk I found a file with all sorts of stuff relating to my adoption, none of which I'd ever seen. There were some letters from the social services and some family correspondence and some other bits and pieces. When I was little they told me that they'd really wanted to have a nice baby like me, and that they'd chosen me specially, but that was a lie. They did it out of Christian charity. That's what they actually said. I found a copy of a letter my dad had written to the adoption people in which he said that he felt it was his "duty to take in this unfortunate child".'

'I still don't understand,' said Theo. 'In order for them to

304

adopt you they must have been registered with the adoption service for quite a long time first.'

'No, they weren't. This was in 1962, it wasn't like it is now. These days there are less than five hundred babies a year available for adoption: then there were twenty-seven *thousand* a year – you could virtually hand-pick your baby, and there weren't the endless waiting lists and interrogations that there are now. The Abortion Act of 1967 changed everything for obvious reasons and after that adoption became hard. Anyway, I'd always got on reasonably well with my parents, although I'd never have said we were close. But when I saw all that stuff I felt totally . . . different about them: it was as though that part of my life had closed.'

'But didn't you feel, with their deaths, that another part of your life might open?'

'I – I don't know what you mean.'

'Didn't it make you want to find your real mother?' I looked at him. 'Don't you want to find her?' *Did I?* 'I think you do.'

'Well –'

'When are you forty?'

'June the first. I think.'

'You think?'

'Well, I'm not totally sure. That's what was on my birth registration anyway.'

Theo furrowed his brow. 'I think your fortieth is the catalyst. You do want to find her, don't you, Rose?' I had another sip of beer. 'I think you've wanted to find her for some time. That's your problem. You do and at the same time you don't. You're such good fun Rose, but you cast a long shadow and I believe that that's the reason why.'

'That's not the reason at all,' I said quietly. 'And you're wrong to assume that it is, Theo, because I've never told anyone the truth.'

'But I think the truth is that you've never forgiven her for giving you up.'

'If only it were that simple.'

'What do you mean?'

'I –' I bit my lip.

'Think Rose, they used to say that life begins at forty, so why don't you make that the watershed to make *your* life start again? Don't you want to know your mother?' I looked at him, and felt a tightening in my throat. 'Don't you want to see her face?'

'I –' I felt tears prick the back of my eyes.

'Don't you want to talk to her and ask her questions about, well, who you are?'

'I –' By now my cheeks were burning and Theo's features had started to blur.

'You do Rose,' he said urgently, 'I know you do.' I stared at my lap. 'Don't you?'

'Yes,' I croaked. 'I *do*. I do want to know her. I *do* want to find her. Of *course* I do – but I *can't*.'

'You can!'

'No. I can't. It's not that straightforward.'

'It is.'

'It *isn't*!'

'Why not?'

'I can't say.'

Theo passed me his handkerchief and I pressed it to my eyes.

'Rose,' he said, 'I don't want to hurt you, but I think I know the reason.'

I looked up at him and stared. 'You can't possibly know,' I whispered hoarsely.

'I think I do. I've guessed.'

'Guessed what?'

'Well – that you're afraid. You're afraid that your mother might not want to know, and you just can't stand it because it would be as though she'd rejected you twice.'

'Sorry, Doctor Freud – your diagnosis is wrong.'

'I think it's right. And it's totally understandable, because you felt your mother had rejected you so badly before.'

'I didn't *feel* she'd rejected me. She *did* reject me,' I said hotly. 'Anyway, that's got nothing to do with it,' I added as a hot tear rolled down my cheek.

'Then why can't you find her, Rose? There are all these adoption agencies, and private detectives and people who'll do an internet search. It would be quite easy for you to track her down, surely?'

'No it wouldn't!'

'Why not?'

'Because . . .'

'Because what?'

'Because it just *wouldn't* – that's why.'

Theo's face expressed a mixture of compassion and total non-comprehension.

'Rose,' he said gently. 'Tell me in words that I can understand. Why can't you find your mother? She gave you up for adoption so there must be paperwork available by which she can be identified.'

'No, there *isn't*,' I said. 'That's the whole point. There isn't any paperwork. There isn't anything.'

'Why not? Was it destroyed? Maybe there was a fire and it was burnt,' he added. I shook my head. 'Then what's the reason?' he persisted. '*Why* can't you try and find her.'

'Because,' I said as a wave of blackness engulfed my chest. 'Because I wasn't just "given up for adoption" as you say.' I stared at him, my temples throbbing. I could hear the beat of my heart.

'What do you mean?' he said. 'I don't understand.' Right, I thought. This is it. *Now.*

'I was *found*,' I said. 'I was . . . found. I was abandoned.' My hands sprang up to my face.

'Oh Rose.' There was a few seconds' silence, then Theo's hand reached out for mine.

'I was thrown away. Like a piece of rubbish. I was discarded. I was ditched. I was dumped. I was left, unclaimed, like so much excess baggage. *There*,' I wept. 'Now you know. That's what really happened to me, Theo.' My mouth ached with sobbing, and my breath came in ragged gasps.

'Oh Rose,' he said again as I cried like a child, shudderingly, inconsolably. 'I'm so sorry . . . but where? Where were you found?'

'In a fucking supermarket trolley in a fucking car park!' I wailed.

'Oh, Christ.' He was lost for words. 'And . . . when did you find this out?'

'When I was eighteen,' I said reaching for a tissue. 'I saw the registration of my birth for the first time on my eighteenth birthday. And where it said Mother's Name it said "Unknown" and where it said Father's Name it said "Unknown," and where it said Place of Birth it said "Unknown". And then it added "Found in the Co-Op car park in Chatham, Kent, on 1.8.62". For the date of birth it said "Unknown, but probably on or about 1.6.62" because I was judged to be about eight weeks old.'

'Eight weeks?'

'Yes, she kept me for eight weeks,' I sobbed. 'Eight *whole* weeks; two months – and then she did that. That's what's always hurt more than anything else. Knowing that she'd kept me that long. Knowing that she'd fed me and held me and cuddled me . . .' I stopped.

He came and sat beside me on the sofa and I felt his arms encircle me. 'Poor Rose,' he whispered. 'Poor Rose.'

'And when I got back home and told my mum what I'd seen she said: "Oh yes I do vaguely remember something in the paper about a baby having been abandoned." But she never mentioned it again, and nor did Dad. And I never mentioned it either, because I was filled with hate after that. I no longer wanted to find my real mother in the way I had before. I just couldn't believe that she'd done that to me, and so I cut her right out of my heart. I cut her out like a tumour, Theo – I "vanished" her – because that's the only way I could survive. I put her in a compartment in my head, and shut the door, and that door's been locked ever since.'

'You've lived with this for over twenty years,' he said softly, 'and never told anyone?' I nodded. 'Oh Rose. It's tragic,' he said simply.

'It is for me.'

'It is for her too. Poor woman,' he murmured. 'To have felt so desperate. She must think of you every day. So did your adoptive parents read about you in the newspaper?'

'Yes,' I whispered. 'They lived in Ashford, which is about thirty miles away, but someone had left a copy of the *Chatham News* in my dad's shop, and in it was the story about me. And my mother worked for the council and she knew the woman at Kent social services so they applied to adopt me, and they did. And the reason they did it was because they felt it was their "Christian duty", as they put it. And when I read that, in that letter of my father's, I just felt something in my heart shut off.'

'And your birth mother never came forward?'

'Never. They gave her four months, but she never did.'

'She must have felt too ashamed, or too confused.'

'I have no way of knowing what she felt.'

'Gosh Rose, you were a foundling,' he said wonderingly. A foundling. For some reason, it sounds so much better than 'abandoned'.

'Yes,' I croaked. 'I was. I was a foundling, Theo. I was found. And I feel I've been lost all my life.' We sat there saying nothing for a minute or two, the silence broken only by my stifled sobs.

'How were you found?' he asked quietly. I pressed the hanky to my eyes then looked at him. 'I mean, what was with you when you were discovered?'

'After my parents died I found out. Because in that file I found the newspaper report in which it said that I'd been wrapped in a cotton blanket – it was August so it wasn't cold; and there was a note pinned to it asking whoever found me to take care of me, and saying that my name was Rose. There was also a small blue plastic box.'

'What was in it?'

I looked at him, then took a deep breath. 'I'll show you. I've never, ever, shown a soul.' I went up to my bedroom, opened my jewel case, took it out then went downstairs. 'It's probably all she had,' I said as I showed it to Theo. 'One gold charm.' It was an Aladdin's lamp. I'd sometimes rub it, in the hope that a genie would appear and bring her back. 'That's how I'll know,' I added quietly. 'That's how I'll know for sure that it's her, and that's how she'll know that it's me. That's what Victorian women used to do,' I went on, calmer now. 'When they left their babies at the foundling hospitals they'd leave something – a piece of embroidery, or a necklace, or a playing card – even a hazelnut – in case they ever saw their child again. Then they could ask them what was with them when they were left, so that they could identify them beyond doubt.' I glanced at the clock. It was midnight. Mothering Sunday had arrived.

'Poor Rose,' Theo whispered, shaking his head. 'You've carried this for so long. I understand so many things about you now. I understand that business with the newspaper for a start.' I looked at him. 'And I think I understand why your marriage didn't work.'

'It certainly didn't. It was a mess. He loved me and left me,' I said bitterly. 'Just like she did.'

'I think you *made* him leave you.' There was a pause, just a beat, like a rest in music, silent and yet redolent, while I thought about what he'd just said.

'I made him leave me?'

'From what you've told me, I think you did. It's as though you were trying to create a situation whereby you'd be rejected again. As though, deep down, you think that rejection is what you really deserve.'

I looked at him. 'Maybe I do think that.' I bit my lower lip and sniffed, then I heard Theo say, very gently.

'Look for her Rose. It's not too late. Try and find her.'

'I would Theo – but I can't. There's absolutely nothing to go on; no records, so she has to look for *me*. Abandoned babies are hardly ever reunited with their birth mothers.'

'Well, I still think you should try. I'll help you Rose.'

'Will you?'

He nodded. 'Yes. I will. I lost my mother when I was nine,

so I'd love to help you find yours. You could put an advertisement in the local paper, in Chatham.'

'Hmmm.'

'It's worth a shot isn't it?'

'Maybe.'

'I think you'd like to try at least, wouldn't you Rose?' I looked at him and felt my eyes fill again.

'*Yes*,' I whispered. 'I would.'

Chapter Eighteen

I've always noticed the stories in the newspapers of course. You'd be surprised how many there are. The baby boy abandoned on a golf course, the baby girl found in a carrier bag. Infants found under hedges, in shop doorways and church porches, and one recently found in a skip. It's not a Grimm tale, but a grim reality and, strangely, there are more now than ever before. Sixty-five are found every year in this country, a quarter of whom are never claimed. It often happens in late December, so at least I was spared the cold. The newborn bundles are usually named after the policemen who find them or the nurses who revive them. Then there are all the foundlings in fairy tales and plays. Perdita in *The Winter's Tale*, or Hansel and Gretel left in the wood. Baby Moses found by the Pharaoh's daughter; Romulus and Remus suckled by the wolf. I know all these characters and their stories inside out, and I've identified with them all.

Sometimes I've been tempted to tell the twins, but a deep sense of shame held me back. I felt I must have been a very bad and unappealing baby for my mother to do what she did. So why then did I choose to tell Theo? Why *did* I . . . ? I don't really know. Maybe because Mother's Day was looming, when it always weighs on my mind, or perhaps because I find him so sympathetic; or maybe he just wore me down. But I don't regret it. I feel lighter. I feel lifted. At last, at *last*, someone knows.

From what I've read, few foundlings feel any animosity towards their mothers, just a desire to understand. But I had always harboured a real hatred towards mine; not because she abandoned me, but because she kept me for those eight weeks first. If she'd given birth to me in a hedge and left me there I'd have been able to forgive her, and even pity her. But she looked after me with evident care, and *then* she ditched me. That's what I just don't get.

In my situation you find yourself clutching at straws. I don't know my true date of birth for example, but at least I know my Christian name really is Rose. The social services people gave me a temporary surname, Stuart, after the man who first found me and picked me up. There was one baby I read about who was discovered wrapped in a tea towel in a lay-by in Yorkshire. He was called William Daniel Redhill. William after Shakespeare, whose birthday it was; Daniel after the ambulance man who attended him, and Redhill after the road in which he was found by a couple on their afternoon walk. All things considered, that's not too bad. He could easily have been William Daniel Tooting Broadway, for example, or William Daniel B105. And then there was the baby found in the doorway of a Burger King. Imagine . . .

Today I showed Theo the box file of my stuff. In it were the papers from the children's home where I'd been kept for three months while my parents applied to adopt me, and the note which my mother had left. *Please look after my baby*, it said, in large, faded, slightly wobbly, round handwriting. *Her name is Rose*. There were the clothes I'd been dressed in, and the edition of the *Chatham News* in which I'd made page two.

'"Baby Left In Car Park",' Theo read out loud from the brittle and yellowing newspaper. 'That's probably why you became a journalist,' he added; 'because you began your life in the news. "The baby was found gurgling happily where it had been left, in a shopping trolley, aged about eight weeks." I don't like you being referred to as 'it,' he said pulling a face. '"The baby was found at 4.30 p.m. on August 1st by the Co-Op's assistant manager, Stuart Jones." August the first,' he repeated. 'So *that's* the significance of August the first for you.' I nodded. 'I remember from New Year's Eve. I thought it might be your birthday.'

'No, it's my Founders Day,' I quipped.

' "The baby was found in a healthy condition," he read on, "and was wrapped in a cotton blanket. It was wearing a white pram suit and had a bottle of milk with it. Police are appealing to anyone who was in the car park at the time and who saw a woman carrying a baby to contact them." '

'No-one ever did.'

I picked up the pram suit and buried my face in it, as though I might sniff some faint aroma of my mother; some lingering residue which might lead me to her, like a blood-hound, forty years on. But all I could detect was the musty smell of old cotton and the dry scent of dust and age.

'Have you worded your ad properly?' Theo asked. I showed it to him.

' "On August 1st 1962," ' he read, ' "an eight week old baby girl was found in the Co-Op supermarket car park behind Chatham High Street. Do you know anything about the circumstances of this baby's abandonment? If so please write in total confidence, a.s.a.p., to Box number 2152." '

Theo phoned the *Chatham News* and placed it, using his credit card, and I paid him back. I didn't want anyone there recognising my name and running a story on me. The replies were to be addressed to Theo, and he asked them to send him a copy of the paper. It arrived within the week. Thirty thousand people would have read my notice – surely *one* of them might know. Someone must have known that my mother was pregnant; but then on the other hand, maybe not. I've had letters from distraught schoolgirls, six months gone, who'd had not the faintest idea. It seems incredible, but it does happen.

'Someone knew something,' said Theo, as he looked at the advert, 'but the question is whether they'll tell. Your mother might have sworn them to lifelong secrecy.'

'She might well. Can I swear *you* to secrecy, Theo? I don't want anyone else knowing about this until I hear something, if I ever do. You won't tell Beverley will you? I'm fond of her but I just don't want her to know.'

'Of course I won't. I'm very discreet. I mean, have I ever repeated to you any of the things that she's told me?' I shook my head. 'Anyway, I think we should keep the ad in for at least a month,' he added firmly. I smiled at the word 'we.' I was touched by his determination to help me find my mother; it was as though he took a personal interest in sleuthing her down.

For the first week I was on tenterhooks. I'd wake early, sick with anxiety, waiting for the loud clatter of the letter box. Then I'd rush downstairs to see if Theo had any letters with a Chatham postmark, stamped 'confidential' – but so far, he didn't. During the day my heart would race at the thought of what I'd started. It was like awaiting the results of some critical test.

'Are you all right Rose?' Beverley asked me on Wednesday morning as we went through my mailbag.

'What?'

'You seem a bit distracted, that's all.'

'Oh, no, no. I'm fine.'

'It's as though your mind's not quite on the job.'

'Really? Oh no, it's . . . nothing.'

'And this reply you've written here,' she said, 'I don't think it's right.'

'What?'

'Well, I don't think you've given good advice.' She handed me the letter again and I read it.

Dear Rose, I have fallen in love with a clerk in my local bank, but I don't know how to tell him. I'm not very good at relationships since I was raped when I was twenty and have avoided men since then.

'What did I tell her?' I asked Beverley.

'You told her to slip him a note.'

'Oh.'

'But that's not the point, is it Rose?'

I heaved a painful sigh. 'No,' I said. 'It's not.'

'The point is that she needs to have the significance of her choice – a man safely behind a pane of glass – pointed out to her. She also needs to have it gently suggested to her that the rape is still affecting her and that she would almost certainly benefit from some professional help on that score.' Beverley's face expressed a mixture of disappointment and surprise. I felt about two inches tall.

'You're right, Bev,' I murmured. 'My advice was terrible. Will you draft that one?'

'Yes, sure.'

'I *am* distracted at the moment actually,' I added. 'It's no excuse, but I'm obviously not thinking straight.'

'Is it because of Ed?' she asked gently. I fiddled with my stapler. I couldn't tell her about my mother.

'Well, yes, it is. In part. I'd decided that I was over him, and I was almost looking forward to moving on. But now he's come back into my life and I'm not sure about *anything* any more. My whole perspective has somehow changed.'

'Do you really think you could give things another go then?'

I shrugged. 'That's what I'm trying to find out. I was a *hopeless* partner, Bev. I know that now, and, for the first time, I think I also know *why*. And Ed really wants us to try again.'

'But do *you*?' I began to doodle on my pad. 'Do *you* want to try again?' she reiterated gently.

'Bev, a recent survey revealed that seventy-five per cent of married couples who'd experienced infidelity stayed together afterwards. Apparently the success of the marriage after the affair depends on the acceptance of both sides that they were mutually responsible for the situation, and on a sincere commitment to change.'

'How interesting,' said Beverley giving me one of her funny, slightly piercing looks. 'But Rose, do you *want* to give things another go with Ed?' she persisted.

I looked out of the window. 'Yes, I think I do, but . . .'

'. . . but what?'

'Oh, I . . . don't know.'

'Don't you?' she said. I fiddled with my earring. 'What's holding you back?'

'I'm . . . not sure.'

'Really?' she said. And now I doodled two stars on my pad, and then Saturn with its hula-hoop rings. 'Well you've just got to do what *you* feel is right,' she said quietly.

'Hmm. That's true. By the way,' I went on, 'have you heard from your friend yet, the one who knows Mary-Claire Grey? I want to know why she left Ed. He says that he dropped her because she complained all the time, but I'd be interested in knowing what she had to say.'

'I don't think Gill's spoken to her yet, but when she does I'll let you know.'

'And how's your romantic life?' I asked her as we began leaflet-stuffing the envelopes. 'Since you've been asking about mine. Fair's fair.'

'True. Well, it's . . . hhm, I'm not quite sure. It's quite hard for the two of us to get together at the moment.'

'Well it's a bummer that Hamish lives in Scotland,' I said as I fished out my *Blushing* leaflet. 'And he travels quite a lot too doesn't he?' She nodded, then sighed. 'Long distance relationships are never easy,' I concluded wearily.

'Yes,' she said feelingly. 'I know.'

On Saturday I met Ed in Whiteleys and we saw the new Nicole Kidman film then we went for a Chinese in Poons.

'You look happy Rose,' he said as we nibbled on some crispy seaweed.

'I *am* happy.' I thought of the advert again. There'd been no reply so far, but I still felt upbeat – at last, at *last*, I had hope. I wanted to stand up right there in the restaurant and shout, 'I'm looking for my mother everyone, and maybe I'm going to find her!' But I didn't. I bit my tongue.

'There's a real twinkle in your eye,' Ed remarked.

'That's because . . . it's so nice to see *you*.'

He smiled. 'You seem . . . different,' he said wonderingly. 'Like you were when we first met. Just happy and vivacious and bright. When you became an agony aunt that all changed and you became . . .'

'Agonised?'

'Well, obsessed. As though nothing else in your life existed but the problems of strangers.'

'I know,' I said, as I sipped my green tea. 'But I'm not like that now.'

'Why do you think that is?'

'Oh, all sorts of reasons,' I replied vaguely. 'Ed, did you know that our nearest star, Alpha Centauri, is so far away – twenty-five million million miles – that it would take a space rocket, travelling at thirty thousand miles an hour, a hundred thousand years to reach it?'

'Er, no, I can't say I did.'

'And did you know that there are small neutron stars – the collapsed cores of exploded supernovae – which are so dense that a piece the size of a paperclip would outweigh Mount Everest?'

'Oh.'

'And that there are more sun-like stars just in the visible universe than there are blades of grass on the earth?'

'Mmm. How do you know all this?'

'From Theo's book. He let me read the proofs. Astronomy's a fascinating subject you know; I mean, here we are having dinner, but all the atoms and particles of which we're made came into being in the Big Bang fifteen billion years ago. Don't you find that thought *amazing* Ed?'

'Well,' he shrugged. 'I suppose I do.'

'And did you know that on Jupiter there's a storm raging which is the size of the earth? And bolts of lightning a thousand miles long?'

'Oh really?' The waiter brought our king prawns.

'Don't you find it *incredible*, Ed. Just the thought of all those billions upon billions of stars?'

He shrugged again. 'I don't give it much thought. To me they're a bit like the wallpaper really – they're just *there*. Or rather they're not usually there as the weather's so bad. Young

Theo's obviously made quite an impression on you,' he added tetchily as he lifted a skein of noodles.

'He's a very interesting chap.'

'And I suppose he's got an enormous telescope has he?'

'Yes he has actually, although it's a refractor, not one of the more modern reflectors and I – oh really Ed.' I lowered my chopsticks. 'Don't be childish. We're not involved.'

'You talk about him as though you were.'

'No, I *don't*. I keep telling you. He's just my flatmate.'

'He's more than that.' I felt my heart race. 'Isn't he?' I looked at him. 'Isn't he?' he insisted.

'All right,' I conceded. 'He *is*. Yes, Theo is more than just my flatmate – he's my friend. He cares about me – I know that now – but that's as far as it goes. Please don't spoil the evening Ed,' I added softly, 'we've had such a lovely time.'

'Yes,' he agreed quietly. 'We have. I'm sorry Rose,' he said rubbing his temple. 'I know I had no right to ask, but I can't help feeling possessive about you. I mean, you are still my wife.'

'It's okay,' I sighed. 'I'm not cross. Theo's like a . . . younger brother,' I explained. This seemed to satisfy Ed and he managed to smile. 'He's like a younger brother,' I repeated. But for some strange reason I suddenly pictured him on the morning after the burglary, naked but for a towel. Ed called for the bill. He peered at it, then frowned.

'That old trick,' he said with a slightly forced smile.

'What?'

'"An optional twelve and a half per cent service charge has been added to your bill." If it's already been added it's hardly optional is it?'

'Oh, honestly, Ed. Never mind.' I smiled inwardly at his indignation, because I know where he's coming from. I know where Ed's coming from, and I know where I'm coming from. We're all carrying our childhoods around.

'And would it be very forward of me to invite you back to my place for a coffee?' he asked as we ambled out arm in arm. 'Given that we're married and everything.'

'Oh, thanks, Ed, but no.'

'Is that "no way"?' he asked quietly.

'No. It's no, as in, "not now".'

'Playing hard to get are you?'

'Not really. I just want to take things nice and slow.'

'You're right,' he said as we stepped onto the down escalator. 'After all we rushed things before. But can I see you again in a few days?'

'Yes,' I said happily. 'You can.'

Ed offered to drive me home, but I hailed a passing cab, hugged him goodbye and jumped in. And as I sat in the back, I felt a deep happiness creep over me, and a kind of gratitude. For I knew I was being given a rare chance to put right things that had gone badly wrong. I was being given the opportunity to find my mother – my *mother*! – and to try and redeem my failed marriage to Ed. How many of us get second shots at one ruined thing in our lives, let alone two?

When I got back Theo was sitting at the kitchen table, reading the *Guardian*. He glanced up as I came in, and, despite our recent closeness, gave me a slightly chilly, disinterested smile.

'Nice evening?' he asked with studied politeness.

'Yes, I . . . went to the pictures.'

'With Ed?'

'Yes, that's right. With Ed.'

'Your husband.'

'My husband,' I echoed. It felt odd saying it.

'Are you going back to him then?' I was used by now to Theo's frankness but his question took me aback. *Was* I going back to him?

'I don't know. All I know is I've been thinking about what you said the other night, about how perhaps, subconsciously, I'd wrecked my marriage. And I decided that you might well be right and so I . . .'

'Want to give it another go?'

I shrugged. 'Maybe. I don't really know.'

'I guess I'd better start flat-hunting then,' he said matter-of-factly. He picked up the property section and began flicking through it with exaggerated interest. 'The spring's a good time to buy.' So that's what this was about. Knowing that I was seeing Ed again was making him insecure because he was worried he'd have to leave.

'Honestly Theo, there's no rush. My situation isn't about to change and I, well, I like having you here.'

'Do you?' he said quietly. He looked up from the paper.

'Yes,' I said. 'I do. You're just so . . . Oh Theo, you're so nice. And I must have seemed such a nightmare when you first came here.'

'Yes, you were.' I winced. But then, as I say, Theo can be a bit lacking on the diplomacy front sometimes.

'I was only a "nightmare" because I was terrified at the thought of living with a total stranger. And I was very unhappy.'

He closed the paper. 'I know.'

'But I feel different now, and I know that it's largely thanks to you. And honestly, I'm not about to move back in with Ed, really I'm not, I'm –' Suddenly my mobile rang. It was Ed, checking that I'd got home safely. 'Yes, I've just walked in the door. Hm, it was a lovely evening,' I murmured. 'Me too. See you soon. Goodnight. I'm sorry Theo, where were we? Oh yes, Ed. I'm just taking things day by day.'

'Well, it's just that I'll be getting the cheque from my wife's solicitors soon so I was thinking that maybe I should start to look for my own place.' My happy mood suddenly evaporated like the rush of steam on a pan of seared scallops. I felt a deep, deep pang.

Maybe I could get back with Ed, but we could keep our own houses, so that I could carry on living with Theo. Yes, that was the answer, I told myself happily, then I'd have the best of both worlds. Ed and I could be like Mia Farrow and Woody Allen before things got nasty – living on opposite sides of Central Park. Or Peter Cook and his wife who had adjacent houses, or Margaret Drabble and Michael Holroyd. And I was just trying to figure out how this might work in reality when the phone rang. It was twenty to twelve. I picked up the handset expecting heavy breathing, but instead it was Bella, on her mobile, in tears.

'What's the matter?'

'It's Bea,' she hissed. 'Andrew and I went to Aubergine for dinner tête-à-tête and she came along. I tried to conceal where I was going, but she followed me.'

'Oh dear.'

'He was really annoyed. So the evening ended very badly and he's just stomped off. She's being so difficult,' she groaned. 'She's coming to *everything* and it's driving him mad. I don't know *what* to do.'

'Do you want me to talk to her?'

'No. Because then she'll know that I've been discussing her with you. But she just won't take the hint. I wouldn't mind so much if she actually liked Andrew, but she doesn't; she's just doing it to spoil my fun.'

'I don't think that's true. She's basically competing with Andrew for you. She doesn't want him to take you away. She doesn't realise how selfish it is, but it can't go on. You'll just have to get better at outwitting her.'

'Mmm,' she sighed, 'you're right. Anyway, how was your evening with Ed?'

'Do you know, it was rather nice.'

'Well you certainly sound happier than I've heard you for ages.'

'Yes,' I said, 'I *am.*' I was happier than I'd been for a long, long time, and I knew I had Theo to thank for that. For the past three years – since my parents died – I'd tormented myself with the thought that I might look for my mother. But I'd been in this awful dilemma about it, because although, deep down, I *did* want to, I resented her too much to try. But now that Theo had pushed me into it I felt liberated. I felt free. What would I say if I actually met her I wondered as I put the phone down. 'Hi Mum! Long time no see.' Or would I call her 'Mummy'? Or 'Mother'? Or would I call her by her Christian name? And what would I do after such a hiatus?

Show her my school reports? Give her forty birthday and Christmas presents all in one go? And how long would it take us to tell each other about our lives? Days. No, weeks. No – *months*.

'You are the weakest link!' I heard Rudy shout. Yes, I thought ruefully. She *was* the weakest link when she should have been the strongest, but now we had the chance to put things right.

'Theo, thank you so much for all your support about my mother,' I said as I went back into the kitchen. 'I'm very grateful because there's no way I would have started this search if it weren't for you.'

His stiffness suddenly evaporated, and he smiled one of his lop-sided little smiles. 'That's okay, Rose. I'm sorry I badgered you, but I felt that you did really want to find her, reading between the lines.' I smiled. Theo had read between my lines, with a hundred per cent accuracy, where I hadn't read between them myself. 'But you might be disappointed,' he added, 'so you'll have to prepare yourself for that.'

'I know. But even if I never find her, just *wanting* to makes me feel so much better. The fact that I don't hate her any more.'

'I don't think you ever really did hate her,' he suggested quietly. 'You were just angry with her, that's all.'

'Yes,' I agreed. 'I was. I was just *so* angry,' I added. 'I think that's why I was so uptight. But now it's as though a wall in my mind has come down. Now there's the possibility that we might actually meet; or maybe just speak to each other over the phone. Hearing her voice would be like a resurrection, as though she'd died but come back to life.'

'But it could take months until you hear anything – if you ever do – so you can't afford to get your hopes up too much. And you need to have things to look forward to Rose, to distract you while you're waiting.'

'You're absolutely right. I do.' I glanced at the noticeboard where there was an invitation from Beverley to the Dogs of Distinction prize-giving ceremony, marked *Theo & Rose. Theo*

& Rose, she'd written. *Theo & Rose*. I liked seeing our names linked like that.

'Well I'd certainly like to go to this,' I said as I took it down. 'Are you going?'

Theo looked affronted at the question. 'Of *course*! It's Trevor's big night.'

The ceremony was the following Thursday evening at the Kensington Roof Gardens. Theo and I went in the taxi with Beverley and Trevor who were both a bundle of nerves.

'It's not the winning, Trev,' she said to him again as we bounced along, 'it's the taking part.' He raised one sceptical eyebrow then she got his brush out of his coat pocket and tidied his fur.

'He looks gorgeous,' I said as she groomed him. 'If there was an award for most handsome hound he'd get it. Who's dishing out the prizes?'

'Trevor McDonald?'

'What, the real one?'

'You mean the *other* one,' she corrected me.

'Right,' said Theo, as we turned off High Street Kensington into Derry Street, 'we're here.'

As we got out of the taxi in the deepening twilight, we saw the other competitors going in. There were setters and spaniels and collies and retrievers, pugs and King Charles cavaliers. We got the lift up to the top floor, where the champagne reception was in full swing. As we went in we spotted a gigantic box of *Dogochox*, the competition's sponsors, and there were photographers everywhere.

'The puparazzi are out in force,' I remarked as Theo pushed Bev through the throng. 'And there's a film crew. Ooh, isn't that the actress, Emily Woof?'

'Yes it is. And Sue Barker's over there.'

'How many finalists are there?' I asked Bev.

'Twelve. Here,' she handed me a press release. 'This is what we're up against.' I glanced through a few of the other nominations. There was George, a bull mastiff, who had alerted passers by to a fire in his house and who had saved the lives of his two companions – a cat and a hamster. *Firemen broke into the house and rescued George, who kept barking at them until they went back in to save the cat and the hamster, who had to be revived with oxygen.* Then there was Whiskey a blind Labrador, whose favourite pastime is climbing mountains and who had scaled Ben Nevis, Snowdon and Sca Fell. *He guides himself with his well-adapted nose, and is hoping to conquer Mont Blanc next.*

'Wow!' I breathed as I read on. *Rupert, a Pets As Therapy dog, visits hospitals and children's homes and even encouraged one little boy, who was thought to be dumb, to speak.* A retriever called Popeye, a Hearing Dog, had saved his owner from a heart attack by dialling 999. And Storm, a Customs and Excise dog, had sniffed out four million pounds worth of hard drugs, and Misty had raised a million pounds for charity by walking from Land's End to John o'Groats. There were guide dogs, and dogs who'd saved people from raging rivers, and who'd rescued children lost on Welsh hills. No wonder the anagram of 'dog' is 'God' I thought as I read last the citation. *Trevor, a golden Labrador from Helping Paw, has become indispensable to his owner, Beverley, after she had a devastating accident three years ago. 'Life without Trevor is simply not worth living,' Beverley says. 'When I got him I felt that all my birthdays and Christmases had come at once.' In addition to helping her with all her household chores, gardening and shopping, Trevor writes a weekly column for the Daily Post, whose circulation, according to official ABC figures, he has raised by a staggering 10 per cent. He has also been an energetic and successful fund-raiser for Helping Paw – a truly talented dog!*

As we circulated at the champagne reception Trevor was interviewed by several journalists about his role in Beverley's life.

'How many commands has he got? . . . Five hundred? . . . Is there anything he can't do? . . . How would you manage without him Beverley? . . . Does he ever get a day off?'

'Can he do a trick for us?' I heard one of them ask.

'No,' Bev protested. 'He can't. He's a professional assistance dog, not a circus performer.'

'Good point,' said Theo under his breath.

A gong suddenly sounded and we were summoned in to dinner. By now the atmosphere had become more intense.

'– Don't worry Trixie – you're a very *special* little dog.'

'– Patch – don't bite your claws!'

'– Stop that Fido! Stop it! Right now!'

'– Oh God, he's been *sick*!'

'– It's just nerves.'

There were about a hundred and fifty people plus the nominated dogs who sprawled under the tables, receiving scraps from their owners who were far too anxious to eat. As the wine flowed, the collective mood now became distinctly competitive.

'– Snoopy was a finalist at the Golden Bonio award too you know.'

'– So was Shep.'

'– Well Frisky was second in his class at World of Dogs last year.'

'– And Whiskey can count.'

'– Wags can count *and* spell. Quite difficult words actually.'

'– Well Trudy can type – really fast.'

Bev looked at me and rolled her eyes. I tried to talk to my neighbour but he was engaged in oneupdogship with the person on his right.

'– Woofy's got five "O" levels.'

'– Bobby's got eight. And two "A" levels.'

'– I bet he hasn't got his pilot's licence though!'

'– No, but he's learning to drive.'

Theo was trying not to laugh while Beverley looked vaguely appalled. It wasn't Trevor's fellow competitors who were the problem so much as the other dog lovers who'd paid to attend. Suddenly a wine glass was clinked to call the room to attention, and the other Trevor McDonald got to his feet. He welcomed us all, then read out the nominations. I looked round the room; knuckles were white.

'We have come here this evening to honour these Dogs of Distinction,' he began as I clutched my napkin. 'The difference they make to the lives of their owners, as well as the wider community, is incalculable. Their sense of duty, personal and public, is unparalleled. Choosing the winning dog from such a field has been a near-impossible task. Thankfully that didn't fall to me, but to the panel of judges who have now made their choice. Ladies and gentlemen,' he went on, opening the shiny gold envelope. 'I know you're all in suspense, so I'll be brief. I am delighted to announce that this year's Dogochox Dog of Distinction is . . .' he pulled out the card, and a hush fell. He laughed. '. . . my namesake – Trevor McDonald!' I gasped with delight. Theo hugged Beverley, whose face was a mask of astonishment, then stood up to help get her chair through the throng. He wheeled her up to the stage, accompanied by Trev as everyone applauded. But behind the polite clapping I could already hear slightly, well, bitchy things being said.

'Fix!' someone behind me whispered. 'Just because he's got the same name.'

'It's because of his media contacts,' said another. 'You know, because of that column he writes.'

'– You don't really think *he* writes that do you?'

'– No, I think it's *her*.'

'– Never mind darling, we'll try again next year.'

'– Is there any more booze?'

And now Beverley was on the podium, Trevor alongside, amiably wagging his tail while she received the prize. Another hush descended as a technician attached a small clip-on microphone to her lapel, and she spoke.

'Ladies and gentlemen,' she began shyly. 'I'd like first of all to thank Dogochox at whose invitation we're all here. And next I'd like to thank the panel of judges for choosing Trevor to be the winner of this year's award. He's prouder and more privileged than he – or I – can possibly express. He's asked me to make a very short speech on his behalf, basically to say . . .' she drew in her breath, '. . . that he politely declines to accept.'

A collective gasp went round the room.

'– *What??*'

'– Wass going on?'

'– What's she talking about?'

'Trevor feels that he can't accept this prize, however prestigious, for the simple reason that he feels that it's . . . wrong. It's wrong to put one brilliant and brave dog above another,' she went on, her voice audibly shaking. 'And so he'd like to share the prize with all his fellow nominees which means we have the trophy for one month each. As for the £1000 cheque, I suggest that it be donated to some animal charity of our choice. Thank you very much everyone, and well,' she smiled and then shrugged, 'that's it.'

'Wow!' I heard someone say behind me. Beverley was surrounded by photographers and journalists as everyone shook their heads in plain disbelief.

'– How *amazing!*'

'– A bit controversial though.'

'– What a nice dog!'

'– What a nice woman.'

'– Well I think they've got a good point.'

Now, as the shock subsided, Beverley and Trevor were given a huge round of applause, then she called all the other dogs up onto the stage and flashbulbs were popping and journalists were frantically tapping into their laptops. Beverley's mobile rang, and I saw her get it out, and a huge smile lit up her face.

'Hi!' I heard her say – the clip-on microphone was still attached to her jacket – 'he won. He won!' she shouted. 'Sorry, it's a very bad line. He won – but he's refused it. Yes, that's right.' She was clearly telling Hamish what had happened, her face radiating joy and relief. 'Well he didn't feel it was right,' I heard her add. 'No, I agree with him one hundred per cent. How's it going where you are?' she asked. 'It's hot is it? Ooh, lucky you.'

I opened *The Times* the next morning to find a photo of Beverley and Trevor on page two headlined 'FUR FLIES AT CANINE AWARD'. The *Daily News* facetiously dismissed it as a 'Puplicity

Stunt'. The *Daily Post* had a big photo of the two Trevor McDonalds together, headlined, *Well I Never, Trevor!*! *The Daily Post's columnist, golden Labrador Trevor McDonald, sensationally declined to accept the Dog of Distinction award at yesterday's ceremony,* I read as I sat at my desk. *Newscaster Sir Trevor McDonald (no relation), presenting the honour, was taken aback by his namesake's decision not to accept the prize. 'I was flabbergasted,' Sir Trevor commented afterwards. 'But Trevor had clearly given it serious thought.'* I looked at Beverley as she opened the day's post.

'Bev, you and Trev are famous.'

She shrugged. 'It's just our fifteen minutes, that's all. It'll soon blow over,' she said calmly, 'and then life will be nice and humdrum once more.'

'Everyone's talking about Trevor,' said Bea when she rang me later that morning. 'He's becoming quite a celeb. He'll be opening supermarkets before long and appearing on *Have I Got News for You*. Perhaps I ought to get him back in the shop,' she mused, 'he'd be a tremendous draw.'

'Sorry, Bea, but I need him here. Anyway, how's the business going?'

'It's actually going rather well. We've had three new commissions just this week. The only fly in the ointment is Bella's chronic lack of concentration,' she added bitterly. 'Her mind's not on the job. But that's because she spends far too much time thinking about that idiot, and I just know that something's going to go wrong.'

'Bea,' I said. 'If you don't give them some space it *will* go wrong. Don't spoil it for Bella. It's up to her who she dates and maybe this is her big chance.'

'I'm not spoiling things,' she said hotly, 'I'm protecting her, and she'll thank me for it one day. Honestly Rose, I just know that Andrew's going to let her down with a nasty bump.'

'Let her be the judge of that Bea. I agree that he's a creep but – and tell me to get lost – I think you should let Bella make her own mistakes.'

'Hmm. Well the same might well be said of you and Ed.

You're not going to move back in with him are you Rose?'

I fiddled with the phone cord. 'No, of course not. Don't be absurd.'

'I'd like you to move back in,' Ed said the following night as we sat sipping Sauvignon in Bertorelli's. He took my hand in his and held it to his lips. 'I miss you, Rose. I'm so lonely without you.'

'Ed,' I said quietly, 'it's too soon. After all, there's no hurry is there? I'm just very relieved that we're getting on so well.'

He stroked my fingers, then sighed. 'But it's a month since we've started seeing each other again. That's quite a long time.'

'It isn't, Ed, it's quite short.'

'But we're *married*, Rose.'

'That's got nothing to do with it.'

'Why do you hesitate?' he asked gently as he kissed my hand again. 'Can't we bury the past?' For some reason I had a sudden vision of Theo, standing in Holland Gardens, his hand on my shoulder, his breath warm on my cheek, pointing out the stars. 'Why do you hesitate, Rose?' Ed repeated quietly.

I fiddled with my wine glass. 'I don't really know.'

'You must know.'

'Well, I suppose because we made such a hash of it before, I want to be quite sure that we don't get ourselves in a mess again.'

'Well,' he said, 'I have an idea. Easter's coming up, so why don't we go away?'

'Oh . . .' I felt my face flush.

'Just for the long weekend.'

'I see.'

'Wouldn't that be nice?'

'Hmmm.'

'How about it? Just you and me, Rose, on a nice little Easter break somewhere warm, hm?'

Up until now Ed and I had been having purely platonic

dates, if we went away that would change. Even though he was my husband and I still found him desperately attractive, something made me demur.

'We could go to Paris,' he went on. 'I know a sweet little hotel.'

'The Crillon?' I said with a laugh.

'Er, not quite. Or we could go to Florence if you like, or Rome.'

'But . . . who would look after Rudy?'

'Theo would.'

'But he might be away himself. He goes off sometimes, star-watching, or giving talks. He's making quite a name for himself on the lecture circuit actually. He's a brilliant speaker.'

'Well, think about it Rose, and let me know. Would you like another drink?'

I shook my head. I'm drinking less these days.

'Ed,' I said suddenly. 'It's really nice seeing you again like this, and going out together, but –'

'But what?'

'Well, why do you want me back?'

'Why do I want you back?' he repeated.

'Yes. I need to know. Is it simply because I'm the devil you know, and you don't want to have to start again with someone new, because, if so, that's not good enough.'

'No,' he said with a wry smile. 'It's not that at all.' He drew in his breath. 'The simple truth is that I love you, Rose. I was devastated when you left, even though I deserved it, and I'd like to put things right. Life's too short, and too precious, to live with huge regrets, and I feel we have a real chance to be happy again. Think about Easter,' he said as the bill arrived. 'I've accumulated loads of air miles: we can go wherever you like.'

Over the next few days I did give it some thought – it was a seductive idea in many ways. We could go to Prague, I reflected, or Barcelona; we could go to Madrid, or Venice or Nice. I imagined us driving down the Grand Corniche, stopping for lunch in Antibes; I visualised us wandering

332

around the Prado, or strolling through St Mark's Square. I saw us clambering up a Tuscan hillside, a sea of wild flowers at our feet. We'd never been anywhere when we were together, apart from on honeymoon, because I'd never had time. It seemed incredible to me now that I could ever have been so obsessed with my work. Edith Smugg didn't reply to all the letters personally, she simply answered as many as she could. And if one of my readers was behaving as I had done to Ed, then I'd have to tell them that it just wasn't on.

Theo was right. I could see that now as clear as day. Out of a perverse 'wish' to be rejected, I'd neglected Ed's needs; he deserved another chance. People don't have affairs for no reason, I reflected. They don't just happen, out of the blue. Ed hadn't been in *love* with Mary-Claire, she was simply a cry for help. I could be a better partner now, I decided, because I finally understood a few big things about myself. It was as though Theo had shone a torch into the darkness of my mind and shown me the tangled mess.

The next day I decided to tell Ed that I *would* like to go away with him. We could have a really lovely weekend somewhere and, in any case, I desperately needed a break – I hadn't had a holiday for over a year. Going with Ed wouldn't commit me to moving in with him, it was just another step on the way. And I was sitting at work, drafting replies, and mentally packing for Cap Ferrat or Vienna or Rome or wherever, when the phone rang.

'*Daily Post* problem page,' said Beverley pleasantly. 'No. No, it's not, but she's here. Who shall I say is calling? Oh.' Her tone of voice suddenly changed. 'I see.' I glanced at her. She looked serious. 'I'll just put you through.'

'Who is it?' I whispered.

'It's Chelsea and Westminster hospital.' Oh, they probably wanted to get me on some committee or other. What a bore.

'Mrs Wright?' said a business-like female voice.

'Er, yes,' I said, taken aback at being addressed by my married name.

'This is Senior Staff Nurse Howells here.'

'Oh.'

'I'm afraid your husband has had an accident. I think you'd better come in.'

Chapter Nineteen

I was there within half an hour. All I knew was that Ed had broken his arm very badly, and fractured two ribs, and that he'd been severely concussed. He'd been up a ladder and it had slipped from under him and he'd fallen fifteen feet. If it weren't for the fact that he'd landed on the grass he could have been killed, the nurse had said. I felt sick. The taxi drew up outside the hospital main entrance and I half walked, half ran through the long corridors to the admissions ward on the fourth floor. Ed was in the far bay, by the window. I parted the mauve curtain, and there he was, his eyes closed, a huge bruise on his brow like a small thunder cloud, his face grey and mottled with pain. I gently touched his left hand, and his eyelids flickered, then slowly opened.

'Rose,' he whispered. 'You're here. I –' he was suddenly seized by a spasm of pain. He clenched his teeth and the sinews in his throat flared like flying buttresses, while drops of sweat beaded his brow. 'Uuuuuuh,' he groaned. '*Uuuuhhhh*! The pain.'

'Ed, you're lucky to be alive.'

'I know.'

'What on earth were you doing?'

'Clearing leaves out of the gutter,' he croaked. His mouth looked dry. I held a glass of water to his lips. 'I had a day off,' he explained, 'and I was trying to fix a few things round the house.'

'Why didn't you get a roofer to do it?'

He rolled his eyes. 'I don't know. Don't give me a hard

335

time,' he murmured. 'I'm in agony.' At this the corners of his mouth turned up slightly. 'And you're my agony aunt.' I looked at his arm, in its fibreglass cast, and its pristine white sling. It was his right arm. Shit.

'The nurse says you've broken your humerus.'

'That's why I'm not laughing,' he groaned.

'And you've cracked two ribs, and badly sprained your wrist.' I looked at his red, swollen fingers protruding from the cast. 'This is going to be tricky, Ed.'

'I know. When I said we should have an Easter break this wasn't quite what I had in mind. You should have heard the noise when my arm snapped, Rose. It was deafening. Uuuuuuhhh,' he groaned again.

'How did you get help?' I asked as I helped him sip some more water.

'My mobile was in my pocket, and I just managed to punch in 999 with my left hand. Then I fainted. I was out cold when they came.'

'The nurse said you were lucky you didn't have to have surgery. She says it's a closed fracture, so your arm will heal without pins.'

'Thank God,' he shuddered. 'I couldn't have stood having an operation. I couldn't have stood it,' he repeated vehemently. 'The injections. I loathe hospitals,' he croaked. 'Get me out of here, Rose, I absolutely *loathe* them.'

'I know.' Ed's always had a phobia about hospitals ever since he had appendicitis as a boy. His local hospital didn't treat it properly and he got peritonitis and nearly died.

'But at least this is a nice hospital,' I said soothingly.

'It *isn't* a nice hospital. It's a horrible hospital! They're *all* horrible, just get me out of here Rose.'

'Okay, okay – try to keep calm.'

'Mrs Wright?' The curtain had drawn back and standing there was Nurse Howells. 'Could I have a word? Your husband's going to be fine,' she whispered as we stood outside his bay. 'We're just going to keep him in tonight for observation because he took a bad knock to his head. But we're worried about him going home alone. Now, I understand that you're separated, but on friendly terms.' I nodded. 'He'll need help for at least ten days.'

'I see.'

'The ribs will heal of their own accord in due course, but the break to his arm is quite bad. There's no nerve damage, but he's going to be incapacitated for a while. Is there any chance you could help out?'

'Well, yes. Of course I will,' I said.

'He'll be discharged tomorrow after the ward round. Could you come and collect him at twelve?' I looked at Ed. He had closed his eyes again. The painkillers were making him drowsy.

'Ed,' I murmured as I bent over his bed. 'I'm going to come home with you for a few days to help.'

'Oh,' he smiled faintly. 'That'll be nice. You'll think I did this deliberately, to get you back, but I didn't.'

'I know you didn't,' I smiled. 'Do you want anything before I go? A newspaper? Some mints? Some orange juice?'

He shook his head. 'I just want to sleep.'

'Okay,' I stroked his forehead. 'I've got to go back to work now, but I'll come and collect you tomorrow. And don't worry, Ed,' I kissed his cheek. 'You were very lucky, and you're going to be fine.'

On the way back to the office I decided what I'd do. I'd spend two days at Ed's house, then go back to my house for a night, then I'd go back to Ed's for another two days, and carry on like that, so that he wasn't on his own for long.

'You could take your laptop and work there while I hold the fort here,' Bev suggested when I got into work. 'In any case it's Easter so there won't be much going on, and I'm sure Theo will look after your house.'

When I got home, Theo was in the kitchen, cooking. He was wearing his *Astronomy is looking up*! tee shirt with a photo of the M33 Whirlpool galaxy. He looked at me and smiled.

'Theo,' I began, 'I'll be staying at Ed's for a bit. You see –'

'So it's all lovey-dovey again is it?' he said dismissively.

'No. No it's not like that. It's just that he's broken his arm.' I told him about Ed's accident and Theo visibly relaxed.

'I see. Well, that's . . . bad luck.'

'So what I'm going to do is spend two days at his house then come back here for a night, and then go back to Putney. But I'd be really grateful if you could look after Rudy when I'm not here.'

'Yes, of course I will.'

'Still no replies to my ad?' I added tentatively.

'No. I'd tell you straight off if there were. But it's got two more weeks to run, so there's still hope.'

'Yes,' I said. 'There is.'

At twelve the next day, Good Friday, I collected Ed in a taxi, and we went back to Blenheim Road. I'd asked the driver to go as smoothly as possible, but with each pot-hole and speed bump Ed was possessed by pain. When we drew up outside number thirty-seven I paid the driver, got Ed's keys out of his bag, then opened the door. It felt strange to be going into his house again, when I'd left it in such fury seven months before. As I put the key in the lock I remembered how I'd stomped out in September with my boxes and bags, insults spewing from my lips like a stream of lava. As I pushed on the door I remembered how I'd sat and watched the house in November, tears streaming down my cheeks. And now here I was back again, the past forgiven, and understood.

Ed stood in the hall, gingerly cradling his right arm while I refamiliarised myself with the house. The large, square hallway, the kitchen leading off to the back, the sitting room on the left, the wide staircase, the deep red dining room off to the right. I felt like Jane Eyre with a broken Mr Rochester as I settled him on the sofa with a cup of tea.

'If only I were ambidextrous,' he said. As he lifted the cup awkwardly to his lips I realised, sinkingly, that he'd need help with everything – dressing, washing, bathing, shaving, writing, shopping – the works. What he really needed was an assistance dog, I realised, idly wondering if Trevor had any mates.

'How's the pain now?'

'Bad,' he groaned. 'Especially my ribs. It hurts to breathe.'

'I'll give you another painkiller. Here.'

'I want two.'

'You can only have one, they're very strong. Now do you need to call anyone?'

'Yes, my mum.'

So I brought him the cordless phone and dialled her number. And as he spoke to her, I went into the kitchen to make lunch. I glanced out of the window into the large walled garden, and at the purple wisteria coming into full flower, and I remembered my dream again. In it I'd hurled crockery at Ed – I'd really wanted to hurt him – but now here I was looking after him like the proverbial ministering angel, all passion spent. I imagined the grass covered with feathers from the slashed duvet, and the fragments of Wedgwood strewing the path. Now I imagined Mary-Claire standing at this very window, looking out. But she'd gone and it was as though she'd never existed, and now Ed wanted me back.

Lying on the grass was the ladder, so I went outside, retracted it and put it back in the shed, and when I got back inside Ed was still on the phone. I opened the fridge and saw a box of eggs, and some smoked salmon. Good, that would do for lunch. As I shut the door something in the tone of Ed's voice made me pause.

'Mum, don't give me a hard time,' I heard him say, his voice rising. 'I've just broken my arm for God's sake . . . Look, we've been over this and you know my feelings . . . I'm sorry, but that's how it is . . . No, I can't bring myself to do it . . . Because I *can't*. He'll just have to try someone else.' He was obviously talking about Jon. Perhaps he wanted another loan. He'd borrowed some money from Ed six years before, and he still hadn't paid all of it back. That was the cause of their rift I think, though I'd never liked to ask. But from the tone of the conversation I could tell that his mother was trying to build bridges.

'Yes, Rose is here,' I heard him add. 'Yes. Maybe, Mum. I don't know.' I heard him ring off so I went and got the phone.

'Is your mum okay?' I asked. 'She must be so relieved it's not worse.'

'She's . . . fine,' he replied. But he clearly didn't want to say any more about the conversation and I wasn't going to probe. I replaced the handset and began cooking lunch.

'Scrambled eggs and smoked salmon okay?' I asked.

'Sounds lovely. But will you cut mine up?'

'Of course. I'll bring it to you there if you like, on a tray.'

'No, it's okay. I'll come in.' So I helped him out of the sofa then we went into the kitchen and sat there eating quietly, looking out.

'Just like old times, eh Rose?'

'Well, not quite.'

'No. Not quite. And it's not quite as good as Venice, is it?' I smiled. 'Never mind,' he added. 'We can go when I'm better.'

'Hmm.'

'And where are you going to sleep?' he asked as I cut up his smoked salmon.

'In the yellow room.'

He smiled ruefully. 'Not with me?'

'No.'

'Pity,' he said.

'Sensible. You have three broken bones apart from anything else.'

'You're very severe, Nurse Costelloe,' he said with a disappointed air. 'And how long are you going to stay?'

I explained that I'd be there for at least a week. 'You'll probably be back at work not long after that, won't you Ed?'

'Yes,' he sighed. 'I probably will. Thanks for helping me Rose.' He took my right hand in his left one and lifted it to his lips. 'The pain's worth it if it means I have you here with me. I hope you'll stay with me always.' My heart turned over at his affectionate words, and I thought, yes. Maybe I will . . .

*　　*　　*

I was surprised by how quickly Ed's house felt familiar to me again. I'd cook for us both, using Theo's recipes – although the Aga took some getting used to – and I'd help him change for bed. I'd get him up in the morning, and cover his cast with a plastic bag as he got in the bath. I'd scrub his back and wash his hair, and I'd hold up a towel as he stepped out. I'd put toothpaste on his toothbrush and shaving foam on his cheeks and I'd make his bed. I felt like Trevor must feel with Beverley. I found the sudden intimacy of it all disturbing when I'd been so distant and guarded before. Seeing him naked again was unsettling, but I told myself that I was simply his carer. Except I wasn't. I was his wife.

On Monday night I went back to Camberwell. I wanted to check on things in the house and collect my laptop. Theo was out, but on the kitchen table were sheaves of estate agents' details. He'd circled some of the properties in red ink – a small house in Kennington, a garden flat in Stockwell – it made me feel panicky, and terribly sad.

'Oh God,' I breathed as I looked at them, 'I don't want him to leave. Theo's so lovely. He's just so lovely,' I repeated. 'He's changed my life. Oh God, I'm such a mess. I don't know *what* to do.'

I just wanted my life to go on as it had before, with Theo and I happily cohabiting, and sharing cooking and Scrabble and jokes; and going to the pub with Bev and Trev, and star-watching on clear, cold nights. I glanced up through the conservatory roof. Twilight was descending and I could just make out Venus shining quite low in the navy blue sky. Rudy suddenly woke up and started chattering and preening, so I fed him, and cleaned his cage. And I grabbed yesterday's paper to line it with, and had a quick look at the crossword. One down, 'Far meteor, destroyed,' six letters. It was an anagram of meteor. 'Remote'. Theo would soon be remote I realised dismally. He'd probably be gone in a few weeks. Although I consoled myself with the thought that buying a property can take an age. He had to find somewhere first – and he's very busy at the moment – and then he'd have to have the survey done. Then there's the conveyancing and all the argy bargy with the other side. And then he'd have to wait for them to move out. Maybe he'd be gazumped I thought optimistically, then felt a guilty pang. But it would probably take him, what, at least two months to move – maybe even three. I breathed a sigh of relief . . .

I drove over to Putney early the next morning so that I could help Ed get up. As I let myself in and pushed open the door I found a few envelopes scattered on the mat. There was one handwritten letter, with a Hull postmark: I guessed that it was from Jon. But when Ed came downstairs and saw it on the kitchen table, he put it straight in the bin.

'Aren't you even going to read it?' I asked him.

'No.'

'Why not?'

'I don't need to. I know what it says.'

'Is it from Jon?' I asked.

'Yes.'

'And you're still not speaking to him?'

'No.'

'I know it's none of my business,' I said as the toast popped up, 'but I think it's an awful shame.'

'You're right,' said Ed. 'It isn't any of your business.' I flinched. 'I'm sorry, Rose,' he said. 'That was very rude of me. My family rows are not your fault.'

'I think you're lucky having a brother to have a row *with*,' I said as I twisted open the marmalade. 'I wish *I*'d had a brother.' Then I thought, maybe I *do*. Maybe I do have one, and maybe I'll meet him. I shivered with anticipation again.

Also in the post were some papers for Ed from work; so he sat outside, at the garden table, reading them in the warm spring sunlight, while I worked on *Ask Rose* inside.

'Shout if you want another cup of coffee,' I yelled as I switched on my laptop.

'Thanks.'

I was just making notes on some of the letters, as I do, when my pencil broke. I got out my sharpener and went over to the bin and began to turn it, and as the wooden shavings dropped into the wicker waste paper basket I looked down, and suddenly stopped. For there, at the bottom, was a torn up letter in the same distinctive handwriting I'd seen only this morning. It was another, earlier letter from Jon. He must be absolutely desperate, I thought. Involuntarily, I found myself stooping to pick a piece up. *Please Ed,* I read, in small, neat handwriting. *I know we've had our differences, but you're my last chance.* Poor chap, he was clearly in dire straits financially: I wished that Ed would do something to help. But obviously I couldn't say anything as I didn't know the situation, and nor had I ever met Jon. Now I noticed something else in the bin, a piece of paper with a list of numbers, in Ed's handwriting – he'd clearly been working something out. *Mortgage, Putney* he'd written. £300k. No wonder he didn't want to lend his brother any more money, he probably didn't have it to spare. And then, beneath, I read, *R's equity, Camberwell. £200k? If R puts in, say, £150k, then Putney mortgage = £150k which = £700 p.c.m.* I felt my heart sink. I went outside.

'Ed, what's this all about?' I asked as I placed the note in front of him.

'What's what about? Oh.' He blushed.

'I found it in the bin – it was quite open, so I wasn't snooping – and I'm wondering if you could explain?'

'Yes, of course I can. I was just being *practical* darling,' he said expansively. 'I want you to move back in with me, you know that – it's no secret. So I was simply doing the arithmetic about what would happen if you sold your house.'

'But I don't want to sell my house,' I protested. 'I like living there.'

'I know you do. It's *totally* hypothetical at this stage of course, but if, later on, you *did* sell it, and we shared costs here – which, after all, is quite normal for married couples, Rose – then we'd have enough between us to have a really nice life. We'd be able to travel and go skiing and have fun, and do all the things that we never got a chance to do before.

Or if you didn't want to live here, I'd happily sell up and we could buy a similar house together somewhere else. We could have a whole new start, Rose, so I was just doing some quick sums to see how it would work out. It was my harmless little fantasy, that's all.'

'Oh.' My indignation seeped away like groundwater. 'Well, I'm not making any major decisions yet.'

'I know you're not. And you don't have to. After all, there's no rush.'

I went back inside and tackled my e-mails. I like to deal with them quickly as they soon stack up. There were several draft letters from Beverley for me to approve, and an additional e-mail from her telling me that she'd heard back from her friend Gill Hart. 'Gill has now spoken to Mary-Claire,' she'd typed, 'but I'd rather tell you what she said, in person, if you still want to know.' Yes, I thought. I do. Mary-Claire had thrown herself at Ed, she'd stolen him from me, and then she'd dumped him. I was more than curious as to why.

That night I went over to London FM and did my Tuesday night phone-in, not with Minty, as she's on maternity leave now, but with her stand-in Tess. We did alcohol problems, bereavement, paternity suits, mothers-in-law, domestic violence and holiday hell. And I didn't really enjoy it that much to be honest, and I was feeling pretty tired as I got in the cab, and wondering whether I couldn't get Beverley to take over from time to time – if she'd like to – which I think she probably would. And I was also feeling despondent about the fact that I still haven't had a response to my ad, when Bea phoned me on my mobile, in tears.

'Rose,' she wept. Oh God. She'd obviously had a row with Bella again. I braced myself for the details. 'Rose?'

'Yes, what is it Bea?'

'Something – uh-uh – terrible's happened.'

'What?'

'It's a – uh-uh – disaster.'

'*What* is?'

'I don't know how we're going to cope.'

'Cope with what?' I felt sick.

'Well – uh-uh – it's just so *awful* . . .'

'*What's* awful?' I persisted.

'Well – uh-uh . . .' she blubbed.

'Tell me for God's sake. Have you been burgled?'

'No,' she gasped.

'Is it the business?'

'No, it's not. It's Bella,' she sobbed.

'What about her?'

'Uh-uh . . .'

'Just *tell* me, Bea!'

'Uh-uh,' she blubbed. I couldn't stand it.

'*Tell* me!'

'Uh-uh-uh – she's been *dumped*!'

I stared out of the window as the shock registered. 'Andrew's dumped her?'

'Yes. Yes, he has. The *bastard*.'

'When?'

'Earlier tonight. I was waiting for you to finish your phone-in.'

'So what happened?' I asked, though I could guess. He'd obviously got fed up with Bea playing giant gooseberry and finally decided he couldn't stand it any more.

'He's such a cad,' Bea sobbed bitterly. 'I *told* you he'd let her down.' Oh.

'Has he gone off with someone else?'

'No,' she said, 'that's not the reason.'

'Then what is?'

'Uh-uh-uh.'

'What *is* the reason?' I pressed her. 'Why did he do it?'

'Because Bella's *pregnant*!' she sobbed.

Chapter Twenty

'I told you,' Bea wept as I sat in the twins' kitchen the following evening. 'I told you he'd let her down, and he has.' I suddenly recalled Bea's confident prediction that Bella was 'heading for a fall.' Andrew would let her down with a 'nasty bump,' she'd said recently: how prophetic that comment now seemed. But the most surprising aspect of Bella's abandonment was not that it had happened, but Bea's reaction – it was totally weird. I thought she'd be relieved, happy even, but she was incontinent with distress.

'It's just so *awful*,' she said again. 'The rejection. I don't know how I'll cope.'

'How *you'll* cope? But Bea –' I glanced at Bella who'd been sitting there silent and dry-eyed with shock, '– it's not you who's been rejected here.'

'But it's as though I *have* been,' she sobbed.

'Er, why?'

'Because we're so alike, of course. Oh *God*,' she wailed. 'It's just so *dreadful*!'

'But you didn't even like him.'

'I *know* . . .'

'So why do you care about him leaving?'

'Because he's hurt my twin, that's why; and if he hurts her, he hurts me too because we share each other's pain. And what was *so* awful,' she went on, her face shining with tears, 'is that he accused her of trying to trap him. He said she'd done it deliberately – isn't that vile?'

'Yes,' I said indignantly. 'It *is*.'

'But I did do it deliberately,' said Bella quietly. I looked at her. It was the first time she'd spoken since I'd arrived.

'What?' said Bea.

'I did do it deliberately,' she repeated calmly. 'I told him I was on the pill. It was a lie.' I looked at Bea. Her mouth was an 'o'. 'But I wasn't trying to trap him,' Bella explained. 'I just wanted to have a baby; and now I am. To be honest, now it's sunk in, I'm not really that bothered that Andrew's gone.'

'But I thought you were nuts about him,' I protested.

'Well, yes, that's true. I was. But then, recently, I'd come to realise that I wasn't quite as nuts about him as I had been to start with.'

'Well you gave a jolly good impression that you were,' said Bea crossly.

'That's because I was hoping it would improve. So if I appeared enthusiastic it was because I was trying to convince myself, as much as him. But I did want to get pregnant,' she concluded, 'and now I have.'

'That's a bit cynical,' Bea sniffed.

'Not really – because I'd be quite happy for him to stick around. But the fact that he's run a mile doesn't particularly bother, or even surprise me.' I mentally anagrammatised his name again. 'I'd begun to realise how immature Andrew is,' Bella went on. 'So I guess fatherhood would shatter his delusions of youth. I mean, why do you think he's forty-seven and still single?'

'Hmm,' I said. This was true. 'When's the baby due?'

'In early November. I conceived when we went skiing. That's why I went,' she explained. 'I know it was terribly selfish of me to go, Bea, and I'm very sorry, but I knew I'd be ovulating that week – and I did. I peed on those sticks, and I ovulated, and I got pregnant, and now I'm happy; so don't worry about me. And if Andrew wants to be a proper father that's absolutely fine – but if he doesn't, well that's fine too. I'm thirty-eight,' she added. 'I knew there weren't going to be many more chances of getting pregnant and so I decided I'd better grab this one while it was there.'

So Bella hadn't gone mad after all. Far from it. She'd been perfectly rational in her pursuit of her goal.

'Oh,' said Bea quietly. 'I see.'

'That's why I got cross with you for coming on the dates,' Bella went on. 'I was worried that you'd drive Andrew away before I could get pregnant – you nearly did.'

'I was only trying to protect you.'

'From what?'

'From disappointment.'

'I'm far from disappointed,' Bella said.

'But why didn't you tell me this *before*?' Bea demanded crossly.

'Because I thought you'd disapprove. You're much more conservative than I am, Bea, and I think you *would* have done. But I began to see that marriage wasn't on the cards, because if Andrew had never married anyone before, then why on earth would he marry *me*?'

'Well . . .' I shrugged. 'What a . . . turn up.'

'So you don't . . . *mind* being dumped then?' asked Bea.

'Mind? No. Not really. I was a bit shocked at first, but now I'm just happy that I'm pregnant,' Bella explained equably.

'But what about the business?' I asked. 'Won't it be tricky with the baby?'

'No,' she replied calmly, 'it'll be fine. We'll need someone to cover for me for a few weeks, but after that I'll be back. As luck would have it there's a nursery just round the corner, so I'll put the baby in there. Don't worry, Bea,' she went on. 'I'll still work with you. I'll do the accounts and I'll look after the shop, I shan't mind now, so it'll be fine.'

'Well, that's brilliant,' said Bea, visibly brightening. She blew her nose. 'And I'll go to the antenatals with you, and the NCT classes, and I'll help you look after the baby. We'll bring it up together.'

'Yes,' said Bella. 'We will. We'll bring it up together, and we'll *both* be its mother. We'll be a *double* mum. It's going to have two mothers, it's going to be a terribly lucky baby, it's –' Her self-control had suddenly vanished, and her eyes were shining with tears. 'Oh Bea!' She looked at her sister, then flung her arms round her, and now they were both crying.

'Oh Bella,' said Bea, 'I'm so happy! I thought you were going to leave me.'

'Don't be silly. I'd never do that.'

'We're going to have a baby,' Bea sobbed. 'We're going to have a *baby*!'

'Yes,' wept Bella happily. 'We *are*.'

I felt wrung out by my latest encounter with the twins and by the various convulsions in their lives. And I found myself envying that baby having two devoted mothers in its life. I imagined it being bounced on both their knees, and being fed by their alternate hands, and having its bed-time story read to it in motherly stereo, one on either side; I imagined them both playing with it in the bath and doing 'one, two, three, *wheeee*!' in the street. It would have double helpings of maternal love, the lucky little thing. And I thought again now of my mother, and wondered whether we'd ever meet. I'd begun to believe that we probably wouldn't; time was getting on. The ad had been in for a month – it was nearly May – and there hadn't been a single reply.

'Do you want to keep it in for a few more issues?' Theo asked me when I went back to Camberwell yesterday evening.

I shook my head. 'Four's enough.'

He got a beer out of the fridge and then offered me one. 'You're probably right. And did you phone NORCAP?' he asked as he got down two glasses.

'I did. They said my chances of finding her were virtually nil.'

'Really?'

'Yes. Because most women who've abandoned their baby have lived with this sorrow and remorse all their lives. They're not going to want to have it all churned up again decades later, are they? It's *such* a can of worms. I mean, how could my mother ever look me in the face, knowing what she'd done?'

'Hmmm. And are you sure you don't want to do any national publicity?' he asked as he leaned against the worktop.

I shook my head. 'I could easily write a feature, or get someone to interview me, but I don't want people to know about it in case they judge her; I want to protect her from that. And I want to protect myself from disappointment in case we never meet. I wouldn't want people asking me about it for evermore, I'd rather they'd never known.'

'But I still think *someone* must know something,' Theo said as he sipped his Becks. 'I mean, you can't hide a child. By the way,' he added, slightly awkwardly, 'I went to see a flat in Stockwell today.'

'Oh,' I said casually. 'And?'

'And I liked it.'

'Uh huh.' I stared at my shoes, aware that my heart was racing.

'In fact I've put in an offer on it.'

'I see.' I felt as though I'd stepped into quicksand.

'But it's a silly offer,' he shrugged, 'so I know the vendors won't accept it.'

'Well . . . fingers crossed.'

'But I get the cheque from my wife's solicitors in a few days, so I thought I ought to start looking for a place of my own. I've been here six months,' he added. Six months? It felt like six weeks. And at the same time it felt like he'd been here for ever. He'd somehow got under my skin.

'So you're leaving then?' I murmured, desolation sweeping over me.

'Well . . . yes. I guess I am. But in any case, Rose, your life seems to be changing.'

'Does it?'

'I mean, you spend a lot of time with Ed.'

'That's only because of his accident.'

'*Is* it?' I nodded. 'But you're practically living with him again.'

'Well, that's because he needs my help. It's only temporary.'

'Really?' I nodded again. 'But you were already beginning to see quite a bit of him before he broke his arm and so, well . . .'

'Well, what?'

'Well it makes me feel a bit . . . unsettled, I suppose.'

'But why the rush to move out?'

'Because, well . . . Look Rose,' he said forcefully, 'I'm about to start my next book and I don't want any emotional upheavals in the middle of that.'

'Emotional upheavals?'

'I mean, upheavals,' he corrected himself. 'So I thought it would be best all round if I found a flat now.'

'Okay,' I sighed, 'it's up to you.' I comforted myself again with the thought that it would probably take him several weeks to move in. 'You must do whatever you think.'

'But you'll let me know if you hear anything about your mother, won't you?' he went on quietly.

'Yes, of course. If I ever do.'

'It must be hard for you, waiting, but try not to think about it.'

I decided that Theo was right. In any case, something else had begun to prey on my mind – another emotion to add to the weird mix of conflicting feelings I was currently experiencing. The fact that Bella was pregnant had made me feel . . . not quite myself. And now, as the days passed I recalled how I'd felt when Bea had first told me the news. My initial, instinctive reaction wasn't shock, or even surprise. It was envy. It took me aback. But Bella was having a baby, and I realised for the first time in my adult life that I'd like to have one too. I found myself looking at babies in their buggies, and noticing pregnant women on the bus, and reading baby articles in newspapers and magazines and looking at baby books. Bella had been let down not with a 'nasty bump,' but with a rather nice one it now seemed to me.

Since discovering I'd been abandoned I'd felt that I could never have children. How could I, I reasoned, knowing what my mother had done? I'd somehow imagined that I might abandon *my* baby: it was as though I couldn't trust myself. So I'd shut my heart to the idea of kids but now I could hear the door creaking ajar. I was thirty-nine, almost forty, so there wasn't long. Perhaps Ed *is* my best bet, I reasoned. We've had our problems but he wants me back, so maybe I could have a baby with him. On the other hand, he'd never been keen on having kids; but maybe, like me, he could change . . .

In the meantime he was slowly recovering, although he was still in a great deal of pain. I took him to outpatients and they put on a new cast and said that his bones were beginning to heal. He was adapting quite well by now to being one-armed, and was hoping to go back to work the following week.

'But it's so lovely having you here Rose,' he said, affectionately as we sat in the garden on Thursday morning. I looked at the camellia with its fat pink blooms and at the scarlet flowers of the Japanese quince. He leaned forward and kissed me. 'I don't want you to leave me again.'

'Maybe I won't,' I said. I watched a blue tit fly into the nesting box hanging from the lilac, a short, fat worm in its beak.

'I hope you stay.' Ed kissed me again. 'I hope you stay for good.'

'Ed, can I ask you something about Mary-Claire?' He nodded. 'Something that's been bothering me?'

'What?'

'She wasn't pregnant was she?'

'No. She wasn't.' I'd shocked him. 'Why do you ask?'

'Well, I just wondered whether that might have been the real reason why you split up with her.'

'No, I told you, she just . . . *whined* all the time. In any case it wasn't a real relationship, Rose. It was . . .' he ran his left hand through his hair, '. . . a mess. But why did you want to know that?'

'Because I think I'd like to have a baby.'

'Really?' He turned towards me. 'You didn't before.'

'I know.' I watched the blue tit wriggle out of the box and

fly off. Its mate must be sitting on eggs.

'Is it because Bella's having one?' he asked.

'Well, yes, partly, if I'm honest – but not just. It's simply that I feel different about motherhood now. I wasn't bothered before, but now I think I am; but you'd always said you didn't want kids.'

'Well I didn't really,' he sighed. 'I just remember what a dreadful struggle my own childhood was. There were so many of us competing for so little, because of my mum being widowed so young. Family life was horribly stressful, so I've never wanted to replicate it.'

'But we wouldn't have those stresses, Ed. We have enough money, don't we?'

'Hmm. But even so . . .' he screwed up his face. 'I mean, a colleague of mine has three-year-old twins and their nursery fees alone cost twenty grand a year. Twenty grand a year, Rose – and they're still only infants! Think how much more they're going to cost. We wouldn't be able to have such a nice lifestyle if we had kids would we?'

'I wouldn't care. I think I would like to have a baby,' I said. 'So if I *were* to come back to you permanently – which is still a big "if" – then that's something you need to know.'

'Is that a condition?' he asked.

'That makes me sound manipulative. Let's say it's simply a wish.'

'Well, okay, then, I'll think about it.' He reached for my hand. 'I'm just so glad you're here, Rose. I think I had a lucky break, falling off that ladder, because it brought you back home.' Home? 'Are you glad you're here, Rose?' He stroked my fingers. 'Are you?'

'Of course,' I heard myself say.

The next day I left food in the fridge for Ed and went into the office, as Beverley was off sick. She's got the 'flu poor girl. I wearily trawled through letters about difficult in-laws, bedwetting, gambling, jealousy, teenagers, head lice and drink. The monotony of it was broken only by several text messages from Ed – he's really into it. VVCAMCS? I read just before lunch. What the hell was that? I looked it up in Serena's dictionary: *Voulez-vous couchez avec moi ce soir?* UDoIt4Me popped up half an hour later. No translation needed there. TDTU appeared at three-thirty – Totally Devoted To You: and at four, CW2CU.

'Can't wait to see you too,' I said as the letters scrolled lazily across the screen.

Then at six I went back to Hope Street to feed Rudy and to pick up my post. As I opened the front door I saw the answerphone winking away: on it was thirty seconds of uninterrupted stertorous breathing, this time with an odd clicking sound. I rang the telephone company again to talk to them about barring the calls but as usual I couldn't get through; and I wasn't prepared to listen to *Für Elise* for forty-five minutes so I hung up and read my post. There was a card from Henry, still in the Gulf, and a reminder about the new kickboxing class. I looked at the flyer. *Come and kick ass with Stormin' Norman's Advanced Tae-Bo class:* I decided I couldn't be fagged. I went into the kitchen to feed Rudy and saw Theo's mail on the table in a small pile. On the top was a letter, open and unfolded, from an estate agent, Liddle and Co. It said that his offer on the flat had been accepted, 'subject to contract'. Oh *shit*! *As the vendors are moving abroad they would like to exchange as quickly as possible and have therefore requested a ten day exchange.* A ten day exchange? Ten days? It normally takes at least ten *weeks*.

'I don't want him to go,' I muttered as I cradled my cup of tea. 'Theo's lovely. I want him to stay.' I glanced at the noticeboard – there was the invitation to his book launch at the Royal Astronomical Society the following Wednesday. I stared at his name. Theo Sheen . . . then suddenly I heard the trill of my mobile phone – it was Ed. He sounded excited and happy and wanted to know when I was coming back. So I cleaned Rudy's cage, fed and watered him, then drove back to Blenheim Road. As I dawdled at a red light I remembered how irritated I'd felt when Theo had moved in, and how I'd wanted to be with Ed. And now I was rather irri-tated at the idea of moving in with Ed, and wanted to be with Theo.

'I'm such a *mess*,' I muttered dismally as the lights changed to green. 'I should write to an agony aunt.' How would I sign it – 'Confused of Camberwell'?

I parked the car in my usual place, and was just rum-maging in the detritus of my handbag for the keys when the door opened.

'Rose,' said Ed. 'Come here.' He folded me to him with his left arm, kicked the door shut, then kissed me. 'It's so nice to see you again,' he murmured into my hair.

'You only saw me this morning,' I laughed.

'I know, but I've really missed you. And there's something I want to say. I couldn't wait to tell you.'

'Tell me what?'

'Well, I've spent all today thinking about what you said and –' He smiled, one of his heartbreaking smiles. 'The answer is "yes". I think we should have a baby.' I stared at him.

'You *do*?'

'I've been turning it over in my mind all day. And if that's the price for staying with you, then I'm more than happy to pay.'

'Do you really *want* a baby though Ed?'

'Yes, I do. If you do.'

'But you must want it for yourself, not just for me.'

'I want it for *us*,' he said. 'Does that convince you?' I nodded, slowly. 'So come on, then.' He grabbed my hand. 'We might as well make a start.'

'Ed,' I said, as I followed him upstairs, 'I don't want you to get me pregnant just to keep me with you.'

'I'm not. I want to get you pregnant to make you happy, and to make me happy.' He kissed me again. We went into his bedroom, and he drew the curtains with his left hand. I remembered how desolate I'd felt when I'd seen him draw them last November: it was as though he was shutting me out. But now here we were again, and I was inside, helping him to undress. He winced as I removed his shirt, carefully pulling it off his right shoulder. Then I undid his trousers, and he pushed them down and stepped out of them and kicked off his shoes. And now I pulled my cotton jumper over my head and wriggled out of my skirt. He kissed me, then we lay down on the bed, and he guided my hand downwards, and his breathing began to increase. Then he kissed me again, and tried to slide on top of me, and I felt the fibre glass cast scrape my skin. Suddenly his face contracted with pleasure. No, not pleasure.

'Oh fuck! My *arm*,' he breathed. 'Ooohhh!' He winced, red-faced with discomfort as he redistributed his weight. 'Blo-ody hell!' he reiterated, closing his eyes and drawing his breath through his clenched teeth.

'Well Ed, maybe we shouldn't, you know, do it, until you're better.'

'No, honestly. I'll be fine. Right, where were we? Let's try again.' We shifted again, our legs tangled, and he gingerly turned onto his back, and tried to pull me on top, but suddenly his face creased again.

'Ed, what's the matter?' I put my hand on his chest.

'It's my ribs. Ow, don't touch them – it's agony – I can't breathe!'

'Look, let's not push it,' I said. 'You've got three broken bones. Why don't we just cuddle instead.'

He nodded, defeated, and pulled me to him. 'Okay, but it's frustrating, isn't it?'

'Hmm.' Although the truth was I felt strangely relieved. We lay there like that for half an hour, my hand on his chest, half-waking, half-sleeping; and for some strange reason I found myself wondering what it would be like to lie in bed with Theo like this, face to face, our limbs pleached and plaited, like rope. I remembered the pattern of pale freckles, like faint galaxies, which spangled Theo's back. I remembered his slim, muscled torso, and his broad shoulders, and his sinewy hands and feet; I remembered his strong, muscular calves and I – What was I *thinking*? This was mad. This is mad, Rose, I told myself angrily. This is just crazy. Get real. You're only fantasizing about Theo because he's leaving, but the fact is your life's changing too. You want to have a baby; Ed's happy for you to have one so you're going to come back to him and that's *that*!

And now I summoned up all kinds of clichés with which to justify my return to Ed. I felt like Serena as I mentally groped for some comforting maxim. 'A bird in the hand is worth two in the bush'. 'You don't look a gift horse in the mouth'. 'You have to take the rough with the smooth'. *'Carpe Diem'*. Suddenly the phone at Ed's bedside rang.

'Yes? Oh hi, Ruth.' It was his sister. 'Yes, getting better, slowly, thanks.' I noticed the upward inflection of her voice; she was asking him something. 'Hmm, she did,' he said. 'Look it's not very convenient right now, Ruth. Yes I know, I know. I know *all* that,' he added, irritably. In the background I could hear Ruth's voice rising. 'But I just can't do it. No. Because I can't. Look, I've just come out of hospital and I'm not going – yes, yes, yes – I *know*. Well he should have thought of that six years ago, shouldn't he? Look, I can't talk any more.' He put the phone down, then stared at the ceiling, his jaw flexing. I saw a small blue vein pulsing by his eye.

'Do you want to tell me about that?' I asked him quietly, as I studied his profile.

'No,' he replied. 'I don't.'

'Is it Jon again?' I asked. He nodded. 'What's the problem?'

'The whole family are . . . getting at me. Putting me under terrible pressure. As though I haven't done enough for him in the past.'

'So he wants more money?'

'What? Hmm. Anyway, let's change the subject,' he said, wrapping his left arm round me. 'What shall we talk about?'

'I don't know.'

'I do,' he said turning to me and smiling. 'Let's discuss babies' names.'

*   *   *

'What a week,' wrote Trevor in his column on Monday:

The brouhaha over Dogs of Distinction has finally died down but I've been dog-tired because a) we've had the hall carpet replaced with some rather tasty parquet so I had a lot of clearing up to do after that – and b) our Bev's not been well. She's had the flu. Yeah – in May. I ask you! But she was completely poleaxed, poor kid. So yours truly has been in assistance overdrive what with all the to-ing and fro-ing to the chemists, collecting prescriptions – and no time to see my mates. Then there's been all the running up and down stairs with paracetamol, boxes of tissues, Lemsips and the rest. Plus bringing her the letters – being careful not to slobber on them – and the phone – and the paper which she was too weak to read. Luckily her mum came for a bit which gave me a chance to catch up on the chores, do the laundry, a bit of gardening – that kind of thing. But Bev's desperate to get better in time for our friend Theo's book launch later this week. He's written this brilliant astronomy guide called *Heavenly Bodies*, fully illustrated, and priced at a very reasonable ten quid. And then – thank Dog! – Bev's Beloved rang to say he's back in town for a month so that's cheered the poor girl up. As I say, she's been a bit up and down with that one, what with not quite knowing how keen he was, and then him being away so much. But he's been round to ours for dinner a couple of times, and I must say he seems to be a nice enough bloke: house-trained and everything, bright eyes, glossy coat, and she's dead keen, so I've got my paws crossed . . .

'It was very nice of you to plug Theo's book, Trevor,' I said to him as Beverley and I made our way to Piccadilly for the book launch three days later. We'd been frantic at work – it was Bev's first day back – so there'd been no time to chat. But now, as we sped up St James's in the back of the cab, we relaxed.

'Well Trevor adores Theo,' Beverley remarked. 'He'd do

anything to help him. Ooh, dog hairs, Rose. On your sleeve, sorry about that.'

'Really? I couldn't care less.' As I looked at Trev I suddenly understood why, despite my former aversion to dogs, I liked this one so much. It was because I recognised that we had a great deal in common, Trevor and I.

'It's awful to think of Trevor being dumped on the motorway, like that,' I said. 'Poor little thing.'

'I know,' Beverley sighed. 'He was only a baby. He was very lucky to survive.'

'Hmm.'

'I think it's had a big psychological effect on him,' she went on. 'I'm sure that that's why he chose a caring profession. He needs to feel needed.'

'Really?'

'Don't you think so?'

'I . . . don't know. All I know is that Ed could do with a dog like you to help him, Trevor,' I remarked as I stroked his ears.

'How *is* Ed?' Beverley asked. 'I've been meaning to ask you, but we've had no time to chat today. Is his arm healing?'

'Yes it is, thanks. He's going back to work on Monday – he'll have been off for two weeks. It hasn't been easy,' I sighed.

'Theo said you've been spending a lot of time over there.' I shrugged, then nodded. 'So is it going well then?'

'No, not really. In fact he's moving out. I wish he wasn't,' I added dismally. Beverley gave me one of her old fashioned looks.

'I meant Ed, Rose, not Theo. I was talking about *Ed*.'

'Oh. Oh . . . of course.'

'Is it going well?' she repeated as I looked out of the window.

'I suppose so, yes. In some ways.'

'I do hope I won't be losing you as a neighbour,' she said quietly.

'I don't know, Bev. Maybe . . .'

'Are you going to move back in with him then?'

'Well, no. Or at least, not yet, I . . .' Suddenly, as we turned right into Piccadilly I saw a woman pushing a buggy. She looked radiantly, unassailably happy. 'But then on the other hand,' I said, 'yes. Yes it's quite possible that I'll go back to Ed. I'm just trying to . . . work it all out. To be honest, I'm rather confused. Bev,' I went on after a few moments. 'You know I asked you about Mary-Claire Grey, and why she left Ed?' She nodded. 'Well, I've decided I don't want to know.'

'That's okay,' she replied. 'I guessed you didn't, as you haven't mentioned it again.'

'I just feel it's all in the past.'

She looked at me and nodded. 'Sure.'

'And in any case she would probably have been rude about him, so I wouldn't really want to hear.'

'Of course. In any case,' said Bev as she fiddled with Trevor's lead, 'I've . . . forgotten the reason, whatever it was. So everything's changing then?' she added brightly. This wasn't so much a question as an observation. Into my mind flashed Theo's room, which would soon be empty.

'Yes. Everything's changing,' I said.

The cab pulled up in the entrance of the Royal Academy, the driver dropped the ramp, and I pushed Beverley through the cobbled courtyard of Burlington House. In front of us was the RA, and to our left we saw 'R. Astronomical Soc.' emblazoned in chiselled gold lettering over a door.

'This is very venerable,' Beverley observed. I pushed her wheelchair up the ramp, and we went in through the glass doors into a Wedgwood blue pilastered hallway, with a black and white marble tiled floor. We followed the crowd through into the Fellows' Room on our right. It was oak-panelled with gleaming oil paintings of eminent astronomers and was already quite full. On the right was a glass cabinet with some antique telescopes and, on the left, a table with copies of the book. It was the first time I'd seen it as it had been published so fast. Beverley and I both bought one then we made our way through the mostly male throng.

'– my new Takahashi's got very nice adaptive optics.'

'– I prefer a Newtonian reflector myself.'

'– fascinating lecture on helio-seismology.'

'– there was a brilliant fireball in Ursa Major last week.'

'– did you see the occultation of Saturn?'

'– too cloudy, but there's going to be a perihelic opposition of Mars.'

'Star bores!' whispered Beverley with a laugh. Trevor trotted ahead, parting the crowd for us as if he were a border collie carving up sheep.

'Hey!' Theo exclaimed, as he caught sight of us. 'My two favourite women!'

'Congratulations!' we said.

He saw that we were holding copies of his book. 'I hope you didn't pay for those.'

'Of course we did,' said Bev. 'It looks lovely,' she added.

'Yes it does. But it was touch and go that we'd have them in time for the party as they only came back from the printers this afternoon.'

'Well we'd like you to graffiti them. But please write clearly Theo as your handwriting's so atrocious,' Bev giggled, 'and could you sign it to me and Trev?'

'What wonderful pictures,' I murmured as I flicked through it. There were photographs from Hubble of glittering star clusters and of the Stingray Nebula like a vast pink and green fish. There was one of a sun in its death throes throwing out great shells of red and mauve gas. There was another of a cartwheel shaped galaxy – the result of two galaxies crashing – spinning through the blackness of space. There was a photo of Neptune, as blue as the sea, with a swirl of streaky white cloud. And here was the Shoemaker-Levy comet smashing into Jupiter, and the sun setting on Mars. The images were so utterly beautiful, they made my soul ache. I sighed, then turned to the opening pages ready for Theo to sign. He'd dedicated the book to the memory of his maternal grandfather, Hugh Adams, 'who first encouraged me to look up'. On the opposite page was the list of acknowledgements; to my amazement, I read my own name.

362

'Thanks Theo,' I heard Beverley say as she read his inscription. 'That's really nice.'

'Theo,' I said, 'you didn't have to acknowledge me – I didn't *do* anything.'

'You did. You let me live in your house, and that made me feel a lot happier and so I was able to work.' I smiled. Theo's hand hovered over the page for a moment, and then he began to write. As he did so I looked at him, and thought of how he would soon be leaving me, going beyond my sphere: and now the astro-babble seemed to fade to silence as I remembered the last six months.

– *You'd look great as the Botticelli Venus . . .*
– *You could easily attract a man of my age . . .*
– *Are you up for it . . . ?*
– *A galaxy's a city of stars . . .*
– *The thought that your mother might be out there, somewhere . . .*
– *There's life beyond every relationship, Rose . . .*
– *I could teach you, if you like . . .*
– *Now add the lemon grass and the ginger . . .*
– *Look for her – it's not too late.*

'There you are,' he said as he handed me the book. I read his inscription. *To the celestial Rose, who drew me into her lovely orbit. With love and gratitude, Theo.*

'Oh that's so . . . nice,' I said impotently. Tears pricked the backs of my eyes. 'It's just lovely, Theo. I don't know what to say.' We stood there, smiling at each other awkwardly, drawn together by gravity, or perhaps simply pushed together by the press of the crowd.

'Tell me again when you're going?' I said.

'Well I exchanged today and the flat's vacant for possession so I'll be completing in a day or two.'

'I didn't think it would happen so quickly,' I said. 'It's really taken me aback.'

'Me too. I thought it would take me months but it's only been a fortnight. I'll miss you, Rose,' he added suddenly. My heart did a swallow dive.

'I'll miss you too,' I whispered.

'Really?' I nodded. 'So we'll both miss each other then.'

'Looks like it, doesn't it?'

'Yeah.' He smiled his funny, lop-sided smile. 'It does.'

'It's been lovely having you staying with me.'

'Really?'

I nodded. 'You've made, well, a big difference to my life.'

'I have?'

I nodded again because I found I couldn't speak. Theo was leaving me.

'Rose,' he said.

'Yes?' My eyes were stinging and my throat ached.

'Rose, I –'

'Theo!' An attractive blonde had come up to him and laid her hand on his arm. She was from the publishers; she looked brisk and official.

'Oh hello Camilla,' he said.

'Theo, can I just drag you over to meet this guy from Channel 4, the one I told you about? He's heard you lecture and thinks you're going to be the new Patrick Moore. Then Felicity from the *Mail* wants to do an interview with you. She says you're going to be to star-watching what Jamie Oliver is to cooking – you know, The Naked Astronomer!' Theo laughed. 'And then I want you to meet Clare from the Discovery Channel, she's got a few ideas she'd like to discuss.'

'Sorry Rose,' said Theo. He shrugged. 'I've just got to talk to some people.'

'Of course,' I smiled. 'You go.' He disappeared into the crowd, which seemed to suck him in like a black hole, and I couldn't see him any more. And now, all around me, people were talking about him.

'– He's really going places, that boy.'

'– He'll get a TV series, I'm sure of it.'

'– Well he's very telegenic.'

'– Oh yes.'

'– And that attractive Yorkshire accent.'

'– He's a populist, but his science is sound.'

Theo's life is going to change hugely, I realised. This book is a watershed and nothing will be the same after this. It'll take him into a whole new sphere, and everything will change. He'll leave Hope Street and move into his flat and maybe we'll stay in touch for a while. And then the phone calls will gradually stop. And I'll open the *Post* one day at the gossip column and see that he's got engaged. And I'll have a huge pang of regret and I'll be out of sorts for a few days and my friends will wonder what's up. But then I'll decide to be sensible, and to think of him simply as that nice boy who lived with me for a while, and who taught me to look up . . . Theo was at a major crossroads. His life would be very different after this. So would mine, for I was at a crossroads too. But there was no question which was the best direction for me to go in – Wright.

Chapter Twenty-One

I hardly saw Theo for the next three days. He was busy doing interviews about the book, and to-ing and fro-ing to his solicitors and the estate agents, and I was still looking after Ed. But on Monday, Ed went back to work. I drove him in as he can't risk being jostled or barged on the tube. As he had to be there by nine, I got in to work earlier than usual. To save Beverley, I opened the mail.

'What have we got today?' I wondered out loud as I ripped into the first envelope.

Dear Rose, I read, *I suffer from premature matriculation and my girlfriend is threatening to leave me. Please can you help?* I was fairly sure he didn't mean he'd passed all his 'A' levels at twelve. I sighed, fired off a short letter, enclosing the relevant leaflet, logged it, then opened the next. *Dear Rose, I don't know what to do – I feel so bad because for the past two years I have been having an affair with a married man, but it wasn't international.* Oh God. *Dear Rose, I recently got married to a man with a rather unfortunate surname. When I announce myself people snigger and make all sorts of unfunny remarks. I'd like to revert to my maiden name but I know that this will offend my husband and his family. What should I do? Mrs T. Bottie.* Why didn't she think of that *before*? To avoid hurting her husband's feelings I advised her to hyphenate both names, continental style – as long her maiden name wasn't 'Bigg'.

Then there was a letter asking about wedding etiquette for a couple who'd both been married before. *With me exchanging vows for the third time and my fiancée for the fourth, we're very*

367

worried about the ceremony. Not least because it turns out that my fiancée's ex-husband but one once dated my father's new girlfriend, and it didn't end very well. Plus my ex-stepdaughter is threatening to boycott the wedding if her father's new boyfriend is there, but I can't not invite him as his ex-wife is my accountant and has stuff on me about my VAT. I'm having sleepless nights, Rose, and can imagine scuffles on our big day. What should I do? Don't bother getting married, I was tempted to write back. With a track record like yours what's the point? Instead I suggested that they should invite *no-one* to the service but throw a party, at a later date, in a very large venue, so that the warring factions could be kept apart.

I glanced at the clock – it was ten to ten. Beverley would be here soon. There were a couple of cross-dressing letters, I'd leave them for her as she does those ones very well. Now I opened another letter on blue Basildon Bond. The handwriting, though slightly shaky, looked vaguely familiar, although I couldn't think why. Suddenly my mobile phone beeped, announcing a text message. LUL, scrolled across the tiny screen, then O:-) Ed. Mystified, I looked it up in Serena's dictionary. *Love You Lots ... Angel.* I smiled, not least at the effort that Ed must have put into it, painstakingly tapping out the letters with his left hand. The phone beeped again, and I read *CantW2XU!* I laughed. But then what does the ad say? 'Touch someone with a text message,' and I *did* feel touched. In fact I felt suddenly cheerful and uplifted as I turned back to the letter in my hand.

Dear Rose, I have a problem, and am very much hoping that you might be able to help me. I'll try my best, I thought. *Just over a year ago, I was diagnosed with leukaemia. You can imagine the shock. Apart from the odd nosebleed, and a couple of infections, I'd had no idea there was anything wrong. I was 35, in the 'prime' of life, supposedly, and my wife had just had our first child. The main treatment for acute myeloid leukaemia is chemotherapy. I've had three lots and I've responded quite well each time, but unfortunately my remission period has been very short.*

'Morning Rose!' I heard Beverley say brightly. 'Rose? Are you okay?' she asked. I looked up.

'Oh sorry – hi, Bev. Hi Trev.'

'You look serious. Is it a bad letter?'

'Yes,' I replied as I read on. 'It's sad.'

The doctors have told me that the disease has now progressed from the chronic, to the accelerated stage, and that my only hope is bone marrow donation. But I have an unusual blood type, and so far no match has been found, either in my family or on the national database of bone marrow donors. Poor bloke, I thought. *All my family have been tested – my mother, uncle, aunts, cousins and siblings – all except one. My brother. He's refusing to do it because we fell out six years ago, over money, and he has not spoken to me since.*

I felt the skin on my neck begin to prickle. I was aware that I could hear myself breathe.

Rose, it's time for me to drop the mask. I know from my mother that you are seeing Ed again and, although I've never met you, I assume that you have some influence with him. The doctors have told me that without donor bone marrow I have between four and six months to live. So I am writing to you now, in despair, to ask you to intercede with him on my behalf. I felt as though I were falling. The letter began to shake in my hands.

'Rose, are you all right?' I heard Beverley say.

'What?'

'You look rather upset.'

'I am.'

'Is it a really sad letter then?' she asked as she turned on her computer.

'*Yes,*' I murmured. 'It is.'

Ed has ignored the three letters I've sent him, so my mother, my sister, Ruth and my two brothers have all tried to persuade him, without success. But Ed has the same blood group as I do, and is therefore my best chance of a match. Rose, I love my wife and daughter and I don't want to leave them. I'd like to see Amy take her first steps. I'd like to push her on the swings in the park. I'd like to walk her to school. I'd like to have the chance to live my life, but time is fast running out. So if there's anything you could say, to make Ed think again, we would be so very grateful to you. Jon Wright.

The words were blurring. I turned over the pages, and re-read the address. The Royal Infirmary, Hull.

'Rose, are you all right?' I heard Beverley ask. I looked out of the window at the sky then dropped my gaze to the Thames. 'Are you all right?' she repeated gently.

'No, Bev. I'm not.'

'What's happened?'

I didn't reply. I couldn't. I was lost for words. Now I remembered the phone calls from Ed's mother and sister and his determined refusal to budge. I remembered the letter he'd thrown away, without reading: I remembered the fragment I'd found in the bin. What was it that was written on it? *Please Ed, I know we've had our differences, but you're my last chance* . . . I'd assumed that it was money Jon was asking for. But it wasn't money – it was life.

How could Ed *not* do it? I asked myself. How was it possible that anyone could be so selfish, so ungenerous, so . . . *mean*? That small word was hardly adequate to express such epic paucity of spirit, such a monumental failure of the heart.

'Do you mind if I see it?' Beverley asked. I handed it to her, and watched her expression change from compassion, to shock, to gob-smacked non-comprehension as she neared the end. 'His own brother?' she said wonderingly. Her eyes were wide with indignation. 'Oh, Rose.' We looked at each other in speechless bewilderment. She shook her head.

'I know.'

'I knew he was a *mean* man,' she said, her lips pursing, 'but this is something else!'

'How could you know that?' I asked her. 'You've never met him.'

'Because of Mary-Claire. My friend Gill told me that *that's* why Mary-Claire left Ed – because she found him so terribly mean. She said he'd made her pay rent when she was living with him, even though he'd asked her to move in. She said he'd make her go Dutch so often she can practically speak it, and that he'd never treat her, or tip. She said he was the

370

most attractive man she'd ever met, but that his lack of generosity had been a massive turn-off.'

'Too right,' I said. 'It *is*.' So that's what Ed meant when he'd said that Mary-Claire had 'whined' and 'complained' all the time. No wonder he hadn't wanted to tell me why she'd left him.

'But you must have noticed it yourself, Rose,' I heard Beverley say quietly. 'You were *married* to him. Didn't you see?' I looked out of the window as I considered the question.

'Yes I guess I did. I *did* see it, sort of, but I was so besotted with him at first that I must have overlooked it. Then I got the agony column and was frantically busy, so it didn't really impact on me. I did notice the small things, but I indulged them because I knew Ed had had a deprived childhood and that can leave a lasting mark.'

'His childhood's got nothing to do with it,' said Bev hotly. 'I know people who had *dreadful* upbringings and they're incredibly generous. Hamish for one! He grew up in a Glasgow tenement, and struggled for years while he studied music, but he's *always* trying to pay. Ed's background is irrelevant,' she reiterated indignantly. 'He's one of these people who just can't *give*.' Yes, I thought. That's right. As usual, Bev had put her finger right on it. Ed can't give. He can't give, or rather he won't give, because he doesn't want to. He's never really known how.

Now I thought of how he'd never give money to charity, or the homeless, and how he'd always try to beat people down in shops. He said he found it 'humiliating' to tip in taxis and so he never did. He'd try and stop me taking champagne to parties because he said our hosts would be 'offended' at their age. And he'd complained if I'd sent the odd cheque here and there to my readers, so I'd stopped telling him after a while. After all, it was my money – I could do what the hell I liked – but he'd said I was 'hopelessly gullible' and 'naive'. I picked up my bag.

'Rose, where are you going?'

'Out. I'll be back by lunch.'

As I drove over Blackfriars Bridge towards the City I thought of all the other things about Ed which my initial infatuation had led me to suppress. The engagement ring, for example. The one I'd never had. Ed had said that there was 'no point' as our engagement was only six weeks. And our cheap honeymoon, in Menorca, out of season, in his mother's small flat. *Would you like some raffle tickets, Sir? No thanks.* That's how I'd recognised his voice at the ball. I thought about how his chief objection to having children was because of 'all the expense'. And now I recalled him saying that if a baby was what it took to keep us together, he was happy to 'pay the *price.*'

I parked on a meter behind Liverpool Street then went up the steps, and through the gleaming glass doors of Paramutual Insurance, and got the lift to the tenth floor.

Ed Wright, Director, Human Resources, announced the plate on his door. *Human Resources*? I wanted to laugh.

'Does your husband know you're here, Mrs Wright?' asked his secretary, Sarah.

'No,' I replied sweetly. 'It's a surprise.' I knocked once then went straight in without waiting.

'Rose!' Ed looked amazed. His office smelt of leather and wood polish. There were several large files on his desk. 'How lovely,' he laughed, pushing himself out of his chair with his good arm and coming towards me. 'What a treat. But what on earth brings you here?'

'Well,' I began as I shut the door. 'I need your help with a letter I've had this morning.'

'One of your readers' problems?'

'Yes.'

'And you think *I* might be able to solve it?' he said quizzically.

'I do.'

'Well, that's flattering – I'll try my best. It must be urgent,' he added as I sat down opposite him.

'Oh yes, it is. In fact it's very urgent,' I explained. I took Jon's letter out of my bag and pushed it across his desk. 'Would you read it please?'

He took it in his left hand, sat down again and then, as he recognised the handwriting, his features stiffened and he looked up.

'Listen Rose, I –'

'Read it!' I said.

'But –'

'Read it! Just read it. The whole thing.'

'Well . . . okay then,' he sighed. He read it quickly, pursed his lips, then folded it up.

'Why haven't you done it, Ed? What the hell are you thinking?'

He heaved a painful sigh. 'You don't understand.'

I felt my jaw slacken. 'What's *not* to understand? Your brother's terminally ill. That's all there is to it.'

'But Jon and I don't get on. Yes, it's all very sad, but there's no relationship now. We haven't spoken for six years.'

'So *what*?'

'So I suppose I just don't feel that . . . brotherly any more. It doesn't really affect me because . . . well,' he shrugged, 'it just doesn't. There's no contact.'

'But that shouldn't make *any* difference, Ed, and in any case it's not even true. Jon sent us that lovely lamp for our wedding, remember? Even though you didn't invite him. *He's* kept the door open, so he clearly doesn't see it the way you do.'

'But . . .'

'There isn't a "but". Your brother's desperately ill and he needs your help, and you're going to give it to him and that's that.'

Ed sighed, and shook his head as though this were a matter of regret, not life or death.

'I can't, Rose. I just . . . can't. I wouldn't do it for a stranger, and Jon has become a stranger, so I don't feel like doing it for him. I'm sorry, but it's too late.'

'It *isn't* too late. At least, not yet. But it very soon will be if you don't get yourself to Hull.'

'They can do more chemotherapy, he might be okay.'

'He says it doesn't work for long.'

'Or they can take stem cells from his own blood. That's a new technique. I read about it in a newspaper article.'

'If it was likely to work don't you think they'd *know*?'

'Anyway I *hate* hospitals,' he said, shuddering. 'I loathe them. You know that. I have a real phobia about them. And I've only just come out of hospital and I'm not going back in. I'm still in a lot of pain actually,' he said touching his plaster cast.

'You know what, Ed? I don't give a fuck. And in any case it's your own stupid fault because you were too mean to pay a roofer to clear the gutter – so you did it yourself and you fell!'

'That's not true,' he protested, though his throat had reddened.

'It *is* true!'

'Well they charge ninety pounds an hour.'

'Worth every penny, Ed. Look how much more it's cost you – and me.'

'I hope you don't regret helping me,' he said peevishly.

I looked at him and blinked. 'Yes, actually – I do. I *do* regret it now that I know that you've been refusing to help Jon. I find it . . .' I groped for a word which with to convey such staggering selfishness '. . . *amazing*, that you could have ignored his pleas for so long. Where's your heart, Ed? Do you have one? Or are you a medical freak?'

'But the donation procedure is very unpleasant, Rose, it involves several injections in your pelvis. There's a lot of discomfort.'

'What's that compared to death? Jon will die if you don't help him. You've got no choice.'

'I do. I do have a choice, actually, and I choose not to do it. As I've tried to explain – but you refuse to understand – I don't feel sufficiently . . . involved.'

'You're right,' I said, sitting down. 'I don't understand. I don't understand at all. I thought blood was supposed to be thicker than water. It clearly isn't in your case.'

'No,' he said slowly, 'that's right. It *isn't* thicker than water. And it isn't in your case either, Rose, because if it were, then your natural mother would never have given you up for adoption would she?' I felt winded, as though I'd been punched. 'Sometimes, Rose, family relationships can be ruptured beyond repair. You, of all people, should understand that.'

'This has *nothing* to do with me. My mother . . . gave me up,' I went on carefully, 'when I was tiny, so there was no real relationship there. But Jon's been your brother for thirty-six years. Your refusal to help him is despicable,' I said quietly. 'I feel so ashamed of you.'

'Well I'm sorry you feel that way, Rose,' he said calmly. 'But in any case you're probably wasting your breath abusing me, as I might not even be a match.'

'No, you might not be, that's true. But then, on the other hand, you might well be as you've got the same blood group, so you must try. It's one thing for Jon to die because no suitable donor was available; it's quite another for him to die because his own brother refused to help. Do it Ed.'

'No. I won't. I just . . . don't think I can.'

'Do it today. Phone the hospital. Phone them right now. Here's the number,' I handed him a piece of paper with all the details. 'Ask them what you have to do. You know,' I added, 'you don't realise how lucky you are.'

'Lucky? What do you mean?'

'Exactly that. You're lucky,' I repeated.

'In what way?'

'Because you've been given the chance to do something really great for someone: something . . .' – I groped for the right word, then I thought of Theo and suddenly found it – '. . . something *grand*. Not many people get an opportunity like that, to make their lives big and meaningful – not narrow and selfish. You should seize this chance, Ed, and you need to seize it, because it'll make you a much better man.'

'I just . . . can't.' He was shaking his head.

I stood up. 'Yes you *can*, and you *will*! Or are you too, too mean?'

'I'm not mean!'

'You bloody well *are*. I've noticed it in small ways often

enough but I never really saw it 'til now. But that's why Mary-Claire left you, isn't it Ed?'

He reddened. 'Oh, she was a pain. She just whinged all the time. She expected me to subsidise her,' he said, his mouth twisting with distaste. 'As though I don't have commitments of my own. That house is very expensive to run.'

'I'm sure it is. But then you insisted on buying such a big place, even though you didn't want kids. And it's a huge expense on your own and you're really pushed. No wonder you never have any spare cash.'

'That's right – I don't, so I really didn't see why Mary-Claire should live there for free.'

'You know, Ed, I never though I'd sympathise with Mary-Claire Grey but right now I'm on her side. And that's why all your previous girlfriends left you, isn't it? Because you're so bloody tight. You're incapable of generosity, Ed, either of the pocket or the heart. Those two things are connected, and now I know just how ungenerous you are. I'd overlooked it because I was besotted with you, but I'm not any more. There's no way I'd stay with you now, knowing this. It's over. I'm not coming back.'

'I thought you wanted to have a baby,' he pointed out calmly.

'No. I don't. Not with you. Not now.'

'Don't leave me Rose,' he said suddenly. He looked stricken. 'Please. Don't. We've got this chance to start over. We could be happy again – the way we were when we first met.'

'No. It's not true. I've done my bit for you Ed, and I'm staying in Hope Street. That's my real home – my little house in Hope Street – not your poncey great Putney Palace. That's partly why you wanted me back isn't it? Because you thought if you could only get me to sell up and move back in with you, your house would be so much more affordable. That's what those little calculations of yours were really about. Well I'm not interested in living with you again, Ed. I don't want to. Not ever. But you can call the hospital – now.' He stared at me.

'Do it,' I said quietly. 'While I'm here. Phone them.' Ed looked out of the window at the City skyline then turned back to me.

'You think you're such a great person, don't you Rose?' he said calmly. 'Kind-hearted Rose, the ever-popular agony aunt, always helping people with her great advice. Sorting out their problems.'

'No, I don't think that. I've know I've got loads of faults, but at least I don't think I've ever been mean. But it's your defining characteristic, Ed. You can't give – except to yourself.'

'And you can?'

I looked at him, shocked. 'Yes. I can give, actually. And I do. I give to my readers. I want to help them. That's giving.'

'Oh really Rose, don't flatter yourself. You give to them to be loved and admired. You give to them because you want them to thank you and think what a wonderful person you are. You don't give to them free of charge. In return you want acknowledgement and recognition. Don't you? My God, you even have a "Grateful" file!' I stared at him, shocked. 'Haven't you?' My face burned. 'I saw it. When you moved out.'

'Well, that's just . . . irony. It's a . . . joke.'

'That's crap. You *do* want people to be grateful to you, and to need you – because you've felt so inadequate all your life, because your own mother didn't want you. You never talked about her to me, but do you think I didn't work that one out?'

'Stop turning this onto *me*,' I snapped. 'This conversation is about *you*. And I'm not "advising" you Ed, I'm *telling* you that you're going to help Jon and that's all there is to it. Phone that number now.'

'You can't make me,' he said calmly.

'No. I don't suppose I can. But I'm quite happy to write to your managing director if you don't do it.'

'Oh yes. Saying what?'

'Saying that you'll need to take a few days off work to go

377

into hospital in an attempt to save your brother's life. There's no way you'll be able to refuse to do it after that.'

'But I've only just come back to work.'

'I don't care. I'll write to him – no I won't, I'll phone him – if I hear that you haven't contacted Jon's hospital by six o'clock tonight.' I picked up my bag and opened it. 'I've said everything I came to say. Here are your house-keys.' I put them on his desk. 'I'm off.'

'Yes, off you go,' he said. 'Back to Camberwell. Back to your little toyboy astronomer with his great big telescope.'

'Oh don't be pathetic!'

'Well you're obviously in love with him. Or perhaps you're just star-struck. But I'm sure he'd give you a nice big bang!'

I stared at Ed. 'I'll ask my solicitor to press on with the divorce,' I said quietly. 'You'll have to manage on your own now. Goodbye.'

'That's it,' I said to myself, as I got the lift down to reception. 'That really is it. Finally. No going back. It's over.' My knees trembled and I thought I might cry reactive tears, but my disgust with him kept them at bay.

'His own brother,' I repeated wonderingly. 'His own brother.' What an impoverished soul. As the automatic doors opened and I stepped out I felt a sudden rush of freedom. I wanted to throw back my head and shout. It was as though I'd been liberated – no more agonising, and weighing up, and to-ing and fro-ing; the decision had been made. I was free. And in that moment I realised that I'd known, deep down, that I could never go back to Ed, but now I understood why. I knew he'd get nasty of course – hence all that crap he threw at me about why I'm an agony aunt. I became an agony aunt because I *genuinely* want to help people and because I'm good at it. Suddenly my mobile phone rang. It was Theo.

'Hi!' I said, as I unlocked the car door. My heart expanded. I was so glad to hear his voice.

'Rose, I've got something to tell you.' His tone of voice was serious. My heart sank, and then suddenly soared – his flat had fallen through! He'd been gazumped. Someone had beaten him to it. He wouldn't be leaving me yet.

'Yes. What is it?' I said.

'Well I'm at home, and the second post's just arrived. I've had a reply to your ad.'

Chapter Twenty-Two

I got in the car and headed straight back. As I sped down Bishopsgate I called Bev and asked her to cover.

'All right, but don't be too long. What shall I say if anyone asks where you are?'

'Tell them I'm at a conference.'

'On what?'

'On, er, oh I don't know – Positive Parenting.'

'So where are you really?'

'In the City – I've just been to see Ed. But something very urgent's come up at home and I've got to get back.'

Theo said that he hadn't opened the letter: I wondered what it would say. 'Dear Box number 2152, I read your ad in the *Chatham News* and I would like to confess that it was I who left you in that supermarket car park forty years ago. I'm terribly sorry about this and I know you must think badly of me, but . . .' But *what*? What excuse could she possibly have? 'But I was thirteen and didn't know I was pregnant/I was married and having an affair/I was forty and I already had six kids and I just couldn't feed any more.'

I'd speculated so often as to who my mother might be and now I was about to find out. My body burned with adrenaline: I felt dizzy, breathless and sick. Every time I had to stop at a light I'd thump the wheel with the heel of my hand. If the car in front dawdled for so much as a fraction of a split nanosecond, I'd hoot. I was in an agony of anticipation – and also of deep, deep dread. Because all my adult life I'd snubbed my past, but now my past was coming looking for me.

I'd often thought about my parallel life – the one I would have had with my mother if she hadn't abandoned me – and I'd wondered what that life would have been like. She could have been anyone so the possibilities were endless. She could have been poor or rich, British or foreign, fat or slim, bright or dim – I was about to replace decades of fantasies and imaginings with the truth. But the truth might not be that palatable. In fact it might well be vile. What if she'd been a prostitute, for example? Or what if I'd been born as the result of a rape? My mother could easily have been an alcoholic, or a drug addict. On the other hand she could have been a deb. And what about *him*? My father? I was about to discover who he was too. I'd assumed he was a good-looking rotter, a good ten years older, but perhaps he was the same age. Maybe they were infatuated teenagers, like Romeo and Juliet, and their parents' didn't get on. His folks didn't think she was good enough – bloody cheek! – and they'd forced him to give her up. And so she'd gone bananas and dumped me in a shopping trolley one sunny day.

I was also, probably, about to learn my true date of birth. Maybe it wasn't June the first. Maybe it was June the eighth, or June the twelfth, or maybe I'd been born in May. I had no history and no identity, other than the one I'd been given, and now I was about to find out.

I might discover too whether I had any siblings. In one way I hoped that I did, but at the same time I hoped that I didn't – because it would crucify me to think that she'd had more children and kept *them*, having abandoned *me*. And where had my mother lived after she'd ditched me, and what had she done after that? She might have stayed in the area – we could have passed in the street – or maybe she'd moved up to town. Perhaps, driven by guilt, she'd worked obsessively hard and become a top businesswoman, or a scientist or a judge. Now, as I turned into Hope Street, all these possibilities jostled for space in my mind, rudely shoving and barging each other as they struggled to make themselves heard.

'– Your mother went to art school and became a painter.'

'– No, she went to RADA and became a star.'

'– She became a primary school teacher actually.'

'– She was a pianist!'

'– Get real – she was a drunken slut!'

'– No, no, no, she became an obstetrician.'

'– Bollocks! She worked for the Beeb!'

I parked the car and ran into the house. In the hall were Theo's boxes, packed and taped shut ready for the next day. I felt my heart contract.

'Theo!' I said breathlessly. I picked my way past his large suitcase and into the kitchen. I looked at him, and smiled.

'Hello Rose,' he said gently. 'Are you ready?' I nodded. Then he handed the letter to me. Holding my breath, as though about to dive into a river, I ripped open the large brown envelope stamped *Private and Confidential* and pulled out a small cream one. It was addressed to the box number in neat blue biro capitals, but the feel of it made my heart sink. For I'd thought it would feel thick to the touch, containing, as I'd expected it to, several pages of explanation, apology and a detailed family history – instead it was disappointingly thin. It felt like the letter you receive when you know you haven't got the job. I handed it back to Theo.

'You open it,' I said.

'No, it's yours. You should do it.'

'I want you to. Please, Theo. You started this after all.'

He pursed his lips. 'Well . . . all right.' He drew his thumb along the flap and pulled out a single sheet of white vellum, written just on one side. He scanned it, nodded slowly, raised an eyebrow, then handed it to me. The address was twelve Cross Street, Chatham, Kent.

Dear Advertiser, I read your notice in the Chatham News with interest. But before I make any enquiries I would like to know two things. Is the name of the baby girl referred to in the advert by any chance 'Rose'? And does this person have any distinguishing marks? It was signed Marjorie Wilson (Mrs). There was no phone number, just the address.

'Do you think she's my mother?' I asked Theo. He looked at it again.

'No. If she were she wouldn't need to ask you your name. Your mother knows what your name is, and where she left you and on what day of what year. I also think from the trembly handwriting that this woman's too old. I guess she simply knows your mother – or used to know her.' My heart did a bungee jump. She knew my mother. This letter was from a woman *who knew my mother!* 'You'd better write back to her straight away.'

'And should I offer to meet her?'

'Not yet. Just tell her that your name is Rose and see what else she has to say.' I nodded, then went to my desk.

Dear Mrs Wilson, I wrote. My hand shook with nervousness. *Thank you very much for your recent letter. Yes, the relevant name is Rose, which is my name, and I do have one distinguishing mark – a birthmark in the shape of India at the top of my left leg. If you have any information whatsoever about my natural mother, whom I am trying to trace, then would you please phone me, a.s.a.p., on either of the above numbers and I'll call you straight back. Thank you so much for responding, and I look forward to hearing from you soon.* I signed myself 'Rose Wright' to protect my identity, just in case she ever reads the *Post*. Well, I am still Rose Wright, I reasoned as I stamped it. Or rather Rose Wrong: Rose very, very Wrong to have thought I could go back to Ed. We were light years apart.

I ran to the post box on the corner and dropped it in, then glanced at my watch. It was half past two. I knew I should be getting back to work, but I just couldn't face it. It had been such a tumultuous few hours.

'What a morning,' I murmured as I pushed on the door. And now, suddenly, the stress of it all caught up with me. Jon's letter, and the thought of him lying in hospital, dying; the memory of my row – and final break – with Ed; the knowledge that this Mrs Wilson might lead me to my mother – my mother, my MOTHER! – the fact that Theo was leaving me. A wave of emotion broke over me like a tsunami. I sank onto a kitchen chair.

'Rose!' said Theo. He was taking his cookery books off the shelf. 'Rose, what's the matter?'

'It's just, oh . . . everything,' I said. I looked at the half-empty shelf and felt my eyes brim. 'It's been . . .' my throat constricted, and I could barely speak, '. . . an overwhelming day.'

'You're obviously under huge emotional stress,' he said gently. Then he came and sat next to me and covered my left hand in his. 'You know that your mother's probably not very far away now,' he murmured. I nodded. 'And I guess it's frightening.' I nodded again. It *was*. Because for years it had all been safely hypothetical: but now it was about to be real. 'You're doing the right thing in looking for her,' Theo said gently. 'You really are, Rose – don't cry.'

'I'm not crying just because of her,' I wept. 'It's all the other things as well.'

'Like what?'

I shook my head. 'Oh – uh – uh – I can't tell you. It's just that I've had the most . . .' I threw my eyes up to the ceiling, '. . . the most *extraordinary* day.' I felt too ashamed of Ed to tell Theo about Jon's letter. 'Plus you're leaving,' I wailed. I looked at the boxes standing in the hall and felt my mouth twist with grief. 'You're leaving me, Theo. Everyone does. They love me and leave me – like *her*.' I felt his arm go round my shoulder as a tear snaked down my right cheek. 'Oh God, what a morning,' I wept. I was crying so much I could feel tears gathering in the hollow at the base of my throat. 'I'm sorry,' I mumbled as he passed me a piece of kitchen roll. 'You must think I'm always blubbing.'

'I don't.' The kitchen towel was soaked with a mixture of tears and mascara.

'I must look such a mess.'

'You do.' Theo reached out and ran his thumb beneath my right eye, then my left. 'But you're a lovely mess, Rose.' I tried to smile.

And now I studied his face, and realised how much I'd miss it. I looked at his blue eyes, behind their steel-rimmed frames, and at the faint line scored into his brow. I looked at his strong, lightly stubbled jaw line, and at the generous curve of his mouth. Ed had thin lips, but Theo's were full ones I now saw, or rather, *felt*. For instinctively I'd inclined my head towards his, just a fraction, his gaze now locked in mine. And then I inclined my head a little more. I couldn't help it. It was as though I was being pulled towards him by gravity, and suddenly I could feel the soft pressure of his mouth on mine.

'Sorry,' I said pulling back. I'd shocked myself. 'I kissed you.'

'Yes,' he said. 'I spotted that too.'

'You see I'm not quite myself today,' I stuttered.

'Didn't you want to kiss me then?' I looked into his eyes again, and noticed the flecks of pale green in the blue. 'Didn't you?' he repeated gently. 'Didn't you, Rose?'

'Yes,' I whispered. 'I did.'

'Well that's absolutely fine then,' he murmured. 'Because I'd quite like to kiss you too.'

An electric charge shot through me as he took my face in his hands. And he pressed his mouth to mine, his light stubble scraping my skin. He was kissing me again, at first gently, and then harder, parting my lips with his tongue. We stayed there, like that, for a few minutes, just kissing.

'Oh Rose,' he said. And now he pulled me into a standing position, and we kissed for a little longer. 'Oh Rose.'

I felt his hands begin to explore the inside of my shirt as he pushed down the straps of my bra. My hands went down to his waistband, and began to undo his jeans. And he slipped my shirt off my shoulders, still kissing me, and now we were going upstairs. We were going upstairs together, and I could hear our combined tread on the steps. And I opened my bedroom door and pulled him inside, and we fell on the bed in a tangle of limbs. He pulled down my skirt, and stepped out of his jeans, then quickly took off his shirt. And now I saw his broad shoulders, and his chest, and his lean, muscled stomach.

'Oh Rose,' he sighed as he kissed my breasts, first one and

then the other. Then he lifted himself up. And as he poured himself into me, with increasing urgency, I suddenly knew. I'd got it. At last. I'd finally realised what the anagram of Theo Sheen is – 'He's the one.'

'He's the one,' I sighed as he moved above me. *'He's* the one,' I reiterated as he came with a great shudder. 'Theo Sheen – he's the one.' He fell forward, panting, his back wet with sweat, and his right cheek pressed hard against mine. We lay there like that for a few minutes. Now he turned over and I locked my arms round his chest, our knees drawn up, his pelvis folded into the hollow of mine. I gazed at the gold freckles which spangled his back, like stars. I traced them with the tip of my finger, and imagined what constellations they might be. This one on his right shoulder looked a bit like Orion, and the light smattering on his left one, the Plough. That 'W' shaped one at the base of his neck could be Cassiopeia, and these four here, the Southern Cross.

'I've wanted to do that for so long,' I heard him say quietly.

'Really?'

'Yes. But you didn't see it. Did you?'

'No. I thought you were just being . . . kind to me,' I murmured. 'Kind and empathetic.'

'You didn't read between the lines.'

'No,' I murmured. 'I guess I didn't. And when did you . . . first . . . ?' I ventured.

'Oh, I don't know, months ago.'

'Really?'

'Hmmm.' I was amazed. 'I was dimly aware that I was attracted to you when I first came to see the house,' he murmured. 'I must have been because you were so bloody tricky, and yet I wasn't put off.' He turned over now and gazed at me. 'But it was when you came out to star-watch with me on New Year's Eve. That's what did it. Your reaction was so passionate. I felt you had a lovely soul . . .'

'Thank you.'

'. . . and that I'd touched it.'

'You had.'

'But I thought you were a bit crazy.' I laughed. 'You were so prickly, Rose.'

'Thorny.'

'Hmm.'

'That's what people say.'

'A bit neurotic.'

'I guess I was.'

'And you were clearly very troubled about your mother, and about your marriage, so I was naturally wary of you. I was upset enough myself at that time about Fiona so I didn't want to take the risk. Plus you were my landlady – it was all very awkward. And then Ed was around again, and I didn't know how you felt, or what you really wanted to do. I just wanted a *sign* from you that you liked me, Rose. A sign. But I didn't get it. Until now.' We stayed like that for a minute or so, just looking into each other's eyes. 'You're such an enigma to me, Rose,' he added quietly. 'Such a . . . puzzle.'

'I've *been* puzzled all my life.'

'I know. And that's why you like doing anagrams, because you're an anagram yourself.'

I could see the truth of that. For *I* had been 'muddled,' *I* had been 'disordered,' *I* had been 'mixed up,' 'confused' and 'upset'. Because the letters of my life had been in the wrong order, but Theo had helped me to sort them out.

'Eros,' said Theo gently. 'That's your real anagram. And you *do* look like the Botticelli Venus, you know.' He ran his fingers across the high ridge of my collar bones. 'You've got such lovely clavicles.'

'You flatterer.'

'And attractive ankles.'

'Really?'

'Oh yes.'

'And of course my hair's mad.'

'It is. It's absolutely barmy,' he said, as he wound a ten-dril round his finger. 'I think you're lovely, Rose. I've always

388

thought so. A bit crazy, but lovely.' I gazed at his face. What a day.

'What a day,' I breathed. 'I will never, ever forget this day. Four huge, and totally unexpected things have happened to me and it's still only lunchtime.' I shook my head.

'Like what?'

'Like . . . this,' I replied softly. 'And hearing about the ad.' My heart turned over, and my mother's imagined face loomed up before me.

'What else has happened today?'

I sighed, then told him about the letter from Ed's brother. His mouth went slack with shock.

'Christ, how *awful*. So what did you do?'

'I went to see Ed, in his office, and I told him he had to do it. And then I left him. For good. And that's the other thing that's happened to me today. I've finished with Ed.'

'You've left him?'

'Yes.'

He pulled me to him, even closer. 'Good. No going back?'

'No,' I said emphatically. 'No going back. It's *over*.'

'Because of what you found out about his brother.'

I nodded. 'It made me feel sick. How could I stay with him now, Theo, knowing that? And he was so vicious to me as well.'

'Was he?'

'Yes. It was only because he was cornered, but he was *vile*.'

'In what way?'

I cringed at the memory. 'He said this awful thing.'

'What?'

'Well, he accused me of being an agony aunt for all the wrong reasons. He said I was doing it for myself. Out of egotism.'

'Really?'

'Yes,' I said irritably. 'He did. Out. *Rageous*,' I breathed, freshly incensed.

'Well, aren't you?' said Theo quietly. I looked at the ceiling. There was a crack in it.

'No,' I replied firmly. 'I'm not.'

389

'Then why *are* you doing it?'

'Because I know I can.'

'I see.'

'That's the only reason, Theo.'

'But you must enjoy it.'

'Of course I do. I don't deny that – being an agony aunt is a bit like lighting a fire for a freezing man – you get back a little of that warmth yourself. And, yes, that's a very nice feeling. But Ed said I really do it so that people will feel grateful to me and need me, and like me and admire me, because I feel so . . . inadequate.'

'That's what he said?'

I felt my lips purse. 'Yes.'

'Well, that wasn't very nice of him.'

'It certainly wasn't.'

'But maybe there's a bit of truth in that.'

'What?'

'Maybe there's a bit of truth there,' he repeated.

'Oh. Well, thanks very much. How typically tactful of you, Theo. So you think my career's just a crutch, do you?'

'No. Not entirely,' he replied. 'But the fact is that for twenty years you've been carrying around this huge psychological burden which you've only just begun to address . . .'

'Well, yes. I have had that . . . issue,' I conceded. I suddenly visualised myself as one of those ants carrying a load four times its own size.

'And I just wonder whether you would have wanted to be an agony aunt if you hadn't felt so troubled yourself?'

I looked at him. Would I? 'Yes. Yes, I would.'

'Are you sure Rose?' he asked quietly. Cheek!

'Look, I hope you're not on Ed's side,' I said indignantly, sitting up. 'Because what he said was vicious and mean-spirited.'

'Don't be silly Rose. It's not like that. I'm just saying that from what I've learned about you – wonderful though you are – I think you probably *are* an agony aunt as much for yourself as for your readers. Maybe Ed's got a point there.'

'Well thank you!' I exclaimed as I reached for my shirt. 'It's nice to know you share his high opinion of me.'

'I do have a high opinion of you.'

'Oh yeah?'

''Course I do. But all I'm saying is, well, why not be honest about the fact that your motives are maybe a bit mixed?'

'Because I'm not going to admit to being some emotional cripple who needs to prop herself up with the problems of others.' How *could* I admit to that? I mean, Christ! – it would make me no better than Citronella Pratt! 'I am an agony aunt,' I said, as I stood up. 'Because I want to help people, that's all.'

'Rose, I don't doubt that, but the question is *why*.'

'Why?' I said staring at him.

'Yes. *Why* do you want to help people?'

'Because . . . I'm good at it, that's why. And because I know I can make a real difference to their lives. I have saved marriages,' I said. I thought of the itchy-fingered arsonist. 'And perhaps even lives. I've been able to, well, yes, to rescue my readers from their problems. They depend on me.'

'I'm sorry, Rose, I don't think that's true. I think you probably depend on them to quite an extent.'

'Oh, well, thanks, Theo – that's *great!*'

'Look, it's nothing to feel bad about. We all have deep seated motives for doing what we do. All I'm saying is there's no shame in acknowledging it, that's all.'

'I see. So you think I should go round telling everyone that the reason I'm an agony aunt is because I'm such a pathetic inadequate – is that it?'

'No, I'm not saying that.'

'I do it out of altruism.'

'Really?'

'Of course I do! Because why the hell would anyone spend all day thinking about other people's ghastly, boring, sordid, and quite often, pathetic, problems if they didn't have to?'

'That's *exactly* my point. Why *would* anyone? Unless they enjoyed feeling needed. And I think that you do.'

'I *don't*!'

'You do, Rose. And it's nice to feel needed. There's nothing wrong with that. And after all, you must feel that your mother didn't need you . . .'

'No,' I said bitterly. 'She *didn't*! She didn't need me. She didn't need me at *all* – so she threw me away!'

'So maybe feeling that you're needed by your readers makes you feel better about that. And it's quite understandable.'

'Well thanks very much. Look, why don't you just stop getting at me?' I snapped as I zipped up my skirt. 'I've had quite enough.'

'I'm not getting at you Rose,' he said as he stood up. 'I think you're grand. I'm just saying that you should wise up to yourself a bit more. I mean, come on – you're nearly forty. Don't you know yourself yet?'

'Yes, I do know myself actually! I'm very self-aware.'

'I'm not sure that you are. I mean, there are things you miss, Rose. *Big* things. Important things.'

'Oh I see,' I said, my pulse racing. 'So not only am I an agony aunt for the wrong reason, I'm not even very good at it. In fact I'm pretty crap at it according to you.'

'No, you're not. But I'm not sure that you're a natural agony aunt, in the way that, well, Bev is for example.'

'Bev?' I felt as though I'd been slapped.

'Yes. She's really astute. She doesn't miss anything. Maybe because her disability has made her such an acute observer. She's a *natural* agony aunt.'

'Oh well, thanks very much,' I said as I put on my shirt. 'This is really great. So not only am I a crap agony aunt, doing it under false pretences, to make myself feel better about my mum dumping me forty years ago, I compare unfavourably to Bev – is that it?'

'No, I didn't mean it like that.'

'Well if Beverley's so wonderful why don't you go out with *her* then?' I muttered as I buttoned my shirt. 'I always thought you liked her. I was convinced for months that you did. Poppet!' I spat.

392

'Yes, I *did* like Beverley. I *do* like her. I like her a lot – but not in that way.'

'And she obviously likes you – "Sweetie!" Well, after what you've just said to me, she can bloody well help herself!'

'Rose, I can assure you that Beverley has no romantic interest in me whatsoever and never has had.'

'Look,' I said as I pulled on my shoes. 'Let's just forget about this. You make love to me, and then you lay into me and totally undermine me and do your best to make me feel bad. I know you're a blunt Yorkshireman and all that, but I just don't get it.'

'I'm not "laying into you" Rose. I think you're a wonderful person.'

'So why are you being so nasty to me then?'

'I'm not.'

'Yes you bloody well are! You're being rude and nasty – downright offensive – and I don't think it's on. I've had enough of it today, what with Ed being so vile – so I'm not taking it from you as well. So why don't you just . . . fuck OFF!' He flinched. I'd shocked him. 'Just fuck right off!' I repeated.

'Don't worry,' he said icily. 'I *will*. You're right, Rose. This was a mistake.' We stared at each other, my heart was pounding so hard I'd thought he'd hear it. Suddenly from somewhere I heard *If you'd like to swing on a star, carry moonbeams home in a jar* . . . Theo groped for his mobile in his shirt pocket.

'Hello? Yes, it is. Oh hello. Have I? Oh. Well that's grand. I thought it would be tomorrow. Well, as it happens, that suits me down to the ground. Yes. I'm on my way now.'

'Where are you going?' I demanded as he pulled on his boxer shorts.

'To the estate agents. That was my solicitor to say I've just completed on the flat – a day early, as it happens – so I'm going to collect the keys.'

'Are you coming back here afterwards?'

He stepped into his jeans and then pulled on his shirt. 'No.

393

I'm not. I'll go straight to the flat. I was going to leave tomorrow, but as my stuff's all packed I might as well leave today. Not least because I now know what an impossible bloody woman you are. Let's forget this Rose,' he said, as he pocketed his phone. 'I wouldn't touch you with a bargepole. You're a *mess.*'

'Yes,' I shouted as he walked out of the room. 'Let's! Let's forget it and you can just – get lost! You pretend to care about me,' I added as he ran upstairs to his room, 'but you've really hurt me.'

'I haven't hurt you,' he said as he reappeared with his duvet. 'I've just tried to get you to be a bit more honest, that's all.'

'But it's none of your business whether I'm honest or not!'

'No,' he conceded. 'That's true. You're quite right Rose. It's got nothing to do with me. Anyway, I'd better get going, I've got loads to do.'

'Yes you'd better,' I yelled as he ran downstairs. 'You've loved me so now you'll leave me! Won't you? *Won't* you?'

'Goodbye Rose.'

'Yes goodbye! Goodbye and good bloody riddance you bastard! You can just fuck off! You can just fuck RIGHT off and NEVER come back.'

I heard him moving his boxes out of the hall, and putting them in the back of the car. Then he slammed the front door, and I heard the squeak of the gate, and I was wondering whether to run after him when my mobile phone rang. It was Bev.

'Rose, aren't you coming in?' she said anxiously. Oh shit. I looked at my watch. It was four.

'Oh, God . . . I don't think I can, I feel so awful.'

'But I'm snowed under here. I need you,' she added.

'I'm sorry, Bev, but I've had a hell of a day and it's getting worse.'

'Look Rose,' she said, 'I don't know what's going on with you at the moment, but I just don't feel your mind's on the job.'

'No it isn't,' I agreed. 'I've got far too many things going on in my life at the moment to be able to care about anyone else.'

'Do you want to talk about it sometime? Maybe I can help.'

'No, thanks Bev, I don't. I just want to lie on my bed and go to sleep and never wake up. And Theo's just left, and we quarrelled but the point is, he's the one.'

'He's the *what*?'

'He's the one. Theo Sheen. He's the one.' Suddenly I heard the ring of the doorbell. 'Sorry, I've got to go.' I ran to the door and threw it open, hoping to see Theo standing there, his arms held wide, an apologetic expression on his face. But it wasn't Theo at all.

'Good afternoon Madam.' It was them. They were back again.

'Have you heard the Good News?' I stared at them. 'Have you heard the Good News?' they repeated politely as they held out a copy of *The Watchtower*.

'No,' I said sharply. 'I haven't. I haven't heard the good news. I've heard nothing but bad news. I'm *so* depressed – will you come in?' They stepped inside and followed me into the kitchen. 'Would you like a cup of tea?' I asked. As I put on the kettle I glanced at the yawning bookshelf and felt a sharp pain in my chest, as though someone was trying to saw through my sternum. 'You see, he's the one,' I explained miserably. 'I didn't realise it until now. But he is.'

'Yes, Madam, He *is* the one. The one and only.'

'I know. And it's taken me all this time to see.'

'Don't worry, for He will forgive you.'

I laughed darkly. 'I don't think so – he was terribly cross. You see, I really offended him, but I like him so much and I just want him back in my life.'

'Then pray, Madam. That's all you have to do. Pray, and He *will* come into your life.'

'I do feel like praying,' I said as I felt my eyes fill again. 'I've never had much truck with religion frankly, but when

I'm desperate, yes, I pray.' I grabbed a bit of kitchen towel and pressed it into my eyes.

'Don't worry,' said the woman. 'He is all loving.'

'Yes,' I said as I got down the teapot, 'he is. He's very decent and loving, and the thing is, he's the one. I've only just worked it out, today. And you see the reason I know he's the one is because I told him.'

'You told him He's the one?'

'No, I didn't tell him that. I told him about my mother, and *that's* why he's the one, because I chose to tell *him*, and nobody else. You see, I told him this enormously significant thing about my past.'

'You can tell Him anything. He hears what you say.'

'Yes,' I said as I got down the mugs. 'He does hear, or rather he did. But if only I'd realised before.'

'Sometimes it takes people a long time to come to God,' said the man gently.

'No, not God. Theo.'

'Yes, Theo. Theo means God. You can call him Theo, God, Jehovah – whatever you want. We know what you mean – and He knows too.'

'No, Theo – my flatmate – *he's* the one.' They shifted slightly uncomfortably on their seats. 'And I've hurt him.'

'But He will forgive you.'

'Do you really think so?'

'Yes. He will forgive you,' said the man soothingly. 'Because He is your friend.'

'Yes, he is. He *is* my friend,' I said. 'That's exactly what he's been. Is P.G. Tips okay?'

'You just have to trust in him,' they said.

'And I *do*,' I replied as I got out the milk. 'I know I *can* trust him. But you see today we went to bed together for the first time, and I'd just broken up with my husband who I'd been temporarily reconciled with, but with whom I've now *definitely* broken up because I discovered that he'd refused to donate bone marrow to his younger brother who's very ill with leukaemia – I know, absolutely awful, I could hardly believe it myself – and then I came home because Theo had an important letter for me – about my mother actually, who I've never met – and then I was feeling rather upset about everything and Theo put his arm round me and then I kissed him and the next thing I knew, we were in bed! But *then* it all went horribly wrong because he accused me of being an agony aunt for the wrong reasons in order to make myself feel better about the fact that my mother didn't want me – which she clearly didn't otherwise she wouldn't have abandoned me in a supermarket trolley when I was a baby – and you see, I'd just broken up with Ed – that's my husband – who I finally dumped this morning after nearly being reconciled with him, and I said, "no, Theo, it's not true. I'm an agony aunt because I do genuinely *like* helping people," but he basically said I was fooling myself. So I shouted at him and he stormed off to the estate agents to collect the keys to his new flat because he's moving out today: and you see that's what makes it all so *awful* – the fact that I didn't know how he felt about me. Or rather I didn't *see*: I didn't read between the lines: because he told me today that he'd liked me for months, but I hadn't realised it because I was blind; and then we quarrelled viciously and I told him to eff off; it's all just a horrible mess and now he's gone and I'm going to be here all on my *own*. I'm going to be here all on my own, *without* him and I can't *stand* it, and I don't know *what* to *do*!' They stood up. 'Oh God I've got *so* many problems,' I wailed.

'Problems! Problems!' shouted Rudy.

'I'm having the most extraordinary day. I just needed someone to talk to. Would you like a biscuit?'

'No thank you Madam. We have to go.'

'But you haven't been here that long.'

'Well,' they said, shifting slightly from foot to foot, 'we have other calls to make.'

'Have another cup of tea then?'

'No, really.'

'Or some cake? I'm sure I've got a Battenburg somewhere.'

'Thank you – no. God bless you Madam, and don't worry. Jehovah loves you. Goodbye.'

'Will you call again?' I said as they opened the front door. 'Please. Please will you come again? Come again soon won't you!' I called after them as they went down the garden path. But they'd opened the gate, and had gone.

I looked at the clock – it was half past five. No time to go to work now. I went upstairs to Theo's room, and, heart pounding, I opened the door. The cupboard door was ajar, the wire hangers clinking gently against each other in the slight breeze. The mantelpiece was empty, the outline of his mother's photograph clear in the dust. His telescope was no longer by the window, the stuff on his desk had been cleared. And now I remembered his diary, and the time when I'd shut his window during the storm. His writing was so hard to read, but now some of it came back. *Rose is very . . . ctive* – that must have been attractive – not active – I now saw – *but I something her something a b . . . pole.* Touch her with a bargepole. That's what he'd shouted at me just now. I stared at his bed. The mattress was stripped. I lay down it and put my head on his slipless pillow, and closed my eyes. I imagined him lying here night after night, while I was lying on my bed, beneath. I slipped my hand underneath and felt something – an old tee shirt. I pressed it to my face.

'Oh Rose,' I said. 'You've messed up.' I felt as derelict as a condemned building, waiting for the crunch of the wrecking ball. And tonight I had to go and do my phone-in: I felt so bad – I couldn't be on my own. I had to talk to someone. I just *had* to. I glanced at my watch. It was twenty to seven. Bev would be back, she wouldn't mind. I'd chat to her until I had to go to the radio station, that's what I'd do. I got up, and went down into the bathroom, and washed my face, noticing a thread of Theo's hair in the sink. I opened the medicine cabinet and saw that the top shelf was stripped of his things. My toothbrush was standing there solitary and forlorn; my towel the only one on the rail. I went downstairs, picked up my keys and went next door. I rang the bell, and there was Trevor. He wagged his tail.

'Hi Trev,' I said, as he let me in. I followed him down the hallway, his claws clicking on the new parquet, and called out 'Hi Bev! It's only me. I've just come round for a chat and to say I'm really sorry about not coming into work today but you see –' I stopped. 'Oh!' I exclaimed softly. 'Er, hello,' I said uncertainly. I felt my face flush.

'Hello Rose,' Henry replied.

Chapter Twenty-Three

I laughed to cover my surprise – and my embarrassment. Henry stepped forward and kissed me on the cheek. 'Henry,' I exclaimed, wonderingly. 'Er, what are you –?' I stopped myself just in time. And then, as I looked from one to the other, I saw. Beverley's face was shining with happiness. It was obvious.

'We're just having a drink before supper,' Bev said. 'Would you like to join us? Henry darling would you get Rose a large G and T – I think she's had a really bad day.' As Trevor got the gin out of the drinks cupboard, Henry got the tonic out of the fridge.

'Well,' I exclaimed softly. I smiled, then shrugged. 'Why on earth didn't you tell me?' I asked as Henry got down a glass tumbler. Beverley blushed.

'Well, for all sorts of reasons,' she began, 'not least because we didn't know for sure ourselves until quite recently.'

'Which was when?'

'Do you really want to know?'

'Yes. If you want to tell me.'

'At the twins' party.'

'Really?' I cast my mind back. I didn't remember seeing Henry talking to Beverley at *all* that night.

'That was when it got going,' Beverley explained. 'When I got home afterwards I took off Trevor's coat, and found Henry's business card in the pocket. He must have slipped it inside as he left.'

'That's exactly what I did.'

'And he'd scribbled "call me!" on the back of it, and so the next day, I did. And we met for lunch, didn't we?' They smiled at each other. 'And then we met a couple of times after that . . .'

'But then I had to go to the Gulf.'

'But we wrote, and we spoke on the phone.'

I suddenly remembered Bev getting a call on her mobile at the Dogs of Distinction award. That must have been Henry I now saw. Yes, of course it was, because I'd heard her comment on the fact that he was somewhere 'hot'.

'Gosh,' I said, smiling, 'so when did it first . . . ?'

'Start?' asked Bev. I nodded.

'At the ball,' Henry explained as he dropped some ice into my drink. 'I took one look at Beverley and I thought, what a fantastic girl. In your lovely ballerina costume,' he added, stroking her hand. And now I suddenly remembered Henry lifting her out of her wheelchair and whirling her round, her face radiant with laughter. Of *course*. 'But then Bea was flirting with me like mad,' he added as he handed me the glass. 'And then she asked me out a few times.'

'And I knew about that from you, Rose,' said Bev. 'So I couldn't confide to you that *I* liked Henry because I was worried that you might tell her. And also, from what you said, I believed that she and Henry were getting on like a house on fire.'

'Well I thought they *were*,' I said, as Henry smiled and rolled his eyes. 'So *that's* why you seemed not to like Bea much, is that right Bev?'

'Yes. I was as jealous as hell. And then you asked me to help her in the shop, and I couldn't very well say 'no,' but I didn't really want to do it. But I'm so glad I did because that's how I met Henry again. He came in one day to take her out to lunch. And I was sitting there, looking at him out of the corner of my eye, feeling awful. But while she was downstairs getting her coat I was amazed to find that Henry was being very, well, attentive to me, weren't you?'

He smiled. 'Yes,' he said. 'I was. I pretended I was interested in Trevor,' he explained. 'Not that I'm *not*,' he added with a laugh.

'You were very attentive,' Bev repeated. 'Slightly flirtatious even – I was surprised, and quietly thrilled.'

'But I was too embarrassed to say anything,' said Henry. 'And I didn't want to hurt Bea. So I had to end that – and I'm not very brave in that way so it took me quite a long time.' So there really *had* been 'another woman' I realised. 'And then of course I didn't know whether or not Beverley even *liked* me,' he continued.

'I was nuts about you!' she laughed.

'But I couldn't have known that because I thought you liked Theo,' he went on.

'Well that's what *I* thought,' I said. 'I thought you and Theo clicked at the ball, Bev. And when I danced with him you seemed to be giving me a rather peculiar look.'

'But Rose, I wasn't even looking at *you*. I was looking at *Henry*. He was dancing cheek to cheek with Bea, and I felt dreadful.'

I cast my mind back to that night. 'I see.' I glanced at Bea's notice board, and saw the Valentine card pinned to it. 'And I thought that was from Theo as well,' I said pointing at it. She shook her head.

'It was from me,' said Henry. 'I knew that Beverley was your next door neighbour, so it was easy to work out the address. But I didn't have the courage to tell you that I liked her. I did try once or twice, but every time I'd start, you'd immediately tell me how well Beverley was getting on with Theo.'

'Well I thought they *were*. And I kept *on* thinking that, Bev, because you seemed to spend time with him.'

'Well, he'd come round, and we'd chat. I found him very sympathetic and good fun, and he'd help me do a few things in the house.'

'But he called you "Pet" and you called him "Sweetie".'

'Oh that was just for a laugh! You didn't take that at face value, did you Rose?'

'Well, yes actually – I did.'

'Then you should have read between the lines. It's easy to flirt with someone if neither of you are really interested. It's much harder to flirt with someone you *like*. In any case Rose, I didn't fall for Theo, because I'd already fallen for Henry.' Henry smiled.

'But hang on, what about that Scottish bloke – Hamish?' I asked. 'The one Trevor kept mentioning in his column?'

'Well,' she laughed gently, 'he was a red herring.'

'Doesn't he exist?'

'Oh yes – he does. He's an old friend of mine, and we have seen each other a few times lately as he's been rehearsing in London, so that was all perfectly true. But I just wanted to put people off the scent about Henry, because by then, I was hooked. But we were worried that Bea would be hurt if she knew, so that's why I couldn't tell you, and so I pretended that it was Hamish I was keen on. But I did tell Theo the truth, though I swore him to secrecy.' *Ah.*

'Well he never said a thing to me.'

'No, he wouldn't have done. He's very discreet.'

And now I remembered that entry in his diary. *Henry is clearly very keen on Bea.* Except I now saw that with Theo's awful handwriting, it wasn't 'Bea,' he'd written, but 'Bev'. *Henry is clearly very keen on Bev.* Theo had seen it, that night, at the ball, where I'd completely missed it. My head was beginning to swim.

'And in any case,' Beverley added, 'Henry and I didn't know ourselves whether or not our romance would develop, did we darling, so we both thought it best to keep quiet.'

'So it was never Theo,' I said.

'Never.'

'Well I got that wrong then.'

'You did. And in any case Rose, I could see – and he eventually told me this himself – that Theo really liked *you*. But you didn't seem to realise it.'

'No,' I said bitterly, 'I didn't.'

'You didn't read between the lines.' People keep saying that to me today.

'It's true.' I emitted a mirthless laugh. 'I didn't read between the lines.'

'Rose, you do sometimes miss things,' said Bev gently. 'Quite big things, actually.'

I looked at her. 'That's just what Theo said. But you see I'd never imagined he'd be interested in me as he's ten years younger.'

'Why not? His wife's thirty-eight.'

'But I didn't know that for quite a while; so although, yes, I found him attractive, I always assumed he'd go for someone his own age. I know you're six years older as well Bev, but I thought ten would be pushing it a bit.'

'Not really,' she shrugged. 'His twenty-nine to your thirty-nine hardly makes you Mrs Robinson, does it? You're both grown-ups.'

'Hmm. That's true. But I'd never been out with a younger man. Why didn't you *tell* me that he liked me?' I added. 'It would have made my life a lot easier.'

'Well I tried to hint at it, but you didn't see. In any case you were still obsessing about Ed. And then you had enough on your plate with all that trouble with Electra and Serena; and then Ed was around so I didn't want to encourage Theo about you, in case he got hurt again. He's had his heartbreak as well, remember. But I did give him advice.'

'Like what?'

'I just told him to spend time with you. To be domestic with you. To teach you to cook, for example.'

'He did teach me to cook.'

'To watch telly and play games.'

'We did.'

'Because it's by spending time with someone, doing the daily domestic things, that you can often get very close. Proximity can draw people together.'

'Hmm,' I sighed. 'I know. Gravity is the mutual attraction between every bit of matter in the universe,' I went on softly.

'And the closer the matter is, the stronger the attraction. That's what Theo told me.'

'It's true.'

'But it's all gone horribly wrong. Theo's just moved out, and oh God,' I put my head in my hands – 'I went to bed with him today.'

'You did?'

'But then we quarrelled.'

'Over what?'

'Well, I'd left Ed just beforehand – over Jon's letter – and Ed had accused me of being an agony aunt for the wrong reason.'

'Really?' said Beverley. 'What did he say?'

I told her.

'Ed said that?'

'Yes. And I told Theo, and he agreed.'

'I see,' she said carefully.

'Great timing, don't you think?'

'Well, Theo's lovely, but he can be slightly tactless sometimes.'

'You're telling me!'

'It's just a bit of northern bluntness, that's all.'

'I know. But he really wounded me – so I told him to fuck off and never come back.'

'Oh Rose,' Bev said.

'I know. And he'd just completed on the flat so he said he was going to go today instead of tomorrow, and he has gone and oh, it's a *nightmare*, Bev.' The thought of his empty bedroom made my heart hurt. 'And it's my phone-in tonight, and I feel *so* wretched and I – What a day,' I repeated, blankly, as I sipped my drink. I shook my head. 'What a day. The most extraordinary things have happened, and they're still happening. I've got it together with Theo, and then we quarrelled and he's left; and I've discovered that you two are together when I hadn't a clue; and then there was that letter from Ed's brother this morning – and my row with Ed – it's all been too much. And now I've got to do my phone-in and sound coherent and take an interest in everyone else's problems when I've got such *huge* issues of my own.' At this I thought again of my mother, and of Mrs Wilson's letter, and my eyes began to fill. And suddenly there were tears snaking down my cheeks, and my head had sunk onto my chest.

'I'm sorry,' I sobbed, 'it's the gin. It's making me emotional.'

'It isn't the gin,' said Bev.

'No. You're right. It isn't the gin. It's my life. It's everything. Oh God, I feel wretched,' I sobbed. 'I'm sorry, you two. I'm glad you're so happy, but I'm just feeling *so* bad.'

Suddenly I was aware of Trevor's wet nose on my hand. He was trying to push something into my lap. I lifted my head. It was the phone.

'It's okay Trev,' said Bev gently. 'Rose doesn't need to call anyone right now. She's got Henry and me.' I looked into Trevor's big, concerned-looking eyes, the colour of sweet sherry, and buried my face in his fur.

'Oh Trevor,' I said, half laughing, half crying, '*thank* you! That's so lovely of you.' Beverley clicked the phone off then handed it back to him.

'Okay, Trev, put it back. Good boy.' I heard the click of his claws on the parquet as he trotted out into the hall. I looked at the clock, it was five to nine. My car would be coming at ten past. I stood up.

'I'd better go.'

'Will you be okay Rose?' said Henry.

'Yes,' I said. 'I'll be fine. Thanks for . . . everything. Well, what a turn-up,' I said. 'What a day. What other extraordinary revelations or happenings could there possibly be?'

'Oh there won't be anything more,' said Beverley confidently. 'Law of averages and all that.'

I went home. As I opened the door I was struck again by the emptiness of the house. It felt hollow, and so did I. It was as though someone had scooped out my insides with a large spoon and all that was left was my shell. As I shut the front door I saw that the answerphone was winking. My heart did a pole vault. Maybe it was Theo ringing to say that he was sorry that he'd hurt my feelings and that he'd like to see me and did I want to go round to the flat? My hand sprang to the button marked 'Play.' Oh for God's sake! Not *again*! The bloody *bastard* harassing me with his beastly slow breathing. It went on for about ten seconds, and I was about to hit Stop and then Erase when I suddenly heard something else. The sound of sniffing. As though someone was crying. How *weird*.

It's okay Trev. That was Beverley! *Rose doesn't need to call anyone right now.* What the hell? *She's got Henry and me.*

Oh Trevor, I heard *my*self say now. *Thank you. That's so lovely of you.*

That was your. Last. Message, intoned the electronic voice. I stared at the machine. Then I played the message again. Then again. Then again. Then once more. And now, at last, I understood. I picked up the receiver and dialled.

'Bev. It's me. Listen, you have my number on speed dial don't you?'

'Yes I do. It's on the first memory button actually.'

'*Ah*,' I said.

'Why do you ask?'

'Because I've just worked out who my heavy breather is.'

'Really? Well you must call the police.'

'No. I'm not going to do that.'

'Why not?'

'Because it's Trevor.'

'*What*?'

'It's Trev.'

'What do you *mean*? Trevor would *never* make nuisance phone calls,' she exclaimed indignantly.

'Yes, I *know*. But he must have been accidentally biting the memory button sometimes when he went to pick up the phone.'

'Oh . . .' she said slowly. 'Oh . . . Well . . .' – I heard her voice fade slightly – 'looking at it now I suppose he could be doing that, yes . . . But I wouldn't have known because I just click it straight off.'

'And that's why I've been hearing heavy breathing,' I said. 'And that's why it was much worse the other day, because he had a cold. But just now I heard all *our* voices on it as well. But how the hell did Trevor manage to conceal the number every time?'

'Because I have 141 pre-programmed in. It makes me feel safer knowing that my number can't be traced.'

'Ah,' I said, faintly. 'I see. Well, mystery solved, Bev. Thanks.' As I put down the phone I thought again about the pattern of the calls, which I'd monitored closely, and now, suddenly, it all made sense. Trevor was very sensitive to weeping – I'd seen that myself, tonight – and he only brought Beverley the phone when he knew she was miserable. That's why the calls were so random. And that's why there had been fewer recently, because she'd clearly been happier, because Henry was back. And *that's* why there'd been that odd clicking sound lately. Because Bev used to have carpet in the hall, but she'd just had that parquet put down. Here was yet another amazing revelation to add to all the day's others. I'd discovered I'd been stalked by a dog.

I looked out of the window. The car was pulling up. I picked up my bag and went outside. My heart sank at the thought of having to do a phone-in. I wasn't up to it tonight. We passed a sign for Stockwell and my heart turned over. I imagined Theo in his new flat. The address was seared on my memory – 5 (a) Artemis Road – I'd seen it on the estate agents' blurb. I imagined him unpacking boxes, and filling cupboards, and sorting stuff out. And I had a sudden fantasy that he'd be listening to the radio while he was doing it, and that he'd have it tuned to London FM. And he'd be so moved by the sound of my voice that he'd feel compelled to call in. And he'd be put through to me and ask me if I'd forgive him for his quite inappropriate frankness, and was I free for dinner tomorrow night? And I'd say, 'Of course I'm free Theo. I'm going to be free every night. Because I've finally worked out that you're the one.'

I sighed as I saw the illuminated sign for London FM on the corner of City Road. I remembered how the day had started with Jon's letter. I'd ring the hospital first thing. Tonight all I had to do was to concentrate on my phone-in, but I found it terribly hard. I heard my own, slightly bored voice with a kind of detached interest as I took the listeners' calls.

'Yes, I'm sure your mother-in-law *is* a "vicious old trout," but calling her one is not exactly going to make relations more cordial is it? . . . Well, let's face it, the fact that he's taken out a restraining order on you is not a good sign, no . . . Just clapping your hands over both ears and shouting "I'm not listening, I'm not listening," is not a good way to resolve conflict with your partner . . . Yes, I'm afraid that the lack of sex IS going to be an impediment to your getting pregnant . . .'

Their voices droned away in my headphones like bees; or rather they whined like mosquitoes, and were just as irritating. Why can't they sort out their own bloody problems I thought angrily. I felt like a gigantic ear.

'And on line five,' said Minty, just back from maternity leave, 'we have Jean from Croydon, whose husband is making unreasonable demands on her.'

'What does he want you to do Jean?' I asked wearily.

'He wants me to . . .' She paused, then coughed with embarrassment. Oh God. It was obviously disgusting. I braced myself for something sick. 'He wants me to wear a wetsuit,' she said delicately. 'And I kind of don't mind in one way, but I feel a bit silly in it. Do you think I should agree?'

'Well if you're going scuba diving or wind-surfing it's probably an excellent idea,' I said. 'Otherwise, I don't recommend it. No.'

'And, er, now,' said Minty, looking at me oddly, 'we have Derek from Luton, whose marriage has just collapsed. Go ahead Derek.'

'It's awful,' he said in a nasally voice. 'My wife's just gone off with her blooming tennis instructor. I ask you! He's only twenty-eight, and she's forty-five so I don't know what she sees in him.'

'I haven't the faintest idea either,' I said. 'But maybe they have great sets. And who's our next caller Minty?'

'Er, well, it's Margaret from Wimbledon who has a problem with her neighbours,' Minty replied uncertainly.

'So what's the problem Margaret?'

'Well, for a start they don't keep their front garden tidy,' she said censoriously. God I hate women like this. 'But what is *really* annoying me,' she went on, 'is that when they're in their back garden they keep throwing snails over the fence onto *my* side! What can I do to stop their anti-social behaviour?'

'What can you do? Well I suggest you strike back with a few of your own. The giant African Land Snail would be very good for this purpose, but do be careful, Margaret, as they weigh about ten pounds and you could be done for GBH.' Minty gave me another odd look, then glanced at the computer screen again.

'Right,' she said brightly, 'and, er, just time for *one* more question.'

'Hi my name's Natalie, I'm from North Fields. And I want to know whether or not I should tie the knot. My partner wants to, but I'm perfectly happy to continue cohabiting, so I'm wondering what to do.'

'So you want to know whether or not you should marry your partner?'

'Yes.'

'You want me to tell you.'

'Yes, I do.'

I looked down at the e-mail print-outs on the desk. 'Well,' I said, 'I can't.'

'What do you mean?'

'I mean, I don't know.'

'What do you mean, you don't know?'

'I mean exactly that. I don't know. If *you* don't know how the hell should *I* know?'

'Because you're an agony aunt. I thought you'd be able to advise me.'

'I'm sorry, Natalie, but I *can't*. You marry him if you want to; and if you don't want to, don't. But it's *your* life. *You* decide.'

'But I need you to help me make that decision. That's why I'm asking you.'

'Well don't ask me. I haven't a clue.'

'Can't you help me then?'

'No, I can't. My life's a complete shambles at the moment, so why should I be able to help anyone else?'

'But that's why we ring in,' said Natalie. 'To ask you. That's what it says on your column. "Ask Rose".'

'Well don't Ask Rose,' I said. 'Don't Ask Rose anything any more, because quite frankly, Rose doesn't want to know.'

Minty's eyes were like satellite dishes. And now, all of a sudden, it came back to me in huge pink, flashing neon letters. What Katie Bridge had said. *We're only agony aunts because we're trying to heal some damaged part of ourselves*. It was true, I now saw. It was *true*.

'Today, I was accused of being an agony aunt for the wrong reason,' I said quietly. 'Not out of altruism – but out of egotism. I was very indignant about this. But actually, as I sit here now, this evening, feeling not the slightest interest in any of your problems, and in fact wondering why you don't just take responsibility for your own lives, and make your own decisions, I realise that it's quite true. I'm an agony aunt because I've enjoyed feeling needed – that's probably why I'm not really that good. I thought I *was* good,' I went on wearily. 'In fact I thought I was a brilliant agony aunt. I thought I had such intuition and insight – that I was so skilled at reading between the lines. But the truth is, I'm not that good at it, because today I've discovered just how many big things I've missed. In fact, if I'm really being honest, I'd say I'm actually pretty second-rate.'

'Er, I think you're being very hard on yourself Rose,' said Minty, her face flushing.

'No, I don't think I am. I wanted to help people – and I thought I could. I even fancied that I was rescuing them from their problems' – I suddenly thought of Theo – 'but the one who really needed rescuing was me.' I looked at the e-mail print outs in my hand, then slowly ripped them in half. 'I've had it with agony,' I said. 'I've really had it. I don't want to be in agony any more.'

'Well, that, er, brings us to the end of the programme,' said Minty brightly. 'So thanks to everyone who's called in. And do join us again next time for *Sound Advice* with Rose Costelloe of the *Daily Post*.'

'No,' I said. 'Don't join me, because I'm sorry everyone, I won't be here.' I slowly turned and looked through the glass partition at Wesley who was gawping at me like a stunned cod.

'What the hell are you thinking of?' he demanded as I pushed on the heavy studio door.

'I'm really sorry Wesley,' I croaked. 'I know that was unprofessional of me.'

'Yes! It was!'

'But you see I'm under so much pressure at the moment. I've got so many problems – I just can't cope.' I dropped the ripped-up e-mails into the bin. 'I've had it, Wesley. I just can't do it any more.'

'But you can't leave us in the lurch like this. I mean who the hell am I going to get instead of you at such short notice?' Who? Well, it was obvious.

'Beverley McDonald. She's a natural,' I said.

Chapter Twenty-Four

I don't sleep well at the moment, but then I've got a lot on my mind. I lie there, staring into the dark, aware of the comfortless silence of the house and the slow tick-tock of my clock. If the World Service hasn't sent me off by two, I count stars – it's better than sheep. I picture the constellations – thanks to Theo's book I know lots of them now – then tick them off. Ursa Major, Ursa Minor, Cassiopaeia, Capricorn . . . Cygnus, Aries, Lynx . . . Aquarius, Perseus, Pisces, Pegasus . . . the Pleiades, Sagittarius, Grus . . . – only another ninety-nine point nine, nine, nine billion or so to go I tell myself; then I list the brightest ones. Sirius, Canopus, Vega, Aldebaran . . . Capella, Polaris, Crux . . . Rigel, Betelgeuse, Alpha Centauri . . . then I go through the galaxies and their type. I start with the Milky Way (spiral), Andromeda 1 (elliptical), Small Magellanic Cloud (irregular), Large Magellanic Cloud (irregular spiral), NGC 6822 (irregular), M33 (spiral). And if I get stuck on those I list all the famous comets – Halley's, Hale-Bopp, Shoemaker-Levy, Temple-Tuttel, Ikeya-Seki, Comet Schwasmann-Wachmann – then I list Jupiter's moons. Io, Europa, Calypso, Ganymede . . . Adrastea, Metis, Thebe . . . Himalia, Elara, Lysithea, Leda . . . Ananke and Pasiphae. If I'm still conscious, I run through Saturn's moons too, but I'm usually out by then.

Heavenly Bodies has done very well. It's at number five in the non-fiction top ten and is apparently selling two thousand a week. I'd like to congratulate Theo, but I haven't heard from him and I can't bring myself to get in touch. And I know what you're thinking, but I just can't help it – I'm afraid it's the way I am. If I feel that someone's hurt me I retreat into my shell, like a snail drawing inward. Then I mentally lock the door.

In any case Theo's very busy. I know that from Bev. She said he's doing publicity for his book, and sorting out his flat and writing a pilot for a new series, *Star-Struck*, on Radio Four. But I'm not busy myself – far from it – because Ricky heard my phone-in last week.

'Well . . .' he said, as I sat in his office the following morning. 'Well, well, *well*.' He lightly bounced the tips of his fingers against one another. 'That was quite a little perform-ance last night.'

'Yes,' I said quietly, 'I know. I'm . . . sorry, Ricky. I was in,' I sighed, '. . . a bit of a state.' And I waited for him to tell me to remove myself and my belongings from the building forth-with. But, to my surprise – and relief – he didn't.

'I'm not going to sack you,' he said with uncharacteristic sympathy. 'You've done the *Post* too much good for me to do that. But you're clearly having some kind of a crack-up, so I suggest you take three weeks off.'

I was only too happy to oblige as I hadn't taken any leave for fifteen months. And with all that's happened – and with my looming birthday – I've been glad to have time to think. So Beverley's been looking after the column, with the help of a temp, and she's been doing the phone-ins too. I tuned in on Thursday and she was brilliant. I imagined her sitting there in the studio, with Trevor, both wearing headphones, both making notes, as Betrayed of Barnes or Balding of Brighton phoned in to have a good whine. I imagined Henry listening too, dressed in velvet and high heels, beaming with partnerly pride. Henry and Bev. Bev and Henry. How come I never spotted that? But then, as I've discovered recently, there are lots of things that I've missed.

I haven't decided what I'll do next: Ricky says we'll talk when I go back to work. But while I reflect on my future I've been decorating the house – nothing radical, just a paint job – and I've been doing the garden as well. I've had the patio repaved, and I've bought some terracotta pots and I've put in a pergola and some new plants. I've been to a few exhibitions, and some films and plays, and I've been reading a lot. Yesterday, in between coats of paint in the sitting room, I read *A Brief History of Time*. And I was thrilled because I actually understood it – or at least I think I did. Did you know that if you were to get sucked into a black hole you'd get 'spaghettified,' all the atoms in your body stretched into infinite strings? And if you were to survive that, it's perfectly possible that you'd get sucked through a wormhole at the bottom and find yourself in another universe. Because our universe might not be, well, the centre of the universe: I mean, it might not be the only one. There might be a multiverse, like a honeycomb, or like adjoining bubbles in the bath. For all we know there might be as many universes as there are stars in the sky, each with its own physical laws. So I've been contemplating the cosmos in this way, and chatting to Rudy, and trying not to think about my mother or about the fact that I'll be forty next week. Four. *Oh . . .*

I used to think of forty as being a bit like Tierra del Fuego. One knew that it was there, on the map somewhere, but that it was a very long way off. And now, to my surprise, there I am.

'What are you going to do?' asked Bella a few days ago as I wandered around Mothercare with the twins. Her bump's just beginning to show now.

'What do you mean, what am I going to do?'

'Well you've got to do *something*,' said Bea.

'You should celebrate it,' said Bella as she looked at tiny sleep suits for newborns.

'What's to celebrate?' I said.

'Forty's only a number, Rose.'

'Rather a high one,' I pointed out bleakly.

'It could be a lot worse.'

'Yes,' said Bella as we looked at soft toys. 'It could be fifty, for example.'

'Or sixty.'

'It could be eighty-three.'

'Hm. That's true.'

'Forty's nothing these days,' said Bea confidently. 'In fact forty's the new twenty.'

'No, it's the new thirty,' Bella corrected her.

'It's the new twenty now, actually. I read it in *Vogue*.'

'It is not.'

'It *is!*'

'It *isn't.*'

'It is!'

'Don't argue,' I said. 'Forty's still *forty* as far as I'm concerned.'

'We'll be forty next year,' said Bella blithely as she picked up a white bunny, with a blue ribbon round its neck, 'and we won't mind at all. We'll tell everyone our age, and we'll have a *huge* party, won't we Bea?'

'We certainly will.'

'We'll invite at least a hundred people.'

'No, that's too many. We'll have fifty.'

'A hundred.'

'Fifty.'

'But *I* want a hundred!'

'Fifty's plenty,' said Bea vehemently.

'Oh all right then, fifty it is.'

'You *must* have a party Rose,' they said, in unison.

'Why?'

'Because we say so.'

'But there isn't *time*. My birthday's next Saturday – who'll come at such short notice?'

'The people who love you, that's who. Have a party, Rose,' said Bella.

'Have a party,' added Bea.

'Have a party, Rose,' they chorused.

I looked at them. 'Okay. I will.'

So I am. I'm having a small drinks party, or rather a

'Fortification'. I've e-mailed fifty people about it, of whom over half have said that they'll come. Then I thought I'd better get in caterers but they're all already booked up – or they're too expensive – so I'm going to have to do the cooking myself. When I say 'the cooking,' I don't mean proper cooking – I mean heating up. Canapés. Bought ones for speed, and two crates of champagne, and several gallons of Pimms. And we can all spill out into the garden if it's not raining – the twins are right. One shouldn't ignore one's fortieth – one should face it with fortitude.

Yesterday morning, I received a couple of early birthday cards and, to my surprise, *Sky and Telescope* magazine too. Theo's mail has been redirected, but this had clearly slipped through the net. As I scribbled in his address I wondered about putting a friendly note on. But I couldn't bring myself to do it, and in any case there wasn't room. Theo clearly doesn't want to talk to me, because if he did, he could easily have called me or e-mailed me or dropped me a line. And he hasn't.

I'd like to have invited him to the party, but I just can't face him: it was so awful when he left. I keep thinking how tactless he was – and how vile *I* was – it makes me cringe; and that's why I haven't been sleeping well, although, for some reason, last night, I did. Because when I woke and put on the radio, I expected to hear the *Today* programme, but instead it was the end of *Excess Baggage*. I glanced at the clock. It said ten-thirty; I'd been asleep for eleven hours. Given my recent insomnia I'd have been glad about this but I had *so* much to do. All the food shopping, for example. I'd left it until that day as I don't have a very large fridge. I shot out of bed, pulling on the first things to hand, without even showering, then set to work. I frantically hoovered and dusted, then tidied the garden, then drove to the big Sainsbury's on Dog Kennel Hill.

Being Saturday, it was heaving of course, and there was no-one to ask where the party food was and when I did eventually find the right section, which was about two miles away, the shelves had run desperately short. Then I had to look for someone to go and get me some more cocktail sausages and mini-roulades, and they took an *age* to come back; and then the queues for the tills were interminable and the woman in front had a problem with her switch card so that took twenty minutes to sort out. So by the time I staggered out with my sixty-two carrier bags, it was already five past three. And then I had to go to the off licence to get the booze and the glasses, and by the time I'd finished there it was four, and my guests would be arriving at seven. So I phoned Bev as I drove back to Hope Street and asked her whether Henry might be able to help.

'No,' she said.

'What?'

'No. He can't. Sorry. He's busy. He's terribly busy this afternoon and he can't help you.'

'Oh. Well, it's only for an hour or so, just to lend me a hand; or maybe you could come a bit early Bev . . . ?'

'No. I'm sorry. I can't. You see, I'm very busy too.'

'What about Trevor?'

'He's busy as well. He's out shopping.'

'Oh,' I sighed. 'Right. Well, see you later,' I said, hoping the brightness of my tone masked my hurt and disappointment, then I phoned the twins. It was engaged, so I had to try three times before I got through.

'Twins!' exclaimed Bea gaily as she picked up the phone.

'Listen, it's me. Could you come a bit early tonight? I've got myself in a mess timewise and I'm in a complete panic.'

'I'd love to,' she said. *Great.* 'But I can't.'

'You can't?'

'I'm really sorry, Rose. But I'm busy.'

'Doing what?'

'Working.'

'On a Saturday?'

'Yes.'

'Oh. Well, can Bella help then?'

''Fraid not.'

'Why?'

'Well . . . because she's . . . working as well.'

'But I'm in a state,' I said. 'In fact I'm frantic.'

'Oh *dear*. But I'm afraid we're both working and so we both can't help you.'

'But this party was your idea! And I've got *all* these people coming and I've only just done the shopping!'

'Don't worry, Rose – you'll be *fine*. Happy birthday, by the way,' she added cheerily. 'See you later! Bye.'

'Well *thanks!*' I hissed as I took out my earpiece. 'What a *useless* pair.' I parked the car in my usual space, then opened the boot and took out the bags. I scooped them up – they went all the way up both arms – then, with the key between my teeth, and turning it with the tips of my fingers, I just managed to open the front door.

'Shit, shit, *shit*,' I said crossly as I staggered into the hall, arms about to snap off.

'Welcome to *Weekend Woman's Hour*!' I heard Rudy say in Jenni Murray's voice. As Rudy burbled away about female circumcision I kicked shut the front door then looked at the telephone table. Great. The post had arrived. Better late than never, I thought, as I surveyed the pile of cards. I'd open them later I decided; then I suddenly stopped. Hang *on* a mo . . . How, I wondered, had the letters managed to jump from the doormat onto the hall table and neatly stack themselves up?

'Serious health and human rights issues . . . legislation needed . . .' And why was Rudy still talking about female circumcision? And what on earth was that noise? And why could I smell cheese straws? It must be Henry. Of course it was – the sweetheart – he *was* going to help me. It was just Bev's little joke. I stood in the kitchen doorway and gawped.

'Happy birthday, Rose,' said Theo brightly. My heart did a triple somersault and five flick-flacks. 'Many happy returns. You've picked a nice, sunny day for it,' he added warmly.

'. . . resistance to infringing the mores and traditions of another culture . . .' I looked at Rudy. He was asleep. It really was *Woman's Hour* – the radio was on.

'What are you doing here Theo?' I enquired coolly. He was wearing his *Astronomers Do It At Night!* tee shirt.

'What am I doing? I'm making cheese straws.'

'That's not what I mean.'

'I thought you could do with some vol au vents too. About, what, eighty? That would be two each wouldn't it – you're expecting over thirty people aren't you?'

'What I mean is . . .'

'And I reckoned you ought to have something sweet too so I made you these . . . ta da!' He opened the fridge with a theatrical flourish and I could see rows of filled brandy snaps.

'Theo,' I said as he turned off the radio. 'How long have you been here?'

'About an hour and a half.'

'Did you break a window?'

He looked offended. 'What do you take me for?'

'Then how the hell did you get *in*?'

He put his right hand in the pocket of his jeans and pulled out a bunch of keys. 'I forgot to give you these back when I left. Didn't you notice?'

I shook my head. 'No.'

'I only found them yesterday, when I unpacked my last box of books – they'd fallen in. That's why I've come,' he explained. 'To return them.'

'Well, thanks very much.'

'I didn't like to post them, of course. Far too risky. So I thought I'd better deliver them in person.'

'Uh huh.'

'And I was wondering whether you'd bite my head off, or blaspheme at me, so I took Bev's advice.'

'Oh – and what did she say?'

'She said that it was her opinion that you probably wouldn't. She also mentioned that you were in a panic about the party so I thought I'd better help you out on the catering front.'

'I see.'

'She said she thought you wouldn't mind if I just let myself in.'

'Oh really?'

'In fact she said she thought you'd be quite pleased.'

'She did, did she?'

He came up to me and took the carrier bags out of my hands. 'Hello Rose.'

'Hello Theo.' Here he was again – the Milky Way kid.

'I see you've been missing me,' he said breezily as he began to unpack the shopping. I stared at him.

'What makes you think that?'

'Male intuition. It's unerring. There are things we men just . . . *know*. In any case it's obvious that you've been finding it hard without me,' he added as he opened the fridge again and put in the smoked salmon.

'Really?'

'All the redecorating you've been doing for example. It's classic displacement activity.'

'Is it?'

He nodded knowledgeably. 'Oh yes. I see you've been busy in the garden too. Which reminds me, I've got you a present. Hold on.'

He went over to the kitchen table, picked up a carrier bag and handed it to me. I looked inside.

'A rose for Rose,' he said as I pulled it out.

'Zephérine Drouhin . . .' I said as I read the label. 'I've never heard of that one.'

'It's a very special rose.'

'In what way?'

'It's got no thorns.'

'But surely all roses have thorns?'

'No. Not this one. It's a thornless Rose,' he explained again. 'So naturally it reminded me of you. It's a climber – deep pink; I thought it'd look nice on that new pergola of yours.'

'Well, yes, it would look nice there,' I said politely. 'Thank you. That's very kind.'

'I've got you another present too.'

'You have?'

'But you can't have it just yet.'

'Oh. So Beverley told you I wouldn't mind if you just . . . turned up, did she?'

'That's right. I wrote to her.'

'When?'

'Yesterday morning. Or rather, I sent her an e-mail. Do you want to know what it said?'

'I'm not sure that I do.'

'It said, "Dear Bev, I've got this problem. I fell in love with my landlady but, being a bit slow on the uptake in some ways poor dear, she didn't realise it for six months. And then, on the day she did finally get it we had this awful row. She told me to 'fuck RIGHT off and NEVER come back!!' Do you think she really meant it? Stumped of Stockwell."'

'And what did Beverley say?'

'She e-mailed me back straight away saying that, no, in her considered opinion, she didn't think you'd meant it at all.'

'Oh really?'

'She said she thought it was just your way of expressing affection.'

'I see.'

'So, encouraged, I decided to come round.'

'You seem confident of a warm reception.'

'Oh, I am.'

'Isn't that a bit complacent?'

'No. Because I know for a fact you're mad about me.'

'Am I?'

'Yes. You're nuts about me.'

'No I'm not. I'm just being civil and polite.'

'That's balls. You're being a right old frosty-face, but you're crazy about me, Rose.'

'What makes you so sure?'

'Two things. Point number one – you're wearing my old tee shirt.' Oh *shit*.

'Well, it was . . . convenient. I was in a panic this morning and everything else was in the wash.'

424

'And point number two –'

'Theo's so *lovely*!' yelled Rudy in my voice. 'I don't *want* him to leave. He's *lovely*! I want him to stay.'

Theo smiled his lop-sided smile. 'That's point number two. He began shouting it at me the minute I got here. I felt quite encouraged.'

'Well . . . I wouldn't take too much notice – he's a bird brain.' We stared at each other for a few seconds, then I felt my eyes suddenly fill.

'I thought you were going to love me and leave me,' I said quietly.

He shook his head. 'No. I'm going to love you and love you.'

'Ah.'

'Would you like a hug then Rose?'

I nodded, slowly. He pulled me to him, and wrapped me in his arms and I felt his breath in my ear. 'And is it all right if I give you a kiss?' he whispered. 'As it's your birthday and everything.' I nodded again. Then Theo pressed his lips to mine, very gently, and we stayed like that for a minute or two.

'Your glasses have steamed up,' I said.

He took them off, and rubbed them on the hem of my tee shirt and squinted at me. 'You know you look *much* better with them on.' Then he hugged me again, rocking me gently from side to side, like silent slow dancing. I felt a tear slide down my cheek.

'I'm sorry,' I croaked. 'I wanted to make it up – but I didn't know how.'

'I'm sorry too. I'm a blunt bugger, aren't I?'

'Well yes, you are blunt. You're also very sharp. And that's why I got so annoyed. Because I knew, deep down, it was true. I didn't just enjoy being needed – I *needed* to be needed. But now I've given it all up. Or, rather, it's given *me* up. No more agony.'

'I know,' he said. 'Bev told me. But what will you do?'

'I haven't a clue. Ricky said he'd try and find me something else. It won't pay as well, but I'll manage somehow.'

'*We*'ll manage,' Theo said.

An hour or so later, the canapés were nearly done, I'd showered and put on a frock and the house was filling up with my friends. I should have called the party a *Fortissimo* rather than a Fortification I thought happily as I listened to the swelling noise.

Every time we say goodbye . . . sang Ella.

'I fry a little . . .' crooned Theo as he quickly cooked another batch of cocktail sausages.

Every time . . . we say goodbye . . .

'I Crisp 'n' Dry a little . . . Here Rose – slap some honey and tarragon on this lot. And don't forget the paper napkins.'

The twins were passing round the smoked salmon blinis while Henry was pouring the Pimms. I'd been worried that Bea would be hurt at seeing him with Beverley, but she'd told me she couldn't care less.

'Oh I've got over him,' she'd said airily the day before. 'Remember, Rose, I'm having a *baby* – my life has moved on. In any case I genuinely don't mind because I like Bev,' she'd added. 'She's a jolly good egg.' And now there Bea was, chatting animatedly to Beverley, who looked like the second happiest woman there.

'Thank you for what you said to Theo,' I whispered to her a few minutes later as Bea stepped into the garden.

'Well, I didn't say much.'

'But your advice was great. Ask Bev,' I added with a giggle.

'Ask Bev *and Trev*,' she said. 'That's what Ricky wants to call it.'

'Really?' I stroked Trevor's ears. 'Well, why shouldn't a dog be an agony aunt – I mean, uncle?'

'But I want to thank *you*, Rose,' Bev murmured.

'Why? I didn't do anything.'

'You did! You helped me find a fantastic man – and a wonderful new career!'

I shook my head. 'No, Bev. They found *you*. I'm just so glad you're happy,' I added.

'Oh Rose, I *am*. I'm jumping for joy.'

Now, as I went into the garden with the tray of vol au vents I caught snatches of conversation.

'– We've been horribly out of touch with Rose.'

'– Well we hadn't seen her for over a year.'

'– No, not astrology – astronomy.'

'– But then I guess she's had a lot going on.'

'– Bella and I can't drink, Henry. We're pregnant.'

'– Nice garden.'

'– Oh, all right then – just a splash.'

At ten o'clock Theo produced a cake, decorated with red marzipan roses, and everyone toasted me with champagne and sang *Happy Birthday*. And as I blew out the four large candles I leaned in too far and the ends of my hair caught fire.

'Flaming June!' cried the twins, then helped pat it out. There was a singeing smell. 'Speech!'

'Well, I don't have much to say, except that I'm glad that you're all here, and that I have such – lovely – people with me today to help me celebrate. I do feel . . . fortified.'

At eleven people began to drift away in taxis, muttering about babysitters and last trains, and by half past eleven they'd all gone. I surveyed the debris. Stray napkins fluttered amongst the flowerbeds; crisps and Twiglets speckled the grass. Wine bottles lay like felled skittles on the patio, and there was a small lagoon of spilled Pimms. The light fittings were threaded with the rainbow strings from party poppers and two ashtrays overflowed. Red wine had been spilt on the pink tablecloth which was hummocked and hillocked with salt.

'What a mess,' I said to Theo with a sigh. 'It's just . . . lovely.'

'Yes,' he smiled. 'It is. It's a lovely, happy mess.'

'Shame to clear it up really,' I said as I gathered up discarded gift-wrap.

'Hmm.'

'What a great evening though.'

'Oh yes. It was grand.'

I smiled at him. Grand. 'You're grand, Theo,' I said.

'Hey, you haven't opened my present yet,' he said. 'I mean your other one.' Theo put his hand in his pocket and pulled out a small box. 'Here.' I removed the red tissue paper and lifted the lid. Inside was a gold charm bracelet, with one charm on it – a star.

'Thank you, Theo.' I kissed him. 'It's *lovely.*'

'It's so that you'll have a charmed life. I shall give you a charm every birthday.'

'I wonder how many I'll end up with then?'

He smiled. 'Oh, *lots.* And you've already got one charm, Rose. I mean, apart from the star.'

'Yes.' I thought of the Aladdin's lamp. 'I know.'

'And I thought, maybe you'll want to put that one on it too, one day.'

'Yes. You're right. Maybe I will.'

'Still no news?' I shook my head. 'Well, best not to think about it. Give it another week, then you could write to Mrs Wilson again and see if she'll tell you anything more. I'll put all your cards on the mantelpiece shall I?' He went into the sitting room, and I began to collect up the plates and glasses. Then he reappeared with some envelopes in his hand.

'Hey,' he said. 'These were on the hall table. I picked them off the mat when I arrived.' Of course. In my panic to get ready I'd forgotten about them. There were three birthday cards, a phone bill and two letters, one marked *Confidential*, which had originally been sent to me c/o the *Post*. Beverley had redirected it. I tore it open. It was handwritten, and very short.

Dear Rose, We have never met, but I wanted to let you know that although Jon is still very unwell, he is at last beginning to show signs of improvement following his bone marrow transplant last week. To our huge relief – after a year of anguish – Ed was found to be a very close match. Thank you so much, Rose, for the part you played in his recovery. We will love you for ever. Claire Wright.

'I've got you, under my sink . . .' I heard Theo croon as

he began to wash up. 'I've got you deep in the . . . are you all right there Rose?'

'What?'

'What's up? You look sad.'

'No. No, I'm not sad at all.'

'Is it serious then?' I nodded. 'Can I see?' He dried his hands and I handed him the letter.

'Thank God for that,' he breathed. 'So he finally did the right thing. Do you feel differently about him now?' he asked me as he handed it back. Did I feel differently about Ed now? That was a *very* good question.

'Yes,' I replied truthfully. 'And no.' And now, as Theo began to wash the glasses, I looked at the second letter which was A5 size, thick to the touch and franked, rather than stamped, with a promotional postmark saying 'New Horizons!' Some promotional thing I presumed. I began to open it, then turned it over and saw that it was from Australia and that it was addressed to 'Rose Wright'. My heart stopped. Then I felt it start to beat again, my hand visibly trembling as I ran my thumb along the rest of the flap. Heart banging like a tom-tom I pulled out a sealed envelope, inscribed *To Rose* and a letter, typed on two sides. It was from a man called Dennis Thornton, writing from an address in Adelaide. As I began to read I felt as though I were barely breathing – all the air emptied out of my lungs.

Dear Rose, I don't quite know how to begin this letter, but I believe – in fact I know – that I am your stepfather . . .

'This is it,' I said to Theo. 'It's come.' I glanced at the clock; I wanted to know exactly what time it was. It was a quarter to twelve. It was a quarter to twelve on June the first. I would remember this moment for the rest of my life. Theo turned off the taps, and leaned against the worktop as I read on.

Six weeks ago a family friend, Marjorie Wilson, wrote to my wife, Rachel – your birth mother – My mother's name is Rachel, I thought wonderingly. Her name's Rachel. It was as though a light had been switched on.

Mrs Wilson's letter was short, the purpose of it being to enclose a copy of the notice you had placed in the press about your abandonment in 1962. Mrs Wilson tactfully suggested that Rachel, with whom she had kept in sporadic, but friendly touch, might find it interesting. She was quite right. Since then I have spoken to Mrs Wilson by phone, and she said that something about your advertisement – and the date mentioned on it – had made her think. She told me that she had always had her doubts about what really happened to the baby she had delivered, and helped to care for, in the summer of 1962. After contacting you, and satisfying herself that you really are that baby, she then wrote to my wife.

Rose, I have known about your existence only for the past two years. I knew that there was something in Rachel's past which distressed her, some 'bad thing' which she said she'd done. Once, tipsy and tearful at a christening (she always hated christenings), she said she felt she had been 'punished' for it, whatever it was. She never said what this 'bad thing' was, and I never asked her, but in October 2000, she told me the truth.

Even after thirty-eight years the memory of how she had given birth to you, and then abandoned you, distressed her terribly: I felt so sorry for her – and for you. Rose, it's not for me to explain what happened, but for Rachel. So I enclose a letter for you, which she dictated to me eighteen months ago. I hoped so much that I would be able, one day, to pass it on to you. That day has now come . . .

My mum's called Rachel, I thought again happily. Her name's Rachel, and she's written me a letter and I'm going to meet her. I picked up the envelope and, even at the distance of four decades, I recognised her large, round handwriting from the note she'd left that day. I wondered how soon we'd be able to get together, and would I call her 'Rachel' or 'Mum' . . . ?

Rose, I am very sorry to have to tell you that Rachel died last year, on March 10th, in the Mary Potter hospice here in Adelaide. She was 53. That's why she at last unburdened herself to me about you, because she knew she had only a few months to live. She wanted so much to be able to put things right, to gain some degree of 'closure' on it, as the psychiatrists say, but she didn't know how. She told me how bitterly she regretted what she had done, and how she wished she had searched for you. I asked her why she hadn't done so, and she explained that although she had longed to find you, she felt too ashamed. She was also afraid. Afraid that if she did trace you, you'd reject her – 'and who could blame her?' she said. Rachel thought it very likely that you knew you'd been abandoned. She said that she couldn't therefore assume you'd want anything to do with her, and in any case she said it was 'too late'.

No. No, I thought. I shook my head. If only she'd looked for me I'd have come.

And so, in order for her finally to find some peace, I persuaded her to write you a letter that I could give to you, should you ever make contact. It gave her great solace, in the final weeks of her life, to know that she had 'spoken' to you at last.

Now I put down Dennis's letter, still unfinished, and opened Rachel's. I couldn't wait any longer. I was opening the letter my mother had written to me. It was dated January the first, 2001.

Dear Rose, Today is New Year's Day, a day for fresh starts and resolutions. Although I won't be able to have a fresh start myself (barring some miracle) I can make, and keep, a resolution – to write to you, the daughter I abandoned nearly forty years ago – to say how truly sorry I am. I also want to tell you that, since then, I have thought of you every single day. I've hoped and prayed that, despite the bad start you had, your life has been happy and fulfilled.

I'm sorry too, that having gone to all this trouble to trace me, and having succeeded (which is why you're reading this) you find that I've abandoned you all over again. What a useless non-mother I've been to you, Rose. What a let-down. What a real 'dropkick,' as we say here in Oz. I am quite sure you must have hated me . . . Yes, I thought dismally. I did. But I console myself with the thought that maybe the fact that you've searched for me means that you've been able to partly conquer your anger and contempt. Or perhaps you're simply curious to know where you come from. Oh no – it's more than that. Anyway, Rose, although I can never expect you to forgive me for what I did (and why should you?), I would at least like to try and explain. So here is the story of what happened, and of what your origins are, and of how you came to be.

431

I grew up in Sittingbourne, in Kent. My parents were decent people, slightly strict I suppose in their outlook, Catholic, and working class. My father, Jim, worked in the paper mill while my mother, Eileen, who was rather delicate, looked after my younger sister, Susan, and me. I've got an aunt, I thought. Her name's Susan. Aunt Susan. Auntie Sue. *We lived in Kemsley, an estate built for the paper mill workers, at number 10, Coldharbour Lane. In 1960, when I was fourteen, the Pennington family moved in next door. There were three boys, all tall and rather good-looking, if a bit skinny, and the eldest one, Ian, became friendly with me.* That's my father, I thought. Ian Pennington. That's my father's name.

Ian was seventeen then, but, to me, he seemed like a real man. I had never had a boyfriend and I developed a huge crush on him. He was very lively, and attractive; he was also ambitious and bright. He was at Borden, the boys' grammar, school, and he was going to go on to college and become a journalist, like an uncle of his who worked for The Times. *Anyway, Ian would collect me from school sometimes, and we'd go to the pictures, or the milk bar, or he'd take me for a spin on his motorbike. For two years our friendship was simply that – a friendship – nothing more. But in September 1961, when he was eighteen, Ian left Kemsley to go to Kings College, London, to study History. He was really happy that National Service had just ended, enabling him to go straight up. I was fifteen then (I was born July 25th, 1946), and still at school. We wrote to each other, and in one of his letters he suggested that I come and visit him one weekend. I remember how excited I was. So I went up on the train one Saturday in mid-October: it seemed such a grown up thing to do. I'd told my parents I was going up to the West End with a friend, to look in the shops, but it wasn't true. Ian met me off the train at London Bridge and we went to his digs at Kings College Hall down in Camberwell. He had a nice bedsit there, and we were very happy to see each other again and, well . . .*

By December it was obvious what had happened. My parents went mad – and being Catholic there was no way I could 'get something done about it'. Ian's parents were also furious, and accused me of being a 'wicked girl' and of 'trying to ruin' their son's life. So a family summit was called, and Ian came home and the first thing he said was 'You can all stop arguing, because I'm going to marry Rachel'. So, smiles of relief all round. Except for one problem – I was under age.

At that time sex with a minor carried a prison sentence; so, in order to keep the 'scandal' under wraps, my parents devised a plan. They took me out of school – the leaving age was fourteen in those days – and kept me at home. They pretended to everyone that I had glandular fever and that I'd be out of circulation for quite a while. My friends couldn't visit me – I remember how bored I was – but of course I had to play along. And in any case I didn't want to see anyone. I had always thought of myself as being quite 'proper,' but suddenly I'd become one of 'those' girls. Except that, unlike most of 'those girls,' my young man was going to stand by me. That's what we all believed.

When the delivery date came nearer, I was to be sent to Chatham, sixteen miles away, to be 'looked after' by an old friend of my mother, Marjorie Wilson, a former midwife, whose husband had been killed in the war. I would stay with Mrs Wilson for a few weeks, as her paying guest, and she would deliver the baby, and show me how to look after it, then Ian would come for me. I would turn sixteen on July 25th and we would get married the following day, at the Register Office, having filled out the necessary forms in advance, including a parental consent form for me. I would then move to London with Ian, and live with him in digs while he finished his degree.

During this time Ian often wrote to me, so I never had any doubt that he would keep his word. Looking back, I remember how happy I felt, despite it being such a stressful time. I loved Ian, and I was going to be with him – and with you – for the rest of my life. I was never an ambitious 'career girl,' Rose – I had no big plans. I knew I'd be quite happy being 'just' a wife and mother: you and Ian would be my universe. So, in early June I went by taxi, in the dead of night (because of course I was huge by then) to Mrs Wilson's place. She was a kind person, and she'd delivered thousands of babies, so my parents knew I'd be fine. And if there were any complications there was a hospital not far away. But I had a straightforward birth after a four hour labour. You were born at three a.m. on June fifteenth. June fifteenth. So my date of birth was a fortnight out.

I called you Rose, because I could already see that you had my colouring – fair skin and red hair. As you can see from the enclosed photo ... I shook the envelope, and out fell a faded snap of a pretty woman, in her mid-thirties, standing in front of Ayers Rock ... *my hair is titian – and it's curly and thick. Or rather it was. I've lost a lot of it now because of the chemo. But all my life it's been a mass of springy red curls, and I could see that you were going to have that too. You were very good and smiley and calm, Rose: you hardly ever cried; and despite the stresses of new mother-hood, and my frustration at having to remain 'hidden' for another few weeks, I felt perfectly fine. I was just waiting for Ian to come. I trusted him completely, and I had absolutely no doubts that he would.*

He came to see me three days after you were born; he'd just fin-ished his first year exams. Then he took a job in a paint factory in Battersea for the summer, knowing that with me and a baby to sup-port, he'd need to make some spare cash. He wrote to me, and I knew that the next time he'd come would be on July 26th, my sixteenth birthday, when we'd go to the register office and get married. At the same time, we would also register your birth (just within the six weeks they give you to do it), under both our (married) names. My parents visited me once during this time, and saw you, and they were so relieved that everything was going to turn out all right and that I'd soon be 'respectable' again. Their plan was a good one, and it was working out well. Or so we thought.

On the morning of July 25th, Mrs Wilson had a phone call to say that her sister, who lived in Lincoln, had been taken into hos-pital, and could she look after the kids. She said she didn't know how long she'd be away but guessed it would be at least a couple of weeks. So she knew that, by the time she got back, I'd be long gone. She was happy to leave me on my own in the house for the couple of days before Ian came, and she trusted us to leave it safely locked up. She left me a few groceries, and wished me well, and I was sad when she'd gone because I'd got to know her quite well, and she'd been kind to me. But at the same time I was very excited about Ian coming to fetch me, and about getting married and starting my new London life. But it wasn't to be. Because that afternoon there was a ring at the bell. Mrs Wilson had told me not to answer the door, but I looked out of an upstairs window, and was surprised to see my dad standing there. And I couldn't work out why he'd come. My parents didn't have a phone so he hadn't warned me that he'd be arriving. He'd obviously just got on the train. And as I went downstairs to open the door I thought that maybe he'd come because it was my birthday, and I was very touched. But that wasn't the reason at all. He looked awful. And he told me that he had some terrible news and that I had to be very brave. I was bracing myself for him to tell me that Mum was very bad, or worse. Instead he told me that Ian had been killed, that morning, on his motorbike. He'd skidded on a roundabout and had gone under a lorry. He'd died in the ambulance.

I was so shocked I felt I'd been shot. My dad sat with me for a bit – I can still remember how grey his face was – then after an hour or so he said he'd have to go. And I said I'd pack my things, because I assumed that I'd be going home with him now – but he just looked at me and shook his head. Then he gave me an envelope with fifteen pounds in it, which he said was all he could spare. And suddenly the penny dropped. I realised that my parents wouldn't want me at home now. They were very sorry for me, but they wouldn't want me as I was, unmarried, with a baby, because I wasn't going to be 'respectable' after all.

I don't want to judge my parents too harshly. It's hard to imagine now, in these liberated days, the awful stigma that existed then towards unmarried mothers. My dad said the gossip in a small community like Kemsley would have been more than they could bear, especially with my mum not being that strong. He also wanted to protect me from all that gossip. So he said I'd have to stay in Chatham, and take you to the local adoption society, where you would be well looked after, and a nice family found, which would be the best thing all round now. He said that once I'd done that, then I could come home.

My whole world – and my future – had collapsed in ruins. It was as though my life had just stopped. I felt as though I'd been cast adrift in a tiny rowing boat, with no oars, in a mountainous sea. You'd have thought that Ian's parents might have wanted to help me, but, like mine, they didn't want to know. Again, I don't want to judge them too harshly – they were grief-stricken – so they just closed in on themselves.

I lay on my bed for five days, just crying. And suddenly, you had started crying too. We were both inconsolable – I thought we'd drown in our tears. I felt so alone, and so distressed, with my grief and my shock and my baby who wouldn't stop crying – I think I was out of my mind. But at the same time, a small voice told me that I'd have to do what my dad said. I knew there was no other way. At a stroke I'd become just another unwed mother – one of 'those' girls. I also knew that even if I did want to keep you – which of course I did – they would never let me. At that time nearly all babies born out of wedlock were adopted – many were forcibly taken away. And how could I have kept you, Rose, as I was then, sixteen years old, with no money, no home and no man? So, although my heart was breaking, I knew I'd have to give you up. So I decided I'd take you to the local adoption society, wherever that was. But at the same time I was determined that they shouldn't know anything about me. I'd just quietly drop you off there, and run.

So, the next morning, the 1st August, I wrote a short note, just saying that your name was Rose, and asking them to look after you, and I put it in an envelope. I also put with it one thing – a gold charm which I cut off the little charm bracelet I wore. I knew that then I'd be able to identify you if, by some miracle, we should ever meet. Then I dressed you in your best romper suit, wrapped a cotton blanket round you, and set out. But, what with being so distressed, I hadn't thought it through. For a start I didn't have a pram, so I had to carry you in my arms. And I didn't know where the adoption society was. I didn't want to draw attention to myself by asking anyone so I just kept walking and I somehow thought I'd see a big sign saying 'Adoption Society' and all I'd have to do is go in. But Mrs Wilson's house was some distance from the centre of town, and I found myself going the wrong way, towards Gillingham, so then I had to turn back. And still I couldn't find it, and after two hours or so I was exhausted walking around with you in my arms although luckily you were asleep. I'd hardly eaten for the last five days so I was pretty weak, and then I had an idea. I decided I'd take you to

436

the town hall instead. I knew that if I took you there someone in authority would take you to the adoption society. I knew the town hall would be near the main street. And although the town was quite empty because of it being the holidays, I still kept away from the main drag. And I found myself walking down this side street, then through a car park behind the Co-Op; and suddenly I had this awful shock. In the distance I saw – or thought I saw – a girl from Kemsley – Nora Baker with her mum: they lived at the bottom end of Coldharbour Lane and Nora went to my school. I began to panic. I couldn't risk them seeing me, but they were coming quite close. And just at that moment you woke up and began crying. and Nora and her mum were crossing the road now, although they still hadn't seen me, and I was terrified. I didn't know what to do. I only knew that I couldn't be spotted by anyone I knew, holding a baby, so I thought I'd just have to put you down. And I suddenly saw this shopping trolley standing there, and before I could even stop to think, I'd just laid you in that. I looked round – no-one had seen me, the car park was empty. And there you were, in the trolley with your blanket and your bottle, and then I glanced to my right and Nora and her mother were getting nearer. And so I began to walk. Without meaning to do it, Rose, I just walked away. And I kept on walking. And walking. I walked away and left you there. And to this day the memory of what I did makes me feel shivery and sick. And my heart was beating so hard I thought I'd die and my face was boiling hot. I was walking very fast now, half running really, keeping my head right down.

Somehow I found my way back to Mrs Wilson's house, and unlocked the door, and I thought, 'what have I done? What have I done?' I knew that by now someone would have picked you up, and called the police. So I quickly stuffed my things into my bag and wrote Mrs Wilson a short note telling her what had happened to Ian, and saying that I'd taken the baby to the adoption society, and that I was leaving now. I signed the note, locked the front door, posted back the keys and then ran. I had only one thought in my head. I had to get out of Chatham because I knew that what I'd just done was a crime. I had abandoned my baby. I was a wicked girl. A common criminal. I'd be punished. I'd go to jail. I'd read about a woman who'd done it to her baby, and she'd been spotted by someone and then arrested, and sent to Holloway. And on the other side of the road was a bus stop, so I stood at it, with my bag, my heart still pounding, and in a few minutes a bus turned up. It said Gravesend on the front, so I got on, and I did feel that I was going to my grave. Ian was dead and my parents weren't going to help me, and I'd just abandoned my child.

So I sat on that bus for two hours, too shocked even to cry, totally terrified. And I kept thinking about you, Rose. I knew that by now you'd have been taken to the hospital, and checked over, and that someone would be taking care of you. I felt insanely jealous at the idea of someone else holding you, and feeding you, but despite the terrible emotions I was experiencing, I knew I couldn't go back. Because if I went back I believed I'd be arrested – and then I'd lose you anyway. Rose, when I think of how quickly the world has changed, and how a girl who did what I had done would be treated today, I feel so angry and resentful. She'd be helped, and counselled, and given welfare payments, and a place to live, and she'd receive compassion and support. But it wasn't like that then. Oh no. It wasn't like that at all.

So that's what happened that day. Perhaps I abandoned you, in a way, because I felt that I'd been abandoned – by Ian and by my mum and dad. That doesn't excuse it, but all I'm saying is that I didn't set out to do it in the way that I did. I meant only to hand you over to the authorities, who I believed would look after you, because I knew there was no other way. Instead, I was panicked into leaving you in a shopping trolley in a car park. How unbelievably callous that must have seemed.

I was aware of Theo sitting quietly at the end of the table. I could hear his gentle, regulated breathing as I read on.

I was so terrified that I might have been seen that I decided it would be best to get out of Kent altogether. So when the bus stopped at Gravesend I got the ferry across the Thames to Tilbury. It was getting dark by then, so I found a boarding house, and it seemed all right so I just stayed there, laying low for a few days, never leaving my room. But I knew my dad's money wouldn't last more than three or four weeks and that I'd have to get some sort of job. But I had no training for anything. I didn't want to go to the employment office in case they'd find out my name, and what I'd done. Anyway, I was walking past a café one day and there was a sign in the window saying that they needed a waitress, so I went inside. I hadn't a clue how to do waitressing but they showed me how to set the tables properly, and how to take the orders, so that's what I did. All I needed was breathing space – I was too distressed to make any plans. It was very hard work, but I was glad about that because it gave me no time to think. I wrote to my parents – without giving them my address – telling them that I'd given you up for adoption, that I was safe, and had a job, but that I didn't want to come home. I told them that I couldn't face seeing Ian's parents – which was quite true. And I told them I'd write to them again when I was 'settled' somewhere, and not to worry about me. I was functioning on automatic pilot, just working my shifts, and sleeping – hardly eating – and trying not to go mad.

One day, about a month later, I was bringing this man the bill – he seemed to me so much older than I was, but he was only twenty-three. Anyway, he struck up a bit of a conversation with me, and he asked me if I'd go to the pictures with him sometime. And although I was wary, I was also so lonely, and sad, and he seemed very nice. So something made me say yes. I just wanted to have someone to talk to, as much as anything, as I felt so unhappy and alone. He said his name was Dennis Thornton. I didn't tell him what had happened to me – I didn't even tell him about Ian – and he had the decency not to ask. He told me, much later, that he'd thought my sadness was because I'd been disappointed, or maybe jilted. He'd also wondered whether I'd had a backstreet abortion. It's only recently that he's learned the truth. Anyway, Dennis told me that he'd just finished his National Service, and that he'd done some odd jobbing but that he was sailing to Australia, from Tilbury, in six weeks' time. He said that there were wonderful opportunities 'down under' and that the passages over there were very cheap. Over the next month or so he asked me out a few more times, and he was always very considerate and gentlemanly and I was beginning to feel quite sad that he was leaving. He'd been a very nice friend. And we were sitting on the harbour in late September, watching the boats sailing in and out when he suddenly asked me whether I'd consider going to

Australia with him. It gave me an almighty shock. He said he'd pay for my ticket, and we could see what we thought of it out there, and if we didn't like it, we could always come back.

I thought of all the terrible things that happened to me. I had lost my fiancé and my baby and my future; I was also still worried that I'd be arrested for abandoning you if the authorities ever found out. The idea of starting my life over in a new, warm country, far away, suddenly seemed very, very appealing. So I took a deep breath, and said yes. We sailed on the S.S. Ormonde – it took nearly seven weeks, and was far from luxurious – in fact at times, in rough seas, it was hell. But on December first we sailed into Adelaide – I felt as though I was being reborn – and that's where we've been ever since.

We've had a good life here, Rose, and Dennis has been, well, just the most wonderful man. He's blushing now as I dictate those words, but it's true, and I want you to know. I often used to think that he'd rescued me. We got married in 1965, and he'd worked in a hardware shop to start with, and then he got into the travel agency business which was just starting up then, and he's done very well. He's ended up with his own travel agency, New Horizons, and I did secretarial training and helped him out. And no-one, not even Dennis, ever knew what had happened, and what I'd done nearly forty years before.

I'm so sorry, Rose. I never meant to abandon you in the way that I did. I never told Mrs Wilson the truth – although we kept in touch – and nor did my parents ever know. As far as they were concerned, the matter was closed. You'd been 'given up for adoption,' and, unable to face living in Kemsley again, I'd run away to the other side of the world.

I have just one other thing to tell you, Rose, and I hope you won't be hurt, but I have another child. She's a lovely girl, and her name is Laura . . .

I felt my eyes suddenly fill with unshed tears, which made my mother's words bend and blur. I've got a sister, I thought, my throat constricting. I have a sister. Her name is Laura.

Laura is 32 now, married to a nice man called Alan, who works with Dennis, and they have a sweet little girl, Alice, who's six.

I've got a niece too! I'm an aunt! To my amazement I

realised that I felt only happiness, not resentment. I pressed a tissue to my eyes then read on.

We adopted Laura in 1971. Adopted? *I'm sure you'll find that very strange. But you see, Rose, I couldn't have any more children. They knew it wasn't Dennis's 'fault,' so then they investigated me. Of course the doctor could tell that I'd had a child already – although I swore him to secrecy – and he said that my infertility was 'unexplained'. But I could explain it perfectly well – though I couldn't tell Dennis. I felt that I'd been punished for abandoning you. I had done something wicked and unnatural and so Nature had struck back. That's how I saw it. And Dennis was keen to be a father, so he suggested we adopted, and as he'd done so much for me how could I say 'no'? And in a strange way I felt that adopting an unwanted baby girl would atone, in some small measure, for what I had done to you.*

Anyway, Rose, there it is. That's the story of what happened, and of why I did what I did. I'm sorry. I'm very, very sorry. And I'm sorry, above all, that we shall never meet. But I'm so glad to have taken this chance to talk to you in this way. And although I have no way of knowing whether you will ever read this, I pray with all my heart that you do. With loving thoughts, your mother, Rachel.

I looked at the clock – it was ten past twelve. Then I picked up Dennis's letter again.

Rose, I am so glad that you have searched for your mum, and so desperately sorry that the trail has ended in this way. But I know how very, very happy it would have made Rachel for you to meet us – your family. We are waiting for you. Please come.

Epilogue

Brancaster Beach, North Norfolk,
Two months later, August 1st

'Lost and found,' said Theo gently. 'Then lost again.'

'Yes,' I whispered. 'She was. She was lost for forty years. And so was I.'

'But you're not lost to each other any more.'

'No, although in one way, we still are. But maybe we'll meet again. In some other universe.'

'Yes. Maybe you will.'

Theo and I lay on our backs, in the sand dunes, gazing at the sky, a vast, curving hollow, stretching to infinity. It was as black as anthracite and dense with stars, like gems flung upwards by some unseen hand.

'You must feel so different now, Rose.'

I listened to the waves breaking over the sand with a long, sad *Shhhhhhhh* . . 'I do, I feel . . . complete. I know where I come from now.'

'You come from Camberwell.'

I smiled and pushed my fingers into the cool sand.

'It's funny to think of my origins being there – it's as though I'd gone back to my source. But at long last I feel as though I actually *belong* to someone.'

He reached out his hand.

'You do. You belong to me.'

'And I belong to Rachel's family – her family in Australia, and her family here. I've got *so* many relations.' I shook my

443

head in wonderment. 'So many.'

'You have.'

'I've got a stepfather, and a sister.'

'Half-sister,' he corrected me.

'That's true. And I've a niece.' I thought of the daisy-strewn letter I'd had from Alice last week, and the poem she'd enclosed. *I've got a new auntie called Rose, I've never met her. But when I do, I know my life will be better.* Not bad for six and a half.

'Alice,' I said with a smile. 'And Laura. My sister Laura. And my stepfather, Dennis. They're my family. Not a shared gene among us, but you know Theo, it doesn't matter – it just doesn't matter – because they're my folks.' For water can be just as thick as blood, I'd discovered. And blood can be as thin as water – I mean, look at Ed.

'And Susan's family were great,' Theo said.

'Yes,' I murmured. 'They were.' I thought of our visit to Susan, her husband and three kids, and of how overcome she'd been. She'd smiled at me politely at first, then her face had suddenly crumpled and she'd hugged me, crying, and just wouldn't let go.

'I've wanted to meet you for so long,' she'd wept.

Susan had always known that I'd been born of course, but, like her parents, she believed I'd been adopted, in the normal way, after Ian's death. After Rachel had died she'd even done a search to try and find me, and couldn't work out why she'd drawn a blank. Now she understood.

'How terrible to think of Rachel being driven to do something so desperate,' she'd said as we sat in her garden looking at her family photographs. 'I suppose she must have felt that *she*'d been abandoned – which she had really – so that's probably why she abandoned you. It's awful to think of what she went through. But she never, ever spoke of it to me, Rose, on any of my visits, until I went for the very last time. It was a month before the end, and she mentioned you, and I nodded. Then she told me that she'd "spoken to you". But she was so ill by then that I thought she might be delirious.'

'No, she had spoken to me. It's just that I didn't get to hear what she'd said for eighteen months.' I thought of my mother's words, coming steadily towards me, like light travelling across space from some distant star.

Susan had shown me photos of my father as well. There was one of him and Rachel, when they were teenagers, standing by his motorbike, looking into each other's faces and laughing uproariously, as though they hadn't a care in the world. Less than a year after that photo was taken he would be dead, and she'd be a self-exile, parted for ever from her child. How tragic, I thought. How absolutely tragic; but at long last I had an image of him. My dad. I've got his brow, his chin, and his height. My pronounced clavicles I get from Rachel, evidently. There was one photo of her in her first evening dress.

'Will you want to get in touch with Ian's brothers?' Susan had asked. 'The Penningtons moved up to Scotland not long after he was killed, but I know someone who's got their address.'

'I'd like to write to them, and ask them if they'd like to meet me. It would be nice to think that they would.' And they do want to meet me, so Theo and I are going to see them in the autumn. When we're back from Oz.

I've been to see the house in Kemsley, and the one next door where my father lived, and the paper mill where my grandfathers worked. I've seen my grandparents' graves too, in Sittingbourne. Strangely, I felt as though I was going to meet them. I brought them red roses. I've paid my respects. Susan gave me a copy of the family tree she'd done. She'd put me on it, with my correct date of birth, next to Laura, my sister.

'You'll have to add to it soon,' I'd said . . .

'Ooh, meteor,' I said to Theo. 'No, sorry, it's a satellite.' My charm bracelet jingled at my left wrist as I shifted slightly. On it are the star, and my Aladdin's lamp, and a tiny telescope charm we found in an antique jeweller's yesterday.

'I love this,' I heard Theo say, as we shifted on the sand.

'This reminds me of being a boy, standing on this beach, staring at the sky with my granddad. Looking up . . . Things are looking up aren't they?'

'Oh they *are*. Things are really . . .' I sighed. 'Pretty grand.'

'Yes. Grand,' he echoed as we strained our necks upwards. 'What a nice way to spend my birthday. And your founders day,' he added.

'Hmm. I like August the first now,' I said. 'I used to hate it. I don't any more.' I felt the sand trickle through my fingers. 'Do you think we're alone?'

Theo looked around. 'Yes. Why? What do you want to do?'

'No, I mean, do you think we're alone – in the universe?'

'Oh. Almost certainly not. When you think how many other solar systems there must be, I doubt that a planet like the earth is unique.'

'I wonder what the aliens would make of us?'

'Well, they'd know quite a bit about us already, from our radio and television broadcasts.'

'Oh yes. Of course.'

'Imagine, every single programme that's ever been made, just whizzing through space, for ever and ever. Hitler's opening address to the Berlin Olympics for example.'

'That's bad PR for us earthlings isn't it?'

'I'm afraid it is. The death of President Kennedy. The aliens must be wondering who the hell shot him. It's probably driving them crazy.'

'It probably is.'

'President Clinton – "I did not have sexual relations with that woman".'

'Ha! Bet they didn't believe *that*!'

'All your radio broadcasts on London FM.'

'Oh yes.' I imagined my voice floating through the galaxy. 'They've probably got as far as Mars by now.'

'I wonder if the Martians think I gave my listeners good advice.'

'Hhmm. I wonder. They're probably arguing about whether Tracey from Tottenham should take her husband back, or whether Vince from Vauxhall really is gay. Or perhaps they have their own Martian agony aunts, or inter-galactic agony aunts.'

'They probably do.'

'You don't miss it do you?' Theo added, turning to me.

'Not in the slightest. I don't need it any more. I'm not in agony,' I said happily.

'No, you're not. You're the *Post*'s star feature writer.'

'Correction. I'm their animal correspondent.' I thought of my current commission – an exposé on the 'Turkeys Tortured for Christmas' scandal, which is why we're in Norfolk. I've got to infiltrate a farm and do an investigative piece on the conditions there. Next week it's Heathrow and the trade in smuggled tortoises, and then I've got to write a piece about a retriever who can do advanced calculus – we're going to call it 'Sum Dog!'. So it's not exactly what you'd call 'cutting edge' journalism, but I really don't mind. It's better than nasty neighbours and hair loss, and Ricky's kindly paying me what I got before. In any case, I have other priorities now. My perspective has changed. In so many ways.

'What's the time Theo?'

'Half eleven. Why – are you hungry again?'

'Yeah. Have you got the sandwich bag?'

He leaned over then grabbed a Co-Op carrier. 'Anchovy and strawberry jam?'

'No thanks.'

'Bacon and marmalade?'

'Nope.'

'Smoked salmon and banana.'

'Pass.'

'Apricot and Marmite?' Apricot and Marmite. Now that sounded good.

'Yeah.' He passed one to me and I took a big bite. 'Oh yum.'

'How long do you think this phase will last?' he asked.

'Haven't a clue.'

'I look forward to you eating proper food again, cooked by me.'

447

'This'll do me for now.'

'And are you feeling okay, Rose?'

'Yes,' I said happily. 'I feel absolutely fine. I get the odd palpitation and peculiar pains in my wrists. But the nurse said that's normal at thirteen weeks. Thanks, darling, that was delish.' I lay back again and studied the firmament. 'We'll have to think about names won't we?' I said.

'Bollocks.'

'No we will Theo. The time will fly.'

'No *Pollux*. Castor and Pollux – how about that? The heavenly twins.'

'Well that's a bit outré, in any case they might not be boys.'

'That's true. Calypso and Ganymede then.'

'Hmm. Now you're talking. But what if they're both girls?'

'Thelma and Louise? Bella and Bea?'

'Rachel and Anna,' I said slowly. 'After both our mothers.'

'Rachel and Anna,' he repeated. 'That's really nice. I hope they won't mind the long flight to Oz.'

'No the doctor said they'll be fine. Anyway we've got to go now before I get too big. Three weeks down under,' I said with a happy sigh. 'It'll be so lovely. Meeting the family. And you'll get some good stuff for your radio series.'

'Yes I'll be able to get all my material about the southern sky. I'm looking forward to seeing the Anglo-Australian observatory. And we might even get to see the southern lights. We've got so much to look forward to haven't we, Rose?' he added

'Yes, I smiled, 'we have.'

He suddenly stood up. 'I think the tide's going out. Shall we go for a walk along the water's edge? A little midnight paddle, Rose? Are you up for it?'

I reached out my hand and Theo pulled me to my feet.

'Yes,' I said. 'I am.'